Matters of *the* Heart

DANIELLE STEEL

Matters *of* *the* Heart

RANDOM HOUSE
LARGE PRINT

Published in the United States of America by Random House Large Print in association with Delacorte Press, New York.
Distributed by Random House, Inc., New York.

The Library of Congress has established a cataloging-in-publication record for this title.

ISBN: 978-0-7393-2842-2

www.randomhouse.com/largeprint

10 9 8 7 6 5 4 3 2

This Large Print Edition published in accord with the standards of the N.A.V.H.

This book is a very special book, and it is dedicated to my very, very, very wonderful children: Beatrix, Trevor, Todd, Nick, Sam, Victoria, Vanessa, Maxx, and Zara, who have seen me through just about every minute of my adult life, and all of my writing career, and are the greatest joy of my existence.

This book is special because, counting my published novels, my unpublished novels from my early days, my works of nonfiction (also published and unpublished), my book of poetry, the children's books I wrote for my children—the whole shebang, this is my one-hundredth book. It is an awesome moment in my writing life, and is in great part thanks to the endless, never ceasing, ever faithful and patient, endlessly loving support of my children. I could never have accomplished this without their love and support. So this book is dedicated with all my heart and soul, love and thanks to them.

In addition, I can't reach this landmark event without thanking very special people in my life, who have contributed to this, my amazing agent and friend Mort Janklow, my beloved editor of many years and friend Carole Baron, my also beloved and incredible researcher Nancy Eisenbarth, who provides all the material that makes the books work and has been my friend since we were children. Also my publishers, my editors, and you, my loyal readers, without whom this couldn't have happened.

To all of you, my heart, my deepest thanks, and my love for this very special moment in my life. And always and above all to my children, for whom I write the books, for whom I live and breathe, and who make every moment of my life with them a precious gift.

With all my love,

d.s.

Some of the greatest crimes against humanity have been committed in the name of love.

A sociopath is a person who will destroy you, without a heart, without a conscience, without even a second glance. At first they are too perfect and too good to be true. Then, they remove your heart, and whatever else they want, with a scalpel. The operation they perform is brilliant, often but not always flawless. And when they've gotten whatever they came for in the first place, they leave you traumatized, stunned, and bleeding by the roadside, and silently move on, to do it again to someone else.

d.s.

Chapter 1

Hope Dunne made her way through the silently falling snow on Prince Street in SoHo in New York. It was seven o'clock, the shops had just closed, and the usual bustle of commerce was shutting down for the night. She had lived there for two years and she liked it. It was the trendy part of New York, and she found it friendlier than living uptown. SoHo was full of young people, there was always something to see, someone to talk to, a bustle of activity whenever she left her loft, which was her refuge. There were bright lights in all the shops.

It was her least favorite time of year, December, the week before Christmas. As she had for the past several years, she ignored it, and waited for it to pass. For the past two Christmases, she had worked at a homeless shelter. The year before that she had been in India, where the holiday didn't matter. It had been a hard jolt coming back to the States after her time there. Everything seemed so commercial and superficial in comparison.

The time she had spent in India had changed her life, and probably saved it. She had left on the spur of the moment, and been gone for over six months. Reentry into American life had been incredibly hard. Everything she owned was in storage and she had moved from Boston to New York. It didn't really matter to her where she lived, she was a photographer and took her work with her. The photographs she had taken in India and Tibet were currently being shown in a prestigious gallery uptown. Some of her other work was in museums. People compared her work to that of Diane Arbus. She had a fascination with the destitute and devastated. The agony in the eyes of some of her subjects ripped out your soul, just as it had affected hers when she photographed them. Hope's work was greatly respected, but to look at her, nothing about her demeanor suggested that she was famous or important.

Hope had spent her entire life as an observer, a chronicler of the human condition. And in order to do that, she had always said, one had to be able to disappear, to become invisible, so as not to interfere with the mood of the subject. The studies she had done in India and Tibet for the magical time she was there had confirmed it. In many ways, Hope Dunne was an almost invisible person, in other ways, she was enormous, with an inner light and strength that seemed to fill a room.

She smiled at a woman passing by, as she walked through the snow on Prince Street. She was tempted to go for a long walk in the snow, and promised herself she might do that later that evening. She lived on no particular schedule, answered to no one. One of the blessings of her solitary life was that she was entirely at liberty to do whatever she wished. She was the consummate independent woman, she was enormously disciplined about her work, and in dealing with her subjects. Sometimes she got on the subway, and rode uptown to Harlem, wandering through the streets in T-shirt and jeans, taking photographs of children. She had spent time in South America, photographing children and old people there too. She went wherever the spirit moved her, and did very little commercial work now. She still did the occasional fashion shoot for **Vogue** if the layout was unusual. But most of the magazine work she did was portraits of important people who she thought were worthwhile and interesting. She had published a remarkable book of portraits, another of children, and was going to publish a book of her photographs from India soon.

She was fortunate to be able to do whatever she wanted. She could pick and choose among the many requests she got. Although she loved doing them, she only did formal portraits now once or twice a year. More often now, she concentrated on the photographs she took in the course of her travels or on the street.

Hope was a tiny woman with porcelain white skin, and jet-black hair. Her mother had teased her when she was a child and said she looked like Snow White, which in a way, she did. And there was a fairy-tale feeling about her too. She was almost elfin in size, and unusually lithe; she was able to fit herself into the smallest, most invisible spaces and go unnoticed. The only startling thing about her was her deep violet eyes. They were a deep, deep blue, with the slightly purple color of very fine sapphires from Burma or Ceylon, and were filled with compassion that had seen the sorrows of the world. Those who had seen eyes like hers before understood instantly that she was a woman who had suffered, but wore it well, with dignity and grace. Rather than dragging her down into depression, her pain had lifted her into a peaceful place. She was not a Buddhist, but shared philosophies with them, in that she didn't fight what happened to her, but instead drifted with it, allowing life to carry her from one experience to the next. It was that depth and wisdom that shone through her work. An acceptance of life as it really was, rather than trying to force it to be what one wanted, and it never could be. She was willing to let go of what she loved, which was the hardest task of all. And the more she lived and learned and studied, the humbler she was. A monk she had met in Tibet called her a holy woman, which in fact she was, although she had no particular affinity for any formal church. If she believed in anything, she believed in life, and embraced it with a gentle touch. She was a strong reed bending in the wind, beautiful and resilient.

It was snowing harder by the time she got to the front door of her building. She was carrying a camera case over her shoulder, and her keys and wallet were in it. She carried nothing else, and she wore no makeup, except very occasionally bright red lipstick when she went out, which made her look more than ever like Snow White. And she wore her almost blue-black hair pulled straight back, either in a ponytail, a braid, or a chignon, and when she loosened it, it hung to her waist. Her graceful movements made her look like a young girl, and she had almost no lines on her face. Her biography as a photographer said that she was forty-four years old, but it was difficult to assess her age and it would have been easy to believe she was far younger. Like the photographs she took, and her subjects, she was timeless. Looking at her, one wanted to stop and watch her for a long time. She rarely wore color, and dressed almost always in black, so as not to distract her subjects, or in white in hot climates.

Once she unlocked the front door to her building, she bounded up to the third floor with a quick step. She was cold, and happy to walk into her apartment, which was considerably warmer than it had been outdoors, although the ceilings were high and sometimes the wind crept through the tall windows.

She turned on the lights, and took pleasure, as she always did, in the spartan decor. The cement floor was painted black, the white couches and inviting chairs were a soft ivory wool, and nothing about the decor was intrusive. It was so simple it was almost Zen. And the walls were covered with enormous framed black and white photographs that were her favorites among her work. The longest wall was covered with a spectacular series of a young ballerina in motion. The girl in the photographs was exceptionally beautiful, a graceful young blond dancer in her teens. It was a remarkable series, and part of Hope's personal collection. On the other walls were many photographs of children, several of monks in India at the ashram where she had lived, and two enormous ones of heads of state.

Her loft was like a gallery of her work, and on one long white lacquer table, set on sponge-covered trays, all of her cameras were lined up in almost surgical order. She hired freelance assistants when she did assignments, but most of the time she preferred to do all her own work. She found assistants helpful, but too distracting. Her favorite camera was an old Leica she had had for years. She used a Hasselblad and Mamiya in the studio as well, but she still loved her oldest camera best. She had started taking photographs when she was nine. She had attended a specially designed photography program at Brown at seventeen, and graduated at twenty-one with honors, after doing a spectacular senior project in the Middle East. She had married shortly after graduating from Brown, worked for a year as a commercial photographer, and then retired for a dozen years, with only the occasional very rare assignment. She had been back at work for the last ten years, and it was in the past decade that she had made her mark in the world and become increasingly well known. She had been famous by the time she was thirty-eight, when MOMA in New York showed an exhibit of her work. It had been one of the high points of her life.

Hope lit candles around the room and left the lights in the loft dim. Coming home to this room always soothed her. She slept on a little platform, up a ladder, on a spare narrow bed, and loved looking down at the room and the feeling of flying as she fell asleep. The loft was completely different from anywhere she had ever lived, and she loved that about it too. Because she had always feared it so much, this time she had embraced change. There was something powerful about accepting what frightened her most. Her private nemeses were loss and change, and rather than running from them, she had learned to face them with dignity and strength.

There was a small black granite kitchen at the back of the loft. She knew she had to eat, so eventually she wound up there, and heated up a can of soup. Most of the time, she was too lazy to make much of a meal. She lived on soups and salads and eggs. On the rare occasions when she wanted a real meal, she went to some simple restaurant alone and ate quickly, to get it over with. She had never been much of a cook, and made no pretense of it. It had always seemed like a waste of time to her, there were so many other things that interested her more—previously, her family, and now, her work. In the past three years, her work had become her life. She put her whole soul into it and it showed.

Hope was eating her soup, watching the snow fall outside, when her cell phone rang, and she set the soup down, and dug the phone out of her camera bag. She wasn't expecting any calls, and smiled when she heard the familiar voice of her agent, Mark Webber. She hadn't heard from him in a while.

"Okay, so where are you now? And what time zone are you in? Am I waking you up?" She laughed in response, and sat back against the couch with a smile. He had represented her for the last ten years, when she went back to work. He usually tried to push her to do commercial jobs, but he also had a deep respect for her more serious artistic endeavors. He always said that one day she would be one of the most important American photographers of her generation, and in many ways she already was, and was deeply respected by both curators and her peers.

"I'm in New York," she said, smiling. "And you're not waking me up."

"I'm disappointed. I figured you were in Nepal, or Vietnam, or someplace scary and disgusting. I'm surprised you're here." He knew how much she hated holidays, and all the reasons why. She had good reason. But she was a remarkable woman—a survivor—and a dear friend. He liked and admired her enormously.

"I figured I'd stick around for a while. I was sitting here watching the snow. It's pretty. I might go out and shoot for a bit later. Some nice old-fashioned stuff."

"It's freezing out," he warned her. "Don't catch cold." He was one of the few people who worried about her, and she was touched by his concern. She had moved around too much in recent years to stay in contact with her old friends. She had lived in Boston since college, but when she got back from India, she decided to move to New York. Hope had always been a solitary person, and was even more so now. It concerned him, but she seemed content with her life as it was.

"I just got in," she reassured him, "and I was having some chicken soup."

"My grandmother would approve," he said, smiling again. "So what do you have planned at the moment?" He knew she hadn't taken any assignments, since nothing had come through him.

"Nothing much. I was thinking about going up to the house in Cape Cod over the holiday. It's pretty there this time of year."

"How cheerful. Only you would think it's pretty. Everyone else would get suicidal there this time of year. I have a better idea." He had on his "have I got a deal for you" voice, and she laughed. She knew him well and liked him too.

"Like what? What crazy assignment are you going to try and talk me into now, Mark? Las Vegas on Christmas Eve?" They both laughed at the prospect of it. Occasionally he came up with some wild ideas, which she almost always turned down. But at least he had to try. He always promised the potential clients he would.

"No, although Vegas for the holidays sounds like fun to me." They both knew he loved to gamble and took occasional trips to Las Vegas and Atlantic City. "This is actually respectable and quite dignified. We got a call from a major publishing house today. Their star author wants a portrait sitting for his latest book cover. He hasn't delivered the book yet, but he will any minute, and the publisher needs the shot done now for their catalog and layouts for advance publicity in the trades. It's all very proper and on the up-and-up. The only problem is that they have a tight deadline. They should have thought of it before."

"How tight?" Hope asked, sounding noncommittal, and stretching out on the white wool couch as she listened.

"They need to do the shoot by next week, for their production schedule. That means you'd be shooting around Christmas, but he requested you, and said he won't do it with anyone else. At least the guy's got good taste. And the fee is pretty hefty. He's a big deal."

"Who's the author?" That would have an impact on her decision, and her agent hesitated before he said the name. He was an important author, had won the National Book Award, and was always at the top of the best-seller lists, but he was a bit of a wild card, and had appeared in the press frequently with assorted women. Mark didn't know how Hope would feel about shooting him, particularly if he misbehaved, and he could. There were no guarantees that he wouldn't. She usually preferred to work with serious subjects.

"Finn O'Neill," he said, without further comment, waiting to see what she'd say. He didn't want to influence her or discourage her. It was entirely up to her, and it would be perfectly reasonable if they declined since it was on short notice, and Christmas week.

"I read his last book," she said with interest. "Very scary, but an amazing piece of work." She was intrigued. "He's a smart guy. Have you ever met him?"

"Honestly, no, I don't know him. I've seen him at a couple of parties, here and in London. He seems like a pretty charming guy, with a penchant for beautiful women and young girls."

"I've got nothing to fear from him in that case," she said, laughing. She was trying to remember what he looked like from the back of the book she'd read, but couldn't.

"Don't be so sure. You look half your age. But you can handle him. I'm not worried about that. I just didn't know if you'd want to go to London this time of year. On the other hand, it sounds less depressing than the Cape, so maybe that would be a blessing. They'll fly you first class, all expenses paid, and put you up at Claridge's. He lives in Ireland, but he has a flat in London and he's there right now."

"That's too bad," she said, sounding disappointed. "I'd rather shoot him in Ireland. That would be more unusual than London."

"I don't think that's an option. He wants to meet in London. It shouldn't take you more than a day. You can be back in time to get really depressed at the Cape. Maybe for New Year's." She laughed at what he said, and thought about it. The idea had some appeal. Finn O'Neill was an important writer, and would surely make an interesting subject. She was annoyed that she had no recollection of his face. "How do you feel about it?"

At least she hadn't turned him down flat, and Mark thought it would be good for her, particularly if the other option was going to Cape Cod by herself. She had a house there, and had spent summers there for years. She loved it.

"What do **you** think?" She always asked his advice—although she sometimes didn't take it. But at least she asked. Some of his clients never did.

"I think you should do it. He's interesting and important, it's respectable, and you haven't done a portrait for a while. You can't spend all your time taking shots of monks and beggars," Mark said in a light tone.

"Yeah, maybe you're right." She sounded pensive. She still loved the portrait work if the subject was intriguing, and Finn O'Neill certainly was. "Can you get me an assistant over there? I don't need to take one with me." Hope was not a demanding person.

"I'll line someone up, don't worry about it." He held his breath, waiting to hear if she'd do it. He thought she should, and in a funny way, so did she. She was dreading the holidays, as she always did, and a trip to London might be a perfect distraction for her, particularly right now.

"Okay. I'll do it. When do you think I should go?"

"I'd say pretty quickly, so you can be in and out

by Christmas." And then he realized again that it didn't matter to her.

"I could go tomorrow night. I have a few loose ends to take care of here, and I promised to call the curator at MOMA. I could take a night flight tomorrow and sleep on the plane."

"Perfect. I'll tell them. They said they'd take care of all the arrangements, and I'll find you an assistant." It was never a problem finding people to assist her. Young photographers were always dying to work for Hope Dunne, and she had a reputation for being easy to get along with, which was well deserved. Hope was pleasant, professional, and undemanding, and what students or assistants learned from her was invaluable to them. Having freelanced for her as an assistant, even for a day, looked good on their résumés. "How long do you want to stay?"

"I don't know," she said, thinking about it. "A few days. I don't want to rush. I don't know what kind of subject he is. It could take him a day or two to loosen up. Maybe book me for four days. We'll see how it goes. That gives us time if we need it. I'll leave as soon as we finish."

"Done. I'm glad you're doing it," he told her warmly. "And London is fun this time of year. Everything is all decorated and lit up, they're not as PC as here. The Brits still believe in Christmas." In the States, it was becoming a taboo word.

"I like Claridge's," she said happily, and then she

sounded more serious. "I might try to see Paul, if he's there. I'm not sure where he is. I haven't talked to him in a while." It was odd to think that they had been married for twenty-one years, and now she didn't know where he was. Her life these days always reminded her of the Chinese saying, "That was then, this is now." It certainly was. And what a difference.

"How's he doing?" Mark asked gently. He knew it was a sensitive subject for her, but given everything that had happened, she had adjusted remarkably well. As far as Mark was concerned, she defined the terms "good sport" and "incredible human being." Few people survived what she did as well as she had.

"Paul's about the same, I think." She answered Mark's question about her ex-husband. "He's on some experimental medication from Harvard. He seems to be doing pretty well."

"I'll call the publisher, and tell them you're taking the assignment," Mark said, changing the subject. He never knew what to say about Paul. Hope was always gracious about it, he knew she still loved her ex-husband, and had accepted the hand Fate had dealt her. She was never bitter or angry. Mark didn't know how she did it. "I'll call you tomorrow with more details," he promised her, and a minute later they hung up.

Hope put her soup mug in the dishwasher after that, and went to stare out the window, at the steadily falling snow. There were already several inches on the ground, and it made her think of London. The last time she had been there, it had been snowing too and looked like a Christmas card. She wondered if Paul was in London now, but decided not to call him until she arrived, in case plans changed, and she had to see what kind of spare time she had. She didn't want to see him on Christmas, and risk either of them getting maudlin. She wanted to avoid that at all costs. They were best friends now. He knew that she would be there for him if he needed her, and she also knew that he was too proud to call. If she saw him, they would both be careful to keep it light, which was what worked best for them these days. The rest was too hard to talk about, and served no purpose.

Hope stood at the window and watched a man leave footprints in the snow, followed by an old woman slipping and sliding as she walked her dog. Watching them, she couldn't resist. She put her coat and boots on, and went back out, with her Leica in her pocket, not the fancy new one that everyone coveted, which she had too, but the old one she loved best. It was a faithful friend and had served her well.

Ten minutes later, she was walking down the street with the snow falling all around her as she prowled along, looking for the right shots. Without planning it, she arrived at the entrance to the subway, and hurried down the stairs. She'd just had an idea. She wanted to get some shots in Central Park at night, and after that, she was going to head for some of the rougher neighborhoods on the West Side. Snow had a way of softening people's hearts and faces. For Hope, the night was young, and if she felt like it, she could stay out all night. It was one of the advantages she had discovered of being alone. She could work whenever she wanted, for however long she cared to, and she never had to feel guilty. There was no one waiting for her at home.

Later that night she walked back down Prince Street at three A.M., smiling to herself and content with her night's work. The snow had just stopped as Hope let herself into her building, and walked up the stairs to her loft. She took her damp coat off and left it in the kitchen, and reminded herself that she had to pack for London in the morning. Five minutes later, she was in her cozy nightgown and tucked into her narrow bed on the sleeping balcony, and she was asleep as soon as her head hit the pillow. It had been a very enjoyable, productive night.

Chapter 2

When Hope got to the airport, the flight to London was two hours late. She had her cameras in her hand luggage, and sat reading in the first-class lounge until they called the flight. She had picked up another book of Finn O'Neill's and wanted to read it on the trip. It had started snowing again, and after they left the gate, they had to de-ice the plane. In all, they were nearly four hours late taking off, after waiting on the runway for two hours. Hope didn't really care, she always slept on long flights. She let the flight attendant know that she wouldn't be eating the meal, and told her what time she wanted to be woken up, exactly forty minutes before they landed at Heathrow. That would give her time for a cup of coffee and a croissant before they began their descent, and also time to brush her teeth and hair. It was all she needed in order to look respectable enough to go through immigration and go to the hotel.

As she always did, Hope slept soundly on the plane, and was happy to see that they landed without difficulty despite the morning fog. As it turned out, the delay had served them well and had given the winter weather time to clear. And as promised, the car from Claridge's was waiting for her as soon as she cleared customs carrying her camera bag. She had already ordered the rental of all the equipment she needed, and it was being delivered to the hotel that afternoon. She was meeting her subject at his home the following morning. She wanted some time to get to know him and they were going to shoot in the afternoon.

So far, everything seemed easy and was on track, and since she had gotten enough sleep on the plane, she was wide awake as they drove into town, and happy when she saw her room at the hotel. It was one of Claridge's prettier suites, with walls painted a deep coral, floral fabrics, English antiques, and framed prints on the walls. It was warm and cozy, and she ran a bath as soon as she arrived. She thought about calling Paul, but she wanted to wait until she saw Finn, so she could determine what kind of free time she had. If need be, if he was in town, she could see Paul on the last day. She shut her mind to all thoughts of their earlier days, she didn't allow herself to think about it, and slipped into the bath and closed her eyes. She wanted to go for a walk as soon as she dressed and had something to eat. It was two o'clock in the afternoon in London by then. And as soon as she called room service to order an omelette and a cup of soup, her rented equipment arrived, the assistant they had hired for her called, and it was four o'clock before she was able to leave the hotel.

She went for a long brisk walk to New Bond Street, and looked at all the shops. They were brightly decorated for Christmas, and every store she glanced into was full of shoppers. Their holiday shopping was in full swing. She had no one to buy a gift for—she had already sent Paul a framed photograph from New York, and a case of good French wine to Mark. She walked back to the hotel around six o'clock, and as soon as she walked into her room, Finn O'Neill called. He had a deep masculine voice that sounded a little hoarse. He asked for her by name and then exploded in a fit of coughing. He sounded very sick.

"I'm dying," he announced, when he stopped coughing. "I can't see you tomorrow morning. Besides, I don't want to get you sick." It was nice of him to think of and be concerned, and she didn't want to get sick either, but she hated to lose a day. She had nothing else to do in London, unless she saw Paul.

"You sound awful," she said sympathetically. "Have you seen a doctor?"

"He said he'd come over later, but he hasn't shown up yet. I'm really sorry. You were nice to come all the way to London. Maybe if I stay in bed tomorrow, I'll be okay by the next day. Are you in a hurry to get back?" He sounded worried, and she smiled.

"I'm fine," she said calmly. "I can stay as long as I have to, till we get the job done."

"I hope you have a good retoucher. I look like shit," he said, sounding like a little kid, and very sorry for himself.

"You'll look fine, I promise. It's all in the lighting," she reassured him, "and we can airbrush. Just get better. Chicken soup," she recommended, and he laughed.

"I don't want to look like Georgia O'Keeffe's grandfather on the book."

"You won't." It was quite an image. She had looked him up on the Internet, and knew that he was forty-six years old, and now she remembered what he looked like. He was a good-looking man. And his voice sounded young and energetic, even if he was sick.

"Are you okay at the hotel?" he asked, sounding concerned.

"I'm fine," she reassured him again.

"I really appreciate your coming over here on such short notice. I don't know what my publisher was thinking, they forgot we needed a photo for the book, and they just reminded me this week. It's a little crazy, with Christmas and everything. I asked them to contact you, but I didn't think you'd come."

"I had no other plans. I was going to Cape Cod, and it's actually more fun to be here."

"Yes, it is," he agreed. "I live in Ireland, but it's pretty depressing there this time of year too. I have a house here that I use whenever I'm not writing. Have you ever been to Ireland?" he asked with sudden interest, and then succumbed to another fit of coughing.

"Not in a long time," she admitted. "It's very pretty, but I haven't had any reason to go there in years. I like it better in the summer."

"Me too, but the wet, brooding winters are good for my writing," he laughed then, "and Ireland is good for my taxes. Writers don't pay income tax in Ireland, which is pretty cool. I took Irish citizenship two years ago. It works well for me," he said, sounding pleased, and she laughed.

"That sounds like a great deal. Was your family Irish?" Given his name, she assumed they were, and enjoyed chatting with him. It was a good opportunity to get to know him a little better, even if on the phone. The more they talked, the more at ease with her he would be when they finally met and worked together.

"My parents were Irish, born in Ireland, but I was born in New York. Their being Irish made it easier to make the switch though. I had dual nationality, and then finally gave up my U.S. passport. It just made more sense for me, as long as I'm willing to live there. There are some fabulous houses in Ireland, and some beautiful countryside despite the bad weather. You'll have to come and visit sometime." It was the kind of thing people said, although she couldn't imagine doing that, and once she took his photograph for the book jacket, it was unlikely that they'd see each other again, unless she did another shoot with him.

They chatted for a while longer, and he told her what his book was about. It was about a serial killer and was set in Scotland. It sounded eerie, but the plot had some interesting twists and he said he'd give her a copy when it was finished. He said he was putting the last touches on it. She told him she hoped he felt better and agreed to meet two days later, to give him time to get over his cold. And after that Hope decided to call Paul. She had no idea if he was in London, but she figured it was worth a try. He answered on the second ring, and he sounded pleased and surprised to hear her. She could hear the familiar tremor in his voice. Over the years, his voice had changed, and sometimes his speech slurred.

"What a nice surprise. Where are you? In New York?"

"No," she said simply, with a quiet smile. "I'm in London. I came over here to work, just for a few days. I'm shooting a book jacket for an author."

"I didn't think you did that anymore, after your last big museum show," he said warmly. He had always been proud of her work.

"I still do commercial work once in a while, just to keep my hand in. I can't do arty stuff all the time. It's fun to do different things. I'm shooting Finn O'Neill."

"I like his books," Paul said, sounding impressed and genuinely pleased by her call. She could hear it in his voice.

"So do I. He's got a cold, so we delayed the shoot by a day. I was wondering if you were here and wanted to have lunch tomorrow."

"I'd love it," he said quickly. "I'm leaving day after tomorrow for the Bahamas. It's too cold here." He had a beautiful boat he kept in the Caribbean in winter. He spent a lot of time on it. It was his escape from the world.

"I'm glad I called."

"So am I." They agreed to meet at the hotel for lunch the next day. She hadn't asked him how he was. She would be able to judge it for herself when she saw him, and he didn't like to talk about his illness.

Paul had turned sixty that fall, and had been struggling with Parkinson's for ten years. It had changed everything about their life, and his. He had developed a tremor right after his fiftieth birthday, and at first he had denied it, but as a cardiovascular surgeon, he couldn't hide from it for long. He had had no choice but to retire within six months. And then the bottom had dropped out of his world and her own. He had continued to teach at Harvard for the next five years, until he couldn't manage that anymore either. He had retired completely at fifty-five, and that was when the drinking began. For two years he hid it from everyone they knew, except for her.

The only wise thing he had done during that time was make some excellent investments, in two companies that made surgical equipment. He had advised one of them, and the investments had been more profitable than anything else he had ever done. One of the companies went public, and when he sold his shares within two years of his retirement, he made a fortune, and bought his first boat. But the drinking kept everything about their life on edge, and as the Parkinson's hampered him more and more, he was barely able to function. And when he wasn't sick, he was drunk, or both. He had finally gone into treatment for his drinking at a residential facility that one of his colleagues at Harvard had recommended. But by then, their entire world had fallen apart. There was nothing left and no reason to stay together, and Paul had made the decision to divorce her. She would have stayed with him forever, but he wouldn't allow it.

As a physician, he knew better than anyone what lay ahead for him, and he refused to drag her through it. He made the decision about the divorce entirely on his own, and gave her no choice. Their divorce had been final two years before, after her return from her months in India. They tried not to talk about their marriage and divorce anymore. The subject was too painful for both of them. Somehow, with all that had happened, they had lost each other. They still loved each other and were close, but he wouldn't allow her to be part of his life anymore. She knew that he cared about her and loved her, but he was determined to die quietly on his own. And other than her work, his seemingly generous gesture had left her completely alone and at loose ends.

She worried about him, but she knew that medically he was in good hands. He spent months at a time on his boat, and the rest of the time he lived in London, or went back to Boston for treatment at Harvard. But there was relatively little they could do to help him. The disease was slowly devouring him, but for now, he could still get around, although it was a challenge for him. It was easier for him being on the boat, with the crew around him all the time.

They had married when Hope was twenty-one years old, when she graduated from Brown. He had already been a surgeon and professor at Harvard by then, and was thirty-seven years old. They had met when Paul came to Brown to teach for a semester, during a sabbatical he had taken from Harvard. It was Hope's junior year at Brown. Paul had fallen in love with her the first time he laid eyes on her, and their affair had been passionate and intense, until they married a year later right after graduation. And even in the two years since their divorce, she had never loved any other man. Paul Forrest was an impossible act to follow, and she was still deeply attached to him, whether they were married or not. He had been able to divorce her, but not to make her fall out of love with him. She just accepted it as a fact of their life. And even though his illness had changed him, she still saw the same brilliant man and mind within the broken body.

The loss of his profession had nearly destroyed him, and in many ways he was greatly diminished, but not in the eyes of his ex-wife. To her, his tremor and shuffling gait didn't change the man he was.

Hope spent the night quietly in her hotel room, reading O'Neill's book, trying not to think about Paul, and the life they had once shared. It was a door neither of them dared open anymore, there were too many ghosts behind it, and they were better off keeping their exchanges about the present, rather than the past. But her eyes lit up when she saw him the next day. She was waiting in the lobby for him, and saw Paul shuffle his feet slowly as he moved toward her with a cane, but he was still tall and handsome, stood erect, and despite the tremor, his eyes were bright and he looked well. She still thought he was the nicest man in the world, and although his illness had aged him, he was a fine-looking man.

He looked equally happy to see her, and gave her a warm hug and a kiss on the cheek. "You look terrific," he said, smiling at her. She was wearing black slacks, high heels, and a bright red coat, with her black hair pulled back in a bun. Her dark violet eyes looked huge and full of life as she took him in. To her practiced eye, he looked no worse than he had in a while, maybe even slightly better. The experimental medication he was on seemed to be helping, although he was still somewhat unsteady as she took his arm and they walked into the dining room. She could feel his whole body shake. The Parkinson's was so cruel.

The maître d' gave them a good table, and they chatted easily as they caught up with each other and decided what to eat. It was always so comfortable for her with him. They were so familiar with each other, knew each other so perfectly. She had known and loved him since she was nineteen, and it seemed strange to her at times to no longer be married to him. But he had been intransigent about it—he refused to have her saddled with a sick old man. She was sixteen years younger, which had made no difference to either of them, until he got sick, and then it had mattered to him. He had opted out of her life, although they still loved each other, and always had a good time when they were together. Within minutes he had her laughing about something, and she told him all about her recent shows, trips, and work. She hadn't seen him in six months, although they talked on the phone fairly regularly. Even though they were no longer married, she couldn't imagine a life without him in it.

"I looked up your subject on his publisher's website last night," Paul told her as his hands shook while he tried to eat. Inevitably, he had a hard time feeding himself, but was determined to do it, and she made no comment at whatever he spilled, nor reached over to help him. It took every ounce of dignity he could muster to go out to restaurants, but she was proud of him that he still did. Everything about his illness had been an agony for him, the career he had lost that had meant everything to him, and on which his self-esteem had rested, the marriage that had ultimately been a casualty to it, because he refused to drag her down with him. The only real pleasure he had now was sailing, while slowly he deteriorated. Even Hope knew that he was only a shadow of the man he had once been, although out of pride, if nothing else, he tried to hide it. At sixty, he should have been vital and alive, still in the bloom of his life and career. Instead, he was in the winter of his life, alone now, just as she was, although she was so much younger. Paul was slipping ever so slowly out of life, and it always upset her deeply when she saw it. He put a good front on it, but the reality was brutal, especially for him.

"O'Neill is a very interesting man," Paul went

on, looking intrigued. "He seems to have been born in the States, of a noble Irish family, and he returned to reclaim his ancestral estate. There was a photo of it on the Internet too, it's quite a place. It's beautiful, in a fallen-down ancient way. There are some lovely old houses like that in Ireland. I've noticed that a lot of the furniture from those places comes up for auction at Sotheby's and Christie's. They look like French antiques and in many cases are. In any event, he lives in an enormous house, and he's an Irish aristocrat, which I'd never realized before. He went to some ordinary American university, but he has a doctorate from Oxford, and he was decorated by the British, after he won the National Book Award in the States, for fiction. He's actually Sir Finn O'Neill," he reminded her, which jogged a memory for her.

"I'd forgotten that," she admitted. Paul was always a source of endless knowledge for her. And then she looked sheepish. "I forgot to call him Sir Finn when he called me. He didn't seem to care though."

"He sounds like a wild character," Paul said, giving up on eating. Some days were harder than others, and there was only so much embarrassment he could tolerate in public. "He's been involved with a number of very well known women, heiresses, princesses, actresses, models. He's a bit of a playboy, but he certainly has talent. It should be an interesting shoot. He sounds like a loose cannon with some fairly outrageous behavior, but at least he won't be boring. He'll probably try to seduce you," Paul said with a sad smile. He had relinquished all claim to her, except in friendship, long since, and never asked about her love life. He didn't want to know. And she spared him the agony of telling him that she was still in love with him. There were a number of subjects they never touched on, both past and present. In the circumstances, what they shared, over the occasional lunch or dinner, or on the phone, was the best they could do. And this last bond between them was what they clung to.

"He's not going to seduce me," Hope reassured him. "I'm probably twice the age of what he goes out with, if he's as wild as you say." She didn't look interested or worried. He was a subject, not a date, in her mind anyway.

"Don't be so sure," Paul said wisely.

"I'll hit him with a tripod if he tries anything," she said firmly, and they both laughed. "Besides, I have an assistant working with me tomorrow. Maybe he'll like her. And he's sick, that should help."

They chatted amiably after lunch, and dawdled over dessert. Paul made two attempts to drink the tea he'd ordered and couldn't, and Hope didn't dare offer to hold the cup for him, although she wished she could. And after lunch, she walked him out of the hotel and waited while the doorman got him a taxi to take him back to his apartment.

"Are you coming back to New York one of these days?" she asked him hopefully. He had an apartment at the Hotel Carlyle, which he rarely used. And he avoided Boston entirely now, except for medical treatments. Going back to visit his old colleagues was too depressing for him. They were all still at the height of their careers, and his had been over for ten years, far too soon.

"I'm going to stay in the Caribbean for the winter. And then probably come back here." He liked the anonymity of London, the fact that no one knew him. There was no one to feel sorry for him here, and it was painful for him to see the sympathy in Hope's eyes. It was one of the reasons why he hadn't stayed married to her. He didn't want to be an object of pity. He preferred being alone to being a burden to someone he loved. And in making that decision, he had deprived them both. But there had been no swaying him once he made up his mind. Hope had tried to no avail, and finally accepted that he had a right to choose how he wanted to live out his final years, and whatever the reasons, it wasn't with her.

"Let me know how the interview with O'Neill goes," Paul said, as the doorman hailed him a cab. He looked down at her with a smile then, and he pulled the small familiar figure into his arms, and as she hugged him, he closed his eyes. "Take care of yourself, Hope," he said with a lump in his throat, and she nodded. Sometimes he felt guilty for letting her go, but he had firmly believed it was the right thing for her, and he still did. He had no right to ruin her life, in order to serve his.

"I will, you too," she said, as she kissed his cheek and helped him into the cab. It pulled away from the curb in front of Claridge's a moment later, and she stood and waved in the cold, as they drove off. It always made her sad to see him, but he was the only family she had left. She realized as she walked back into the hotel that she had forgotten to wish him a Merry Christmas, but she was glad she had. It would only have brought back memories for both of them, which would have been much, much too hard.

She went up to her room and changed into flat shoes, and a heavier coat. And a few minutes later, she left the hotel quietly and went for a long, solitary walk.

Chapter 3

Fiona Casey, the assistant her agent had hired for her, showed up at Hope's hotel room at nine o'clock the next morning. She was a bright, funny, redheaded girl, who was totally in awe of Hope. She was a graduate photography student at the Royal Academy of Arts, and supported herself by doing freelance work. She was equally impressed that they would be shooting Finn O'Neill, and stumbled all over herself, carrying Hope's equipment out to a rental van. They were due at Finn O'Neill's house at ten o'clock. Hope hadn't heard from him again, so she assumed he was healthy enough to do the shoot.

The driver the hotel had provided for her with the van drove them the short distance to an elegant mews house at a fashionable address. The house was tiny, as they all were on the narrow backstreet, and as soon as she struck the brass knocker on the door, a maid in a uniform appeared and let them

in. She led them into a doll-sized living room near
the front door, which was crammed with weath-
ered antique English furniture. The bookcase was
overflowing, and there were stacks of books on the
floor, and glancing at them, Hope could see that
many of the books were old, either leatherbound,
or on closer inspection, first editions. This was
clearly a man who loved books. The couches were
comfortable, covered in leather, and very old, and
there was a fire burning brightly in the grate, which
seemed to be the only heat source in the room. It
was cold, except when one stood close to the fire.
And in close proximity to the sitting room was a
dining room painted dark green, and a small
kitchen beyond. Each of the rooms was very small,
but had lots of charm.

They sat there for nearly half an hour, waiting
for Finn, as both Fiona and Hope got up to stand
near the fire, chatting quietly in whispers. The
house was so minute that it seemed awkward to
speak too loudly, for fear that someone would
overhear them. And then, just as Hope began wondering where he was, a tall man with a mane of
dark hair and electric blue eyes burst into the
room. The house seemed ridiculously small for a
man his size, as though if he stretched his arms he
could touch the walls and span the room. It
seemed an absurd place for him, particularly after
she had looked up his ancestral home in Ireland on
the Internet after Paul mentioned it to her.

"I'm so sorry to keep you waiting," Finn said in an ordinary American accent. She didn't know why, but after all she'd read about O'Neill and his ties to Ireland, she almost expected him to have a brogue, except that they had spoken on the phone the night before, and he had sounded like any other educated New Yorker, although he looked more European. Whatever his ancestry, he was in fact as American as Hope. And his cold sounded a lot better. He coughed a few times, but no longer sounded as though he were dying. In fact, he looked surprisingly healthy and full of life. And he had a smile that melted Fiona on the spot, as he had the maid offer her a cup of coffee while he invited Hope to join him upstairs. He apologized to Fiona for disappearing with Hope, but he wanted to get to know his photographer a little better.

She followed him up a narrow winding staircase, and found herself in a cozy but larger living room, filled with books, antiques, objects, mementos, old leather couches, and comfortable chairs, and there was a blazing fire in the fireplace. It was the kind of room where you wanted to tuck yourself in and stay for days. Every object was fascinating and intriguing. Some were from his travels, and others looked as though he had treasured them for years. The room was full of personality and warmth, and despite his large frame and long limbs, it somehow seemed the perfect place for him. He let himself down into the embrace of an overstuffed old couch, and stretched out his long legs toward the fire with a broad grin at Hope. She saw that he was wearing well-worn, very elegant black leather riding boots.

"I hope I wasn't rude to your assistant," he said apologetically. "I just thought it might be nice to get acquainted, before we get to work. I'm always self-conscious about being photographed. As a writer, I'm used to observing everyone else, not to having others watch me. I don't like being in the limelight." He said it with a boyish, slightly lop-sided smile that immediately won her heart. He had an immense amount of charm.

"I feel exactly the same way. I don't like being photographed either. I like being at the shooting end myself." She was already thinking about where she could photograph him best. She almost pre-ferred him right where he was, stretching out com-fortably in front of the fire, his head slightly thrown back so she could see his face. "Are you feeling better?" He appeared so healthy and vital that it was hard to believe he'd ever been sick. He still sounded a little hoarse, but he was full of en-ergy, and his blue eyes danced when he laughed. He reminded her of the fairy tales of her youth, and looked like the perfect handsome prince, or the hero in a book, although most of the subjects of his work were fairly dark.

"I'm fine now," he said blithely, and then coughed a little. "This house is so small, I always feel somewhat foolish in it, but it's so comfortable and easy, I could never give it up. I've had it for years. I've written some of my best books here." And then he turned to point to his desk behind them. It was a wonderful old partner's desk, which he said had been on a ship. It dominated the far corner of the room, where his computer sat on it, looking strangely out of place. "Thank you for coming over," he said kindly. He seemed truly grateful, as the maid walked in, carrying a silver tray with two cups of tea. "I know it was a crazy thing to ask you to do, on Christmas week. But they needed the shot, and I'm finishing a book next week, and due to start another right after, so I'll be back in Dublin working. Meeting you in London now made more sense."

"It was fine actually," Hope said easily, helping herself to one of the cups of tea. Finn took the other one, and the maid instantly disappeared back down the stairs. "I had nothing else to do," she said, as he examined her carefully. She was younger than he had expected, and better looking. He was startled by how tiny and delicate she was, and the strength of her violet eyes.

"You're a good sport to come over here right before Christmas," he commented, as she looked at the light and shadows on his face. He was going to be easy to photograph. Everything about him was expressive, and he was a strikingly handsome man.

"London is fun this time of year," Hope said

with a smile as she set down her cup of tea on the regimental drum he used as a coffee table. A stack of beautiful old alligator suitcases sat to one side of the fireplace. Everywhere she looked there was something to admire. "I usually ignore the holiday, so it was fun to come over here. The assignment was a nice surprise and came at a good time. What about you? Will you be spending Christmas in Ireland or here?" She liked getting to know her subjects before she started work, and O'Neill was easy and relaxed. He didn't seem like a difficult person, and he was open and accessible as he smiled at her over his cup of tea. He was extremely charming and appealing.

"No, I'm going to stay here and go back afterward," he answered. "My son is flying over the day after Christmas. He goes to MIT, he's a bright kid. He's a computer whiz. His mother died when he was seven, and he grew up with me. I really miss him now that he's in college in the States. It's more fun for him here in London than in Dublin. And then he's going skiing with friends. We're very close," Finn said proudly, and then looked at her intently. He was curious about her. "Do you have kids?"

"No." She shook her head quietly. "I don't." He was surprised. She looked as though she would. She didn't look like one of those career women who had decided not to have children. She seemed more motherly and there was a noticeably gentle softness about her. She was soft-spoken and seemed nurturing and kind.

"Married?" He glanced at her left hand, and there was no ring.

"No," and then she opened up a little. "I was. My husband was a cardiovascular surgeon at Harvard. Heart-lung transplants were his specialty. He retired ten years ago. We've been divorced for over two years."

"I think retiring destroys people. I'm going to keep writing until they carry me out. I wouldn't know what else to do with myself. Was retiring hard on him? It must have been. Heart surgeons are always heroes, particularly at Harvard, I imagine."

"He had no choice. He got sick," she said quietly.

"Worse yet. That must have been tough for him. Cancer?" He wanted to know about her, and as they talked, she watched the movement of his face, and the bright blue of his eyes. She was glad they were shooting in color—it would have been a shame not to get the actual color of those eyes. They were the bluest she'd ever seen.

"No, Parkinson's. He stopped operating as soon as he found out. He taught for several years after that, but eventually, he had to give that up too. It was very hard on him."

"And probably on you too. That's a brutal disappointment for a man in the midst of a career like that. Hence the divorce?"

"That and other things," she said vaguely, glancing around the room again. There was a photograph of Finn with a handsome young blond boy, who she guessed was his son, and he nodded when he saw her looking at it.

"That's my boy, Michael. I miss him now that he's at school. It's hard getting used to his not being around."

"Did he grow up in Ireland?" She smiled at the image. Like his father, he was good-looking.

"We lived in New York and London when he was small. I moved to Ireland two years after he left for college. He's an all-around American kid. I never really was. I always felt different, maybe because my parents weren't born in the States. All they ever talked about was moving back. So eventually, I did."

"And Ireland feels like home?" she asked as their eyes met.

"Now it does. I reclaimed my family's ancestral house. Restoring it will take me the next hundred years. The place was falling apart when I got it, and parts of it still are. It's an enormous old Palladian home built by Sir Edward Lovett Pearce in the early 1700s. Unfortunately, my parents died long before I got it back, and Michael thought I was nuts to take it on." There was a photograph of it on the mantelpiece, and he handed it to Hope. It was a gigantic classic house, with a large stone staircase in front, and rounded side wings with columns. In the photograph Finn was in front of the house, astride an elegant black horse. He looked very much the lord of the manor.

"It's an amazing house," Hope said with admiration. "It must be quite a project to restore."

"It has been, but it's a labor of love. It will be my legacy to Michael one day. I should have it in decent shape by then, providing I live for at least another hundred years to do it." He laughed as he said it, and Hope handed back the photograph. Now she was sorry she hadn't shot him there. In comparison to the remarkable Palladian palace, his London mews house suddenly seemed ridiculously small, but all his publisher wanted was a head shot, and for that the cozy room they were sitting in was good enough.

"I'd better get my assistant started," Hope said, standing up. "It'll take us a while to set up. Do you have any preference about location?" she asked, glancing around again. She had liked the way he looked when he was sitting on the couch, relaxing and talking about his Dublin house. And she wanted to shoot him at his desk as well, and maybe a couple of shots standing next to the bookcase. It was always hard to predict where the magic would happen, until they connected as she worked. He seemed like an easy subject; everything about him was open and relaxed. And as she looked into his eyes, she could sense that he was the kind of man you could trust, and rely on. There was a feeling of warmth and humor about him, as though he had a good understanding of people's quirks and the vagaries of life. And there was a hint of laughter in his eyes. He was sexy too, but in a distinguished, aristocratic way. There was nothing sleazy about him, even though her agent had warned her that he was something of a womanizer. Seeing him, that was easy to understand. He was enormously appealing, seemed very caring, and was a gorgeous hunk of man. And she suspected that if he turned the charm on at full volume, he'd be hard to resist. She was glad she wasn't in that position, and was only working with him. He had been very complimentary about her work. She could tell from questions he had asked her, and things he referred to, that he had Googled her. He seemed to know the entire list of museums she'd been shown in, some of which even she didn't remember most of the time. He was very well informed.

Hope went back downstairs and helped Fiona sort out the equipment. She told her what she wanted, and then went upstairs to show her where to set up the lights she'd be using. She wanted to photograph him first on the couch, and then at his desk. As she watched Fiona set up, Finn disappeared upstairs to his bedroom, and he reappeared an hour later when Hope let him know that they were ready. She sent the maid up to tell him, and he came back downstairs in a soft blue cashmere sweater the same color as his eyes. It was a good look on him, and his trim form looked sexy and masculine in the sweater. She could see that he had just shaved, and his hair was loose but freshly brushed.

"All set?" She smiled at him, picking up her Mamiya. She told him where to sit on the couch, Fiona gave them a light reading as the lights flashed beneath the umbrella, and Hope set down the Mamiya and took a quick Polaroid to show him the pose and the setting. He said it looked great to him. A minute later, Hope started shooting, alternating between the Mamiya, the Leica, and the Hasselblad for classic portrait shots. She took mostly color, and a few rolls of black and white. That was always her preference for a more interesting look, but his publisher had been specific about wanting color and Finn said he preferred it too. He said that it felt more real to his readers and made it easier for them to connect with him, than in an arty black and white shot on the back of the book.

"You're the boss," Hope said, smiling, as she looked into the camera again and he laughed.

"No, you're the artist." He seemed completely at ease in front of the camera, moving his head and changing his expression by fractions, as though he had done this a thousand times before, which

Hope knew he had. The photograph they were taking was for his eleventh book, and so far, all of them for the past twenty years had been best sellers. At forty-six, he was an institution in American literature, just as she was in her field. It would have been hard to decide which of them was more famous or more respected. They were an even match in their reputations and skills in separate fields.

They shot for an hour, as she praised him for good moves and the right turn of his head, and she was almost sure she had gotten the winning shot in the first half hour, but she knew better than to stop there. She had Fiona move the light setup to his desk, and suggested he take a half-hour break, and maybe put a white shirt on, but leave it open at the neck. He asked if she'd like to stop for lunch then, but Hope said that if he didn't mind, she'd prefer to continue working. She didn't want to break the mood, or to get slow and lazy after lunch. She found that it was usually better to stay on it once she and her subject were working well together. A long lunch or a glass of wine could break the spell for either or both of them, and she didn't want that to happen. She was delighted with what they were getting. As a portrait subject, Finn O'Neill was a dream and he was fun to talk to. The time was speeding by.

Half an hour later, he was back in his living room, in the white shirt Hope had asked for, and sat down at his handsome partner's desk. Hope moved the computer away because it looked so incongruous in that setting. He was a delightful subject, fooling around, telling jokes and stories about well-known artists, writers, his house in Ireland, and the outrageous stunts he had pulled on book tours in his youth. At one point he had tears in his eyes when he talked about his son and bringing him up on his own, without a mother after her death. There were so many magical moments while she talked to him that Hope knew she would have a multitude of great shots to choose from, each one better than the last.

And then finally, after a few shots of him leaning against an antique ladder in front of the bookcase, they were through. And just as she said it, he exploded in laughter with a look of joy and release, and she stole one more shot of him, which could just turn out to be the best one. Sometimes that happened. And he gave her a warm hug as she handed her Leica to Fiona, who took it reverently from her hands and set it on a table with the others. She unplugged the lights and began to break down the equipment and put it away, as Finn led Hope downstairs to the kitchen.

"You work too hard! I'm starving!" he complained as he opened the refrigerator and turned to her. "Can I make you some pasta or a salad? I'm about to keel over from starvation. No wonder you're so small, you must never eat."

"Usually not when I'm working," she admitted.

"I get too involved in what I'm doing to think about it, and it's so much fun doing the shoot." She smiled shyly and he laughed.

"Most of the time I feel that way about working on a book, although at times I hate it too. Particularly rewrites. I have a nasty editor, and we have a love-hate relationship, but he's good for the books. It's a necessary evil. You don't have that with what you do," he said enviously.

"I have to edit myself, but I have clients to deal with who commission the work, like your publisher, and museum curators, who can be pretty tough, though it's different than doing rewrites must be for you. I've always wanted to write," she confessed. "I can barely write a postcard—for me it's all visual. I see the world through a lens, I see into people's souls that way."

"I know, that's what I love about your work, and why I asked the publisher to get you to do the photo for the book jacket." He laughed then as he expertly made an omelette for them both, moving like a tornado in the tiny kitchen. He had already made the salad while they talked. "I hope my soul doesn't wind up looking too black in the shots you took," he said, pretending to look worried, as she looked at him intently.

"Why would it? I didn't see any signs of a black soul, or a dark spirit. Is there something I missed?"

"Maybe a little friendly hereditary craziness, but it's harmless. From what I've read about my Irish relatives, some of them were fairly nuts. But not dangerously so, mostly eccentric." He smiled at her as he said it.

"There's no harm in that," Hope said benignly, as he put their omelettes on separate plates. "Everyone has a little craziness in them somewhere. I spent some time in India after my husband and I split up, trying to figure things out. I guess you could say that was crazy too," she said, as they sat down at the beautiful mahogany table in his cozy dark green dining room. There were paintings of hunting scenes on the walls, and one of birds by a famous German artist.

"How was it?" Finn asked with interest. "I've never been to India myself. I've always wanted to go."

"It was fantastic," Hope said as her eyes lit up. "It was the most exciting, fulfilling time I've ever spent. It changed my life forever, and how I look at everything, including myself. And there are some of the most beautiful spots on earth. I just opened an exhibit of some of the photographs I took there."

"I think I saw a couple in a magazine," Finn said as he finished his omelette and started on his salad. "They were photographs of beggars and children, and an incredible one of sunset at the Taj Mahal."

"I went to some incredibly beautiful lakes too. They're the most romantic places you could ever dream of, and some other places were the saddest.

I stayed at Mother Teresa's hospital for a month, and I lived at a monastery in Tibet, and an ashram in India, where I found myself again. I think I could have stayed there forever." When he looked into her eyes, he saw something very deep and very peaceful, and beyond it, deeper than that, he saw two bottomless pools of pain. He could see that Hope was a woman who had suffered. He wondered if it was only about the divorce and her husband's illness. Whatever it was, he could tell that she had been to hell and back, and yet she was incredibly balanced and peaceful, as she looked across the table at him with a gentle smile.

"I've always wanted to do something like that," he admitted to her, "but I never had the courage. I think I was afraid I might have to face myself. I'd rather face a thousand demons." It was honest of him to admit it and she nodded.

"It was wonderfully peaceful. We weren't allowed to speak in the monastery. It was amazingly restful and healing. I'd like to go back sometime."

"Maybe you need to have some fun instead." Finn looked suddenly mischievous as he said it. "How long are you here for?" He sat back in his chair and smiled at her. She was mysterious and intriguing.

"I'm going back to New York tomorrow," she said, smiling at him.

"That's not enough time to spend in London. What are you doing for dinner tonight?"

"Probably sleeping, after a bowl of soup from room service," she said with a grin.

"That's ridiculous," he said with a look of stern disapproval. "Will you have dinner with me?"

She hesitated and then nodded. She had nothing else to do, and he was interesting to talk to. "I didn't bring any decent clothes with me," she said, looking apologetic.

"You don't need them. You can wear a pair of pants and a sweater. You're Hope Dunne, you can do whatever you want. Will you have dinner with me tonight at Harry's Bar? As far as I'm concerned, it's the best Italian food in the world." She knew it well, but didn't go there often. It was one of the most elegant dinner clubs in London, and anyone and everyone who was important would be there. Women would be dressed in elegant, stylish cocktail dresses, and the men wore dark suits. And he was right, the food was superb.

"I'd love to. Are you sure you won't be embarrassed that I didn't bring anything dressy with me?" She felt faintly awkward, but liked the idea of having dinner with him. Among other things, he was intelligent, interesting, and quick. She hadn't been bored with him for a minute all day. He was knowledgeable on a multitude of subjects, well read, well educated, and brilliant. The opportunity to spend a few hours with him and get to know him better was hard to resist. She had come to London just for him. And Paul had left that day.

"I'd be honored to have dinner with you, Hope," Finn said honestly, and looked as though he meant it. She was the most interesting woman he had met in years. "You can tell me more about India, and I can tell you all about Ireland," he teased her. "And what it's like to restore a three-hundred-year-old house."

Finn told her he would pick her up at the hotel at eight-thirty, and a few minutes later she and Fiona left, after the driver carried out all their equipment. Fiona had been quietly reading a book in the small sitting room, after the maid gave her a sandwich for lunch. She didn't mind waiting for Hope, and had loved working with her that day.

Fiona got all the equipment organized for Hope back at the hotel, and put away her cameras. It was five o'clock by the time she left, and she said it had been a great day. And after that Hope lay down on her bed for a nap, thinking about her conversation with Finn, and his invitation for that night. It was one of the things she liked best about doing portraits. The work itself wasn't exciting, but the people she met were. He was such a talented man, as most of her portrait subjects were. She had always loved his work, and it was fascinating discovering the man behind it. He wrote somewhat eerie, even frightening books. She wanted to ask him more about it that night. And he seemed to be just as interested in her work.

She fell asleep for two hours, and woke in time

to shower and dress for dinner. As she had warned him, she wore black pants and a sweater, and the only pair of high heels she had brought with her, and was relieved that she had brought a fur coat. At least, she wouldn't totally disgrace him at Harry's Bar that night. She couldn't compete with the fashionable women there, but she looked sober, and simple, and decently dressed. She wound her hair in a bun, and put on just a little makeup and bright red lipstick before she left her suite to wait for him downstairs.

Hope was sitting in the lobby when Finn walked in promptly five minutes later, in a dark blue suit, and a beautifully cut black cashmere coat. He was a striking figure and heads turned as he greeted her and they walked out together. Several people recognized him as he escorted her to the Jaguar he had left at the curb. This wasn't the evening she had planned on before she met him, but it was fun being out with him, and she smiled broadly as they drove away.

"This is great. Thank you, Finn," she said warmly, and he turned to her with a smile. The restaurant was only a few blocks away.

"I'm looking forward to it too. And you look terrific. I don't know what you were worried about. You look very chic." It had been a long time since she had been out to a fancy dinner. She didn't do much of that anymore. She rarely went out in the evening now, except to museum parties, or her own gallery shows. Dinners like the one at Harry's Bar were more part of Paul's old world, and no longer hers. She was part of a more artistic crowd in New York, that was more in keeping with her work. They went to little bistros in Chelsea and SoHo, never fashionable restaurants.

The headwaiter greeted Finn warmly, and obviously knew him well. He led them to a quiet corner table amid well-dressed diners from a variety of countries. She could hear people speaking Italian, Arabic, Spanish, Russian, German, and French as well as English. And Finn ordered a martini as soon as they sat down. Hope ordered a glass of champagne, as she looked around. The same cartoons were on the walls. Nothing had changed since the last time she'd been there with Paul. It had been years.

"Tell me how you got started taking pictures," Finn asked as their drinks were served, and Hope took a sip of her champagne.

She laughed at the question. "I fell in love with cameras when I was nine. My father was a professor at Dartmouth, and my mother was an artist. My grandmother gave me a camera for my birthday, and it was love at first sight. I was an only child, so I was good at entertaining myself. And life was pretty quiet in New Hampshire when I was growing up. As long as I had a camera in my hands, I was never bored. What about you?" she asked him. "When did you start writing?"

"Just like you. When I was a boy. I was an only child too, so I read all the time. It was my escape."

"From what?" she asked with interest. Their art forms were different, but their creative talents were nonetheless a bond.

"A lonely childhood. My parents were very close, and I think I felt left out a lot of the time. There wasn't a lot of room for a child in their lives. They were older. My father was a doctor, and my mother had been a famous beauty in Ireland. She was fascinated by his work, and a lot less interested in me. So I developed a rich fantasy life, and spent all my time reading. I always knew I wanted to write. I wrote my first book at eighteen."

"Was it published?" she asked, impressed. And he laughed as he shook his head.

"No, it wasn't. I wrote three that were never published. I finally got published with my fourth. I had just graduated from college by then." She knew he had gone to Columbia and then later Oxford. "Success didn't come till a lot later."

"What did you do until you were published?"

"Studied, read, kept writing. Drank a lot." He laughed. "Chased women. I got married fairly young. I was twenty-five, it was right after my second book came out. I worked as a waiter and a carpenter too. Michael's mother was a model in New York." He smiled sheepishly at Hope. "I've always had a fatal weakness for beautiful women. She was a terrific-looking girl. Spoiled, difficult, narcissistic, but she was one of the prettiest women I've ever seen. She was young too, and things fell apart very quickly when we had Michael. I don't think either of us was ready to have a child. She stopped modeling, and we partied a lot. I didn't have a lot of money, and we were both miserable."

"How did she die?" Hope asked gently. What he was describing sounded more like a divorce in the making than a tragic loss for him, and she wasn't far off the mark.

"She was hit by a drunk driver, coming back from a party in the Hamptons late one night. We'd been separated off and on before, and thank God, she always left Michael with me when she went somewhere like that. She was twenty-eight years old, and I was thirty-three. We probably would have gotten divorced eventually. But I still felt awful about it when she died. And suddenly I was alone with my son. They weren't easy years. But fortunately, he's a great kid, and he seems to have forgiven me most of the mistakes I made, and there were quite a few along the way. I'd lost my own parents by then, so there was no one to help us, but we managed. I took care of him myself. It made us both grow up." He smiled the smile that was half-boy, half-handsome prince that had been melting women's hearts for years. It was easy to see why. There was something so honest and open and ingenuous about him. He didn't try to hide his flaws or his fears.

"You never remarried?" Hope was fascinated by his life story.

"I was too busy with my son. And now I feel like it's too late. I'm too selfish and too set in my ways. And since Michael has been gone, it's the first time I've been on my own. I wanted to savor it for a bit. And being married to a writer isn't much fun. I'm chained to my desk most of the time. Sometimes I don't leave the house for months. I couldn't ask anyone to take that on, and it's what I love to do."

"I feel that way about my work too," she agreed. "It's all-consuming at times. My husband was very good about it, and very supportive. And he was busy too. **Very** busy, at the height of his career. Being a doctor's wife can be lonely too. But it wasn't for me." She hesitated for a minute and looked away, and then smiled wistfully at Finn. "I had other things to do." He assumed that she meant her work, which made sense to him. She had produced an enormous amount of work over the years.

"What did he do after he had to retire?"

"He taught, at Harvard. The academic world was familiar to me, because of my father, although Harvard was more competitive than Dartmouth, loftier maybe, and a little more cutthroat. Teaching wasn't enough for Paul, so he helped to start two companies that made surgical equipment. He got very involved in that, and he did very well with it. I think it's what saved him for the first few years, when he couldn't practice anymore. It took some of the sting out of being sick, for a while anyway, to succeed at something else. And then he got worse. And a lot of things changed. It's hard to see him so sick at his age. He's still a relatively young man." She looked sad as she said it, remembering how he had looked at lunch the day before, having trouble walking and feeding himself, and he was still so dignified and strong, even if he was frail.

"What does he do now? Do you miss him?"

"Yes. But he didn't want me taking care of him. He's very proud. And everything changed for us, after he was sick . . . and other things that happened. Life sweeps you away at times, and even if you love someone, you can't find your way back again. He bought a sailboat three years ago, and lives on it a lot of the time now. The rest of the time, he's in London, and he goes to Boston for treatment, and then to New York for a few days. It's getting harder for him to get around on his own. Being on the boat is easier for him. His crew takes good care of him. He left for the Caribbean today."

"How sad," Finn said pensively. It was hard for him to understand why Paul had let Hope get away. And from the way she talked about him, Finn could tell that she still loved her ex-husband and cared about what happened to him. "I guess it wouldn't be a bad life for a healthy man. I suppose if you're sick, nothing is much fun anymore."

"No, it's not," Hope said softly. "He's part of an experimental program treating Parkinson's at Harvard. He's been doing fairly well until recently."

"And now?"

"Not so well." She didn't offer the details, and Finn nodded.

"So what about you, when you're not running off to Tibet and India and living in monasteries?" He smiled as he asked the question. They had both finished their drinks by then.

"I'm based in New York. I travel a lot for my work. And I go to Cape Cod when I have time, which isn't often. Most of the time, I'm flying around taking photographs, or working on museum shows of my work."

"Why Cape Cod?"

"My parents left me a house there. It's where we spent summers when I was a child, and I love it. It's in Wellfleet, which is a charming, sleepy little town. There's nothing fancy or fashionable about it. The house is very simple, but it suits me, and I'm comfortable there. It has a beautiful view of the ocean. We used to go there for summers, when I was married. We lived in Boston then. I moved to New York two years ago. I have a very nice loft there, in SoHo."

"And no one to share it with?"

She smiled as she shook her head. "I'm comfortable the way things are. Like you, it's difficult being married to a photographer who's never home. I can do things now that I never did when I was married. I float all over the world, and live out of a suitcase. It's the opposite of what you do, locked in a room, writing, but it's not very entertaining for someone else when I travel or even work. I never thought about it as selfish," as he had said about his own work, "but maybe it is. I don't answer to anyone now, and I don't have to be anywhere." He nodded as he listened, and they ordered dinner then. They were both having pasta, and decided to skip the first course. It was interesting to learn about each other's lives, and he told her more about his house in Ireland then. It was easy to see how much he loved it and what it meant to him. It was part of his history and the tapestry of his life, woven into his being and dear to his heart.

"You have to come and see it sometime," he offered, and she was curious about it.

"What sort of doctor was your father?" she asked him over their pasta, which was as delicious as he had promised, and as she remembered. The food there was better than ever.

"General medicine. My grandfather had been a landowner in Ireland, and never did much more than that. But my father was more industrious, and had studied in the States. He went back to marry my mother, and brought her over with him, but she never adjusted well to life away from Ireland. She died fairly young, and he not long after.

I was in college then, and I always had a fascination with Ireland because of them. Their being Irish made it easy for me to get the nationality when I wanted it.

"And tax-wise, it made sense for me to give up my U.S. citizenship eventually. You can't beat no income tax for writers. That was a pretty appealing setup for me, once the books were doing well. And now that I have my great-great-grandparents' house back, I guess I'm there forever, although I don't think I'll ever be able to convince Michael to move there. He wants a career in the high-tech world when he graduates from MIT, and there are plenty of opportunities in Dublin, but he's determined to live in the States and work in Silicon Valley or Boston. He's an all-American kid. It's his turn to find his way now. I don't want to interfere with him, although I miss him like crazy." He smiled ruefully at Hope as he said it, and she nodded and looked pensive. "Maybe he'll change his mind and move to Ireland later, as I did. It's in his blood. And I would love it, but he's not interested in living in Ireland now."

He wondered why she had never had children, but didn't dare ask her. Maybe her husband had been too involved in his medical career at Harvard to want them, and she had been too busy attending to him. She was so gentle and nurturing that she seemed like the sort of woman who would do that, although she was deeply involved in her own career now. She had said they'd been married for twenty-one years.

Exchanging their histories and talking about their artistic passions made the evening go quickly, and they were both sorry when the evening came to an end and they left the restaurant after a predictably delicious dinner. Hope had indulged herself with the candies and chocolates Harry's Bar was known for, after dinner. And Finn confessed that he was always sorely tempted to steal the brightly colored Venetian ashtrays, when they had had them on the tables, when smoking was still allowed. She laughed at the image of his sneaking one into the pocket of his well-tailored dark blue suit. She couldn't see him do it, although she had to admit, it might have been tempting. She had always liked their ashtrays too. They were considered collectors' items now.

He started to drive her back to Claridge's after dinner, and then hesitated before they got there.

"Can I talk you into one more drink? You can't leave London without going to Annabel's, and it's almost Christmas. It'll be lively there," he suggested, looking hopeful, and she was about to decline, but she didn't want to hurt his feelings. She was tired, but game for one more glass of champagne. Talking to him was delightful, and she hadn't had an evening like this in years, and doubted she would again anytime soon. Her life in New York was quiet and solitary and didn't include nightclubs and fancy dinners, or invitations from handsome men like Finn.

"All right, just one drink," she agreed. And Annabel's was packed when they walked in. It was as busy and festive as he promised. They sat in the bar, had two glasses of champagne each, and he danced with her before they left and then drove her back to Claridge's. It had been a terrific evening, for both of them. He loved talking to her, and she enjoyed his company too.

"After a night like this, I wonder what I'm doing, living in solitude outside Dublin. You make me want to move back here," Finn said as they got back to her hotel. He turned off the engine, and turned to look at her. "I think I realized tonight that I miss London. I don't spend enough time here. But if I did, you wouldn't be here, so it wouldn't be any fun anyway." She laughed at what he said. There was a boyish side to him that appealed to her, and a sophisticated side that dazzled her a little. It was a heady combination. And he felt the same way about her. He liked her gentleness, intelligence, and subtle but nonetheless lively sense of humor. He'd had a terrific time, better than he had in years, or so he said. He was also charming, so she didn't know if he was telling the truth, but it didn't really matter. They had obviously both enjoyed it.

"I had a wonderful time, Finn. Thank you. You didn't have to do all that," she said graciously.

"It was great for me too. I wish you weren't leaving tomorrow," he said sadly.

"So do I," she confessed. "I always forget how much I like London." The night life there had always been great, and she loved the museums, which she hadn't had enough time to visit at all on this trip.

"Could I talk you into staying for another day?" he asked her, looking hopeful, and she hesitated, but shook her head.

"I shouldn't. I really ought to get back, and I have to edit your pictures. They're working on a pretty tight deadline."

"Duty calls. I hate that," he said, looking disappointed. "I'll call you the next time I come to New York," he promised. "I don't know when, but I will, sooner or later."

"I won't be able to give you a night as nice as this."

"There are some good places in New York too. I have my favorite haunts." She was sure he did. And in Dublin too. And probably everywhere he went. Finn didn't seem to be the sort of man to sit around at home at night, except when he was writing. "Thank you for having dinner with me tonight, Hope," he thanked her politely as they got out of the car. It was freezing cold, and he walked her into the lobby as she held her coat tightly around her in the icy wind. "I'll be in touch," he promised, as she thanked him again. "Have a safe trip back."

"Enjoy your holidays with Michael," she said warmly, smiling up at him.

"He'll only be here for a few days, and then he'll be off skiing with his friends. I only get about five minutes with him these days. It's of the age. I'm damn near obsolete."

"Enjoy whatever time you get," she said wisely, and he kissed her cheek.

"Take care of yourself, Hope. I had a wonderful day."

"Thank you, Finn. So did I. I'll send you the proofs of the pictures as soon as I can." He thanked her and waved, as she walked into the lobby alone, with her head down, thinking. She had had such a nice time, far more than she'd expected. And as she got in the elevator and rode up to her floor, she was genuinely sorry to be leaving the next day. After London, it was going to seem very dull now to go up to the Cape for Christmas.

Chapter 4

It was snowing again when Hope got back to New York. The next morning she looked out her window at six inches of snow blanketing Prince Street, and decided not to drive to Cape Cod. Being in London had reminded her of how much fun it could be in the city, and when everyone else went shopping that afternoon, the day before Christmas Eve, Hope went to the Metropolitan Museum, to see a new medieval exhibit there, and then walked back down to SoHo through the still-falling snow, which by then had been called a blizzard.

The city was almost shut down. There was no traffic on the streets, cabs were impossible to find, and only a few hardy souls like her were walking home, trudging through the snow. Offices had closed early, and schools were already on vacation. Her cheeks were red and her eyes tearing, and her hands were tingling from the cold when she got back to her loft, and put the kettle on for tea. It had been an invigorating walk, and a delightful afternoon. And she had just sat down with a steaming cup of tea when Mark Webber called her from home. His office was closed till New Year's. There were no assignments likely to come up between Christmas and New Year.

"So how was it?" he asked, curious about O'Neill.

"He was great. Interesting, smart, easy to shoot, terrific looking. He was everything you'd expect him to be, and nothing like his books, which are always so complicated and dark. I haven't started editing the shots yet, but we got some great ones."

"Did he try to rape you?" Mark asked, only half-joking.

"No. He took me for a very civilized dinner at Harry's Bar, and to Annabel's afterward for a drink. He treated me like a visiting dignitary and great-aunt."

"Hardly. Going to the most fashionable restaurant and nightclub in London is not exactly what you do with a great-aunt."

"He was very proper," Hope reassured him, "and wonderful to talk to. He's a man of many interests. I almost wish I'd shot him in Dublin, it sounds like he's more in his element there, but I'm fairly certain we got the shots his publisher wanted. Maybe more than they need. He's cooperative and very pleasant to work with." She didn't add that he looked like a movie star, which he did. "His

London house is the size of a postage stamp, which was a bitch with the equipment, but we managed. The one outside Dublin sounds like Buckingham Palace. I'd have liked to see it."

"Well, thanks for doing it on such short notice. His publisher is damn lucky. What are you doing over the holiday, Hope? Are you still going to the Cape?" It seemed unlikely in the blizzard, and unwise. He hoped not.

She smiled as she looked out the window, at the continuing swirls of snow. There were nearly two feet of it on the ground now, and it was still coming, while the wind blew it into towering drifts. They had promised three feet by morning. "Not in this weather," she said, smiling. "Even I'm not that crazy, although it would be pretty once I got there." Most of the roads had been closed by that afternoon, and getting there would have been a nightmare. "I'll stay here." Finn had given her his latest book to read, she had some photographs she wanted to sort through for a gallery in San Francisco that wanted to give her a show, and she had Finn's shoot to edit.

"Call if you get lonely," he said kindly, but knew she wouldn't. Hope was very independent, and had led a solitary, quiet life for several years. But he at least wanted her to know that someone cared about her. He worried about her at times, although he knew she was good at keeping busy. She was just as likely to be taking photographs on the streets of

Harlem on Christmas Eve, as shooting in a coffee shop for truckers on Tenth Avenue at four in the morning. It was what she did, and how she loved spending her time. Mark admired her for it, and the work that resulted from it had made her famous.

"I'll be fine," she reassured him, and sounded as though she meant it.

After they hung up, she lit candles, turned off the lights, and sat looking at the snow falling outside, through her big windows without curtains. She loved the light, and had never bothered to put up shades. The streetlamps lit up the room along with the candles, and she was lying on the couch, observing the winter scene, when the phone rang again. She couldn't imagine who it would be, on the night before Christmas Eve. Her phone only rang during business hours, and it was always about work. When she picked it up, the voice was unfamiliar to her.

"Hope?"

"Yes." She waited to hear who it was.

"It's Finn. I called to make sure you got back okay. I hear there's a blizzard in New York." His voice sounded warm and friendly, and the call was a pleasant surprise.

"There is," she confirmed about the blizzard. "I walked from the Metropolitan Museum all the way downtown to SoHo. I loved it."

"You're a hardy soul," he said, laughing. His

voice was deep and smooth in her ears. "You'd do well on the hills where my house is, outside Dublin. You can walk for miles, from village to village. I often do, but not in a blizzard in New York. I tried to call my publisher today, and they were closed."

"Everyone is, for the holidays by now anyway, even without the snow."

"And what are you doing for Christmas, Hope?" It was obvious she wasn't going to the Cape now, with a blizzard in New York.

"I'll probably float around, and take some pictures. I have a few ideas. And I want to look at your shoot, and start working on it."

"Isn't there someone you want to spend the holiday with?" He sounded sad for her.

"No. I enjoy spending it on my own." It wasn't entirely true, but it was the way things were. She had learned to accept that, from the monks in Tibet and in the ashram. "It's just another day. How's your son?" she asked, changing the subject.

"He's fine. He's out for dinner with a friend." She realized as she glanced at her watch that it was eleven o'clock at night in London, and it made her think of the pleasant evening they had spent together.

"He's leaving for Switzerland in two days. I'm getting short shrift this time. That's what twenty-year-olds are like. I can't blame him. I did the same thing at his age. You couldn't have paid me to spend time with my parents then. He's a lot nicer than I was. His girlfriend is flying in tomorrow, and at least I'll have Christmas with them, before they leave that night."

"What will you do then?" she asked, curious about him. In some ways, he seemed almost as solitary as she was, although he had a far bigger social life, and a son. But the life he had described in Dublin, when he was writing, was much like hers in her SoHo loft, or at the Cape. Despite their differences in style, they had found they had a lot in common.

"I'm thinking I'll go back to Dublin on Christmas night. I have a book to finish, and I'm working on the outline for the new one. And everyone leaves London like a sinking ship for their country houses. I'd rather be in Russborough then." It was the small town outside Dublin, closest to his house, where he lived. He had told her all about it over dinner. His palatial home was just north of Russborough, where there was another historical Palladian mansion, much like his, only in better shape, he claimed. She was sure his was beautiful too, in spite of its need for restoration. "And you'll go to the Cape after the blizzard?"

"Probably in a few days. Although it will be very cold on the ocean, if the storm moves up there, which they say it will. I can wait till the roads are clear at least. But the house will be cozy once I get there."

"Well, have a nice Christmas, Hope," he said kindly, and there was something wistful in his voice. He had enjoyed meeting her, and he had no real reason to call her again, until he saw the photographs she took. He was looking forward to seeing them, and talking to her again. He felt an odd connection to her, and wasn't sure why. She was a nice woman, and he had felt as though he could get lost in her eyes. He had wanted to learn more about her, and she had told him many things, about her life with Paul, and her divorce, but he had a feeling that there were walls she had put up long before, and no one was invited to go behind them. She was very guarded, and yet warm and compassionate at the same time. She was a woman of mystery to him, as parts of him had been to her. And the unanswered questions intrigued them both. They were people who were accustomed to looking into other people's hearts and souls, and yet had been elusive with each other.

"You too. Have a lovely Christmas with your son," she said softly, and a moment later, they hung up, and she sat staring at the phone, still somewhat surprised by the call. It had been unnecessary, friendly, and pleasant, and reminded her of the nice evening she had spent with him two days before. It already seemed like aeons ago now that she was back in New York. London felt like it was a million miles away on another planet.

And she was even more surprised when an email

from him came in later that night. "I enjoyed speaking to you earlier. I am haunted by your eyes, and the many mysteries I saw in them. I hope we meet again soon. Take care. Happy Christmas. Finn." She noticed he used "happy" instead of "merry," like the English, and she didn't know what to make of his email. It made her slightly uncomfortable, and she remembered her agent's warnings about his being a womanizer. Was Finn just trying to charm her? Another conquest? And yet, he had been totally circumspect with her in London. And what mysteries did he mean? What was he seeing? Or was he only playing with her? But something about the tone of his email, and their conversation that evening, struck her as sincere. Maybe he did normally chase after women, but she didn't have the feeling that he was chasing her. And she was struck by the word "haunted." She didn't answer him until the next day. She didn't want to seem anxious, and she wasn't. She hoped that they would be friends. That happened sometimes with her subjects. There were many who had become friends over the years, even if she didn't see them often, and only heard from them from time to time.

She answered Finn's email as she sat down at her desk with a cup of tea on the morning of Christmas Eve. The world was silent and white outside, blanketed by virgin snow, and it was afternoon in London.

"Thank you for your email. I enjoyed talking to you too. It's beautiful here today, a winter wonderland of perfect snow everywhere. I'm going to go to Central Park to take photographs of children sledding, very mundane, but appealing. There are no mysteries, only unanswered questions that have no answers, and the memory of people who enter and leave our lives, for a short or long time, and stay only as long as they are meant to. We cannot change the patterns of life, but only observe them, and bend to their will with grace. May your Christmas be warm and happy. Hope."

Much to her surprise, he answered her within the hour, just as she was leaving the house in all her snow gear, with her camera over her arm. She heard her computer say "You've got mail," went back to check, and pulled off her gloves to press the button. The email was from Finn.

"You are the most graceful woman I have ever met. I wish I were there with you today. I want to go to Central Park to go sledding with the children. Take me with you. Finn." She smiled at his answer, it was his boyish side surfacing again. She didn't respond, but put her gloves back on, and left the house. She wasn't sure what to say to him, and was hesitant to get into a serious correspondence with him. She didn't want to play a game with him and lead him on.

She found a cab outside the Mercer Hotel less than a block away, and it took them half an hour to get to Central Park. Some of the streets were clear, although many weren't and it was slow going. The driver dropped her off at the south end of the park, and she walked in past the zoo. And eventually she found the hills where children were sledding, some on old-fashioned sleds, others on plastic disks, many with plastic garbage bags tied around them by their parents. Their mothers were standing by, watching, trying to stay warm, and the fathers were chasing them down the hill, picking them up when they had spills. The children were squealing and laughing and having fun, as she discreetly took photographs, zooming in on their faces full of excitement and wonder, and suddenly in a way she hadn't expected it to, the scene shot her backward in time, and a spear lodged in her heart that she couldn't remove, even by turning away. She felt tears sting her eyes, not from the cold this time, and she took photographs of the icy limbs of the trees in abstract patterns to distract herself, but it was useless. She felt breathless with the pain of what she was experiencing, and finally, with tears burning her eyes, she put the camera over her shoulder, turned away, and walked back down the hill. She left the park at a dead run, trying to flee the ghosts she had seen there, and she didn't stop running until she reached Fifth Avenue, and headed back downtown. It hadn't happened to her in years. She was still shaken when she got home.

She took off her coat and stood staring out the

window for a long time, and when she turned away, she noticed Finn's email on her computer from that morning, and read it again. She didn't have the heart or the energy to answer him. She was drained from the emotions she had felt in the park that afternoon. And as she turned away from the computer, she realized with a sinking heart that it was Christmas Eve, which made it worse. She always did everything she could to avoid sentimental situations at Christmas, even more so since the divorce. And now, after watching children sledding in the park, everything she normally hid from had hit her broadside, and knocked her flat. She flipped on the TV to distract herself, and was instantly assaulted with Christmas carols sung by a children's chorus. She laughed ruefully to herself as she turned off the TV again, and sat down at the computer, hoping that answering Finn's email would distract her. She didn't know what else to do. The night ahead of her looked long and sad, like a mountain range to climb.

"Hi. It's Christmas Eve, and I'm a mess," she typed out quickly. "I hate Christmas. I had a visit today from the ghost of Christmas past. It nearly killed me. I hope you're having a nice time with Michael. Merry Christmas! Hope." She hit the send button and then regretted it instantly when she reread her message. It sounded pathetic even to her. But there was nothing she could do to get it back.

It was midnight in London, and she didn't expect to hear from him till the next day, if at all. So she was startled to hear her computer tell her she had an email. It was an immediate response from Finn.

"Tell the ghost of Christmas past to get lost, and lock your door behind him. Life is about the future, not the past. I don't love Christmas a lot either. I want to see you again. Soon. Finn." It was short and to the point and a little scary. Why did he want to see her? Why were they emailing each other? And more importantly, why was she writing to him? She had no idea what the answer was to that question, or what she hoped to get from him.

She lived in New York, he lived in Dublin. They had separate lives and interests, and he was a subject at a photo shoot and nothing more than that to her. But she kept thinking of things he had said to her at dinner, and his eyes when he looked at her. She was beginning to feel haunted by him, which was the same thing he had said about her in his email. It left her feeling a little bit unnerved, but she answered him anyway, reminding herself to keep it businesslike and upbeat. She didn't want to start some sort of sophomoric email romance with him, just because she was lonely and it was Christmas. She was well aware that it would be a big mistake. And he was way out of her league, leading a somewhat jet-set international life, with women at his feet. She didn't want to be one of them, and she had no desire to compete.

"Thank you. Sorry for the maudlin email. I'm fine. Just a touch of holiday blues. Nothing a hot bath and a good night's sleep won't cure. All the best, Hope." It seemed a little better to her as she sent it off, and his answer was quick and sounded annoyed.

"Holiday blues are to be expected, over the age of 12. And what's with 'All the best'? Don't be so cowardly. I'm not going to eat you, and I'm not the ghost of Christmas past. Bah humbug. Have a glass of champagne. It always helps. Love, Finn."

"Shit!" she said as she read it to herself a minute later. " 'Love,' my ass. Now look what you've done!" she said aloud to herself, feeling even more nervous. She decided not to answer it, but took one piece of his advice, and poured herself a glass of wine. His email sat on her screen all night and she ignored it, but she read it again before she went to bed, and told herself it didn't mean a thing. But in spite of that, she thought it was best if she didn't respond, and when she climbed the ladder to her sleeping loft, she told herself she'd feel better in the morning. As she moved to turn off the light, she saw the wall of photographs of the young ballerina. She stood staring at them for a long moment, and then got into bed, turned off the light, and buried her head in the pillows.

Chapter 5

As she hoped she would, Hope felt better when she woke up in the morning. It was Christmas Day, but there was no reason to treat it differently from any other day. She called Paul on his boat, which was her only concession to the holiday. He sounded all right, although he'd caught a cold on the plane leaving London, which was dangerous for him. They wished each other a Merry Christmas, stayed off sensitive subjects, and hung up after a few minutes. After that she took out a box of photographs to edit for her next show, and pored over the images for several hours. It was two o'clock in the afternoon before she looked up, and decided to go for a walk. She glanced at the email from Finn again, and turned off the computer. She didn't want to encourage him, or start something she didn't want to finish or pursue.

And when she dressed and went out, the air felt brisk. She passed people going to visit each other, and others coming out of the Mercer Hotel after lunch. She walked around SoHo and all through the Village. It was a sunny afternoon, and the snowfall of the day before was starting to turn to slush. She felt better when she got back to the loft, and worked some more. And at eight o'clock, she realized that she had nothing to eat in the apartment. She thought of skipping dinner, but was hungry, and finally decided to go to the nearest deli, to get a sandwich and some soup. The day had turned out to be a lot easier than the one before, and the following day she was planning to go to her gallery on the Upper East Side to talk to them about her show. She was relieved, as she put her coat on, to think that she had made it through another year. She dreaded Christmas, but with the exception of the bad moment the day before in Central Park, this one hadn't been too rough. And she was amused to see a row of cooked, stuffed turkeys lined up at the deli, ready for anyone who needed an instant Christmas dinner.

She ordered a turkey sandwich with a slice of cranberry jelly on it, and a container of chicken soup. The man at the deli knew her, and asked how Christmas Day had been for her.

"It was fine," she said, smiling at him, as he looked into the violet eyes. He could tell from the things she bought from him that she lived alone. And from what he could see, she didn't eat much. She was tiny, and at times looked very frail.

"How about a piece of pie?" She looked to him like she needed a little fattening up. "Apple? Mince? Pumpkin?" She shook her head, but helped herself to a container of eggnog ice cream, which she had always loved. She paid, thanked him, wished him a Merry Christmas, and left with her provisions in a brown bag. She was hoping not to spill the soup, and that the ice cream, with its proximity to the lukewarm container, wouldn't melt. She was concentrating on not spilling it, as she walked up the steps to her building, and saw a man with his back to her in the doorway, carefully looking for a name on the bell. He was hunched over to see the names better in the dim light, and she was standing behind him, waiting to open the door with her key, when he turned and she stared, with a sharp intake of breath. It was Finn, wearing a black knit cap, jeans, with a heavy black wool coat, and he smiled as he looked at her. His whole face lit up when he smiled.

"Well, that makes things easier. I was going blind trying to read the names. I lost my glasses on the plane."

"What are you doing here?" she asked in surprise. She was stunned.

"You didn't answer my last email, so I figured I'd come over and find out why." He looked relaxed and totally at ease as they stood talking on the front step, and Hope was shaking as he took the brown paper bag from her hands. She didn't know why he had come, but it frightened her. It seemed so bold and unnerved her.

"Be careful you don't spill it. It's soup," she said, not sure what to say next. "Do you want to come up?" There was nothing else she could say. She couldn't brush past him and go home and leave him on the doorstep.

"That would be nice," he said, smiling, but Hope hadn't smiled yet. She felt panicked to be talking to him on her front step. He had entered her world without invitation or permission or warning. And then he looked at her gently. He could see she was upset. "Are you mad at me for coming?" He looked worried, as the wind whipped her hair.

"No. I just don't know why you did." She looked afraid.

"I have to see my agent anyway, and talk to my publisher. And to be honest, I wanted to see you. You've been on my mind since you left. I'm not sure why, but I can't get you out of my head." She smiled then, and unlocked the front door, wondering if she should go back to the deli for more food. She wasn't sure if she should be flattered, or angry at him for the intrusion, without checking with her first. He was impulsive, and as full of charm as he had been when they met. It was hard to stay angry at him, and her initial reaction of fear began to dispel as they walked up the stairs.

Without further conversation, she led him up to

her apartment and unlocked the door. She went to put the food in the kitchen, and rescue the ice cream before it melted, and then she turned to look at him. He was staring at the photographs on her walls.

"That's the most beautiful ballerina I've ever seen," he said, studying each print closely, and then looking at her with a puzzled frown. "She looks like you. Was that you as a young girl?" She shook her head, and invited him to sit down. She offered him a glass of wine, which he declined. He glanced around the peaceful, spare decor as she lit the candles and then sat down on a couch across from him with a serious expression.

"I hope nothing I said made you feel that you should come," she said quietly, still feeling uncomfortable seeing him in her apartment. She blamed herself if she had led him on or encouraged him, but she didn't think she had.

"You sounded sad. And I missed you, though I'm not sure why," he said honestly. "I had to come to New York at some point anyway, so I decided it might as well be now, before I finish my book and start the next one. I won't want to come for months after that. And I was sad myself when Michael left this morning, earlier than planned. Don't be mad. I'm not here to push you into anything." She knew there had to be plenty of other women available to him, if he wanted them. She just didn't understand what he wanted from her.

She offered to share her sandwich with him and he smiled and shook his head. It had been an incredibly impulsive move for him to come, and she couldn't decide if it was flattering or scary. Most likely both.

"I'm fine. I had a huge meal on the plane, but I'll keep you company while you eat." She felt silly eating a sandwich in front of him while he ate nothing, so she put it aside, and then he shared the soup and ice cream with her. By the time they got to the eggnog ice cream, he had her laughing at the stories he told, and she had started to relax, in spite of the startling visit from a man she scarcely knew. It was awkward seeing him sitting there, stretched out on the couch and totally at ease in her loft.

They were just finishing the ice cream when he asked her about the ballerina again. "Why do I feel as though that's you?" It was particularly odd because the ballerina in the photographs was blond, and Hope's hair was so dark. But there was a similarity between her and the young dancer, a kind of familiar look. She took a deep breath then, and told him what she hadn't planned to share with him.

"That's my daughter, Camille." In answer to what she said, he looked stunned.

"You lied to me," he said, looking hurt. "You said you didn't have kids."

"I don't," Hope said quietly. "She died three

years ago, at nineteen." He was silent for a long moment, and so was Hope.

"I'm so sorry," he said, looking shaken as he reached out to touch her hand, and she looked deep into his eyes.

"It's all right." She told herself silently again, 'That was then. This is now,' as the monks had taught her in Tibet. "You learn to live with it after a while."

"She was a beautiful girl," he said, glancing at the photographs again and then back at Hope. "What happened?"

"She was in college, at Dartmouth, where my father taught when I was a child, although he was gone by then. She called me one morning, with the flu, and she sounded really sick. Her roommate took her to the infirmary, and they called me an hour later. She had meningitis. I talked to her and she sounded awful. I got in the car to go up to her from Boston, Paul came with me. She died half an hour before we arrived. There was nothing they could do to save her. It just happened that way." There were tears rolling slowly down her cheeks as she said it, and she had a peaceful look on her face, as Finn watched her. He looked devastated by what she'd said. "She danced in the summers with the New York City Ballet. She had thought about not going to college and dancing instead, but she managed to do both. They were going to take her in as soon as she graduated, or before if she wanted. She was a wonderful dancer." And then as an afterthought, she added, "We called her Mimi." Hope's voice was barely more than a whisper as she said it. "I miss her terribly. And her death destroyed her father. It was the last straw for him. He had already been sick for years, and drinking heavily in secret. He stayed drunk for three months when she died. One of his old colleagues at Harvard did an intervention on him, and he put himself in a hospital and dried up after that. But when he did, he decided that he couldn't be married to me anymore. Maybe I reminded him too much of Mimi, and the loss. He sold his business, bought a boat, and left me. He said he didn't want me sitting around waiting for him to die, that I deserved better than that. But the truth was too that losing Mimi was so devastating for both of us, that our marriage fell apart. We're still good friends, but every time we see each other we think of her. He filed for divorce, and I left for India. We still love each other, but I guess we loved her more. After that, there wasn't much left of our marriage. When Mimi died, we all did in a way. He's not the person he was, and maybe I'm not either. It's hard to come through something like that in one piece. So there it is," she said sadly. "I didn't want to tell you in London. I don't usually tell people about her. It's just too sad. My life is very different without her, to say the least. It's all about my work now. There's nothing else. I love what I do, that helps."

"Oh my God," Finn said, with tears in his own eyes. Hope could sense that he had been thinking about his own son while she told him the story of her daughter. "I can't even imagine what that must be like. It would kill me."

"It almost did," she said, as he came to sit next to her on the couch and put an arm around her shoulders. Hope didn't object. Feeling him close to her helped. She hated talking about it, and rarely did, although she looked at the photographs on the wall every night and thought about her all the time, still. "The time I spent in India helped. And in Tibet. I found a wonderful monastery in Ganden, and I had an extraordinary teacher. I think he helped me to accept it. One really has no other choice."

"And your ex-husband? How is he about it now? Did he go back to drinking?"

"No, he's still sober. He's aged a lot in the last three years, and he's a lot sicker, so it's hard to tell if it's Mimi or the disease. He's as happy as he can be on his boat. I bought this loft when I came back from India, but I travel a lot, so I'm away much of the time. I don't need a lot in my life. Nothing makes sense without Mimi. She was the center of our life, and once she was gone, we were both pretty lost." The pain she had experienced showed in her work. She had a deep connection with human suffering that came out in the photographs she took.

"You're not too old to marry again and have another child," Finn said gently, unsure of what to say to comfort her. How did you comfort a woman who had lost her only child? What she had told him was so enormous that he had no idea how to help her. He was shocked by the story she had told him. Hope wiped her eyes, and smiled.

"Technically, I'm not too old, but it's not very likely, and it doesn't make much sense. I can't see myself marrying again, and I haven't dated since Paul and I divorced. I just haven't met anyone that I wanted to go out with, and I wasn't ready. We've only been divorced for two years, and she's been gone for three. It was a lot to lose at the same time. And by the time I do find someone again, if I ever do, I will be too old. I'm forty-four now, I think my baby-making days are pretty much over, or will be soon. And it wouldn't be the same."

"No, of course not, but you have a lot of years ahead of you. You can't spend them alone, or you shouldn't. You're a beautiful woman, Hope, you have a lot of life in you. You can't close the door on all that now."

"I don't really think about it, to be honest. I try not to. I just wake up every morning and face the day. That's a lot. And I put everything into my work." It showed. And then, without a word, he put his arms around her and held her. He wanted to shield her from all the sorrows in her life. She was surprisingly comfortable in his peaceful embrace. No one had done that for years. She couldn't even remember the last time. She was suddenly glad he had come. She hardly knew him, but his being there seemed like a gift.

Finn sat there holding her for a long time, and then she smiled up at him. It was nice just sitting with him and not talking. And then slowly he let go of her, and she went to make herself a cup of tea and pour him a glass of wine. He followed her into the kitchen, and helped himself to more of the eggnog ice cream. He offered her some, and she shook her head, and then wondered if he was hungry. It was really late for him, in fact it was the middle of the night in London.

"Do you want some eggs or something? It's all I have."

"I know this sounds crazy," he said, looking sheepish. "But I'd love some Chinese food. I'm starving. Is there any place like that around here?" It was Christmas night and not much was open, but there was a Chinese restaurant nearby that stayed open very late. She offered to call them and they were open, but they didn't deliver.

"Do you want to go?" she asked, and he nodded.

"Is that all right? If you're tired, I can go alone, although I'd love it if you'd come." She smiled at him, and he put an arm around her shoulders again. He felt as though something important had happened between them that night, and so did she.

They put their coats on a few minutes later and went out. It was nearly eleven o'clock by then, and it was freezing cold. They hurried along the street to where the Chinese restaurant was. It was still open, and there were a surprising number of people inside. It was bright and noisy and smelled of Chinese food, people were shouting in the kitchen, and Finn grinned as they sat down.

"This was exactly what I wanted." He looked happy and relaxed and so did she.

Hope ordered for them since she knew their food, and it arrived a little while later, and they both dug in. She was surprised that she was as hungry as he was. They were like starving people as they ate almost everything, and talked of lighter subjects than they had all evening. Neither of them mentioned Mimi again, although she was on their minds. They both chatted as they ate their dinner, and everyone around them seemed to be in good spirits. For some, it was the perfect ending to a Christmas Day.

"This is more fun than eating turkey," Hope giggled, as she finished the last of the pork, while Finn polished off the shrimp and grinned.

"Yes, it is. Thanks for coming with me." He looked at her gently. He was deeply touched by her now that he knew all that she'd gone through. It made her seem vulnerable and so alone to him.

"Where are you staying, by the way?" she asked casually.

"I usually stay at the Pierre," he said, leaning back in his chair. He was full and happy as he smiled at her. "But I took a room at the Mercer this time, because it's close to you." He had really come to New York to see her. It was more pressure than she wanted, but right now she didn't mind. She was having a lovely time with him. And somehow being there with him made sense. They hardly knew each other, but she felt a powerful bond with him now that she had told him about Mimi.

"It's actually a nice hotel," she said, trying to look relaxed about his being so nearby. She was still a little stunned that he was there.

"I don't really care about the room." He grinned ruefully. "I just wanted to see you. Thanks for not being mad that I showed up."

"It's a pretty major gesture, I'll admit." She remembered how stunned she was when she saw him on her front stoop. "But a nice one too. I don't think anyone's ever flown from anywhere to see me." She smiled back at him as the waiter brought them fortune cookies and the check, and she laughed when she read hers, and handed it to him.

" 'You can expect a visit from a friend.' " He laughed out loud, and then read his to her too. " 'Good news is coming soon.' I like these. I usually get the ones that say 'A teacher is a wise man.' Or 'Pick up your laundry tomorrow or else.' "

"Yeah, me too." She laughed again. They walked slowly back to her apartment, and he left her at the front door. He had dropped his bag off at the hotel before he came to see her. And it was nearly one in the morning by then, six o'clock in London, and he was starting to run out of steam. "Thank you for coming, Finn," she said softly, and he smiled at her and then kissed her on the cheek.

"I'm glad I did. And I liked our Christmas dinner. We'll have to make it a tradition to eat Chinese food instead of turkey. I'll call you in the morning," he promised, and she let herself into the building with her key, waved, and watched him walk down the street toward the hotel. She was still thinking about him as she walked upstairs. It had been a lovely evening, and a totally unexpected treat. It was certainly out of the ordinary for her.

She was getting undressed when she heard her computer tell her that she had mail. She went to look, and it was Finn.

"Thank you for a wonderful evening. My best Christmas ever, and our first. Sweet dreams."

This time she answered, as she sat down to her desk. It was all a little overwhelming, and she didn't know what to think. "It was wonderful for me too. Thank you for coming. See you tomorrow."

She glanced at Mimi's photographs as she got up from her desk. She was glad that she had shared her with Finn. In an odd way, for a few minutes at least, it brought her back into their midst. She would have been twenty-two by then, and it was still hard to believe she was gone. It was odd how people came into one's life, and left, and then others came when you least expected them to appear. For the moment, Finn was an unexpected blessing. And whatever happened, she was grateful to have spent Christmas night with him. She was still stunned that he was there. She had decided not to let herself worry about it and just enjoy the time they shared.

Chapter 6

Finn called her the next morning and invited her to breakfast at the Mercer. She had nothing important to do and was delighted to join him. He was waiting for her in the lobby and looked as handsome as he had in London. He was wearing a black turtleneck sweater with jeans, with his dark hair freshly brushed. He looked wide awake when she saw him, and he admitted he had been up for hours, and had walked around the neighborhood at the crack of dawn. He was still on London time.

Hope ordered eggs Benedict, and Finn ordered waffles. He said he missed them when he was in Europe, where they were never quite the same. He said the batter was different and in France they put sugar on them. He poured maple syrup all over them as Hope laughed at him. He had drowned them, but he looked ecstatic when he took a bite.

"What are your plans today?" he asked her over coffee.

"I was going up to the gallery where they're showing some of my photographs of India. Would you like to come?"

"I'd love it. I want to see the show."

They took a cab uptown after breakfast, and he was enormously impressed when he saw the work. It was beautifully hung in a large, prestigious gallery, and afterward they walked up Madison Avenue, and then over to Central Park to walk through the still white snow. In the rest of the city, it was melting and turning to slush, but it was still pristine in the park.

He asked her about India, and then they talked about her travels in Tibet and Nepal. They stopped at a bookseller's cart on their way into the park, and found one of his early books. Hope wanted to buy it and he wouldn't let her, and said it wasn't one he loved. They talked about his work then, their agents and careers. He was impressed by all of her museum shows, and she was in awe of his National Book Award. They admired a great deal about each other, and seemed to share a lot of common ground, and as they came out of the park again, he took her for a ride in a horse-drawn carriage, which seemed silly and fun to both of them as they tucked the blanket around them, and giggled like two children.

It was lunchtime by the time the ride was finished, and he took her to lunch at La Grenouille, which was very chic, and they had a delicious meal. Finn liked to eat well, although Hope often skipped meals. And afterward they strolled back downtown on Fifth Avenue, and as she often did, they walked all the way back to SoHo. They were both tired, but had enjoyed spending the day together. He took her back to her apartment, and she invited him to come up, but he said he was going back to the hotel to take a nap.

"Would you like to go to dinner later, or do you have something else to do? I don't want to take up all your time," he said thoughtfully, although he had come to New York to do just that.

"I'd love it, if you're not tired of me," she said with a small smile. "Do you like Thai food?" He nodded enthusiastically, and she suggested a place she liked in the East Village.

"I'll pick you up at eight," he promised, and kissed the top of her head. She went back to her loft then, and he walked back to his hotel. And although she tried not to, she thought about him for the next several hours. He was thoroughly enjoyable company, interesting to talk to, and suddenly an enormous presence. She had no idea what to make of it, or if she should even try to figure it out.

She was wearing gray slacks and a pink sweater when he came to pick her up. And they had a glass of wine before they went out. He didn't comment on Mimi's photographs this time, but he admired some of Hope's other work. He said he wanted to go to the Museum of Modern Art the next day, to see some of her older work.

"You're the only photographer I know who's in museums," he said with open admiration.

"And you're the only author I know who's won the National Book Award, and been knighted," she said with equal pride. "That reminds me, I never call you 'Sir Finn.' Should I?"

"Not unless you want me to laugh at you. I still feel odd myself when I use it. Although it was pretty exciting to meet the queen."

"I'll bet it was." She smiled broadly, and then she took out a box of photographs she had promised to show him, of Tibet. The photographs were amazing, and she pointed out several of her beloved monks.

"I don't know how you managed not to talk for a month. I couldn't do it," he admitted readily. "Probably not even for a day."

"It was fantastic. It was actually hard to start speaking again when I left. Everything I started to say seemed unimportant and too much. It really makes you think about what you're saying. They were wonderful to me there. I'd love to go back one day. I promised them I would."

"I'd love to see it, but not if I have to stop talking. I suppose I could write."

"I kept a journal while I was there. Not talking gives you time for some fairly deep thoughts."

"I suppose it would," he said easily. She asked him then where he had lived when he grew up in New York. "The Upper East Side," he replied. "The building isn't there anymore. They tore it down years ago. And the apartment where I lived with Michael was on East Seventy-ninth. It was pretty small. That was before the books really took off. We had some lean years for a while," he said without embarrassment. "When my parents died, they had pretty much eaten through the family money. They were fairly spoiled. Particularly my mother. The house in Ireland belonged to her family, and since there were no male heirs, they sold it. I'm glad I got it back. It'll be nice for Michael to have one day, although I doubt he'll want to live in Ireland, unless he's a writer." Finn grinned at the thought and Hope smiled. Ireland was famous for its no-tax policy for writers. She knew a number of them who had moved there. It was irresistible.

They left for the Thai restaurant then, and had an excellent meal. And while they ate dinner, Finn asked her what she was doing on New Year's Eve.

"Same thing I do every year." She grinned. "Go to bed at ten o'clock. I hate going out on New Year's Eve. Everyone is crazy and drunk. It's a great night to stay home."

"We have to do better than that this year," Finn insisted. "I'm not crazy about it either, but you have to try at least. Why don't we do something ridiculous like go to Times Square and watch the crystal and mirrored ball fall down, or whatever it does. I've only seen it on TV, although I imagine the crowd is pretty awful."

"It might be fun to photograph," she said thoughtfully.

"Why don't we try it? If we hate it, we'll go home."

She laughed, thinking about it, and agreed.

"Then it's a date," he confirmed, looking pleased.

"How long are you here?" she asked, as they finished dinner.

"I haven't figured that out yet. I might do some work with my editor before I go back." And then he looked at her carefully. "The rest depends on you." She felt a tingle of nervousness run down her spine then. She didn't know what to answer when he said things like that, and he had a few times. Knowing that he had come to New York to see her was an awesome responsibility as well as a gift. She was just finishing dessert when he looked across the table at her, and took her breath away with what he said. "I think I'm falling in love with you, Hope."

She didn't want him to have said what he just did, and she had no idea how to respond. Let me know when you figure it out? Don't be silly? So am I? She didn't know what she felt for him yet, but she liked him a lot. Of that, she was sure. But as a friend or a man? It was too soon for her to tell.

"You don't have to say anything," he said, reading her mind. "I just wanted you to know how I feel."

"How can you know that so soon?" she asked, looking worried. Everything seemed to be moving so quickly. She wondered if love happened that way at their age.

"I just do," he said simply. "I've never felt like this before. And I know it's fast. But maybe it happens that way sometimes, when it's for real. I think at our age, you know what you want, who you are, and what you feel. You know when you've found the right person for you. It doesn't have to take a long time. We're grown-ups, we've made mistakes before. We're not innocents anymore." She didn't want to tell him that he had a lot more experience than she, but he knew that about her anyway. He could tell. And she had been married for nearly half her life, and single for only the past two years. "You don't need to feel pressured because I feel that way, Hope," he went on. "We have a lifetime to figure it out, or as long as you want." She had to admit, he was sweeping her off her feet. And this was completely different from the time she'd shared with Paul. Finn was wilder, more creative, his whole existence was more free form. Paul had been extremely disciplined in every way, and deeply involved in his work. Finn seemed more engaged in life, and the world. And his was a broader world, which appealed to her a lot. Hers had broadened a great deal too in the past few years.

She was open to new people, new places, new
ideas, like her monastery in Tibet and the ashram
in India, which she would never have thought of
going to before she lost Mimi and Paul.

They walked back to her apartment after dinner,
and this time he came up for a drink. She was nervous that he would try to kiss her—and she didn't
feel ready to yet—but he didn't. He was relaxed,
but gentlemanly, and respected her boundaries. He
could sense too that she wasn't prepared to deal
with more than what they were doing. Walking,
talking, going out for meals, getting to know each
other. This was why he had come to see her, and
exactly what he wanted. And she felt as though no
one had been as devoted to her so soon after they
met. Paul wasn't in their early days, he was too
busy, and he was sixteen years older, which was
very different. She and Finn were almost the same
age, of the same generation, and had many of the
same interests. If she had made a list of everything
she wanted in a man, Finn had it all. But she hadn't
wanted anyone since Paul. And now Finn was here,
big as life. And she had only known him for a
week. But so far, it had been a very intense week,
and they were spending a lot of time together.

They went to the MOMA the next day, and the
Whitney Museum the day after. They went to all
her favorite restaurants, and his. He met with his
agent to talk about a new book deal. And much to
her amazement, she missed him for the few hours

he was gone. Other than that, he was with her every minute, except when he left her at her loft at night. He still hadn't kissed her, but he had mentioned again that he was falling in love with her. She had just looked at him with worried eyes. What if he was playing with her? But even more frightening was the thought that maybe he wasn't. What if this was for real? What would happen? He lived in Ireland, and she in New York. But she wouldn't let herself think about it yet. It was too soon. It just didn't make sense. Except even Hope knew that it did. It made a lot of sense, for both of them. She could base herself anywhere in the world, and they knew it. And so could he. It was an ideal situation. They seemed perfectly matched.

Hope didn't tell Mark Webber, her agent, what was happening when he called. And there was no one else for her to tell. Mark was her closest friend, and she liked his wife as well. They invited her over to have dinner, but she declined. She didn't want to tell him Finn was in town to see her. She knew Mark would be shocked, or surprised at least, and probably fiercely protective and suspicious. She wanted to spend the evening with Finn. So she said she was too busy with some new work, and Mark promised to call again the following week, and told her not to work too hard.

And on New Year's Eve, as they had agreed earlier in the week, she and Finn went to Times Square. She took an old camera with her, to take shots in black and white. They got there around eleven, and artfully wended their way through the crowd that had been waiting there for hours. The characters around them were extraordinary, and Finn enjoyed watching it through her eyes. They were having a great time.

At midnight, the ball fell from the top of a flagpole with lights flashing inside it, and everyone screamed and cheered. There were prostitutes and drug dealers, tourists, and college kids from out of town, every form of humanity around them, and she was so busy taking pictures of them at midnight that she was startled when Finn put her camera aside and stood before her, and pulled her into his arms. And before she knew what had happened, he was kissing her, and everything around them was forgotten. All she was aware of and remembered later was Finn kissing her, and feeling totally safe and protected in his arms, wanting the kiss never to end, and as she looked into his eyes afterward in amazement, she knew that she was falling in love with him too. It was the perfect beginning for a new year. And maybe a new life.

Chapter 7

Finn stayed at the Hotel Mercer for the next two weeks. He met with his agent and publisher, taped two interviews, and saw Hope every chance he got. He was ever present, ever willing to adjust his schedule for her, and wanted to spend every moment with her that he could. Hope was startled by how fast the relationship was moving, although they hadn't slept together, but she enjoyed his company. She was torn between reminding herself that this was more than likely just a passing thing for him, and wanting to believe it was real, and allowing herself to be vulnerable to him. He was so open, kind, loving, attentive, and they had such a good time together, it was impossible to resist. He couldn't do enough for her, and did everything imaginable to please her, with a myriad of thoughtful gestures. He brought her flowers, chocolates, books. More and more, she was letting herself be swept away on the tidal wave of emotions he

engulfed her with. And after three weeks of constantly being in each other's company, he said
something that brought her up short, as they
walked through Washington Square Park one afternoon on their way back downtown from a
long walk.

"You know what this is, don't you?" he said
earnestly, as she had a hand tucked into his arm.
They had been talking about Renaissance art, and
the beauty of the Uffizi Gallery in Florence, which
they had discovered that they both loved, and Finn
was very knowledgeable about. He had many interests and numerous talents, not unlike Hope.
They seemed a perfect match in so many ways.
And he was by far one of the most interesting men
she had ever met, and the most attentive. He was
truly the handsome prince of whom every woman
dreamed, and loving at the same time. He asked
her about all the things she cared about and
wanted, and they were constantly surprised to discover they loved many of the same things. He was
like the mirror image of her soul.

"What is it?" she asked, smiling up at him with
a tender look in her eyes. There was no question,
she was falling in love with him, after knowing him
for only weeks. It had never happened to her before. Not even with Paul. Her romance with Finn
was moving with the speed of sound. "Whatever it
is, it's wonderful. I'm not looking a gift horse in the
mouth." She had a feeling that if she talked to

someone about their budding relationship, they wouldn't understand it, and would tell her to take her time before jumping in. She was, but she also had a powerful sense that this was a man and a situation she could trust. She didn't doubt it. There was no reason to. She knew who he was, and there was a soft hidden side of him that touched her to the core.

"This is fusion," he said softly. "Where two people become one."

She looked at him with an inquisitive expression, startled by the word and asked him what he meant.

"Sometimes when people fall in love," he explained, "they are so close and so well suited to each other, that they blend together, and you can't tell where one person starts and the other ends. They merge, and can't live without each other after that." It sounded a little frightening to her, and not what she had in mind. She and Paul had had a good marriage until he got sick, and Mimi died, but they had never "fused" or become one person. They were two very distinct people, with different personalities and needs and thoughts. It had always worked well for them.

"I don't think I agree with you," she said quietly. "I think you can be just as much in love as separate people, standing beside each other, each one whole and adding to the other, or complementing each other, without 'fusing' and becoming one. That sounds unhealthy to me," she said honestly. "That's not really what I want," she said firmly. "I want to be a whole, individual person, and I love the whole person you are, Finn. We don't need to be one. Then each of us would lose an important part of ourselves that makes us who we are as people." Finn looked disappointed by what she said. It was the first time they had disagreed.

"I want to be part of you," he said sadly. "I need you, Hope. It's only been a short time, but I already feel like you're a part of me." It still didn't sound right to her, even if it was flattering or meant he loved her. It sounded claustrophobic and extreme, especially so soon. They hardly knew each other. How could they fuse into one person? And why would they want to? They had both worked hard to become who they were. She didn't want to lose that now. She was falling in love with who and what he was, she didn't want to fall in love with herself. It felt all wrong.

"Maybe you don't love me as much as I love you," he said, looking worried and hurt.

"I'm falling in love with you," she said, looking up at him with her deep violet eyes. "There's a lot we need to learn about each other. I want to savor that. You're a very special person," she said gently.

"So are you. So are we," he insisted. "Our two parts make one bigger, better whole."

"That's possible," she conceded, "but I don't

want either of us to lose who we are in the process. We've both worked too hard to achieve what we have, to lose that now. I want to stand next to you, Finn, not **be** you. And why would you want to be me?"

"Because I love you," he said, pulling her close to him, and stopping to kiss her hard. "I love you more than you know." The way he said it was touching, not scary, but it was too much in such a short time. "Maybe I'll always love you more," he said, looking pensive, as they walked on again. "I think there's always one person in a couple who loves more than the other. I'm willing to be that one," he said generously, and it made her feel slightly guilty. She thought she loved him, but she had loved Paul for so many years, it was going to take her time to get used to Finn, and settle him in her heart. She had to get to know him better first, and there was plenty of opportunity. They were with each other constantly, except when she went back to her loft to sleep at night. He changed the subject then, and she was relieved. Not only did she have to get used to loving him, his notion of fusion made her uncomfortable, and it wasn't what she wanted in a relationship or had in mind. "What are we doing this weekend?"

She looked thoughtful for a moment before she answered. "I was thinking it might be nice to go to the Cape. I'd like you to see the house. It's very simple, but it's a relic of my childhood. That house means a lot to me." He smiled as soon as she said it.

"I was hoping you'd ask me up there," he said, putting an arm around her shoulders. "Why don't we spend more than a weekend there, if you can spare the time? It might do us both good." He was in no hurry to go back to Ireland. They were both masters of their own fate and time, and he was enjoying the time he was spending with her, getting to know her. And he was in no hurry to get back to his writing, he said. She was more important to him.

"I guess we could spend four or five days, or even a week. It can get very bleak in winter, and cold. Let's see how the weather is when we get there." He nodded and agreed.

"When do you want to go?" he asked, looking excited. She had no pressing assignments at the moment. Her schedule was clear, and so was his, other than the editing he had to finish. They were going to a party at the MOMA that night, and he had a publishing event to attend the following week. They were both enjoying discovering each other's worlds, and in each case, they left the limelight to the other and were happy to take a backseat. It seemed like a perfect balance between two well-known, successful, creative people, whose worlds complemented each other. It was just what she had said earlier, they stood beside each other, without having to fuse into one person. Everything about that idea seemed wrong to her.

"Why don't we go to the Cape tomorrow?" Hope suggested. "Bring lots of warm stuff with you." And then she looked faintly embarrassed to broach a delicate subject, but she wanted to speak up clearly. "I'm not ready for us to sleep together, Finn. Are you okay with sleeping in the guest room?" It had been a long time since Paul, and she wanted to be sure of what she was doing. There had been no one of importance in her life since her husband, which made this a much bigger deal. Whatever it was, if it was going to be lasting or not, she had to figure it out, and what she felt about it, before she took that leap.

"That's fine," he said with an understanding look. He seemed to have an unlimited ability to make her feel comfortable and happy. He let her set the pace, be as close or as distant from him as she felt at any given moment. He was the kindest, most loving man she had ever met. He was truly a dream come true. And if she had been praying for a man to come into her life, which she wasn't when he turned up, he would have been the answer to those prayers. There was nothing about him she didn't like so far, or that made her uneasy, except perhaps his silly ideas about fusion, but she was sure it was just his way of expressing insecurities and wanting to be loved. And she was coming to love him, for who he was, not for being a part of her. Hope was a very independent person, and she hadn't come through all she had by being part of someone else, nor did she want to start now. And she knew that her monks in Tibet wouldn't have approved of that idea at all.

The party they went to at the museum that night was lively and crowded. It was an important event—the opening of a major show. The main curator of the museum came to talk to her and she introduced him to Finn. They chatted for a few minutes, and several photographers snapped their picture for the press. They made a striking pair. It was definitely a milieu where Hope was the star, and Finn was less well known, until they heard his name. But being somewhat in the background didn't seem to bother him in the least. He was warm, friendly, charming, and unassuming, even though he was the famous Sir Finn O'Neill. No one who would have seen him would have thought he was a show-off, or arrogant in any way. He was more than happy to let Hope be the star she was at the museum event, and he seemed to enjoy talking to lots of people and admiring the art. He was in good spirits when they took a cab back to the hotel. They were leaving for Cape Cod in the morning.

"I miss you when we're in a crowd like that," he confessed as she snuggled next to him in the taxi. She had had a good time, and had been proud to be with him. It felt so good being part of a couple again. She didn't need it to complete her, but it was nice having him there, and talking to him about the party afterward. She had missed that since her divorce. Parties were always more fun if you could gossip about them later with a mate. "You looked beautiful," he complimented her readily, as he had several times that evening. "And I was so proud to be with you. I really enjoyed the evening, but I have to admit, I love having you to myself. It's going to be great to have some time alone in Cape Cod."

"Having both in one's life is nice," Hope commented peacefully with her head on his shoulder. "It's exciting to go out and meet people sometimes, and then it's nice to have quiet time alone."

"I hate sharing you with your adoring public," he teased her. "I like it best when we're alone. Everything is so fresh and new right now, it feels like an intrusion when anyone else is around." The way he said it flattered her, that he was so anxious for time with her, but there were definitely times when she enjoyed the company of her peers and colleagues, and once in a while, even their admiration. For her, it had been part of life ever since she'd gone back to work, although she always benefited from solitary moments too. But it touched her that Finn was so anxious to be with her, and to not waste a single moment they could spend alone. They would have plenty of time together at the Cape.

"You have your adoring public too," she reminded him, and he hung his head in embarrassment in a burst of humility rarely seen and that no one would have expected of him. It surprised her at times that for a man so well known in his field, and so strikingly good looking, he didn't seem narcissistic to her at all. He wasn't selfish or self-centered, he took pride in her accomplishments, was discreet about his own, and had no need to be the center of attention. And whatever flaws he had that she had not discovered yet, a big ego was not among them. He was a gem.

They left for Cape Cod at nine o'clock the next morning, in a Suburban he had rented for the week, since Hope no longer kept a car in New York. Whenever she needed one, she rented one herself. Living in the city, it made more sense, and she didn't go up to Cape Cod very often anymore. She hadn't been there since September, four months before. She was thrilled to be going with Finn now, and have the opportunity to share it with him. For a man who loved nature, solitude, and time alone with her, it was the perfect place for them to go.

She was determined not to sleep with him that weekend, and already knew what guest room she would put him in. It was actually the room she had spent summers in as a child, and it was next door to her parents' old room, which she lived in now and had for years.

She and Paul had spent summers there during most of their marriage. And at the time, the simplicity of it had suited them both, although with the windfall he had made from the sale of his company, Paul's life was grander now. And if anything, Hope's had gotten less cluttered over the years. She had no need for luxuries, unusual comforts, or excess of any kind. She was a very unassuming, straightforward person, and enjoyed a simple life. And Finn said he did too.

They stopped for lunch at the Griswold Inn, in Essex, Connecticut, on the way to the Cape, and as they drove past an exit for Boston, Finn mentioned his son at MIT.

"Why don't we stop and visit him?" Hope asked with a bright smile. After all she'd heard about him, she wanted to meet him, and Finn laughed.

"He'd probably fall over if I stopped in to see him. Actually, they're not back yet after the winter break. He said he was going to Paris after skiing in Switzerland with his friends, or he may be back at my place in London. Maybe we could stop in to visit some other time. I'd like you to meet him."

"So would I," Hope said warmly.

They drove on to Wellfleet after Providence and they reached the house at four in the afternoon, as the light was starting to get dim. The roads had been clear, but it looked like it might snow, and it was bitter cold, with a stiff wind. She directed Finn to drive into the driveway, which was slightly overgrown. The house stood apart from all the others, and there was tall dune grass all around. It seemed bleak at that time of year, and Finn commented that it looked like a Wyeth painting that they'd seen at the museum, which made Hope smile. She'd never thought of the house that way before, but he was right, it did. It was an old barn-shaped New England structure, painted gray with white shutters. In summer, there were flowers out front, but there were none now. The gardener she hired to come once a month cut everything back in winter, and he wouldn't even bother to come now until spring. There was nothing for him to do there. And the house looked sad and deserted with the shutters closed. But the view of the ocean from the dune it sat on was spectacular and the beach stretched out for miles. Hope smiled as she stood looking at it with him. It always made her feel peaceful being there. She put an arm around his waist and he leaned down to kiss her, and then she took her keys out of her bag, opened the door, turned off the alarm, and walked in, with Finn right behind her. The shutters were closed against the wind, so she turned on the lights. Dusk was coming fast.

What he saw when she lit the lamps was a beautiful wood-paneled room. The wood was bleached, as were the floors, and the furniture was stark and simple. She had redone the couches a few years before because they were so worn. The fabrics were the pale blue of a summer sky, the curtains were a simple muslin, there were hooked rugs, plain New England furniture, a stone fireplace, and her photographs were all over the walls. It had a stark simplicity and unpretentiousness that made it easy to be there, particularly in the summer, with the breeze coming off the ocean, sand on the floor, and everyone going barefoot. It was the perfect beach house, and Finn immediately responded to it with a warm smile. It was the kind of house every child should spend a summer in, and Hope had, and so had her daughter. There was a big country kitchen, with a round antique table, and blue and white tiles on the walls that had been there since the house was built. The place looked lived in and well worn, and more important, much loved.

"What a wonderful place," Finn said, as he put his arms around her and kissed her.

"I'm glad you like it," Hope said, looking happy. "I would have been sad if you didn't." They went outside together then to open the shutters, and when they came back in, the view of Cape Cod Bay at sunset was spectacular. He wanted to go for a walk on the beach, but it was too late and too cold.

They had brought groceries with them, which they had bought in Wellfleet, and unpacked them together. It felt like playing house and she looked happy. She hadn't done that in years, and with Finn, she loved it. Then he went out to get their suitcases and she told him where to put them. He walked upstairs to their bedrooms, set them down, and looked around. Hope's photos hung in every room, and there were a lot of old photographs of her with her parents, and Mimi with her and Paul. It was a real family summer home that spanned generations and warmed hearts.

"I wish I had had a house like this when I was growing up," Finn said as he strode back into the kitchen, his hair still disheveled by the wind, which only made him look more handsome. "My parents had a very stuffy, boring place in Southampton, which I never liked. It was full of antiques and things I wasn't allowed to touch. It wasn't like being at the beach. This is the real deal."

"Yes, it is." She smiled at him. "I love that about it too. That's why I keep it. I don't get here often enough anymore, but I love it when I do." There were too many memories and friendly ghosts here for her to ever give it up. "It's not fancy, but that's what I love about it. It's fantastic in the summer. As a kid, I spent all my time on the beach, and so did Mimi. I still do."

She was making a salad as she said it to him, and they were going to make steaks on the grill. The kitchen appliances were modern and functional, and often in summer they barbecued, but it was too cold to do that now. Finn set the table, and lit a fire. And a little while later, he made the steaks, and she warmed some soup and French bread they'd bought at the store. They set some French cheeses on a platter, and when they sat down at the kitchen table, it was a hearty meal. Finn opened a bottle of red wine he'd bought, and they each had a glass. It was a perfect dinner in the cozy house, and then they sat in front of the fire, telling stories of their respective childhoods.

Hers had been simple and wholesome in New Hampshire, near the Dartmouth campus, since her father was an English literature professor there. Her mother had been a talented artist, and her childhood had been happy, despite the fact that she was an only child. She said it had never bothered her not to have siblings. She had had a great time with her parents and their friends, and was included at everything they did. She spent a lot of her time visiting her father at his office on the campus. He had been devastated when she decided to go to Brown instead, as a seventeen-year-old freshman, but they had a better photography department. It was where she ultimately met Paul. She met him at nineteen, and married him at twenty-one, when he was thirty-seven. She said that both her parents had died within the first few years she was married. It was a huge loss to her. Her father died of a heart attack, and within a year, her mother of cancer. She couldn't live without him.

"See what I mean?" Finn commented. "That's

what I meant by fusion. It's what real relationships should be, but it can be a dangerous thing sometimes, if things don't work out in a relationship, or one of the partners dies. Like Siamese twins, one can't survive without the other." It still didn't seem like a good thing to Hope, particularly citing her mother's untimely death as an example. Hope had no desire to be anyone's Siamese twin, but she didn't comment. She knew he loved the theory, but she didn't. And for her, it had been a hard blow to lose both parents so close together. She had inherited the Cape Cod house from them, and sold their old Victorian near Dartmouth. She said that she still had all her mother's paintings in storage. They were good, but not quite her style, although she clearly had talent, and occasionally taught a class at Dartmouth, but she had no interest in teaching, unlike Hope's father, who was gifted, much loved, and deeply respected at the school for all the years he taught there.

By comparison, Finn's youth was far more exotic. He had already told her that his father was a doctor and his mother an extremely beautiful woman.

"I think my mother always felt she married beneath her. She had a broken engagement before that to a duke in Ireland. He was killed in a riding accident, and shortly after that, she married my father and went to New York with him, where he had a very substantial practice, but her family was much fancier than his, and she always lorded it over him. I think she missed having a title, since her father was an earl, and she would have been a duchess if her fiancé hadn't died.

"She always had frail health when I was little, so I didn't see a lot of her. I always had some young girl taking care of me, whom they brought over from Ireland, while my mother had the vapors and went to parties, and complained about my father. The home I have in Ireland now originally belonged to her great-grandfather, and I think it would have made her happy that it is back in the family now. It means a lot to me because of it.

"My father was always very disappointed that I didn't want to be a doctor like him, but it just wasn't for me. He made an excellent living and always supported my mother handsomely, but it was never quite enough for her. He wasn't titled, and she hated living in New York. I'm not sure they were ever very happy, although they were discreet about it. I never saw them fighting, but there was a distinct chill in our Park Avenue apartment, which my mother hated, because it wasn't Ireland, although our home was beautiful and filled with antiques. She just wasn't a happy woman. And now that I live there, I can see why. The Irish are a special breed, they love their country, their hills, their houses, their history, even their pubs. I'm not sure you can take an Irish person away and have them be happy somewhere else. They pine for their own country, and it must be in the genes, because the minute I walked into my great-great-grandfather's house, I knew I was home. It was as though it had been waiting for me all my life. I knew it the minute I saw it.

"My parents died fairly young too, in a road accident together. I think if she had lived, and my father hadn't, she'd have gone back to Ireland then. It was all she waited for during all the years of their married life in New York. I suppose she loved my father, in her own way, but she wanted to go home. So I did it for her." He smiled sadly. "I hope you come and visit me there, Hope. It's the most beautiful place on earth. You can walk in the hills for hours, amid the wildflowers, without ever seeing a soul. The Irish are an odd combination of soulful, solitary, and then wildly gregarious in the pubs. I think that's how I am, sometimes I just need to be alone, and at other times I love being around people, and having fun. At home, I'm either locked up, writing, or having a good laugh in the local pub."

"It sounds like a good life," Hope said, nestled in beside him on the couch, as the fire died slowly. It had been a lovely evening, and she felt wonderfully comfortable with him, as though they had known each other for years. She liked hearing the stories of his childhood, and his parents, although it sounded lonely in some ways. His mother didn't sound like a happy person, and his father had been busy all the time with his patients, and neither of them seemed to have had much time for him. He said it was why he had started writing, and was a voracious reader as a child and young man. Reading, and eventually writing, was his escape from an essentially lonely childhood, despite their very comfortable Park Avenue life. Her far simpler life had been much happier with her own parents in New Hampshire and Cape Cod.

Finn and Hope had both married young, so they had that in common. They were both artistic in different fields. They were both only children, and their own children were only two years apart, so they had become parents at roughly the same time. And for very different reasons, their marriages had failed. Hers for complicated reasons, and his officially when his wife died, but he readily admitted that his marriage to Michael's mother had never really worked, and probably would have ended in divorce if she hadn't died, which was traumatic for him and their child. Finn said she was totally narcissistic, beautiful, and spoiled, and essentially badly behaved. She had cheated on him several times. He had been enamored with her beauty as a young man, and then overwhelmed by what it entailed. There was a lot of common ground between Finn and Hope, in many ways, although their marriages had been different, and his son was still alive. But there were many common points, and they were nearly the same age, only two years apart.

When the fire finally went out, she turned off the lights, and they walked upstairs. He had already found his bedroom when he brought the bags up and had seen hers. She had a small double bed in the cozy room that had been her parents', and the bed always felt too big for her now without Paul. The one in the room Finn was staying in was so small that Hope looked embarrassed and said that maybe they should trade, although hers didn't look big enough for him either.

"I'll be fine," he reassured her, and tenderly kissed her goodnight. And then they each disappeared into their rooms. She was in bed five minutes later in a heavy cashmere nightgown with socks, and she laughed when Finn called out a last goodnight in the small house.

"Sweet dreams," she shouted back, and turned over in the dark, thinking of him. They had known each other for so little time, but she had never felt so close to anyone in her life. For a minute, she wondered if his fusion theory was correct, but she didn't want it to be. She wanted to believe that they could love each other, but keep their distinct lives, personalities, and talents intact. That still felt right to her. Thinking about him, she was awake for a long time. She was remembering the things he had said about his childhood and how lonely it sounded to her. She wondered if that was why he was so anxious to be part of someone else. His mother didn't sound like much of one to her. And it was interesting to think that while he said that his mother was beautiful and dissatisfied, he had married a woman who was also beautiful and selfish and hadn't been a good mother to their son. It was odd how, in some cases, history repeated itself, and people re-created the same miseries that had tormented them as children. She wondered if perhaps he had tried to get a different ending to the same story, and hadn't succeeded in the end.

As she thought about it, she heard a thump that sounded like Finn had fallen out of bed, punctuated by a loud "Fuck," which made her laugh, and she went to check on him, padding down the hall in her nightgown and cashmere socks.

"Are you okay?" she whispered in the dark, and heard him laugh.

"The chest of drawers attacked me when I went to the loo."

"Did you hurt yourself?" She sounded worried about him, and felt guilty about the small room he was in.

"I'm bleeding profusely," he said in a tone of anguish. "I need a nurse."

"Should I call 911?" She laughed back.

"No, some hairy paramedic will give me mouth to mouth, and I'll have to knee him in the groin. How about a kiss?" She moved into the room and sat down on the narrow bed that had once been hers, and he took her in his arms and kissed her. "I miss you," he whispered.

"I miss you too," she whispered back. And then hesitantly, "Do you want me to sleep in here?"

He laughed out loud. "In this bed? Now, that would be a contortionist's act I'd like to see you do. That isn't what I had in mind." There was a long silence, and he didn't push. He had promised that they would sleep in separate rooms and not have sex, and he was determined to keep his word, although he would have preferred otherwise, and she felt foolish now for suggesting it.

"I guess this is kind of stupid, huh? We're in love with each other, and I guess no one's keeping track."

"Something like that," he said gently, "but it's up to you, my love. I'm happy to sleep here, if that's what you want. As long as you take me to a chiropractor tomorrow, so he can fix my back." She laughed again, and pulled the covers off him unceremoniously, as he sat up.

"Come on. Let's be grown up." She held out a hand to him and led him to her room, and he didn't object. But he had left the choice up to her. Without commenting on it further, they both climbed into her bed, and as they lay side by side in the small double bed, he took her in his arms.

"I love you, Hope," he whispered.

"I love you too, Finn," she whispered back. And then without another word of discussion or explanation, or mention of fusion, he made love to her as no one ever had in her life.

Chapter 8

Finn and Hope's days at Cape Cod were magical. They woke up late in the morning, made love before they got up. He cooked breakfast for her, and they bundled up and went for long walks on the beach. When they got back, Finn lit a fire in the living room. They spent hours reading, and she took photographs of him. They made love again in the afternoon, cooked together, slept together, talked for hours about everything that mattered to them. She had never spent as much time with anyone in her life.

She found boxes of old photographs of Mimi and her parents, and went through all of them with him. They went to local restaurants and ate lobster, with butter dripping down their chins, laughing at each other in ridiculous gigantic paper bibs, and she took pictures of him that way too. She asked a waiter to take a photograph of them together, and Finn got briefly annoyed and jokingly accused her of flirting with the waiter, which she wasn't.

It was almost like a honeymoon. They stayed for a week, and finally, regretfully, they closed the house. Finn latched the shutters, and they drove back to New York. This time, he didn't stay at the Mercer, he moved into the loft with her. It felt perfectly natural to her now. She was totally at ease with him.

They went to his publishing event the night they got back, and this time he was the center of attention, and she quietly took photographs of him from a distance, smiling softly, and every now and then their eyes would meet across the room. She was proud of him as she watched him, and he was equally proud to have her with him. The only heartache they were facing was that he was going back to Dublin soon.

They talked about it when they got home that night, and Finn looked unhappy, although they'd had a lovely evening.

"When can you come over to see me?" he said, looking like a child about to be abandoned by his mother, or sent away to camp.

"I don't know. I have an assignment, shooting an actor in L.A. the first week in February. After that, I'm fairly free."

"That's less than two weeks away," he said miserably, and then frowned as he asked her the next question. "What actor?"

"Rod Beames," she said casually. She had shot him once before. He was up for an Academy Award for best actor.

"Shit," Finn said, giving her an angry look. "Have you ever gone out with him?"

"Of course not." She was startled by his reaction and the question. "He's a subject, not a boyfriend. I never go out with the people I shoot." And then she laughed as she said it, given what had happened with him. "You're the first," she reassured him. "And the last," she promised, as she leaned over to kiss him.

"How do I know that's true?" He looked upset and worried, and it touched her. Paul had never been jealous, but Finn clearly was. He had made a comment about one of the waiters at a restaurant at the Cape, and accused her half-jokingly of flirting with him, which of course she wasn't. She laughed at Finn, and he apologized. It made her feel very young and desirable that he would even worry about it, but she only had eyes for Finn.

"Because I say so, silly," she said, and kissed him again. "I suppose I could fly to Dublin from L.A., after that. Can I fly to Dublin, or do I have to change planes in London?" She was already figuring out the dates in her head.

"I'll check. What about you and Beames?" He went back to it again.

"About the same as you and Queen Elizabeth.

I'm not worried about her. You don't need to worry about him."

"Are you sure?"

"Totally." She smiled at him, and he relaxed a little.

"What if he asks you out this time?"

"I'll tell him that I'm madly in love with a fabulous man in Ireland, and he doesn't have a chance." She was still smiling, as Finn continued to look at her nervously. It was true. Once they started sleeping with each other, all of her reserve fell away, her guard went down, she trusted him completely, and her heart was his. They had talked about how quickly it had all happened between them, and how much in love they both were. It was what the French called a "coup de foudre," a bolt of lightning that had hit them, and he pointed out regularly that there was no turning back now. He said he was irreversibly in love with her, and she was equally in love with him.

Hope had come to the conclusion that at their age, those things happened, they knew who they were and what they wanted, what had gone wrong in past lifetimes, and they both felt certain that this was forever, even though she felt it was soon to tell anyone. They had been in love with each other for just over a month, and Hope had never been as sure of anything in her life as she was of her love for him, and Finn felt the same. They both knew it was for real, and agreed that it was the best thing that had ever happened to them.

Finn promised to check out the flights for her the next day, and as it turned out, there was a flight to Dublin from L.A. He stayed in New York for another week and they had a wonderful time together. She thought of introducing him to Mark Webber, but decided it was premature. No one would understand how certain they were of each other this early. It was easier not to have to defend it, and just enjoy it privately. And Finn wanted to be alone with her anyway before he left. He said he didn't want anyone taking up their time, which was infinitely precious as the days flew by until he was to leave.

He looked mournful the morning she helped him pack his suitcase. He was miserable about leaving, and still nervous about her photo shoot with Rod Beames. He kept bringing it up, and Hope was beginning to feel silly reassuring him. But since they had met and fallen in love with each other after her assignment to shoot him, he was worried about all her portrait sittings now. She reassured him again and again. And they made love before they left for the airport. She had never made love as often in her life as they had in the past weeks.

They had vaguely discussed marriage, although not in hard and fast terms. It really was too early, but they had both confirmed that the concept was not distasteful to either of them. Finn didn't care what it took, or how they did it, he wanted to spend the rest of his life with her. And she was beginning to think the same thing, although she wasn't sure she needed marriage to do it. She was already more or less living with him, and would be in Ireland as well.

And he had shocked her by bringing up the subject of a baby. He said he wanted to try having one with her. She had gently told him that the project would probably need considerable intervention and assistance, and she didn't feel ready to take that on, at least not yet. She wanted to discuss it later, after they'd been together for longer, but somewhere deep within her, although it sounded crazy, the idea had some appeal. Particularly when she looked at the photographs of Mimi and remembered how adorable she'd been as a baby. The idea of having a child with Finn was scary, but dazzling. And thinking about it made her feel young again. He insisted that they could do it at their ages, others had, including several of his friends. He was pushing hard for the idea, but had agreed to wait at least a couple of months before they discussed it again.

He was silent on the way to the airport and held her in his arms in the limousine. They kissed and whispered, and he promised to call her the minute he arrived. He was taking the night flight, and would arrive too late for him to call her, but it would be morning for him.

"I'll get the house ready for you," he promised. He said he had a lot of cleaning up to do, and he needed to get the furnace man in, so the part of the house they lived in wouldn't be freezing cold. He told her to bring a lot of sweaters and warm jackets, and good solid shoes to walk in the hills. It would be early February when she got there, so it would be rainy and cold. She had promised to stay with him for a month, and was looking forward to it. He had to write in March anyway, and she had assignments set up in New York, so she couldn't stay longer than that. But a month would be a great start, and allow her to settle in. They had just spent four weeks together in New York.

Leaving each other at the airport was like ripping a limb off for both of them. She had never been as attached to anyone, and certainly not this quickly, except Mimi, but not even Paul. Her relationship with Paul, when she met him, had been far more measured and started more slowly, particularly since she was a student then, and he was so much older. He had been very cautious about not moving too quickly. Finn had none of those concerns, and had leaped in with both feet. But at their age, it made more sense. Both of them knew people who had fallen in love in their forties, realized they'd met "the right one" quickly, married within months, and had been happy ever since.

But they both knew that it would still be hard to explain to others. They had fallen madly in love and decided to spend their lives together, in a month.

And Hope was determined not to say anything to Paul yet. She didn't want to upset him, and had no idea how he'd react. She had been alone for so long, and so accessible to him whenever he wanted, even if it wasn't often, she somehow had a sense that he might be unnerved by her being involved with someone. But she thought that once they met, he and Finn could be good friends. Finn had expressed no jealousy about him yet, which seemed a very good thing. Hope would have been bothered by it if he had. Paul was very important to her, and she loved him deeply, in a pure way now, and knew she always would, for however long he lived, which she hoped would be a long time. She had talked to him once in January, and he was still on his boat then, sailing toward St. Bart's. She never mentioned Finn. And Paul could get her on her cell phone anywhere in the world, so even when she was in Ireland, he could call her, and she didn't need to tell him where she was, unless she chose to when he called. But she wanted to be discreet for now.

She and Finn kissed for a last time, and she waved as he went through security and disappeared, and then she went back to the city in the limo he'd rented. It was the first time she'd been alone in a month and it felt strange. It was small comfort that they wouldn't be wrestling with her narrow bed. It was an impossible fit for her and Finn, but he insisted on sleeping with her in it, every night. She had promised to try and fit a larger bed onto her sleeping platform before he came to stay again, but it would be a tight fit.

After he left, the apartment seemed empty without him, and she wandered around aimlessly for a while, then she answered some emails, checked her mail, made some editing notes about photographs for her retoucher, and finally took a bath and went to bed with a book. She missed him, but she had to admit that, for a short time, having time to herself was nice. Finn liked a lot of attention, engaged in interesting conversations with her at all hours, and wanted to be together all the time. And just for a change, it was almost fun to be on her own again, although she wouldn't have said it to him. He would have been crushed.

Her cell phone woke her at three in the morning. It was Finn. He had just arrived. He called to tell her he loved her, and missed her awfully. She thanked him, told him she loved him too, blew him a kiss, and went back to sleep. And he called her again at nine. He told her everything he was doing at the house in preparation for her arrival, and she smiled, listening to him. He sounded like a little kid, and she loved that about him. There was an innocence and sweetness about him that was irresistible. When they were to-gether, it was easy to forget how famous and suc-cessful he was, just as he did about her. It wasn't important to them.

He called her three times a day, and she called him as often, between projects and meetings, gallery visits, and discussions with curators. He sounded fine until the day she was leaving for L.A., and then he mentioned Rod Beames again and re-minded her not to fall in love with him, or even go out to dinner with him, remembering what had happened between them. She assured him that she wouldn't and reminded him that Beames had a twenty-five-year-old wife who was pregnant, and he would surely not be chasing her.

"You never know," Finn said, still sounding anx-ious. "I'd rather have you than any twenty-five-year-old."

"That's why I'm in love with you," Hope said, smiling. She was rushing to the airport and had to get off the phone.

Once she was in L.A., Finn called her constantly. She finally had to shut off her phone at the sitting, and he complained about it bitterly when she turned it back on again after the shoot.

"What were you doing with him?" Finn asked, sounding angry.

"Taking his picture, silly," Hope said, trying to calm him. It was the first time she had ever en-countered jealousy of this nature. It would never have occurred to Paul, nor to her. "I'm all done. I'm back at the hotel. I have a meeting tomorrow morning at the L.A. County Museum about a show next year, and then I'm through. I'm flying out tomorrow. So stop worrying. And I'm not seeing Beames again." In fact, he and his wife had invited her to dinner, and she hadn't accepted because Finn had made such an issue about it. It seemed like a shame to her. She liked having dinner with her subjects before or after a shoot. It was the first time she had ever hesitated to do so, because she didn't want to upset Finn. She hoped he'd get over his jealousy soon. It was a little trying, but flattering at the same time, as though she were some hot young thing that every man on the planet would want to seduce, which she had pointed out to Finn was hardly the case. But he was jealous anyway.

Instead of going out, she had dinner in her room at the Beverly Hills hotel. When Finn called her before he went to bed, he was happy to find her having room service. He was warm and loving with her and could hardly wait for her to arrive.

Hope flew to Dublin after her meeting at the L.A. County Museum, which went well. The flight was long, and by the time she landed in Dublin, she felt as though she had been on a plane for days. In the future, it was going to be a lot easier getting to Ireland from New York.

She went through customs quickly, and Finn

was waiting for her as she came through and swept her into his arms. Anyone who saw them would have thought he hadn't seen her for years, and he was carrying an enormous bouquet of flowers, reds and yellows and pinks—they were the prettiest flowers she'd ever seen. They chatted animatedly as they went to pick up her bags, and then she followed him to his car. She liked listening to the Irish brogues around her, and Finn imitated them perfectly. He swept a low bow as he held open the door to his Jaguar, and she got in holding her bouquet. She didn't say it, but she felt like a bride.

It took them a little over an hour, driving southwest from Dublin, until they reached the town of Blessington, and drove through it. Finn followed the signs to Russborough, on narrow country roads, driving expertly on the left side, and then turned off finally onto a gravel road. The hills he had talked about were all around them, the Wicklow Mountains. There were forests and fields of wildflowers that had sprung up in the February rains. It was cold, but not as much so as Cape Cod. It was mostly damp and gray, and it rained on and off as they drove from the airport. And as soon as they reached the gravel road that was his driveway, he stopped the car, took her in his arms, and kissed her hard. He took her breath away.

"God, woman, I felt like you were never coming. I'm not letting you out of my sight again. Or I'm going with you next time. I've never missed anyone so much in my life." They had only been apart for a week.

"I missed you too," she said, smiling, happy to be there, and she couldn't wait to see his house.

He started the car again then. It was a dark green Jaguar with tan leather seats, very elegant and masculine, and perfectly suited to him. He told her she could drive it anytime, but she was afraid to drive on the wrong side of the road, so he promised to be her chauffeur wherever she went, which sounded fine to her. She didn't need to go anywhere without him anyway. She was here to see him.

They drove along the gravel road for what seemed like forever, with forests in the distance, and a row of trees bordering the road. They sped along a graceful turn then, and suddenly she saw it, and caught her breath. For a moment she was speechless, while he smiled. It always did the same to him, particularly when he'd been away for a while.

"Oh my God!" Hope said, turning to look at him with a broad smile. "Are you kidding? That's not a house, it's a **palace**!" It looked extraordinary. The house was enormous, and looked like the photograph he'd shown her in London, but in real life it was so much bigger, it stunned her.

"Pretty, isn't it?" he said humbly, as he stopped the car and she got out. The house itself was majestic, the staircase looked like the gateway to heaven, and the columns lent it grace. "Welcome to Blaxton House, my love." He had already told her it bore his mother's maiden name and always had. Finn put an arm around her, and led her up the long stone steps. An old man in a black apron came out to greet them, and a moment later an ancient maid appeared wearing a uniform and a black sweater, with her hair in a tight bun. They looked older than the building, but were smiling and friendly, as Finn introduced her to them. Their names were Winfred and Katherine, and he explained to her later that they had come with the estate, and commented himself that they looked nearly as old.

Inside the house, there was a long gallery filled with dusty family portraits in a long dark hall with tapestries and somber furniture. There was no proper lighting, and Hope could hardly see the portraits, as she walked past them. Winfred had gone out to get her bags, and Katherine had disappeared to make them tea. On either side of the gallery were enormous drawing rooms, sparsely furnished in threadbare antiques. Hope noticed several handsome Aubusson carpets in muted colors, badly in need of repair. But the windows were long and wide, and let lots of light in. The curtains were beautiful and old with gigantic tassles but were in shreds, barely hanging by a thread.

The dining room was palatial, and the table could seat forty, Finn told her, with enormous silver candelabra that someone had polished till they gleamed. Next to it was a library that looked like it housed a million books. Finn led her up the grand staircase, to a floor with half a dozen bedrooms, small dressing rooms, sitting rooms. There were ancient furnishings in them, but all the rooms had dustcovers on the furniture, and the curtains were closed. And finally, up another smaller staircase, was the cozier floor where Finn lived. The rooms were smaller, the light brighter, and the furniture and rugs in better condition. Here, there were no curtains at all, and the rooms seemed to be filled with light, even though it was a gray day. He had a fire burning brightly for her, and had filled vases with wildflowers in every room. There was a cozy bedroom with a gigantic four-poster bed, which she knew instantly was his. And as in his mews house in London, there were stacks of books everywhere, particularly in the room he used as an office.

Katherine found them as Hope was taking her coat off, and set down a silver tray in a small sitting room. There was a silver teapot on the tray, a plate of scones, and clotted cream. She curtsied with a shy smile at them both, and left.

"So what do you think?" he asked her, looking anxious. All morning he had asked himself what he would do if she hated it and ran. He loved the place himself, but he was used to its state of comfortable disrepair, and he didn't even see it anymore. He was afraid she would find it gloomy or depressing, and refuse to stay. And instead she was smiling at him and held out her arms.

"It's the most beautiful house I've ever seen," she reassured him, "and I love you more than life itself." As she said it, he felt as though he were sinking into a featherbed of her approval and love, and it brought tears to his eyes.

"It needs a little work," he said shyly, and Hope laughed.

"Yes, it does, a little, but you don't need to rush. It's very comfortable up here. Can we go exploring later? It's a little overwhelming at first." She was feeling in awe of all she'd seen, but she wanted to get to know the house and do whatever she could for him.

"You'll get used to it, I promise." He sat down and poured a cup of tea for her, as she helped herself to a scone. She put cream on one for him too. "Wait till you see the bathrooms, the tubs are big enough for both of us. And I want to go for a walk with you this afternoon. There are beautiful old stables in back, but I haven't had time to think about them yet. There's too much else to do. I keep pouring my royalty checks into it, and this place just scarfs them up and it doesn't even show. I have to start buying some decent furniture one of these days. Nearly every couch and chair in the place is broken. What's here came with the house." Most of all, from what Hope could see, everything needed a good cleaning and a coat of paint, or many coats of paint. But it was easy to figure out that restoring a house like this one would cost a fortune. It would take him years to do it all. And suddenly, she was dying to help. It would be an exciting project for them both.

But before she'd even finished the scone or gotten to her tea, he had dragged her off to his enormous four-poster bed, and lovingly attacked her. He had the door locked and her clothes off in less than a minute, and he made love to her until she was breathless and he was sated. They had a sex life worthy of teenagers, and she never failed to be impressed.

"Wow!" She grinned at him afterward, wondering how she had lived without him for a week. He was definitely habit forming, and their passion totally addictive. He gave her pleasures she had never even dreamed of.

"I'm not letting you out of my sight again," he said, grinning at her, lying naked across what was now officially their bed. "In fact, I may have to chain you to the bed. I'm sure one of my ancestors did something like that at some point. It seems like an excellent idea. Or maybe I'll just chain you to me." She laughed.

He showed her the enormous bathroom then and the gigantic tub. He ran a bath for her, and she was very glad she'd gotten some sleep on the plane. She could see she wouldn't get much here. She slipped into the warm water in the bathtub, and

Finn appeared with her cup of tea, in an exquisite gold Limoges cup. She sat there drinking tea in the bathtub, feeling very spoiled. It was a long way from the simple pleasures of Cape Cod, or her loft in New York. Blaxton House was remarkable, and Finn even more so.

Finn got in with her, and moments later, he made love to her again in the bathtub. As she had in New York at times, and Cape Cod, she wondered if they'd ever get out of the house. Finn insisted that no one had ever turned him on as much in his entire life, which she found hard to believe, but it was nice to hear, particularly after the last several years of her monastic life. Finn was an explosion of joy and lust she had never expected.

Eventually, he let her put on jeans, a sweater, and loafers, and she went downstairs with him. This time they toured each room more carefully. She raised shades, many of which fell as she touched them, and pulled back curtains, so she could see the rooms more clearly. There was beautiful wood paneling, and some lovely moldings on the walls. But the furniture was a disgrace, the ancient carpets badly in need of restoration, and all of the curtains were beyond salvation.

"What if you got rid of everything that's broken or too damaged to save, cleaned it all up, and started painting it room by room? It might give you a fresh start, although it would be empty at first." She was trying to think what she could do to help while she was there, and it would be challenging and creative to work on it with him, or even for him while he was writing. She had nothing but time on her hands.

"It would be more than empty." Finn laughed at her. "It would be totally bare. I don't think there's much here worth saving." Most of the furniture looked awful, and the upholstery was pretty grim in brighter light, some chairs only had three legs, tables were propped against walls, fabrics were dirty and torn, and there was the smell of dust everywhere. Winfred and Katherine were too old to keep it clean. They mostly took care of his rooms upstairs and ignored the rest. The place looked as though it hadn't been cleaned properly in years, and Hope delicately said so. "I didn't bring you over here to do housework," he said apologetically, visibly embarrassed, and she didn't want to criticize his house or make him feel bad. She knew it was his treasure.

"I'd love to do it. It would be a fun project for me. Why don't we sort through it while I'm here, room by room, and see what you want to save."

"Probably nothing. It looks like the 'Fall of the House of Usher,'" he said, looking around, as though seeing it for the first time, now through her eyes. "I can't really afford to do everything it needs." He looked apologetic. He wanted her to love it as he did.

"We can figure it out once we get it clean. That

would be a start. We might even be able to buy fabric in a local market to cover some of the couches.
I'm pretty good with my hands," she said, and he
gave her a lascivious look that made her blush.

"You certainly are!" he agreed, and she laughed.

After they looked around the house, he took her
out to see the grounds. He gave her an old jacket
of his, which was enormous on her, and they went
to see the stables, the gardens, the park, as it was
called, and walked to the edge of the forest nearest
the house. There was a heavy mist falling, so he
didn't suggest they walk into the hills, which he
was anxious to do with her. Instead, he drove her
into the village, and showed her all the quaint
shops. They stopped for a drink at the pub, and
Hope had a cup of tea, while Finn had a tall glass
of warm dark beer. They chatted with everyone
around, and Hope was amused to see grandmothers, children, old men, young ones, and young
women coming in and out of the pub. It was like
the local social club and had none of the atmosphere of bars in the States. It was kind of like a
coffeehouse and bar all rolled into one. And everyone was extremely friendly. The only thing that
bothered Finn was that he said there were two men
looking at her, which she hadn't even noticed. He
was extremely possessive of her, but she wasn't the
kind of woman to give him any worries on that
score, so she wasn't bothered. She had never even
been flirtatious in her youth, and was very straight-

forward, and faithful to her man. Finn had nothing to fear from her.

They drove back to the house and eventually had what the locals referred to as "tea," which was really a light dinner. There were sandwiches, meats, potatoes, cheeses, and a heavy Irish meat soup, all of which filled them both. And after that, they sat by the fire in his little living room upstairs. They went to bed early, and she climbed under the comforter, and this time, before he could make love to her, Hope fell sound asleep.

Chapter 9

On the day after Hope arrived at Blaxton House, she had Winfred, Katherine, and Finn pulling back curtains, taking down shades, and opening shutters so she could better see the condition of the rooms. Finn had given her carte blanche to do whatever she wanted, and by that afternoon, the house was full of light. Torn shades had been disposed of, shredded curtains had been taken down to be more closely examined and were lying on the floor. In the main living room, she had all the broken furniture pushed to one side of the room, and she had made a long list of what needed to be done. In drier weather, she wanted to take the ancient carpets out to air them, but there was no way to do that now. It rained on and off all day. The house was dusty, and she was coughing by the time she finished her rounds on the main floor. There was actually some very good-looking furniture, the arms and legs needed to be reinforced, and most of the upholstery was gone. She wanted to find a furniture restorer in the village, and with so many important manor houses in the area, she was sure that there was one. So far, she had listed sixteen pieces of furniture that needed restoration, and only seven that were broken beyond repair. She had Finn take her into the village to buy wax late that afternoon—she wanted to try and work on some of the woodwork and paneling herself. It was going to be a mammoth job. Winfred and Katherine were impressed with what she was doing, and Finn was in awe. And the next day, she did the same on the second floor. There, she went through all the bedrooms, and found some beautiful furniture under the muslin covers. Hope was having a great time. Finn loved it, and her.

"Good lord," Finn said, smiling at her. "I didn't expect you to restore my house yourself." He was touched by what she was doing. She was a hard worker and she had a good eye. She made him take her into Blessington to find a restorer, which she did, and she made an appointment for him to come out the next day. He took away all the pieces Finn agreed needed to be worked on, and the following day, she had him drive her to Dublin, where she bought miles and miles of fabric, for upholstery, and some for the bedrooms in pastel satins. She made sure that Finn liked all the colors, and she paid for it herself as a gift to him.

And for the next many days, she worked with

Winfred and Katherine to clean all the rooms, and get rid of all the dust and cobwebs. She left some of the shredded curtains hanging, and those that were beyond salvation she threw away. The windows looked better with no covering than with the remains of the old ones hanging there. The house already looked cleaner and more cheerful, and she pulled back the deep green velvet curtains in the gallery, so the house didn't look so dark as one walked in. The place was looking better every day. And Hope said she was having a ball.

"Come on," Finn said one afternoon, "let's get out of here. I want to show you around." He took her to see the other great houses, and she assured him that none were more beautiful than his. Blaxton House looked the most like Russborough House. And her goal now was to help him get his place into shape. It was too big a job for him alone, and she sensed that money was somewhat tight for him, so she tried to do everything on a budget, and paid for things whenever she could, without offending him. Finn was deeply appreciative of all she did. He was well aware that it was a labor of love she was doing for him. And the results were already starting to show.

Whenever he had work to do, she spent time on her waxing and polishing project, and room by room, the woodwork was starting to shine. The broken furniture was out being restored. A local upholsterer had taken the pieces to be re-covered, and upstairs she had found treasures under the holland covers. The master bedroom once uncovered was a marvel of exquisite furniture and beautiful frescoes on the walls. She said it looked like Versailles.

"You are amazing," Finn said in admiration. And when she wasn't waxing, polishing, and pushing furniture around, she was taking photographs of the locals, or digging through antique shops, looking for treasures for his house. She even helped Katherine polish the silver on a rainy afternoon, and that night, they had dinner in the formal dining room, at one end of the enormous table, instead of on trays upstairs. She was wearing jeans and an old sweater of Finn's, which made her look like a little girl. The house was still fairly cold. "I feel like one of those cartoons in **The New Yorker,**" Finn said, laughing, as Winfred served them dinner in the gigantic room. The kitchen was in the basement, and was a relic, but everything in it worked, and Hope had wrought her magic there too. By the time she had been there for two weeks, his house looked as though she had worked on it for months, and it was much improved.

After dinner, she was taking photos of the frescoes on the ceiling in the main living room as Finn walked in and smiled to see her there. She made his heart sing every time he gazed at her.

"How hard do you think it would be for us to paint these rooms ourselves?" she asked, looking vague, as he put his arms around her and kissed her.

"You're insane, but I love you. How did I ever survive before we met? My house was filthy, my life was a mess, and I didn't know what I was missing. Now I know. I don't think I'm going to let you go back to the States." He looked serious as he said it, and she laughed. They were both enjoying working on his house, and it was looking great. She could see why he loved it, and she was enjoying polishing it up for him.

"Why don't we have some of your neighbors in for dinner sometime?" she suggested. "There must be some interesting people here, living in all those big houses. Do you know a lot of them?" she asked with interest. It would be exciting to fill the table in the dining room with lively people, and she wanted to meet some of the locals.

"I don't know any of them," Finn said. "I'm always working when I'm here. I never make time to go out. I do most of my socializing in London."

"It would be nice to invite people over, maybe when the furniture comes back," she said pensively.

"I'd rather be alone with you," he said honestly. "You're only here for a short time, and I don't want to share you with anyone. It's much more romantic on our own," he said firmly. He clearly wanted her to himself, but Hope wanted to meet people and show off the house.

"We can do both," she said sensibly. "We can

meet people, and spend time alone." It seemed odd to her that he had lived there for two years and didn't know anyone.

"Maybe next time," he said vaguely, and as he said it, her cell phone rang and she answered it. It was Paul. And she walked into a little alcove off the living room and sat down to talk. She hadn't spoken to him in weeks. He was still sailing, and said he was fine. She told him she was visiting a friend in Ireland at a fabulous old house. She noticed that he sounded tired, but didn't press the point, and after a few minutes she got off, as Finn walked into the room. "Who was that?" he asked, looking worried. Hope smiled as he sat down next to her.

"It was Paul. I told him all about your house."

"That's nice. Is he still in love with you?" Hope shook her head. "He's too sick to think of anyone but himself. He divorced me, remember? He's just a very special friend now. He's my family. We were married for a long time." Finn nodded and didn't pursue the subject, and he looked relieved by what she had said.

They went for a walk in the hills then, and Hope brought back two baskets full of wildflowers, and put them in vases when they got back. Finn looked at her with a happy smile, and that night he talked again about their having a baby, although he had promised not to for a while. He said he loved her so much, he just couldn't resist. He insisted he wanted a child with her, and she reminded him that it was too soon. She didn't say it to him, but she didn't want to have a baby unless they were married, and that wasn't a certainty yet, although it was looking more and more likely.

"I want a little girl who looks just like you," Finn said wistfully, as he held her after they made love. "I want our baby, Hope," he pleaded with her.

"I know," she said sleepily, "me too . . . but it's not a sure thing at my age anyway."

"It is nowadays. We can get a little high-tech help. The Brits are pretty good at that." He was very persistent about wanting to get her pregnant, but for the moment they were still using protection, so it wasn't likely to happen. It really seemed too soon to her. That was a major decision she wasn't ready to undertake yet. It was one thing helping him fix up his house, another having a child.

"We'll see," she said, as she cuddled into his arms and nestled up against him, smiling happily, thinking that these were the best days in her life, or surely in a very, very long time.

On her third week in Ireland, Finn surprised her by suggesting they go to Paris for the weekend. She hadn't thought of traveling in Europe while she was there, but she loved the idea. He made reservations at the Ritz for them, which was her favorite hotel, and that weekend they flew to Paris. They were going to London on the way back, which was perfect for her, since she wanted to meet with the photography curator at the Tate Modern, and called the day before they left to make an appointment. He was delighted at the prospect of meeting her.

Their time in Paris was everything they had hoped. The room at the Ritz was small but elegant, they walked miles all over Paris, and ate in wonderful old bistros on the Left Bank. They went to Nôtre Dame and Sacré Coeur, and poked around antiques shops, looking for things to take back to Blaxton House. The time they shared was magical, just as it had been so far everywhere else. But Paris seemed even more romantic and particularly special. The city was meant for that.

"I've never been so spoiled in my life." She tried to pay for some of their dinners, but Finn wouldn't let her. He had old-fashioned ideas about it, although he had let her pay for a few things for the house. She wished he would let her do more. His books did well, she knew, but he had a son to support and pay tuition for. He was putting Michael through college, and even without income taxes in Ireland, a house the size of Blaxton House was a major challenge to maintain and support. And life was expensive everywhere. She had so much money from Paul that she felt guilty not helping Finn more. She tried to explain it to him one day over lunch.

"I know it's embarrassing to have me pitch in," she said gently, "but I got this crazy huge settlement from Paul when we divorced. He had just sold his company, and with Mimi gone, neither of us has anything to do with our money. He spends most of his time on the boat. And I have hardly any expenses. Honestly, I wish you'd let me pay for things once in a while."

"That's not my style," Finn said firmly, and then wondered about something. "With Mimi gone, who are you going to leave your money to one day?" It was an odd question, but nothing was out of bounds between them. They had talked about everything, and she had thought of it herself. She had no living relatives except Paul, and he was sixteen years older than she was, and very sick. It was unlikely that he would outlive her, a thought that made her very sad. And all the money she had came from him. He had given her a staggering settlement in the divorce, over her protests, but he had insisted that he wanted her set for life, and whatever was left when he died, was coming to her too.

"I don't know," Hope said honestly, thinking about the money she would leave behind at the end of her life. "Dartmouth maybe, in honor of my father and Mimi. Or Harvard. I don't have anyone to leave it to. It's kind of an odd situation. I give away a fair amount every year now, to various philanthropic causes I care about. I set up a scholarship in Mimi's name at Dartmouth, because she went to school there, and another one at the New York City Ballet."

"Maybe you should fund things that you enjoy."

"I know. It's kind of taken me the last two years to get used to having all this money. I don't need it. I told Paul that when we got divorced. I lead a simple life." And her parents had left her enough to take care of the house on Cape Cod. "Sometimes I feel guilty having it," she said honestly. "It seems kind of a waste." He nodded, laughed, and said he wished he had her problem.

"I keep wanting to put money aside to restore the house, but it's hard with a kid in college and houses all over the place. Or two anyway. One of these days I'll really clean the place up." She was dying to help him do it, but it was too soon for that too. They had been together for two months, which in the real world wasn't a long time. Maybe in a few months, if all went well, he would let her help financially with restoring the house. She really wanted to do it.

After that, they walked in the Tuileries, went to the Louvre, and walked back to the Ritz for their last night. It had been a heavenly weekend, just like everything else they did together. They ordered room service and spent the night in bed, indulging in the luxury of the hotel. And in the morning, they took the train to London, and were back at his tiny house at noon. It warmed her heart to see it, and think of the shoot they had done there. As she had suspected at the time, they had gotten several wonderful photos out of it, and Finn had chosen one he loved for the book, when it was ready for publication. She had framed several others for him, and for herself.

She had her appointment at the Tate Modern Museum that afternoon, and Hope was startled to discover that Finn was annoyed about it, which didn't make sense to her.

"What's up?" she asked him, as they shared one of his terrific omelettes in his kitchen. "Are you mad about something?" He was visibly pouting at her over lunch.

"No, I just don't know why you have to meet a curator today."

"Because they want to give me a retrospective show next year," she explained quietly. "That's a big deal, Finn."

"Can I come with you?" he asked, looking hopeful, and she looked apologetic, but shook her head.

"It wouldn't look serious, if I brought someone along."

"Tell them I'm your assistant." He was still pouting.

"You don't take assistants to meet with curators, only to shoots." He shrugged in answer, and didn't speak again until she was leaving the house. She had called for a cab.

"When will you be back?" he asked coldly.

"As soon as I can. I promise. If you want to walk around the museum while I talk to him, you can. It's excellent." He said nothing and shook his head, and a minute later she went out, feeling guilty for leaving him, which she knew was ridiculous. But he was trying to make her feel that way, and had succeeded. As a result, she rushed through the meeting, didn't cover all the questions she wanted to ask, and was back at his house in two hours. He was sitting on the couch, reading a book and sulking. He looked up with a sullen expression when she walked in.

"Was that fast enough for you?" Now she sounded annoyed, because she had hurried through the meeting, to get back to him. He just shrugged. "Why are you being like this? You're not four years old. Sometimes I have work to do. So do you. It doesn't mean I don't love you."

"Why couldn't you take me with you?" he said with a wounded expression.

"Because we're two separate people, with separate lives and careers. I can't always be part of yours either."

"I want you to be. You're always welcome to join me."

"And most of the time, you are too. But I don't know this curator, and I didn't want him to think I'm a flake by mixing business with romance. It doesn't look serious, Finn."

"We're together, aren't we?" he questioned her with an injured look, which annoyed her even more. She had no reason to feel guilty, and resented what he was doing. And he had succeeded in making her feel bad. It didn't seem fair. She loved him too, but he was acting like a two-year-old.

"Yes. But we're not Siamese twins." It was his fusion theory again, which she had never agreed with. He wanted to do everything together, and sometimes she just couldn't. He couldn't come to shoots either. And she couldn't write a book with him. And however much he wanted it to be otherwise, they were not one person, they were two. She was very clear on that. He wasn't. "That doesn't mean I don't love you," she said gently, and he ignored her while he went on reading.

He didn't respond for a long time, and then he surprised her again. He looked up at her and closed the book. "I made an appointment for you tomorrow. For us."

"With whom?" She was puzzled. "What kind of appointment?"

"With a doctor. A fertility doctor who specializes in people our age who want to have babies." They both knew that his age was not a problem, hers was. He was being kind in how he said it and she looked at him wide-eyed.

"Why didn't you talk to me about it before you

made the appointment?" It seemed a rather high-handed thing to do, and she had told him she wanted to wait, for a while at least.

"I got the name, and I thought it was a good idea to meet her while we were in London. At least we can hear what she has to say, and what she recommends. You might need to start preparing for it now, if we're going to do it in a few months." He was moving very quickly, just as he had with their relationship in the beginning. But this was a much bigger commitment and decision. A baby was forever. And she wasn't sure yet if they were.

"Finn, we don't even know if we want a baby yet. We've only been together for two months. That's a big decision. A **huge** decision. For both of us to make, not just you."

"Can't you just listen to her?" He looked like he was about to cry and she felt like a monster, but she wasn't ready and she felt panicked to be talking to a doctor about it already. "Will you talk to her?" His eyes pleaded with her, and she hated to hurt his feelings and turn him down.

Slowly, Hope nodded, but she wasn't happy about it. "I will. But I don't want to be rushed into this. I need time to make that decision. And I want to enjoy us first." He smiled when she said that, and leaned over to kiss her.

"Thank you, that means a lot to me. I just don't want us to miss out on having a baby of our own." She was touched by what he said, but still upset that he had gone forward with it, without at least asking her first. She wondered if it was his way of getting even for not taking him to the museum meeting with her. But she knew it was more that he was desperate to have a baby with her. The problem was that it was too soon for her, and she had said that to him clearly since he first brought it up. He was very stubborn once he got an idea in his head. He seemed unfamiliar with the word "no."

They went to Harry's Bar again for dinner that night, and Hope was quiet, and then they came home and made love. But for the first time, she felt some distance from him. She didn't want him making her decisions for her, particularly not big ones. Paul had never done that to her before the divorce. Before they had made all their big decisions jointly with lots of mutual consultation. It was what Hope expected of Finn, but he was much more forceful about his ideas. They were two very different men.

And she was even more upset the next day when they got to the doctor. It wasn't an appointment for a consultation, it was a full workup for a fertility screening, with a battery of tests, some of them unpleasant, which she wasn't prepared for. She balked when she discovered what was planned, and said something to the doctor about it, who seemed even more surprised that Hope didn't know what the appointment would entail.

"I sent you a folder of information on it," she said, looking at them with a confused expression. She was a very nice woman, and undoubtedly competent, but Hope was visibly unhappy at the news of what she was expected to do that day.

"I didn't get the folder," Hope said simply, looking at Finn. He was instantly sheepish. He had obviously gotten it when he made the appointment but not shared it with her. For the moment, this was his project, not hers. "I didn't even know about this appointment until last night."

"Do you want to do it?" the doctor asked her bluntly, and Hope felt as though she had her back to the wall. If she didn't, Finn would be hurt, but she was going to be upset if she did. And the tests did not sound pleasant. She thought about it for a long moment, and out of love for him, decided to sacrifice herself.

"All right, I will. But we haven't made a final decision yet about getting pregnant."

"I have," Finn said quickly, and both women laughed.

"Then you have the baby," Hope said quickly.

"Have you ever been pregnant?" the doctor asked her, handing her a stack of forms to fill out, and two brochures about in vitro fertilization and donor eggs.

"Yes, once," Hope said quietly, thinking of her daughter. "Twenty-three years ago." She glanced at the brochure in her hand then. "Would we have to use donor eggs?" Hope didn't like that idea at all. In that case, genetically, it would be Finn's baby, but not hers. That didn't sit well with her.

"Hopefully not, but it's an option. We have a number of tests to run on you first, and we have to check the viability of your eggs. A younger egg is always a surer bet, of course. But yours may still be lively enough for us to use, with a little help." She smiled, and Hope felt faintly sick. She hadn't been ready for this process at all, and wasn't sure if she ever would be. Finn wanted it so badly, he was overriding her. She knew he was doing it because he loved her. But it was a very big deal to her.

"Are we checking my eggs today?" Hope knew it wasn't a small procedure, if that was the case.

"No, we can do that next time, if we need to. We'll check your FSH levels today, and take it from there." She handed Hope a list of the procedures they were going to do, which included a pelvic ultrasound, a pelvic exam, and a battery of blood tests to check her hormone levels. And they wanted a sperm sample from Finn.

For the next two hours, they ran through all the tests, and he made assorted whispered lewd remarks to Hope about helping him with the sperm sample, but she was in no mood for that. She told him to do it himself, which he did, and appeared with it proudly while they did her ultrasound. The doctor announced with pleasure that Hope was ovulating now, and everything looked good on the ultrasound so far. "You two could go home today and give it a try on your own," she commented, "although I'd rather do artificial insemination with Mr. O'Neill's sperm. You could come back and let us do that for you this afternoon, if you like," she offered, with a helpful glance at Hope.

"I don't want to do that," Hope said in a strangled voice. She felt as though suddenly other people were running her life, mostly Finn. And he looked disappointed by what she had just said.

"Maybe we'll try that next month," the doctor said blandly, as she removed the ultrasound wand, wiped the gel off Hope's stomach from the external part of the exam, and told her she could get up. Hope felt drained. She felt as though she were on an express train she hadn't bought a ticket for, and didn't want to be on, to a destination she hadn't chosen in the first place. She had just been reading the travel brochures, and Finn was trying to make the decisions for her, about where they were going and when.

They met with the doctor in her office after all the tests, and she told them that so far everything looked good. They didn't have Hope's FSH count and estrogen levels yet, but her eggs looked good on the screen, Finn's sperm count was high, and she thought that with artificial insemination, they might have a good chance. If that didn't work in the first two months, they would put Hope on Clomid to release more eggs, which could result in multiple births, the doctor warned her, and if the Clomid hadn't worked in four months, they would start with in vitro fertilization. And eventually, if necessary, donor eggs. The doctor handed Hope a tube of progesterone cream and told her how to use it every month from ovulation to menstruation, to stimulate implantation and discourage spontaneous abortion. And she told her to see the nurse on the way out for an ovulation predictor kit. By the time they left the office, Hope felt as though she had been shot out of a cannon or drafted into the Marines.

"That wasn't so bad, was it?" Finn said, smiling broadly at her, delighted with himself when they reached the sidewalk, and Hope burst into tears.

"Don't you care what I think?" she asked him, sobbing. She didn't know why, but it had made her feel as though she were betraying Mimi, replacing her with another child, and she wasn't ready for that either. She couldn't stop crying as he put his arms around her. And she was still crying when they got into a cab and he gave the driver his address.

"I'm sorry. I thought you'd be happy about it once we talked to her." He looked crushed.

"I don't even know if I want a baby, Finn. I already lost a child I loved. I haven't gotten over it yet, and I don't know if I ever will. And it's still too soon for us."

"We don't have time to fool around," he said,

pleading with her. He didn't want to be rude and say that for Hope, at forty-four, time was running out.

"Then maybe we'll have to be happy with just us," she said, sounding anguished. "I'm not ready to make that decision yet, in a two-month-old romance." She didn't want to hurt his feelings, but she needed to be sure. Marriage was one thing eventually. But a baby was something else. "You have to listen to me, Finn. This is important."

"It's important to me too. And I want to have our baby, before we lose the chance."

"Then you need a twenty-five-year-old woman, not someone my age. I'm not going to play Beat the Clock on a decision as important as this. We need time to figure it out."

"I don't," he said stubbornly.

"Well, I do," she said, sounding increasingly desperate. He was so insistent about it that she was feeling cornered and trying to make him back off. She knew how much he loved her, and she loved him too, but she didn't want to be pushed.

"I've never wanted a baby with anyone before. Even Michael was an accident. That's why I married his mother. And I want a baby with you," he said with tears in his eyes as he looked at her in the back of the cab.

"Then you have to give me time to get used to the idea. I felt as though I was being railroaded in that doctor's office. If we'd let her, she'd have gotten me pregnant today."

"That doesn't sound like a bad idea to me," he said, as the cab pulled up to his address. And a moment later, Hope followed him inside, looking miserable and shaken. She was exhausted, and felt as though she'd been dragged behind a horse, holding on by her teeth. It had been a draining emotional experience for her. Finn didn't say anything, and went to pour her a glass of wine. She looked as though she needed it. She started to turn it down, and then thought better of it. She drained it in a few minutes, and he filled it up again, and had a glass himself.

"I'm sorry, darling. I shouldn't have pushed you into it. I was just so excited by the idea. I'm sorry," he repeated gently, and kissed her. "Will you forgive me?"

"Maybe," she said, smiling sadly at him. It hadn't been a pleasant experience for her, to say the least. He poured her another glass of wine, and she drank that one too. She was seriously upset, but started to calm down after her third glass, and then started crying again, and Finn wrapped her in his arms and took her upstairs. He ran a warm bath for her, and she slipped gratefully into it, and closed her eyes. She lay there for a while, unwinding, trying to push the unpleasant doctor's visit from her mind. Being in the warm bath helped, and when

she opened her eyes again, Finn handed her a glass
of champagne and a giant strawberry, and slipped
into the bath with her. Hope started to giggle as he
unwound his long frame into the bathtub with her,
and he had a glass of champagne too.

"What are we celebrating?" She smiled at him.
She was slightly tipsy, but not drunk. But she
needed the wine to get over the afternoon, and as
she finished the champagne in the flute he had
handed her, he took the glass from her hand and
set it down. He had emptied his glass too. And
then as always happened when they bathed together, he began to make overtures that neither of
them could resist. It happened before they knew it,
and without thinking about it. He made love to
her in the bathtub, and then they lay on the bathroom floor on the carpet and finished it. It was hot
and passionate and desperate, with all the agony
and turmoil she had felt that afternoon. All she
knew as she lay there was how badly she wanted
him, and he wanted her just as much. They
couldn't get enough of each other, it was hard and
furious and quick, and after he came, he lay on top
of her, and then gently got up and lifted her in his
arms like a doll and laid her on his bed. He dried
her gently with a towel, and tucked her into bed.
She smiled at him with the slightly glazed eyes
of someone who has had too much to drink.
But there was love and tenderness there too, not
just wine.

"I love you more than anything on earth," he whispered to her.

"I love you too, Finn," she said, as she drifted off to sleep and he held her close.

He was still holding her when they woke up in the morning, and Hope squinted at him. "I think I got drunk last night," she said, slightly embarrassed. She remembered what had happened in the bathtub and after, and how great it had been. It always was with him. And then suddenly, with a jolt, she was wide awake. She remembered what the doctor had said about coming back that afternoon. She had been ovulating, and they had used no protection. She lay back against the pillow with a groan and then looked at Finn. "You did that on purpose, didn't you?" She was angry at him, but it was her fault too, and she was furious with herself. How stupid was that? But maybe nothing would happen. At her age, getting pregnant could take a year or two, not one moment of passion on a bathroom floor, like a kid.

"What?" Finn asked her innocently.

"You know exactly what I mean," she tried to sound cold, but couldn't pull it off. She loved him too much, and suddenly she wondered if she had wanted it too, but didn't want to take responsibility for the decision, so she got drunk and let him do it. She wasn't innocent either. She was a grown woman and knew better. She felt totally confused. "I was ovulating yesterday. She told us both that.

She even offered to do artificial insemination if we wanted her to."

"What we did was much more fun. And this way it's in God's hands, not hers or ours. Probably nothing will come of it," he said benignly, and she hoped that would be true. She sat up against the pillows and looked at Finn.

"What if I do get pregnant, Finn? What would we really do? Are we ready for that yet? At our age? That's a hell of a commitment, at any age. Are we ready to take that on?"

"I would be the happiest man on earth," he said proudly. "What about you?"

"I'd be scared shitless. Of the dangers, the implications, the pressure on us, the genetic risks at our age. And of . . ." She couldn't say the rest, but she was terrified of losing another child she loved. She couldn't go through it again.

"We'll deal with it if it happens, I promise," he said, kissing her, and holding her as though she were a piece of spun glass. "How soon will we know?"

"These days? I think in about two weeks. I haven't been pregnant in years. It's pretty simple to find out now, with a drugstore pregnancy kit." She thought about it for a minute. "I'll be back in New York by then. I'll let you know." At the thought of it, her blood ran cold, and a tiny little piece of her wanted it to happen, because she loved him, but her powers of reason didn't, only her heart. It just didn't make sense. She was totally confused.

"Maybe you shouldn't go back," he said, looking worried. "It might not be good to fly so soon."

"I have to. I have three important shoots."

"If you're pregnant, that's more important." She felt suddenly insane. They were acting as though she were pregnant and they had planned this baby. But only one of them had. Finn. And she had let him do it.

"Let's not go crazy yet. At my age, it's about as likely as getting hit by a comet. You heard what she said. If we ever decide to do it, we'd probably need help."

"Or maybe not. She wasn't sure. I think it had to do with your FSH."

"Let's hope it's high or low, or whatever it's supposed not to be." She got out of bed then and felt as though she'd been hit by a bus. Between the emotions of the day before, and the hangover she had from the wine and champagne, she felt like she'd spent two weeks riding broncos in a rodeo. "I feel like shit," she said as she headed for the bathroom, and he smiled adoringly at her.

"Maybe you're pregnant," he said, looking hopeful.

"Oh, shut up," she said, and slammed the bathroom door.

Neither of them said anything about it on the flight back to Ireland or for the next few days. She went back to waxing and polishing the wood paneling at his house, and he kept telling her to take it easy, which annoyed her more. She didn't want to think about it. She'd had a great time with him in Paris, but she was upset about what had happened in London, both the doctor's visit, and their escapade on the bathroom floor. And the day before she was leaving, the doctor called.

"Great news!" she announced. "Your FSH is as low as a twenty-year-old's and your estrogen level is terrific."

"What does that mean?" Hope asked, as her stomach turned over. She had a feeling she wasn't going to like what she was about to be told.

"It means that you should have an easy time getting pregnant on your own." She thanked the doctor and hung up and said nothing to Finn. He was hopeful enough as it was. And if she had told him there was a serious chance she might have gotten pregnant, he wouldn't let her go back to New York. He didn't want her to go. He was already complaining about being lonely, and wanted to know how soon she would return. She had explained that she had work to do, and had to be in New York for three weeks. As always, it was like leaving a four-year-old.

They spent a peaceful last night together, and made love twice before she left. He looked mournful as they drove to the airport, and she realized that he had major abandonment issues. He couldn't stand seeing her leave, and he was already depressed.

He kissed her goodbye at the airport, and made her promise to call him the moment she arrived. She smiled as she kissed him. It was sweet really, even if it was a little silly at their age, to be so upset about being apart for a few weeks. He was going to finish his book, and she was going to work on his house again when she got back. She reminded him to call the restorers to see when the pieces would be finished, and he handed her a small gift-wrapped box before she left. She was touched by the surprise.

"Open it on the plane," he told her, kissed her one last time, and waved as she headed to the gate.

She followed his instructions and unwrapped it just as the plane took off toward New York. And then she laughed. She held it in her hand and shook her head with a rueful expression. It was a home pregnancy test. And it would be negative, she hoped. But she knew she had to wait another week before she found out. She put the box away and put it out of her mind as best she could.

Chapter 10

Hope was busy almost every waking moment in New York. She did a fashion layout for Vogue, had a portrait sitting with the governor, and helped curate a gallery show of her work. She had lunch with Mark Webber, and told him about her romance with Finn. He was stunned, and warned her again that he was a wild man with women. He had a major reputation for it in New York, which she already knew. But she was sure that he was being faithful to her. He hardly let her out of his sight. She mentioned that to Mark, that Finn constantly talked about their "fusion" as a couple, and was jealous of other men. Even her lunch with her agent bothered him. They were the only two things about him that worried her. She'd never been with a jealous man. And he was very possessive of her. She still needed time on her own. Working in New York was doing her good. It revitalized her, and made her excited about seeing him again. She didn't want to feel smothered by being chained to him, which was what he would have liked. Having a few weeks of her own life brought her perspective and independence again, which was important to her. He seemed to be extremely threatened by everyone she saw. And every time he called her, he wanted to know how soon she was coming back. Like a mother speaking to a child, she kept reminding him that she would be gone for two more weeks.

"Watch out for jealous guys," Mark warned her. "Sometimes they come unhinged. I had a jealous girlfriend once. She came after me with a knife, when I broke up with her and took another girl to senior prom. Ever since then jealousy scares the shit out of me." Hope laughed at the image.

"I think Finn is pretty sane. But he's very needy in some ways. He hates being left. I'm going back in two weeks." She had already been in New York for a week, and Finn was complaining about her absence every day. He sounded miserable and depressed every time they spoke.

"Do you think this is serious with him?" Mark asked, with a look of concern.

"Yes, I do," she said quietly. Very serious. But she didn't want Mark to worry about her, or her work. "I can commute from Dublin, whenever I have work here," she reassured him. "Or fly places from there. It's not that far away. He lives in a remarkable house. It's more like a castle, although it needs to be restored."

Mark was still astounded at what she had told him, but he was happy for her. "Have you told Paul?"

"It's too soon," she said, looking thoughtful. She planned to eventually, but not for a while. She had no idea how he'd react, or if he would be sad. She had spoken to him the day before. He was at Harvard for treatment, and he hadn't sounded well at all, but he assured her he was doing fine. It saddened her, and she worried about him a great deal. He was sounding ever more frail.

Hope did some errands after she left Mark, and then she went home. She knew exactly what day it was, and so did Finn. He had already asked her twice. This was The Day. It was the first day the test would show if she was pregnant or not. She drew a long breath, and walked into the bathroom with the test he had given her. She was sure it was going to be fine, but it scared her anyway. She followed the directions to the letter, set it on the counter afterward, and walked away. The test took five full minutes, and it seemed like an eternity to her. She went to stare out the window, and then walked back to the bathroom, dreading what she would find, and telling herself that she wasn't pregnant. It seemed too stupid to be worrying about this at her age. She hadn't had a scare like this in years. Not since she was in her late twenties, and hadn't wanted to be pregnant then either. Paul had only wanted one child, and Mimi was enough for her. As it turned out, she hadn't been pregnant, and was surprised to find that she was more disappointed than relieved. And it had never happened again. They were always careful, and not as abandoned and passionate as she and Finn. She and Paul had made a careful, conscious joint decision to have Mimi and it didn't happen on a bathroom floor.

She walked back to her bathroom counter as though she were approaching a snake. The test directions had been very clear as to how to read the test. One line you're not pregnant, two you are. Anyone could have figured it out. From the distance, she saw one line, and heaved a sigh of relief. She approached and picked it up just to be sure, and was prepared to let out a scream of delight over the negative result, and then she saw it. The second line. Two lines, although the second one was fainter than the first, which the instructions had said still meant a positive result. Shit.

She stared at it in horror, set it down, and picked it up again. Still two lines. Her urine had done whatever it was supposed to under the white plastic holder. Two lines. She held it up to the light, and then just stood staring at it in shocked disbelief. Two lines. She was forty-four years old, and she was pregnant. She sat down on the edge of the tub shaking, with the test still in her hand, and then she threw it away. She thought about using the second one, but she knew she'd get the same result. She had been ignoring it, but her breasts had been sore for the last two days. She told herself that it meant she was getting her period. But she wasn't. And now she had to tell Finn. He had won. He had gotten her drunk and tricked her and she had let him, and she wondered if somewhere deep within, she wanted this baby too. She loved him, but not even three months after she had met him, she was pregnant with his child. And in some hidden, distant part of her, she wanted it too. She felt panicked and confused. She needed time to absorb the idea, and decide how she felt about it.

She walked into the living room, sat staring into space, and a few minutes later, he called her. She felt guilty doing it, but she didn't want to tell him yet. She already knew what his reaction would be. The one she wasn't sure of yet was her own. It was ten o'clock at night in Ireland, and she knew he was working on his book. He said he had been waiting to call her all day, and wanted to know if she'd done the test. Feeling like a traitor to him, she lied and said she hadn't, as tears came to her eyes. Part of her wanted his baby, and another part of her didn't. She was scared. This was much too real. Somewhere inside her, a new life had begun.

"Why haven't you done it yet?" He sounded hurt, and she couldn't think of a good excuse.

"I can't remember where I put the test. I put it away when I got here, and now I can't find it. I think my cleaner moved it."

"Then buy another one, for chrissake," he said, sounding insistent and anxious. It made her feel cornered again. She was feeling trapped and betrayed by her own body as much as him, and her own whirling emotions. "Come on," Finn said in a pleading tone. "Go out and get another test. I want to know. Darling, don't you?" But she did know, and wished she didn't. She promised him she'd pick up another test that afternoon, and call him when she did. He suggested they wait on the phone together for the results, and she was glad she hadn't done that. He called again two hours later, and she didn't answer the phone. She knew she couldn't hide from him forever, but she needed at least a few hours to compose herself, and figure out what she felt. For now, it was mostly fear with an undercurrent of something else that she couldn't put her finger on yet, and wondered if it was hope.

He called her at midnight again, which was five in the morning for him. He said he'd been up all night, working on the book, and worrying about her.

"Where were you? I was worried sick."

"I had to go out and get some film," she said, stalling him for a minute. Their lives were about to change dramatically. They would be bound to each other forever by this child. She loved him, but this was an enormous commitment, both to the baby, and to him.

"Did you get the test?" He was starting to sound annoyed, and her voice was small when she answered.

"Yes."

"And?"

She held her breath for a long moment and let it out. She couldn't avoid it anymore. "It was positive. I just did it," she lied again. He would have been furious if he knew she had known for hours and didn't call him. "I did it five minutes ago, but I didn't want to wake you up." Her face was sad and her stomach was in a knot, but she tried to sound normal, even happy.

"Oh my God!" He shouted at the other end. "Oh my God! We're having a baby!!" In spite of herself, she smiled at his obviously unbounded joy. "I love you so **much,**" he quickly added, and sounded like he was crying. He was so sweet about it that he slowly pulled her out of her terror, and into the deep waters of his excitement with him. She wondered if maybe it would be okay after all. She hoped it would. She saw Mimi's photographs as she spoke to him, and prayed she would approve. And Hope suddenly panicked again. What if this one died too? She couldn't live through it.

"When will it be?" Finn asked excitedly.

"I think around Thanksgiving. I want to have it over here," she said firmly, trying to make her peace with it as she said it. Suddenly it was becoming real to her. They were having a baby, and she had decisions to make about it. A new life was growing inside her. A tiny person whose father was Finn, a man she loved but scarcely knew.

"Wherever you want. I love you, Hope. For God's sake, take care of yourself. How soon can you come home?" She didn't want to tell him she was home. Now home was with him. And that meant Blaxton House to him.

"I'll be back in two weeks," she said softly, feeling her love for him, and his for her, begin to calm her. She had been in a panic since she did the test that afternoon.

"Should you see a doctor?"

"Eventually. Let me get used to the idea first. I just found out five minutes ago. This is a big step, Finn. A very, very big step."

"You're not sorry, are you?" he asked, sounding worried, and a little hurt.

"I don't know what I feel yet. Scared, impressed, kind of stunned. Happy." She closed her eyes as she said it and was surprised to realize she meant it. She was happy. She wanted his baby. She just hadn't wanted it this soon. She had wanted to be sure first. And now it was a done deal. He got his wish.

"Hurry up and come home," he said in a choked voice. "I love you both."

"Me too," she said, and they hung up. She was

in shock. It was hard to believe she was pregnant, but maybe it was meant to be. Destiny had intervened. She loved him, and this was a huge commitment. She knew they would marry at some point, and would have anyway, although probably sooner now. She would have to tell Paul, and she was sure he would be shocked too. But her life was with Finn now. They had a lot to talk about. A lot to plan. A lot to do. Their life together had begun in earnest, in a very serious way. She tried to sleep that night and couldn't. So much was running through her mind, about him and the baby. All her fears and hopes running together. She felt totally overwhelmed.

When she woke up in the morning, there was a delivery from her florist at her door. Finn had sent her two dozen long-stemmed red roses, and the card read "I adore you. Congratulations to us. Come home soon." She cried when she read the card. Her emotions were up and down. She wanted the baby, she didn't, she loved Finn, and she was scared. Who wouldn't be? And on Thanksgiving she'd have their baby in her arms. It was a lot to think about. And all she wanted now was to go back to Ireland and bury herself in Finn's arms. His wish for them had come true. She suddenly thought of the fusion he had talked about. With this baby, their bond to each other was forever.

Chapter 11

Hope flew back to Ireland, as promised, three weeks after she left. Finn was waiting at the airport, and he picked her up and swept her off the ground. They talked about the baby all the way back to his house. And as soon as she saw it, it felt like home. She was planning to stay for at least a month this time, maybe more. She had no commitments in New York till May. And she'd be ten weeks pregnant by then, a delicate time to travel. Finn wanted her to put her jobs off, and she said she might. She had seen her gynecologist before she left New York, who said everything was fine. Her HCG levels were good, and all was progressing as it should. It was too early to tell much more, and she told Hope to come in when she got back. She told her to take it easy for the first three months. At her age, miscarriage was an issue, so the doctor cautioned Hope not to do anything too wild. But intercourse was fine. She knew Finn would be relieved to hear that, although he wanted this baby so badly, he would even have given up their sex life and had asked her if they should. He'd been happy to know that sex was allowed. It was an important part of their life. He wanted to make love constantly, at least once a day, often more. She had never had a sex life like theirs in her entire life.

As soon as she walked into Blaxton House, she saw that he had put flowers everywhere, the place was immaculate, and Winfred and Katherine were thrilled to see her. It was beginning to feel like home to her. And upstairs in his study, she could see that Finn had worked hard on the book. There were stacks of papers and research all over the desk. And as she walked into the room, he spun her around again and kissed her. She sank into a warm tub, and he took a bath with her, as he always did. It was rare for him to let her take a bath on her own. He said he enjoyed her company too much, and she looked so sexy in the tub. And as always, they wound up going to bed and making love, and he was gentle with her. He was in awe of the baby they had conceived, and the miracle they were going to share. He said it was his greatest dream.

Katherine brought them lunch on trays, and afterward they went for a long walk in the Wicklow Mountains. They had a quiet dinner that night, and the next day she went back to work on the house. The furniture had come back from the restorer and looked terrific, and all the upholstered pieces done in the fabric she'd bought in Dublin had returned and were in place in several rooms. The house already looked brighter, cleaner, and more cheerful, and wherever she had polished the woodwork before she left, it gleamed. She had more ideas about the house, and mentioned them to Finn, but all he wanted to talk about was the baby. He said it would join them forever, and his eyes shone whenever he mentioned it. This clearly was his dream, and it was slowly becoming hers. She still had to get used to the idea. It had been a long time since she'd been pregnant, and it brought back a lot of tender memories for her. Secretly, she hoped it would be a girl, and so did Finn. He said he wanted a daughter who looked just like Hope. The changes that were happening to them, and would be happening to her soon, were a lot to absorb and digest. Again and again, as she looked at him, she had to remind herself that it was happening, and it was for real.

She was going through a beautiful old desk in the library two days after she'd come back to Ireland, trying to decide whether to have it restored or not, or just polish it herself, when she opened a drawer, and at the back of it, found a photograph of a strikingly beautiful young woman standing next to Finn. In the photograph, both were very young. He had an arm around her shoulders, and was so obviously enamored with her that Hope wondered if it was Michael's mother. She had never seen any photographs of her. And there were several more in another drawer of the desk. She wasn't sure if she should mention it to Finn or not, and she was curious. She was staring at one of the photographs when he walked in.

"What are you up to?" he asked, smiling at her. "I've been looking for you everywhere. What mischief are you devising?" he inquired, as he approached and then saw the photograph in her hand. He took it from her, looked hard at it, and instantly his eyes turned sad. She had never seen him look like that when he talked about his late wife before, and she was surprised.

"Michael's mom?" she asked softly, and Finn shook his head as he set the photograph down and looked at Hope.

"No, it's not. A girl I was in love with a long time ago. I was twenty-two at the time, she was twenty-one." It was hard to believe, but judging by the faded photograph, he had been even more handsome then. They were two beautiful young people smiling up from the photo on the desk.

"She's a pretty girl," Hope said evenly. Unlike him, she wasn't jealous, and surely not of a girl he'd been in love with twenty-four years before.

"She was," he said, glancing at the image again. She had long straight blond hair. "Audra. She died two weeks after that was taken." Hope looked shocked when he said the words. She looked so young and healthy, obviously some kind of accident had occurred.

"How awful. What happened?" It reminded her of Mimi again. It was so unfair when young people died before they even had a chance to live. They would never marry, have babies, get old, be grandmothers, or experience all the good and bad things that happened to everyone else.

"She killed herself," Finn said with an agonized expression. "It was my fault. We had a terrible argument. It was stupid really. I was jealous. I accused her of sleeping with my best friend, and I told her I'd never see her again. She swore that nothing had happened, and I didn't believe her. Afterward he admitted that they'd gotten together so he could help her pick out a birthday gift for me. He said later that she was crazy in love with me, and I was equally insane about her. But I was so angry when I thought she'd betrayed me, that I told her it was over, and walked out. She begged me not to, and I didn't find out until after, from her sister, that she was pregnant. She was kind of high strung, and very sensitive. She was going to tell me after my birthday, but she was afraid of how I'd react. And to be honest, I'm not sure how I would have taken that piece of news then. She wanted to get married anyway, and I don't know what I'd have done. In any case, we had an awful fight, I left her and told her I'd never see her again because I thought she'd cheated on me. I went back to her house four hours later to apologize. Her parents were out of town, and I rang the bell forever. She never answered, so I went home. Her sister called me the next day. She had slit her wrists, and they found her. She had left a letter for me. Her sister told me about the baby then. It was an awful time. I think it's why I married Michael's mother when she told me she was pregnant, even though I wasn't in love with her. I didn't want anything like that happening again. I've lived with it on my conscience ever since." As he said it, Hope reached out and touched him, and picked up the photograph again. It was hard to believe that that beautiful young girl had died only days later. It was an awful story, and admittedly, he hadn't behaved responsibly, but he was young. And people did stupid things at any age, not understanding the desperation of others, or how deep their fears or emotions ran.

"Her sister said that their father would have killed her for being pregnant, particularly if I didn't marry her," Finn went on. "He was a nasty piece of work, an alcoholic and very abusive to both girls. Her mother was dead. So she had no one to turn to, or to count on, except me. And I let her down. She thought I'd ended it for good, since I had convinced her of it. So she died." He looked deeply remorseful as he said it, and clearly had been for all of his adult life since.

"I'm so sorry," Hope said softly.

"Her sister died in a freak boating accident not long after. I went out with her for a while, because she reminded me so much of Audra. But it made us both feel worse. It was a very unhappy time in my life," he said with a sigh, and put the photographs away. He had been painfully honest about it. "It's a hell of a thing to have on your conscience. I don't know why I was such an asshole to her. Young, I guess, and stupid and full of myself, but that's no excuse. I didn't really intend to end it with her, I was just pissed and wanted to teach her a lesson for flirting with my friend. Instead she taught me a lesson I never forgot and never will." As he said it, Hope couldn't help remembering the instances when he'd be jealous with her, asking her questions about the subjects of her photo shoots, her ex-husband, her agent, the waiter at the restaurant on Cape Cod, and the two men in the pub in Blessington. He was still jealous, but these days he had it in better control. And he had no reason to be jealous with Hope. And apparently he hadn't with Audra either. The story was awful, and Hope felt deeply sorry for him. She could see in his eyes how guilty he still felt about it all these years later.

"Maybe she had emotional problems you didn't know about," Hope said, trying to comfort him. "Normal people don't do things like that. They don't kill themselves, no matter how desperate they feel." She couldn't imagine Mimi doing something like that, or herself at that age. But whatever the reason, the girl in the photograph was dead.

"Sometimes young girls do," Finn said, "or even older ones. I was never totally convinced that Michael's mother didn't do the same thing. She was drunk, and our life was a mess. She knew I didn't love her, and I don't think she loved me either. She was a very unhappy woman. We were trapped in a loveless marriage, and we hated each other. I didn't want to divorce her, for Michael's sake, but I should have. It's all such a waste sometimes," he said bleakly, and then smiled at her. And for a totally insane instant, Hope had the odd feeling that despite his sense of guilt, he was flattered by the notion that these women had died for him. The thought gave her a chill. And then as though to confirm it, he looked at her strangely and asked her an odd question. "Would you ever kill yourself, Hope?" Slowly, she shook her head, but was honest with him.

"I thought about it when Mimi died. More than once. And when Paul left me. But I couldn't do it. No matter how terrible I felt and how hopeless, I couldn't conceive of doing something like that. I went to India and tried to heal instead. That made more sense." But she was an essentially healthy person, with a firm footing in life, and she had been considerably older, in her early forties at the time. These were very young women, and girls that age tended to be more dramatic and more extreme and intense, although she couldn't imagine Mimi doing it either, for a broken romance, or any other reason. These were obviously troubled girls in desperate situations, one pregnant out of wedlock with an alcoholic father to face and a boyfriend she thought had left her, and the other trapped in a loveless marriage with a child she didn't want and a husband Finn said she hated. It was upsetting to think about. And Finn was quiet as he walked out of the room, and went back upstairs to his office to work on the book.

Hope put the photographs back in the drawer, and decided not to restore the desk. She went for a walk alone after that, and thought about Finn. He had had turmoil and upset with the women in his life, and the death of a young girl on his conscience for more than twenty years. It was a lot to live with. And she thought his question to her had been odd. Maybe he just wanted to reassure himself that no matter what happened, he would never have to face something like that again. And with Hope there was no risk. Suicide was not an option for her. If her daughter's death hadn't destroyed her, she knew that nothing would. She dreaded losing Paul, when that happened, and she knew she would one day. She hoped for him, and for her, that that wouldn't happen for a long, long time.

As she walked along, it was sad thinking about death, instead of birth, and then she thought of the baby, taking hold inside her. The child she and

Finn had conceived was an affirmation of life and hope, and an antidote to all the tragedies that had happened to them both. She saw now, more than ever, what a wonderful thing it was, and realized that that was what Finn had been doing, clinging to life to overcome the shadows of death that had trailed him for years. It was a touching thought and made her love him more than ever. She thought about Audra then, and even not knowing her, silently mourned her loss. Hope was touched by Finn's honesty in admitting his part in the tragedy. He had made no effort to hide or deny it, which was honorable of him. And Hope felt guilty for her momentary thought that he was somehow flattered that she had loved him enough to commit suicide over him. Hope was sure that wasn't true, and was sorry she had even thought it. It had been a sick thought, but for an instant something in his eyes, and his question to her after that, had made her think it. She was glad she hadn't said it to him. He would have been justifiably wounded that she would suspect him of such a thing.

She felt better when she got back to the house, and decided to empty two closets that were full of ancient dusty linens. She was sneezing incessantly at the top of a ladder when Finn found her there late that afternoon. She had been easy to find when he heard the sneezing, and scolded her when he found her.

"What are you doing on that ladder?" he said

with a disapproving scowl, as she blew her nose for the hundredth time and looked at him.

"Getting rid of this mess." Shelf by shelf, she was pulling the yellowed linens down, tossing them to the ground, and as she did, a cloud of dust rose each time, and made her sneeze again. "This stuff must have been sitting here for a hundred years. It's filthy."

"And you're a fool," he said angrily. "Now get off that ladder. I'll do that if you want. If you fall, you'll kill the baby." She stared at him in surprise, and then smiled, touched by his concern.

"I'm not going to fall off, Finn. The ladder is perfectly solid. We found it in the stables." It was the only one tall enough to reach the top shelves in the closets, because the ceilings were so high. But he was serious, and held the ladder for her, as she reluctantly got down. "I'm not a cripple, for heaven's sake, and I'm only a few weeks pregnant." She lowered her voice so no one would hear them, although Winfred and Katherine were both so deaf that it was unlikely they would, and there was no one else around.

"I don't care. You have a responsibility to all three of us now. Don't be stupid," he said, and climbed the ladder for her. And in less than a minute, as he did the same job, he was sneezing too. And a moment later, they were both laughing. It was a relief after the somber discoveries she had made that day. The sad story of Audra was still on her mind, but she didn't mention it to him again, she knew now how painful it was for him, and she felt sorry for him. "Can't we just throw this stuff away?" Finn asked, looking at the heap of yellowed linens on the ground. Most of them were table-cloths no one had used for years, and the rest were sheets for beds in sizes that no longer existed.

"I will, but we had to at least pull them out first. We can't let them sit up there forever." She was be-coming the unofficial mistress of the manor, and Finn was pleased to see it.

"You're such a little housewife," he teased her, and then he smiled down at her from the top of the ladder. "I can't wait till we have a baby running around here. It'll really feel like a home then. Un-til you came along, Hope, it just felt like a house."

She had infused her own life and spirit into it, just by cleaning it up and moving things around, and the furniture she'd had restored looked beauti-ful, although there was still too little of it. The house was mostly empty, and it would have cost a fortune to fill it. She didn't want to overstep her bounds, so she was trying to do her best with what was there, and only added a few things, as small gifts to him. He was deeply appreciative of everything she did. And the results were looking good, although it was obvious that it would take years to restore the house to its original condition, and probably more money than Finn would ever see. But at least he had claimed his mother's family's ancestral home, and she knew what it meant to him.

His love for the house was almost as deep as his love for her. He had come home to his roots, and reclaimed them. It was a major step for him. And he felt as though he had been waiting to do that all his life, and often said that to her. He knew that his mother would have been proud of him, if she were still alive to see it. And Hope loved sharing the experience with him. Her efforts to improve it for him, and return it to its previous glory, were a gesture of love for him.

For the next several weeks, Finn continued to work on his book, and Hope took a few pictures. She took them discreetly in the pub sometimes, mostly of old people, and no one seemed to mind. Most of them were flattered. After Finn finished work in the afternoons, they went for long quiet walks in the hills. He talked with her about his work, and how the book was going. She paid close attention to everything he said, and was fascinated by the process of his work, as he was with hers. As he had even before he met her, he loved the photographs she took. And he particularly liked the series she was doing of old men and women in the pubs. They had wonderful faces and expressive eyes, and seen through Hope's lens, they were transfused with all the tenderness and pathos of the human spirit. They had tremendous respect for each other's work. No one had taken as great an interest in her work before, nor had anyone in his.

They talked about the baby, although she didn't like to dwell on the subject. She didn't want to get her hopes up too much now that she had gotten comfortable with the idea. The first three months were always unsure, and at her age even more so. Once she got past that, she would really allow herself to celebrate the idea. Until then, she was hopeful and excited, but trying to remain calm and realistic, and somewhat reserved. Finn had already given his whole heart to it, and she had long since forgiven him for the hideous afternoon at the fertility doctor in London, and even for getting her drunk and pregnant later that afternoon. The results of it were too sweet to resist, and she loved him more than ever, particularly now with this additional bond. She was feeling mellow, happy, and very much in love.

They were talking about getting married, and they both loved the idea. All Hope wanted was to spend the rest of her life with him, and he felt exactly the same way. And their plans to marry in the near future made her feel very much mistress of his home.

She was emptying drawers in the dining room one day, in her continuing efforts to purge the house of old, meaningless things, when she came upon a lease that had just been tossed into a bottom drawer. And it looked relatively new. She was going to leave it on Finn's desk, and then realized what it was. It was a six-year lease for Blaxton House that Finn had signed two years before. And as she read it, she realized that the house had been rented, not bought. She was floored. He had said the house was his.

She thought about putting the lease back in the drawer, and not mentioning it to him. It wasn't really any of her business, but it troubled her all that afternoon. It wasn't just that he had lied to her, but it seemed so odd to her that he would tell her he owned it, when in fact it was only rented. And finally, she couldn't stand it, and decided to clear the air with him. It seemed like an important point to her. Honesty was a crucial part of the relationship they were building, which they both hoped would last for years, hopefully forever. And she wanted no secrets between them. She had none from him.

She waited until teatime to ask him about it, and they were eating the sandwiches and soup that Katherine provided for them every evening. She made them a hot meal at noon, with hearty meat and vegetables and Irish potatoes, which Finn ate and she didn't. Hope preferred lighter meals, and she was grateful that as her pregnancy progressed, she felt fine. If anything, she ate more than usual, and she hadn't been nauseous for a minute. She hadn't been with Mimi either. In the twenty-three years since her last pregnancy, nothing had changed, and she felt healthier than ever, and looked it. She had the bloom of youth and motherhood in her eyes and on her cheeks, despite her age. In fact, she looked suddenly younger than ever.

She broached the subject carefully as they finished the meal. She wasn't quite sure how to do it, and didn't want to embarrass him or make him feel exposed by what she had discovered. In the end, she decided to just say it.

"I found something in a drawer in the dining room today," she said as she folded her napkin and Finn took a long swallow of wine. He always drank more in the evening when he was writing a book. It helped him relax, after concentrating on the story all day. Hope could see that it was grueling work.

"So what did you find?" he asked, looking distracted. He had done a particularly hard chapter that day.

"The lease for this house," she said simply, looking him in the eye, to see his reaction. There was none for a minute, and then he looked away.

"Oh," he said, and then looked at her again. "I was embarrassed to admit to you that I don't own it. I do, in my heart and soul, but I couldn't afford it. So they rented it to me. I was hoping that in the six years of the lease, I could scrape up the money, but this works for now. I'm sorry I didn't tell you the truth about it, Hope. It's humiliating to admit you can't buy your own family's house, but right now I just can't, and maybe I never will." He looked embarrassed as he said it, but not about the lie. It wasn't really a lie, or not a big one anyway, and she told herself that he owed her no explanations, neither about the house, nor about his financial situation, although he was her baby's father and the man she loved. But for the moment anyway, he was not responsible for her, and probably never would be financially. She didn't need that kind of help from him. And she had thought about it all afternoon since she'd found the lease. The only thing that really bothered her was that they were pouring money, or she was, into someone else's house, which didn't seem smart to her. She was a little startled that he let her do that, but Finn was in love with Blaxton House, whether it was his or not. It had belonged to his ancestors, and to him by birthright, even if it was only leased.

"You don't owe me any explanations, Finn," she said quietly. "I didn't mean to put you on the spot, but I was curious about it. It's really none of my business." He was looking at her, and obviously feeling awkward. "I have a proposition to make you. I'm very fortunate, because of Paul. I have no kids"—and then she smiled, and gently touched his hand—"or at least I didn't for a while, and that's about to change. But Paul was incredibly generous with me, and he has helped me make some very good investments that are continuing to pay off." She didn't hide her circumstances from him, she had no reason to. It was obvious he wasn't after her money, and she loved him. They loved each other, and shared a sacred trust and bond, particularly now with the baby. She trusted Finn completely, and knew she wasn't wrong. He was a good man, and a solid person, even if he didn't have a lot of money. That meant nothing to her. Paul hadn't had much when she married him either. Hope was not interested in money. What she valued was the love they shared.

"The proposition that I want to make you is that I buy this house. If you feel uncomfortable about it, you can pay the rent to me, although I don't see why you should. Or some token amount to make it legal, like a dollar a month, or a hundred a year. I don't give a damn about it. We can ask the lawyers how it has to be. When we get married, I can give it to you as a gift, or put it in trust for you in my will. If we don't marry, and don't stay together, which would make me very sad"—she smiled at him, they both knew that there was no risk of that, from all they could see at the moment—"then we could turn it into a loan, and you could pay me back over thirty years, or fifty for all I care, but I wouldn't pull the house out from under you. This house should be yours, and I'd feel better for you, knowing that you own it now, or that someone does who loves you and isn't going to change their mind and stop renting it to you. This house is yours, Finn. It belonged to your family for hundreds of years. If you'll agree, I'd like to buy it now and protect it for you, and our children. And just to cover all the bases, in case this baby doesn't happen for some reason, I still feel the same way. I don't need the money. I don't know what they're asking for it, but I think it will make a very, very small dent in what Paul gave me." She was being totally honest with him, as Finn stared at her in amazement. It was the nicest thing anyone had ever done for him, and she wanted nothing from him in return. She just loved him.

"My God, what did he give you?" Finn couldn't help asking. She was totally unconcerned about buying the house and what it would cost her. And Finn realized she was doing it for him, out of love.

Hope didn't hesitate when she answered. There was no one else on earth she would tell, except him. She trusted him with her life, their baby, and her fortune. She didn't consider the money hers anyway, it was Paul's, and should have been Mimi's. And now, one day, it would go to this baby, and Blaxton House was part of that baby's heritage anyway, because it was Finn's. She was helping him build a legacy for their child, and if not, out of kindness, for him.

"He gave me fifty million from the sale of his company. He sold it for two hundred net after the sale. I'll get another fifty when he dies, hopefully not soon. And it's carefully invested. I actually made quite a lot of money last year. I guess money breeds more money. That's an awful lot for one woman with few needs. I can afford to buy the house," she said simply. "And I'd like to do that for you. Do you know how much they want for it?" She had no idea what a house like his would sell for in Ireland.

He laughed in answer. "A million pounds. That's less than two million U.S. dollars." It was laughable in comparison to the kind of money she was talking about, which was inconceivable to him. He knew she had money, that was obvious, and she had said that Paul had been extremely generous with her. But he had had no idea she had that kind of money. It was beyond his wildest imagination. "And we can probably get them down on the price for cash, way down. The house is in pretty bad shape, as you know. We might even be able to get it for seven or eight hundred thousand pounds, which would be a windfall for them, and a bargain for us. That would be about a million and a half, in dollars." And then he looked at her sternly. "Hope, are you sure? We've only been together for four months. That's a hell of a gesture." What she was proposing was the greatest gift of his life, beyond his wildest dreams.

"I'd like to fix it up with you, and do everything it needs. It's a shame to let the place go to rack and ruin, particularly if we buy it."

"Let me think about it," he said. He seemed

overwhelmed. He leaned over and kissed her, drained his glass of wine, filled it, and drained that one too, and then he laughed again. "I think I may have to get drunk tonight. This is all a little rich for my blood. I don't even know what to say to you, except that I love you and you're an extraordinary woman."

They both went to bed shortly after that. They were tired, the emotions of the day were too much for him, and he passed out from the wine. They both woke up in the middle of the night. There was a storm outside, and Finn turned to her in the dark, looking at her, propped up on one elbow.

"Hope?"

"Yes." She smiled at him. She was happy with the offer she had made him. It felt right to her, and it was so little money compared to what she had. And it was such a great house for them.

"Can I accept the offer now, or do I have to wait until morning?" He looked like an overgrown boy in the dark, and his eyes were dancing, he was so happy. She was making him the greatest gift of his life. And he was almost afraid she would change her mind and take it back. But he didn't know Hope if he thought that. She was a woman of her word.

"You can accept the offer anytime you like," she said, with a gentle hand on his neck as the wind howled outside. It was raining hard. Spring didn't come easily in Ireland, and it was an odd feeling for her, knowing this was going to be her home now, but she loved it too. And she was proud of his ancestral house, sharing it with him, and hopefully their child, or even children. The future lay brightly before them.

"Maybe we should wait and see if the place falls down tonight. That's a hell of a wind blowing," Finn said with a smile.

"I think it will be okay," she said, still smiling.

"Then I want to say yes to your generous offer. Thank you for giving me back my house. And I promise you, when we get married, when I make the money for it, I'll pay you back. I'll rent it from you, for the same price I pay now. And I'll pay you back in installments, whenever I can. It may take a while, but I'll do it."

"You can do it any way you want. But at least you'll know the house is yours and no one can take it away from you, nor should they. You're the rightful heir."

He nodded with tears in his eyes, even though he was smiling. He was in awe of her again. "Thank you. I don't know what else to say. I love you, Hope."

"I love you too, Finn." He put his head on her shoulder and went back to sleep then, like a child. He looked as though he felt peaceful and safe, as she lay holding him, and gently stroked his hair. And finally, she fell asleep again too, as the storm raged on outside.

Chapter 12

The day after the storm Hope called the bank and made all the arrangements to buy the house, and Finn helped her. They had lost a tree in the night, but they didn't care. It hadn't hurt anyone, and had done no damage. And the owner of the house, who had bought the property as an investment, was happy to accept seven hundred and eighty thousand pounds, a million five hundred thousand dollars. It was a terrific price, and Finn was ecstatic. Hope had the money wired, and since there were no conditions on the sale, Blaxton House was theirs eight days later. Legally, it belonged to her, but she had all the papers drawn up, leaving it to him in the event of her death, and allowing him to pay a nominal rent for now. Once they were married, the house would be put in trust for their child. And if for some reason they didn't marry, or there was no child, he could still buy the house from her, over an extended time.

It was a fantastic deal for him, and one he never could have gotten otherwise. And she was already making plans to restore it to its original beauty. Hope was thrilled to have a free hand for the restoration. There was nothing in it for her, except the joy of making Finn happy, and knowing that they owned the house they were living in, and where their baby would grow up. She reminded Finn again that the deal was not contingent on her pregnancy. If for any reason they lost the baby, nothing changed. And if their relationship failed, she was still willing to let him buy the house from her over time. It was the ideal arrangement for him, and he said she was the most generous woman in the world. Hope insisted it was a blessing for them both. She had asked no one's advice and needed no one's permission. She just did it, and notified her bank to make the wire transfer to the previous owner. Everyone was extremely pleased with the deal. And Finn most of all, but Hope was happy too. He put the deed to the house in his desk drawer like it was made of gold. And then he turned to Hope, and knelt down before her, looking into her eyes.

"What are you doing?" she asked, laughing at him, and then saw his serious expression. This was clearly an important moment to him.

"I'm formally asking you to marry me," he said solemnly, taking her hand in his own. There was no one to ask. She had no relatives except Paul, and that wouldn't have been appropriate, although Finn was grateful to him as well for how generous he had been with Hope. "Will you be my wife, Hope?" Tears filled her eyes as he knelt before her, and she nodded. She was too moved to speak, and cried much more easily now, with their baby in her womb.

"Yes, I will," she said in a strangled voice, and then choked on a sob. He stood up then and took her in his arms and kissed her.

"I promise I'll take care of you all your life. You won't regret it for a minute." She didn't think she would. "I'll get you an engagement ring the next time we go to London. When do you think we should get married?" The baby was due in November, and she wanted to do it before that, if only to legitimize the child. But she didn't want to wait anyway. They were both sure about their love.

"Maybe we shouldn't make official plans till you tell Michael," Hope said, thinking of his son, and not wanting him to feel left out. "Maybe we could get married this summer in Cape Cod." That would mean a lot to her.

"I'd rather get married here," Finn said honestly. "Somehow it would seem more official. We could still do it over the summer, when Michael is here. He always comes over at some point, even if it's not for long."

"I need to meet him first, before we tell him," Hope said sensibly, and they both agreed that they didn't want to tell him on the phone. He knew nothing about her, and suddenly they would be calling to say that his father was marrying a total stranger, and having a baby. It was a lot for Finn's son to swallow at one gulp. Hope wanted to give him time to meet her and adjust to the idea. And she had to tell Paul, and she knew it might be a blow for him at first, knowing she was with another man, and having his child. They needed time for others to get used to their plans. And summer seemed soon enough to Hope, or even fall. That gave them time to get organized too. A lot had happened in a very short time. Their relationship, a baby, and now they were planning to marry. The rapidity of it all still took her breath away. In four months, she had a whole new life. A man, a child, a house. But Finn was wonderful to her and she was sure.

She was busier than ever once they bought the house. It was well into April by then, and she decided to postpone her jobs in New York in May. She didn't want to fly before the end of her first trimester, when the baby would be solidly ensconced. She asked Mark to move all her May commitments to mid-June, and didn't tell him why, although her bank had told him she had bought the house.

"So you bought a place in Ireland," he said with interest. "I'll have to come over and see what you're up to over there. How's everything with Finn?"

"Perfect," she said, sounding ecstatic. "I've never been happier in my life." He could hear it, and he was pleased for her. She had been through some very tough times, and she deserved all the happiness she had now.

"See you in June. I'll get everything worked out. Don't worry about it. Just have fun with your castle or whatever it is." She told him a little about the house, and he liked hearing the joy and excitement in her voice. Hope hadn't sounded like that in years.

And for the next two months, she and Finn never stopped. Hope hired a contractor and started doing the repairs the house needed so badly. They had to put a new roof on, which cost a fortune but was worth it. Windows were sealed that had leaked for fifty years. Dry rot was cut out, and she made arrangements to have the interior of the house painted while they were in Cape Cod for the summer. And she was buying antiques in shops and at auctions, to fill the house with the furniture it deserved. And every time Finn saw her, she was carrying something, dragging a box, climbing up a ladder, or stripping a paneled wall. She boxed up the books in the library so they could work on the shelves. She never stopped, and more than once Finn gave her hell and reminded her that she was pregnant. She still acted as she had when she was pregnant with Mimi, and Finn reminded her that she was no longer twenty-two years old. Sometimes Hope remembered to be careful, and the rest of the time she laughed at him and told him that she wasn't sick. She had never felt better or been happier in her life. This was like the reward for all the sorrow that she'd been through. She believed that Finn was the miracle that God had given her, and she said it to him all the time.

She was working particularly hard one after-noon, packing up the dishes so they could have the inside of the china closets painted, and she com-plained afterward that she had hurt her back. She got in a warm tub and it felt better, but she said that it really ached, and Finn scolded her again, and then felt sorry for her, and rubbed her back.

"You're a fool," he chided her. "Something is go-ing to happen, and it'll be your own goddamn fault, and I'll be pissed. That's our baby you're toss-ing around, while you work like a mule." But it touched him too that she loved his house so much and was doing it all for him. She wanted it to be beautiful now so he'd be proud. It was her labor of love for Finn, and so was their child.

She slept fitfully that night, and stayed in bed the next morning. She said her back still hurt, and he offered to call a doctor, but she said she didn't need one. He believed her, although she didn't look well. He thought that she looked pale, and she was obviously in pain. He came up to check on her an hour later, and found her on the bathroom floor, in a pool of blood, barely able to crawl, as she looked up at him. He panicked when he saw her and rushed for the phone. He called for the paramedics and begged the operator to send them fast, and then returned to Hope in the bathroom. He was holding her when they arrived, and his jeans were soaked with blood. She had lost the baby and was hemorrhaging, and she lost consciousness when the paramedics picked her up and put her on a gurney to carry her out. Finn ran along beside them, praying she would live, and when she came to in the hospital hours later, after they had cleaned out her womb, Finn was staring at her with a dark look. She reached out a hand to him and he turned away and got up. She was crying and he was staring out the window, and then turned to look at her. He looked both angry and sad, and there were tears in his eyes too. He was thinking of his loss, more than hers.

"You killed our baby," he said brutally, and she broke into a sob, and she reached out to him again, but he didn't come near her. She tried but was too weak to sit up. They had given her two transfusions to make up for the blood she'd lost.

"I'm sorry," she managed to say through her sobs.

"All that stupid lifting and carrying, look what it did. You just made it to three months, and now you fucked it all up." He said nothing to comfort or reassure her, and Hope looked heartbroken as he raged at her. "It was a shitty thing to do, to the

baby, and to me. You killed a healthy baby, Hope."
It didn't occur to him that maybe the baby wasn't
so healthy if it hadn't survived past that point, but
there was no way to know now, and she felt bad
enough. "How could you be so selfish and so
dumb?" She was sobbing, listening to him berate
her, and a few minutes later, he stormed out. She
lay in bed, inconsolable, thinking of everything
he'd said to her, and the nurse finally gave her a
shot as she cried incoherently, and when she woke
up hours later, Finn was sitting next to her again.
He still looked grim, but he was holding her hand.
"I'm sorry for what I said," he said gruffly. "I was
just so disappointed. I wanted our baby so much."
She nodded and started to cry again, and this time
he took her in his arms and consoled her. "It's all
right," he said. "We'll do it again." She nodded and
just lay in his arms and sobbed. "Even if I act like
a fool sometimes, I love you, Hope." As he said it,
tears rolled down his cheeks, and hers.

Chapter 13

Hope left for New York two weeks later in June. She was thin and pale and very subdued, and she knew that Finn was still upset. He blamed her fully for the miscarriage, and insisted that only her carelessness had caused it. He refused to accept the idea that age might have been a factor, or it could have happened anyway. He never missed an opportunity to tell her that it was her fault. He kept telling her they'd both feel better when she got pregnant again and did it right this time, which only exacerbated her own unspoken guilt. She had apologized to him a thousand times. Finn acted like she had betrayed him, and their child. She felt like a murderess every time she looked at him, and she wondered if he'd ever forgive her. All he talked about was doing it again. And it was almost a relief to get on the plane to New York and get away from him. And she was by no means ready to do it again, or not this soon at least, if at all. He acted as though she owed it to him. But after losing Mimi, now losing this pregnancy had her in deep mourning suddenly. And she was in disgrace with Finn as well, which nearly broke her heart.

She managed to finish all her assignments in New York, and had been hoping to see Paul since she hadn't seen him in six months, which was far too long. But when she called him on his cell phone, he said he was in Germany, checking out a new treatment for Parkinson's, and he planned to stay there for a while. She was sorry to miss him, but they promised to meet in the fall.

She had lunch with Mark Webber, who thought she looked exhausted and said she was working too hard. But she insisted she was happy, and he hoped she was. But she didn't look as happy to him as she had sounded on the phone. Finn's harsh criticism of her when she lost the baby had hit her hard. There had been a cruelty to it that was hard to get over now. It was the first time he had been unkind to her in the six months they'd been together, and the first time a shadow had come between them.

Mark had gotten her several assignments for the fall, and she wasn't sure if she should take them or not. If she got pregnant again, she knew that Finn wouldn't let her fly to New York. Suddenly something that had been both an accident and a blessing had become a life-or-death project that took precedence for Finn. And for the first time, Hope felt unsure of herself. She felt profoundly guilty, and nervous about doing it again.

She went to see her doctor in New York, who told her that she had to wait at least three months before trying to get pregnant again, and reminded her sensibly that she might have lost the baby anyway, even if she'd stayed in bed. But after everything Finn had said to her, she felt responsible and depressed. She had already decided to put their wedding off till December, since now there was no rush. She was too depressed to plan their marriage.

Finn arrived in New York as soon as she finished her work. He was in better spirits than when she had left him, and he was very loving to her. Hope tried to stay off the subject of the miscarriage, but he mentioned to her several times that he wanted her to see the fertility doctor in London when she went back. He didn't want to waste any time, and he made Hope feel that she owed it to him. She was still feeling too weak and tired and depressed to argue with him and fight back, so she finally said she would. It was easier than battling about it. And they were going to be at the Cape for July and August, while Blaxton House was being painted from top to bottom. And she was sure she'd feel better by the end of the summer, and things would look different and less depressing to her by then. She was still dealing with all the hormonal changes that came from losing a three-month pregnancy, and so much blood. Her body was still in shock. And Finn's harsh reaction, blame, and accusations had shaken her considerably. His behavior about the miscarriage was so out of keeping with his normal, extremely loving style of the past six months. She was anxious for him to calm down again, and felt sure he would.

The best thing that happened once Finn arrived was that his son Michael came down from Boston to meet them in New York for dinner, and Hope thought he was an absolutely terrific kid. He was a bright, open, friendly, well brought up, and all-around lovely boy. He had just turned twenty, and looked a lot like Finn. He teased his father repeatedly, and was fairly bold with him, but she was impressed by how well they got along. It said a lot for Finn that he had single-handedly brought up such a wonderful boy, and Hope thought it spoke well of him as a father that their relationship was so good.

Hope invited Michael to the Cape, but he said he was spending the summer in California with his maternal grandparents, as he did every year. He said he had a job lined up at the San Francisco stock exchange for July and August, and he was excited about it. Spending time with him made Hope miss Mimi acutely again, and that night after he left them, Hope complimented Finn.

"He's a fabulous kid. You did a great job," she said, and he smiled at her. For the first time, she felt as though things were beginning to repair with them. Losing the baby had been a terrible blow to them both. They hadn't wanted to tell Michael at their first meeting they were planning to get married. She and Finn agreed to tell him when he came to Ireland in September. She was excited for him to see all the things they were doing to the house. She couldn't wait to see them herself when they got back. And she was looking forward to having Michael with them. She wanted to get to know him better.

When she and Finn got to the Cape, it was as though nothing bad had happened. He didn't mention the miscarriage again, he stopped accusing her and making caustic remarks that made her cringe. He was as loving, kind, and gentle as ever. He was the Finn she had fallen in love with seven months before, only better. And she began to relax and feel more like herself again. She put on some weight and felt healthy, and they were together every moment. He had brought his manuscript with him, and he said the work was going well.

Her only disappointment was that he refused to meet any of her friends at the Cape. She and Paul had had an open-door policy at the house, and their friends had dropped in often. Finn told her he didn't want that happening, it disturbed his work, and he was uncomfortable meeting them whenever it happened. She took him to a Fourth of July picnic at the home of a couple she had known forever, and Finn was standoffish and unfriendly. Several people told him they loved his work, and even then he was chilly, and insisted that he and Hope leave early.

When she questioned him about it the next day, he said he hated that kind of suburban summer community and had nothing in common with them. And what was the point of meeting them? They lived in Ireland. What Hope realized increasingly was that he wanted her to himself. He complained if she went to the grocery store without him. He wanted to go everywhere with her. It was still flattering in some ways, but there were times when she found it oppressive. And he told her that he liked her Cape Cod house much better in winter than in summer, when it was peaceful and the area was deserted. Without exception, Finn had rejected all her old friends. She hardly saw them herself now that she no longer lived in Boston, and she had always loved the congenial atmosphere at the Cape, but it was clear that that was not going to be part of her life with Finn. Although he had socialized a great deal in his youth and gone out with a million women before her, once in a relationship Finn preferred to lead a quiet life with her, and have no social life whatsoever except with her.

At times it left her feeling isolated. He insisted that it was more romantic that way, and he didn't want to share her. And he was so loving to her that she really couldn't complain. Whatever momentary rift had happened to them around the miscarriage was finally healed and forgotten by the end of the summer. Finn was totally the handsome prince again, and even if she hardly saw her friends all summer, she was relieved that she and Finn were closer than they had ever been. In the end, it was as though the sadness of the miscarriage had only brought them closer and made him more loving. And if she had to sacrifice seeing her Cape Cod friends for that, it was worth it. Her life with Finn, and the well-being of their relationship, was more important.

They went back to New York after Labor Day. Finn had an important meeting with his British publisher that he had to go back to London for. Hope stayed in New York to wrap up a few last details after the summer. She had to see her banker and lawyer, and meet with her agent before she left. She was planning to be back in Ireland by the weekend, and was going to spend September there. She didn't really have to be back in New York until November. She tried not to remember that that was when their baby would have been born. Maybe Finn was right and they would have another. Whatever God decided. She was feeling healthy again and more philosophical about it. And he hadn't mentioned the fertility doctor again since July.

When she saw Mark, he told her he had a fabulous assignment for her in South America in October, and she had to admit it sounded good to her too, but she hesitated to do it. She knew Finn would be upset, and if she happened to get pregnant again, he wouldn't want her to fly, although her doctor said she could. She didn't want to risk his fury again, or a miscarriage, and she looked at Mark sadly and said she didn't think she could do it.

"What's that about?" he asked, looking unhappy.

"I just think it's the wrong time in the relationship for me to be flying all over the world. We're redoing the house, and Finn gets upset when I go away." She didn't want to tell him that she'd recently been pregnant and might try again.

"I think you're making a big mistake, if you let him influence what assignments you take, Hope. We're not interfering in his career, and there is no decent reason for him to interfere in yours. That's bullshit. How about telling him you don't want him writing a book? You both have important talents and careers. The only way it'll work between you two is if you both respect that. He can't manipulate you into not working. Or if he is, you shouldn't let him."

"I know," she said nervously. "What can I tell you? He's a baby. And we're planning to get married at the end of the year. Maybe he'll calm down after that." She hoped so, but for now he made her feel guilty every time she left him, even for work, although he insisted that he was proud of her, and respected what she did. It was confusing information, and a double message that made her feel unsure of herself and insecure.

"What if he doesn't calm down then?" Mark said, looking worried.

"We'll talk about it then. We've only been together for nine months."

"That's my point. It's a little early for him to be fucking with your career. In fact, that should never happen."

"I know, Mark," she said quietly. "He's very needy, in a funny way. He needs a lot of attention."

"Then adopt him, don't marry him. You'd better straighten this out very soon, or you'll regret it later." She nodded. She knew he was right, but it was easier said than done, and with the exception of his poor reaction to the miscarriage, no one had ever been more wonderful to her than Finn. And his unkindness over the miscarriage had been some kind of slip. She was convinced of it, and he had been better than ever in the months since. She was willing to adjust her work schedule for a while to suit him, and she already had three good assignments lined up for November, she didn't need another one. It wasn't worth it. So she turned it down. She had done as much for Mimi when she was young. But Mimi had been her child, not a man. Hope felt that she had already lost so many people she loved in her life that she didn't want to take the chance of losing another. And maybe if she made Finn mad enough, as she had over the miscarriage, he would leave. She didn't want to risk it.

She saw Paul the day she left, and she had been planning to tell him about Finn, and that they were getting married, but he looked so sick that she didn't have the heart to tell him. She had to help him feed himself, he could hardly walk now, and he had aged twenty years in the last one. She was frightened when she saw him. He said the treatment in Germany hadn't worked for him. After that he had gone to spas, and wound up in a hospital with an infection. He was happy to be home in the States. He was on his way to Boston for treatment, and she cried on the way to the airport after she left him. It was terrible watching him slip away and he looked so frail. She was still depressed about it when she got on the plane.

She slept most of the way to Dublin, and it was early morning when she got there. Finn was waiting for her with the broad slow smile she knew so well and loved so much. The moment she saw him, she knew that all was well in their world. He drove her home to Blaxton House, and ten minutes after they got there, they were in bed. He was more passionate toward her than ever, and more loving. They stayed in bed, whispering and talking and making love till noon, and then he took her downstairs to see how beautiful the house looked now that it had been painted. She was pouring a fortune into it, and they both agreed that it was worth it.

It felt wonderful being back there again, and she felt like the mistress of the manor. Michael was coming to visit them in a few days. And she was happy to have some time alone with Finn before that. She was beginning to think that he was right, and being alone was better. Every moment they shared was loving and romantic. It was impossible to complain about that. And by the end of the afternoon, after surveying their domain with pleasure, they walked back up the stairs hand in hand and went back to bed.

Chapter 14

When Michael arrived, Finn went to pick him up at the airport, and Hope decided to wait at the house. She didn't want to intrude on them, they had so little time together. And she was happy to have him there. She had arranged one of the newly painted guest rooms for Michael, with an enormous bowl of yellow flowers. She'd bought some magazines in town for him, and tried to think of everything he might like. She knew how much he and Finn loved each other, after their years alone while Michael was growing up, and she was looking forward to getting to know him better. Finn was taking him to fish at the Blessington Lakes for a few days, he had made arrangements for hang gliding, and was planning to rent some horses. He wanted him to have a good time, and Hope was willing to do anything possible to help them, even if that meant keeping out of their way, but Finn had told her not to worry about it.

And this time, they were going to tell Michael about their wedding plans in December. Since it had turned out to be a winter wedding after all, Hope had agreed that it might be better in Ireland, although she also liked the idea of getting married in London, to make it easier for people like Mark to come. Finn loved the idea of doing it at the tiny church in Russborough, with a reception at the house, and said he didn't care if they did it all alone. Finn wasn't sure if Michael would come from Boston, and said it didn't matter to him. The only one important to him at the wedding was Hope. He didn't need a single other soul to be there. This was a far cry from the highly social animal she had believed him to be when they met. In reality, Finn was nearly a hermit. And the only person he wanted to be with was her. He said it was a sign of the immensity of his love for her, and she believed him. The ultimate tribute of Finn's love was that he wanted to devote every waking moment to her.

When Michael arrived from the airport with his father, he gave Hope a friendly hug, and commented on the changes in the house. He was enormously impressed.

"What happened? Did you win the lottery, Dad?" Michael teased him. There was always a faint edge to their exchanges and Michael's comments, but they were harmless. They were the kind of things said between men, one growing into power and manhood, the other trying to hold on to it for dear life. And as Hope watched them, she wondered if that was why Finn was so desperate to have a baby. It was a way of hanging on to his virility and his youth, and proving to himself and the world that he was young. Hope thought that there were other ways to prove it.

She showed Michael around, through all the changes and restorations they'd done. The painting that had been done over the summer was a vast improvement over the dingy walls. She had finally gotten rid of the rugs and had the beautiful old floors redone. It looked like the same house, but so much better, and Michael complimented her politely on everything he saw.

The two men left for the lake the next day, and were gone for three days. After that, Michael wanted his father to go to London with him for two days, and Hope stayed home to work. She didn't really get the chance to spend time with Michael until the day before he left. He had to get back to MIT for the beginning of his junior year, and Finn was in the village buying the newspaper when she sat down to breakfast with Michael. Katherine had made them both eggs, sausages, and tea, and Michael seemed to like it. He was quiet at first as they both ate their breakfast. Finn had told her that he hadn't mentioned their upcoming marriage yet, and she didn't want to be the one to do it. It wasn't her place. It was up to Finn, and she wondered when he was going to tell him. His son was leaving the next day.

"Your father misses you terribly," she said to open a conversation with him. "After all those years of living together, it must be a big change for you too, to be away from him." Michael looked up from his sausages and stared at her blankly, but didn't comment. "I'm sure all those years alone with each other made you very close." It was a little awkward talking to him, and Michael was pleasant and polite with her, but not really chatty. She wondered if mother figures made him uncomfortable, since he hadn't had one, which made her sad for him. "Your father has told me how much fun it was when you two lived in London and New York." She was struggling for conversation, as Michael sat back in his chair and looked Hope in the eye.

He summed it up in one sentence for her. "I didn't grow up with my father." He didn't sound angry when he said it, or disappointed. He said it as simple fact, and Hope was stunned.

"You didn't? I . . . he told me . . . I'm sorry. I must have misunderstood." She felt as though she sounded like a moron, and she did. Michael looked unconcerned.

"My father says a lot of things that sound good to him at the time, or make him look good. He rewrites history, like in his books. He gets confused between fact and fiction. It's just the way he is," he said without condemnation, but it was an incredibly damning statement about Finn, and Hope didn't know what to say in response, nor what to think.

"I'm sure I'm the one who's confused," she said, backing down in a panic. But they both knew she was covering up the awkward moment and making excuses for Finn.

"No, you're not," Michael said, as he finished his sausage. "I grew up with my grandparents in California. I hardly ever saw my father until I went to college." That was only two years before, and that meant that their years together in London and New York were a lie, or a fabrication, or wishful thinking, or something. She didn't understand, and tried not to let Michael see how upset she was. "I know my father cares about me, and he wants to make it up to me now, but we've been strangers for most of my life, and in some ways we still are."

"I'm sorry," Hope said, looking devastated. "I didn't mean to bring up a painful subject." She felt terrible, but the boy across the table from her didn't even look upset. He was used to Finn with all his quirks, and apparently telling stories was one of them, according to his son.

"That's why he's such a good writer. I think he actually believes the stuff he says, once he says it. From that moment on, it's true for him. It's just not true for anyone else." He was amazingly understanding about it, and Hope couldn't help thinking that his grandparents had done a good job with him. He was a healthy, whole, sane, well-balanced young man, not because of Finn, as it turned out, but in spite of him.

"I assume these were your mother's parents?" She decided to check that out, and he nodded. "Your mother died?"

"When I was seven," he confirmed, fairly un-emotionally, which surprised her. At least that much was true, but the rest of his childhood was a fantasy of Finn's. And then she thought of something.

"If you don't mind, Michael, I hate secrets, but I think this would be embarrassing for your dad. I'd rather we not tell him we had this conversation. I don't want him to be upset at you for telling me." But she was extremely upset herself, with good reason. It was a very important subject to lie about, the entire youth and childhood of his son, and his relationship with him. She wondered why Finn had done it, and had no idea how she'd ever broach the subject with him. She didn't want him to feel cornered, but she knew that at some point, they'd have to clear it up. But Michael nodded easily at her suggestion.

"This isn't the first time it's happened," he said simply. "My father usually tells people I grew up with him. I think it's embarrassing for him to ad-mit I didn't, and he never saw me, or not often." She agreed with him, but still, it was disturbing.

"Don't worry about it. I'm fine. I won't say anything to him." And almost as soon as he had said
the words, Finn walked in with a broad smile. In
spite of herself, Hope found herself staring at him,
and then roused herself from her reverie and stood
up to kiss him, but it didn't feel quite the same. She
knew now that he had lied to her, and nothing
would be comfortable between them until he told
her why.

The three of them went to the local pub for dinner that night, and over beer Finn said something
about he and Hope planning to get married sometime. Michael nodded and seemed pleased for
them in a remote way. He thought Hope was a nice
woman, and he didn't have a lot invested in his relationship with Finn, or her, and now she knew
why. Finn and his son hardly knew each other, if
what Michael said was true. And she had no reason
to disbelieve it, it had the ring of truth when he
said it. One of them was lying, and she had the
sinking feeling it was Finn.

He didn't invite his son to the wedding, or even
say there was one planned, and for the moment,
there wasn't. But Hope had wanted a small cere-
mony, attended by their closest friends, and surely
Finn's son. She realized then that Finn really
wanted to do it alone, just as he had said. That
sounded sad to her, but she didn't comment. She
had very little to say that night, and she and
Michael avoided looking at each other. She hugged

him the next day before he left, and thanked him for coming to see them.

"I hope you come back to visit us anytime," she said, and meant it.

"I will," Michael said politely, and thanked her for the hospitality. Finn drove him to the airport then, and she realized how strange his visit had been. It did have the feeling of strangers or casual acquaintances getting together, and not father and son. Given what Michael had told her the day before, she was surprised that he came at all.

She was still thinking about it when Finn came back from the airport, and she looked at him strangely. Finn picked up on it and asked her what was wrong. She was about to say nothing, and then decided to be honest with him. She felt she had no other choice. She needed to know why he had told her the story he had. If she was going to spend the rest of her life with him, she had to know and believe that he was telling her the truth, and he hadn't.

"I'm sorry . . . ," she said, apologizing in advance, "I hate to bring this up, and I don't want to get Michael in trouble. We were talking yesterday and I said how much you loved him, and how much it meant to you that he grew up alone with you." She took a breath and went on. "And he told me he grew up with his mother's parents in California. Why didn't you tell me that before?"

She looked into Finn's eyes, and he looked immediately sad.

"I know. I lied to you, Hope." He came right out and admitted it, without stalling or hesitating. "I felt terrible about it. I can tell from all your stories about Mimi what a wonderful mother you were to her. I didn't think that you would understand that I had given my son to my ex-wife's parents. I tried to take care of him," he said, as he sat down with his head in his hands. They were outside, and he was sitting on the stump of the tree that had fallen, and then he looked up at her. "I just couldn't do it. I wasn't up to it, and I knew I wasn't enough for him. They were good people and they loved him, so I let them take him. They were threatening to take me to court at the time, for their daughter's son, and I just didn't want to go through that and fight them, or put Michael through it, so I let him live with them. It was agony for me, but in the long run, I think it was better for him. He's a great kid. They did a good job." He looked up at her miserably then. "I thought if I told you that, you'd think less of me, and I didn't want that to happen." He reached up and put his arms around her waist and drew her to him, as she looked down at him, in sadness for him. "I just wanted you to love me, Hope, not disapprove of me." He choked on a sob as he said it, and a tear rolled down his cheek. She felt terrible for him.

"I'm sorry," she said, holding him close to her. "You don't have to win my approval. I love you. You can tell me whatever the truth is. It would have been hard for you to bring up a child all alone." Others had done it, but she could see how difficult it might have been for him. And she felt bad that he had felt he had to lie to her so she would love him. "I love you, whatever you've done. Believe me, I've made my share of mistakes too."

"I don't think so," he said, holding her tightly, his face pressed against her stomach, and then he remembered something, and looked into her eyes. "Aren't you supposed to be ovulating today?" She laughed, he never seemed to lose track of her cycle now, but she could better understand his desperation for a baby. He had missed all of Michael's childhood, and after what he had just said to her, she could forgive him for lying about it. Particularly since he was so remorseful once she knew the truth.

"Will you promise me something?" Hope said, and he looked at her intently. "Whatever the truth is, just tell me. The truth is never as bad as a lie." He nodded. "A lie can unravel the whole tapestry of a relationship. The truth only hurts for a minute."

"I know. You're right. I believe that too. It was cowardly of me." He had lied to her twice now, once about owning the house, and now about bringing up Michael, and both times because he

was embarrassed by the truth. She couldn't understand it. But she felt much better having talked to
him about it. He was easy to forgive, and she loved
him, clay feet and all.

He stood up then, put his arms around her and
held her, and then he kissed her, and then asked
her about ovulating again.

"I don't know, you tell me. You seem to know
better than I do. I always lose track. Maybe we
should just wait until we're married. It's only a few
months." She was still disappointed that he hadn't
invited Michael to the wedding, and wanted to get
married alone. She had promised Mark Webber he
could come, and he would be sad if he couldn't,
and she would too.

"You don't have time to wait until we're married,
to get pregnant," Finn said somewhat unkindly.
"We're not getting any younger."

"You mean I'm not," she said bluntly. But at
least she understood his rush now. He was making
up for lost time, and he was right. At her age, her
biological clock was booming, not just ticking.
"Let's see what happens," she said vaguely. She was
afraid of another outcome like the one in June,
whatever the reason, although she knew how important it was to him, so she hadn't ruled out getting pregnant again. And a tiny part of her was
afraid that if she didn't cooperate, he might find a
younger woman who could far more easily give
him babies, but she didn't say that to him.

"Maybe we should go back to the doctor in London and let her work her magic," he suggested, as they walked up the front steps.

"We did fine on our own last time," Hope reminded him. "I'm sure we can again." Finn didn't seem as sure and had more faith in science, although white wine and champagne had served them well six months before. He made her check with the ovulation kit that night, but she wasn't ovulating. They made love anyway, just for the fun of it, which she thought was better. Finn was still the best lover she'd ever had, and the incident with Michael was forgotten. She was sure Finn would be honest with her in future. He had no reason not to. She loved him, and that was all.

Chapter 15

They went to London in October, but not to the fertility doctor. They stayed at Claridge's, checked out the antique shops, and went to two auctions at Christie's. Hope was a little taken aback when Finn bid on a spectacular armoire and a partner's desk, each of which went for close to fifty thousand pounds. He had gotten carried away in the auction, and apologized profusely for it later when they went back to the hotel. He offered to sell them again at Christie's, if she didn't want to spend that much money. But she loved them too, so they went to pay for them the next day and she didn't really mind, although she'd been stunned by the price at first. She had never bought furniture that expensive before. He was remorseful for the rest of the day. But they had gotten two beautiful pieces. They had them shipped home, and flew back to Dublin that night. It was a beautiful October night when they got there, and they were both happy to get home. The house was quiet and peaceful, and they figured out where they would put the new antiques. They agreed on everything. And the only damper to the evening was that she discovered she'd gotten her period, and Finn was bitterly disappointed. He got morose about it that night, and had too much to drink, and then he got angry at her and told her it was her fault she wasn't pregnant, and she wasn't trying. But there wasn't much she could do, unless she started taking fertility drugs, which she didn't want to do, and even the London doctor had said she didn't need. He just had to be patient.

The following day she was relieved that he was in better spirits. He said his new contract had come from his publisher, for a hell of a lot of money. He signed it, and drove to the DHL office to send it, and then took her out for a nice dinner that night in Blessington. He said the contract was a major one for him, for three books. It put him in a festive mood, and he seemed to forgive her for not getting pregnant. That was becoming a major issue between them. It had been four months since the miscarriage, and he was more anxious than she was about it. But she was still ambivalent, and Finn wasn't. He wanted a baby. Now!

Their new antiques arrived from London a few days later, and they looked fabulous when the movers placed them. Finn said they were worth every penny she had spent on them and she had to agree. And as they both knew, she could afford it.

She was talking to Mark on the phone the next day about the three shoots she had lined up for November, and the future show at the Tate Modern, and he made a comment about Finn.

"That's too bad about his contract. He must be upset about it." Hope was confused the minute he said it. They had celebrated his signing it only a few days before.

"What do you mean?"

"I hear they dropped him. He failed to deliver his last two books, and his sales have plummeted. I guess people think the subjects are too weird. They scare the hell out of me," he added. "There was an article about it in **The Wall Street Journal** yesterday. They dropped him, and they're even threatening to sue him to recover monies for the two books he didn't deliver. It's amazing how people can fuck things up for themselves, not having discipline and living up to their contracts." Hope felt sick as she listened, and wondered if he was embarrassed again about what had happened. But he could have shared it with her, and celebrating a new contract was pushing it. She wondered what he had signed and sent back.

From what Mark was saying, it certainly wasn't a new contract. Maybe it was legal papers. Or nothing. She didn't want to admit to Mark that Finn hadn't told her. And she never saw **The Wall Street Journal** in Ireland. Finn knew that, so theoretically, he was safe. She hardly read the papers at all, except the local ones. They were living in a bubble at the foot of the Wicklow Mountains. Finn had counted on that. But it was a pretty shocking story, and if it was true, she knew he must be in dire financial straits, and even more so if they sued him, which was probably why he hadn't told her. He was like a kid hiding a bad report card from his parents. But Hope also realized this was far more serious. He was lying to her about what was happening in his life, not just the past. And all he wanted to talk to her about was getting pregnant.

She thought of something else then, and checked the bank records after she talked to Mark. Finn hadn't paid the rent he owed her monthly since they bought the house in April. She didn't care about the money, and she never mentioned it to him so as not to embarrass him, but it was a clear sign that he was having money troubles and hadn't told her. She knew that if he had the rent money, he would have paid. And he hadn't. She had never thought to check, since it was just a token payment anyway.

She used it as a way of opening the topic of conversation that night, and asked him if everything was all right, since she had noticed that he hadn't paid his rent. He laughed when she asked him.

"Is my landlady getting impatient?" he asked as

he kissed her, and sat down to dinner with her in the kitchen. "Don't worry about it. The signing money for my new contract should be here in a few days." He didn't tell her how much it was, but her heart sank. He was lying to her again. She didn't know whether to be angry with him, or frightened, but his ability to skirt the truth, distort it, or just fabricate it, was beginning to unnerve her, and a red flag went up in her head. She didn't ask him about it again, but he had just flunked the test, and it remained an obstacle between them for the next several weeks while she worried about it, and then packed for her trip to New York.

Finn walked in while she was closing her suitcases and instantly looked like an abandoned child. "Why do you have to go?" he asked petulantly, as he pulled her onto the bed with him. He wanted her to stop and play, and she had a lot to do before she left in the morning. But she was upset with him anyway. He still hadn't told her the truth about his contract, and if everything Mark said was true, his current publishing situation was disastrous. He was still working on his book, but she had never realized, when she saw him do it, that he was already two books late. He never told her, and seemed almost cavalier about it. It was stressful for her knowing he wasn't telling her the truth, and she didn't want to confront him yet again. His publishing life really wasn't her business, but knowing he was truthful was important to her.

And for the moment, he clearly wasn't. "I want you to cancel your trip," Finn said as he held her down on the bed and tickled her. And in spite of herself, she laughed. He was like a child sometimes, a big, beautiful boy, but he was also lying to his mommy, and they were man-sized lies and getting bigger. The current one was huge. And she was sure that he was lying to her out of shame. There had never been any real competition between them. They both had successful careers, in different fields, and were stars in their own right. But if he had been fired by his publisher and was getting sued, it put him at a disadvantage, and probably hurt his ego, in the face of her steady, solid, constantly rising career. She didn't know what to say, and he wasn't talking about his publishing problem at all.

"I can't cancel my trip," she told him. "I have to work."

"Fuck it. Stay here. I'm going to miss you too much." She almost asked him to come with her, and then realized that she needed a break. They were always together. And it was hard to work with him around. He needed constant attention, and wanted her to himself. That was fine at the house in Ireland, but it was impossible when she was trying to work in New York, and she was actually looking forward to a few weeks in her SoHo loft. She had promised Finn she would be back in Ireland by Thanksgiving, which was three weeks away.

"Why don't you finish your book while I'm gone?" The weather was depressing in Ireland that time of year, and it sounded like he needed to do that. Maybe it would keep him from getting sued by his publisher. She had looked up the **Wall Street Journal** article on the Internet after talking to Mark Webber, and the situation sounded frightening to her. In his shoes, she would have been panicking, and perhaps he was, and so hiding it from her to save face. They were suing him for more than two million dollars, and interest, three million in all. It was a very, very big deal, and he had no way to pay for it, she knew, if he lost. Fortunately, the house was in her name. She had thought of putting it in his, and was planning to as a wedding present, but now she was glad she hadn't, and she would keep it in her name if he was still being sued by the time they got married. But she was feeling uneasy about the marriage too. He had told too many lies, and it was hard to put it out of her mind. She also knew how unusual it was for a publisher to sue an author, and not handle it behind closed doors. They had to be truly furious with him to have it go that far.

Finn was in a black mood the next day when he took her to the airport, and for the first time since she had met him, she was relieved when the plane took off. She put her head back against the seat and spent the rest of the flight trying to figure out what was happening. She was feeling confused.

Most of the time, he was the most lovable man she had ever known. But then there had been his viciousness when she lost the baby, his anger, and blaming her unfairly. His obsession with getting her pregnant again, his sudden willingness to spend her money, the lie he had told her about owning the house, the one about bringing up Michael, and now this huge mess he was in with his publisher that he hadn't said a word about. There was a knot in her stomach the size of a fist, and she was relieved to get back to her comfortable apartment and her own life, just for a few weeks. She suddenly needed space and air.

It was too late to call him when the flight got in, and for once she was relieved about that too. Their exchanges seemed dishonest to her, because there was so much he wasn't saying, and that she couldn't say, because he had no idea what she knew. The dream was turning into a nightmare, and she needed to sort it out before it irreparably destroyed what they had.

She had given herself two days to get organized before she had to do the first shoot, and she went to see Mark Webber the next day. He was surprised to see her in his office. She never dropped in without calling first, and he could see she was upset. He led her into his private office and closed the door behind him. She sat down across the desk from him, and looked at him with worried eyes.

"What's up?" Mark always cut to the chase, and

so did she. She didn't beat around the bush. And she was way too worried to do so now.

"Finn never told me about the lawsuit with his publisher, or the canceled contract. In fact, he told me he just signed one, which is apparently bullshit. I think he's embarrassed to tell me, but it makes me nervous when people do that." Listening to her made Mark nervous too. He had always been uneasy about Finn. He had only met him once or twice. He thought he was very charming, and a little slick. "I've never done this in my life," Hope said, looking apologetic. "But is there some way we could get some kind of investigation, to tell us everything, past, present, whatever? Some of it is none of my business, but at least I'd know what's true and what isn't. Maybe there are other things he's not telling me. I just want to know." Mark nodded, and he was relieved to hear her say it. He had always meant to suggest it to her, ever since she said she was in love with him and planning to get married. Mark thought an investigation was a good idea in some circumstances, and in her case essential.

"Look, Hope, you don't need to apologize to me," he reassured her. "You're not being nosy, you're being sensible. You're a very rich woman, and I don't care how nice the guy is, you're a target. And even the nicest guys in the world run after money. Let's just find out what kind of shape he's in, and what he's done with his life."

"He doesn't have any money," Hope said quietly. "Or at least, I don't think so. Maybe he does. I just want to know everything, right from the beginning. I know he grew up in New York and Southampton, and then he moved to London. He has a house there, and he moved to Ireland two years ago. The house we live in was his great-great-grandfather's. And he was married about twenty-one years ago, he has a twenty-year-old son named Michael. His wife died when Michael was seven. That's about all I know. Oh, and his parents were Irish. His father was a doctor." She gave Mark Finn's date of birth. "Do you know someone who could check all this stuff out, so no one ever knows?" It was still embarrassing for her to be prying into the life and history of someone she loved as much as Finn, and wanted to trust. She had in the beginning, but less so now, because of his lies. Finn had an explanation for each one, but she was uneasy about it.

"I know the perfect guy for this. I'll call him myself," Mark said quietly.

"Thank you," she said, looking miserable, and a few minutes later, she left Mark's office, feeling overwhelmed with guilt. She felt terrible for the rest of the day, especially when Finn called and told her how much he loved her and how miserable he was without her. He said he almost wanted to get on a plane and come to New York, but she reminded him gently that she had to work. She was even nicer to him than she would have been normally because she felt so guilty about what Mark was doing on her behalf. But Mark was right, it was smart. And if they didn't find any skeletons in his past, or problems, except the lawsuit, Hope knew she didn't need to worry and could marry Finn in peace. It was getting down to the wire, and they had been talking about getting married on New Year's Eve, less than two months away. She wanted to know before that that everything was fine. And nothing was feeling good to her right now. Her instincts were screaming, and she was feeling sick and stressed.

Hope found it unbelievably hard to work the next day. She was nervous and distracted, and couldn't make a decent connection with her subject, which was unheard of for her. She finally forced herself to concentrate with enormous effort, and she managed to do the shoot, but it wasn't one of her best days. And the rest of the week was pretty much the same. Now that she knew someone was checking on Finn, she wanted to get the information, deal with it, and put it behind her. The suspense was killing her. She wanted everything to be all right.

And that weekend she went to Boston to see Paul, who was in the hospital at Harvard. He had caught a bad respiratory flu on the boat, and they were afraid of pneumonia. The captain of his boat had arranged to have him sent to Boston by air ambulance, which had probably saved him.

Paul was doing better but not great, and he slept through most of Hope's visit. She sat next to him, holding his hand, and now and then he opened his eyes and smiled at her. It was painful to think that he had once been a vital man, brilliant in his field, full of life in every way, and now it had come to this. He looked so old and frail, and had just turned sixty-one. His whole body was shaking. And at one point, he looked at her and shook his head.

"I was right," he whispered, "you wouldn't want to be married to this." As he said it, tears filled her eyes and she kissed his cheek.

"Yes, I would, and you know it. You were stupid to divorce me, and it cost you way too much money," she teased him.

"You'll have the rest pretty soon, except for what Harvard gets." He could barely speak, and she frowned as she listened to him.

"Don't say that. You're going to be fine." He didn't answer, he just shook his head, closed his eyes, and went to sleep. She sat with him for hours, and flew back to New York that night. She had never felt so lonely in her life, except when Mimi died, and then she had had him. Now she had no one, except Finn. She tried to talk to him about it on the telephone the next day.

"It was so sad seeing him that way," she said as her voice trembled, and tears rolled down her cheeks, which she wiped away. "He's so sick."

"Are you still in love with him?" Finn asked coldly, and Hope just closed her eyes at the other end of the phone.

"How can you say that?" she asked him. "For chrissake, Finn. I was married to him for twenty years. He's the only family I have. And I'm all he has."

"You have me," Finn answered. Everything was about him.

"That's different," she tried to explain to him. "I love you, but Paul and I share history, and a child, even if she's not here anymore."

"Neither is ours, thanks to you." It was a cruel thing to say, but he was jealous of Paul, and wanted to hurt her in whatever way he could. It was a side of Finn that she deplored. And telling her that the miscarriage was entirely her fault didn't make it true. It just made him seem mean. It wasn't a part of him she loved, although there were many other parts that she did. He was wonderful to her in many ways.

"I have to go to work," she said, cutting him off. She didn't want to get into discussing the miscarriage with him again, or his jealousy of Paul, particularly now. If he was going to be foolish about that, it was his problem, not hers. It was very disappointing to hear him talk to her that way.

"If I were that sick, would you be there for me?" He sounded like a child as he asked.

"Of course," she answered, sounding bleak. Sometimes his bottomless pit of need was impossible to fill. She felt that way right now.

"How can I be sure?"

"I just would. I'll call you tonight," she said, glancing at her watch. She had to be uptown in half an hour.

When she got there, it was another long, hard day. She was in a terrible mood. Finn seemed to be upsetting her constantly all of a sudden. He was unhappy that she was away, and said his writing wasn't going well. And Hope was waiting to hear from the investigator Mark had hired, and nervous about what he was going to say. She hoped that everything would be okay. It didn't make up for the fact that Finn was lying to her about his current publishing situation, but at least if everything else was in order, she could tell herself that he was reacting badly to a difficult situation. That would be forgivable at least.

She didn't hear from Mark until the end of the week. The investigator had been told to send the information through him. Mark called Hope on Friday afternoon. He asked her if she could come to his office, he said he had some files and photographs to share with her. He didn't sound particularly happy, and Hope didn't ask him any questions until she got to his office. She was nervous all the way uptown. Mark's face gave nothing away until they sat down. And then he opened the file sitting on his desk, and handed a small ragged photograph to her. His face was grim.

"Who's that?" Hope asked him as she stared at it. It was a photograph of four little boys, and the photograph was yellowed and tattered.

"It's Finn." When she turned it over, she saw that there were four names on the back. Finn, Joey, Paul, and Steve. "I'm not sure which one he is." All four were wearing cowboy hats, and they looked very close in age. "It's him with his three brothers." As Mark said it, Hope shook her head.

"Someone made a mistake. He's an only child. It must be a different O'Neill. It's a pretty common name." That much she knew was true. Mark just stared at her, and then read down the page. "Finn was the youngest of the four boys. Joey went to federal prison and is still there for hijacking a plane to Cuba a hell of a long time ago. Before that, he was on parole for bank robbery. Nice kid. Steve was killed by a hit-and-run driver when he was fourteen, somewhere on the Lower East Side where they lived. Paul is a cop, in the narcotics division. He's the oldest. He gave the investigator this photograph. We promised to get it back to him. Their father died in a bar fight when Finn was three. He was a jack-of-all-trades. The mother, according to Paul, was a maid for some fancy people on Park Avenue, and she and the four boys lived in a one-bedroom walk-up apartment in a tenement on the Lower East Side. The boys slept in the bedroom, she slept on the couch in the living room. I think her name was Lizzie. She died of pancreatic cancer about thirty years ago, when the kids were still young. Apparently, they went to hell in a handbasket. Pretty shortly thereafter, Finn and one of the others were in foster care, and Finn ran away.

"He worked as a longshoreman when he was about seventeen, after their mother died, but his brother says he was always the smart one and told a hell of a good story. He's been doing just that ever since, and making a nice living at it, until recently." Mark looked at the file in front of him with blatant disapproval as Hope listened in painful silence. He hated doing this to her, but she had wanted the information, and now she had it. Just about nothing Finn had told her about his early life was true. Yet again, he had been ashamed to tell the truth, in this case about his humble and rocky beginnings compared to hers. She felt deeply sorry for him and what Mark had described of Finn's youth. "His brother says he did manage to go to City College, and after that he never saw any of them again.

"Their mother named him after some Irish poet, which I suppose was prophetic. He says she was kind of a dreamer, and always told them fairy tales before they went to sleep, and then drank herself into oblivion on the couch. She never remarried, and it sounds like she had a pretty miserable life and so did they, you have to feel sorry for them." He handed her a photograph of Finn then when he was about fourteen. He was a handsome boy, and it was clearly Finn. He didn't look that much different now, and the face was the same. "There was no money. Eventually, their mother lost her job and she was on welfare, until Paul could help her on his policeman's salary. But that couldn't have been easy, since he was already married and had kids himself.

"Their mother died in the charity ward of a welfare hospital. They never had a dime. There was no apartment on Park Avenue, no house in Southampton. No father who was a doctor. Their grandparents came from Ireland, via Ellis Island, and if there is any ancestral tie to the house you're living in in Ireland, Paul O'Neill knows nothing about it, and strongly doubts it. He said their grandparents and great-grandparents were potato farmers who came to this country during the Great Famine, like a lot of other people, but they would never have owned a house like yours. After Finn was a longshoreman, he seems to have done a lot of things, waiter, chauffeur, doorman, barker at a strip joint. He drove a truck and delivered papers, and I guess he started writing fairly young and sold some stories. After college, his brother doesn't know a lot about what happened to him. He thinks he got some girl pregnant and got married, but he doesn't know who she was and he never saw the kid. He hasn't been in touch with him for years.

"And according to the investigator, Finn is in deep shit financially. He's in debt up to his ears, he's had a number of bad debts, and his credit rating is a disaster. He declared bankruptcy, which is probably why he eventually went to Ireland. He doesn't seem to be able to hang on to money, although he's made a fair amount with his writing in recent years. But now his publishers are pissed at him, so that's gone up in smoke too. It sounds like the best thing that ever happened to him was walking into you a year ago. And let me tell you, this is going to be one hell of a lucky sonofabitch if he marries you. But I don't think I'd say the same for you.

"There's nothing wrong with his background, or with having been born poor. A lot of people have come up from situations like that and made something of themselves. That's what this country is all about. And you have to admire the guy for crawling out of a pit like that. His credit is a mess, but that's not the end of the world, if you want to help him with it. What I don't like," Mark said, looking over the file at her, "is that he lied to you about damn near everything. Maybe he's ashamed of where he comes from, which is sad for him. But marrying a woman and claiming you're someone and something you're not doesn't show much integrity on his part, and it's none of my business, if you love the guy, but I don't like the smell of it for you. The guy is a first-class liar. He's invented a whole history for himself, including aristocratic ancestors, titles, doctors, and an entire world of people who don't exist. Or maybe they do, but if they do, or did, none of them are related to him, which frightens me."

He handed Hope the file without further comment, and she glanced through a neatly typed, fully documented report by the private investigator. Mark told her they were searching further, and promised additional information on his background in the next two weeks. But they seemed to have been very thorough so far, and as Hope looked back at Mark, she felt sick. Not because what she had heard was terrible, or unacceptable, but what she knew now was that Finn had lied to her about every fact and detail. It made her heart ache to think about it. He had had a miserable childhood in a walk-up tenement apartment, with a drunken mother, a father who had died in a bar fight, and he had wound up in foster care, which must have been nightmarish for him too. And instead of trusting her and sharing it with her, he had invented a mother who was allegedly a spoiled Irish aristocratic beauty and a father who was a Park Avenue doctor. It was no wonder he clung to her like a lost child every time she walked two steps away from him. After a childhood like that, who wouldn't? But the problem was that he had lied to her about so many things. It made her wonder what else he had lied about, and what secrets he was keeping from her. He hadn't even told her that his publisher had fired him and was suing him. So he was continuing to lie to her right up to today. There were tears brimming in her eyes as she looked at Mark across the desk.

"What are you going to do?" Mark asked her gently. He felt sorry for her. After a man like Paul, she had fallen into the hands of Finn. Mark knew she was in love with him, but his fear for her was that Finn O'Neill might be hiding something worse. And Hope was afraid of that too. She had had eleven glorious, exquisitely happy, fabulous months with him, with the exception of the miscarriage and his reaction to it. But other than that, everything had been loving and great. And now their whole life seemed to be unraveling, and Finn with it. It was extremely depressing.

"I don't know what I'm going to do," she said honestly. "I have to think about it. I'm not sure what this means. I don't know if he's too embarrassed to admit how he grew up and is trying to save face, which isn't admirable, but maybe I could live with. Or if he's a profoundly dishonest person." Mark suspected that that was more likely, and even that he was after her for the money. In Finn's current situation, that seemed easy to believe, and the same thought had crossed Hope's mind too. She wanted to give him the benefit of the doubt, and believe the best of him. She loved him. But she didn't want to be blind and foolish either. She had wanted this information, now she had it, and she had to digest it and come to her own conclusions. And she didn't want to say anything to Finn. She didn't want to hear any more lies from him. It would only make the situation worse, until she figured out what to do.

"They don't have anything yet on Finn's marriage. They know the woman's name, and the dates and circumstances seem to coincide with what you said. So maybe he told the truth about that, and not his childhood. They're doing some more investigating, and verifying her cause of death. You said it was a car accident. The investigator said he'd have that for us by next week, or at worst by Thanksgiving."

"I'll be back in Ireland by then," she said sadly.

"Be careful, Hope," Mark warned her. "Be cautious about what you say to him. There's a possibility that even if you love him, you don't know who and what this man is. He's probably just a very creative liar, which is what makes him such a good writer. But there's always the possibility that he could be something far worse. You never know with people. Don't corner the guy and stick this stuff in his face. Use it for yourself, to make a good decision. But be very, very careful how you handle him. You don't want to wake up a sleeping demon.

For what it's worth, his brother says he's a sociopath. But he's not a shrink. He's just a cop who has a crazy brother. And remarkably, no one has ever blown Finn's cover, not even his brother, which is amazing. Paul O'Neill says Finn would lie about the time of day. It certainly looks like it from all that, although most of it is harmless. It's just sad. Just be very careful you don't help him turn it into something worse. If you embarrass him with this, he could get very nasty with you." He was seriously worried about her, particularly after reading everything he had. His suspicion was that Finn O'Neill was a pretty sick guy, and it was hard to believe, under the circumstances, that he wasn't after her money. And he had her to himself, far away in Ireland, in a big, deserted house in the countryside. Mark Webber didn't like it at all.

"The sad thing is that until now no one's ever been as nice to me. He's the sweetest person on the planet, except for once or twice when he got mad. But generally, he's a kind, loving, lovable guy." And she had believed every word he said.

"And a pathological liar, from the sound of it. If you corner him, even accidentally, he may not be so nice." Hope nodded. She was well aware of it herself, and he had been vicious to her about the miscarriage, which for some reason he took personally, as though she had lost the baby on purpose to hurt him. She wondered if that was what he thought, although it was beginning to occur to her that her having his child would give him a far more powerful claim on her. It was hard to know his motivations anymore, or where the truth lay. "I want you to do something for me, Hope. The law firm we use at the agency has a Dublin office." He smiled then. "Every writer who wants to stop paying income tax moves to Ireland, so about a dozen years ago, the firm opened an office there.

"I checked with them this morning. The man running the Dublin office now worked with us for several years in New York, and he's a good solid man, and an excellent attorney. I got his phone number this morning, and his cell phone, and they're going to contact him and give him your name. He may even have done some work for you while he was here. He's American and his name is Robert Bartlett. If you have any kind of problem, I want you to call this guy. And you can always call me. But I'm a lot farther away. He could drive down from Dublin anytime you want to see him." As soon as he said it, Hope shook her head.

"Finn would have a fit, and he'd be suspicious. He's jealous of everyone, and if this guy is under a hundred, Finn would go insane." Mark wasn't reassured by what she was saying, but handed her his numbers anyway from the notepad on his desk.

"I think he's somewhere in his forties, if it matters. In other words, he's not a kid, nor some doddering old guy. He's a nice, sensible, grown-up, savvy, respectable guy. And you never know, you may need his help one day." Hope nodded, hoping that she wouldn't, and tucked his numbers into the inside pocket in her purse.

It hadn't been a happy meeting and Mark was sad to see her leave, particularly in these conditions. She was in the middle of a messy situation, with a man who was a loose cannon, dishonest at best, and she had some difficult decisions to make. He didn't sound dangerous to Mark, from everything Hope had said, but it wasn't going to be pleasant for her dealing with it. He hated knowing she was so far away.

"I'll be okay," she reassured him, and then thought of something before she left. "Be careful if you call me. I'm going to leave this file in a locked drawer in my apartment. I don't want Finn to find it. And please don't refer to it if you call."

"Of course not," he said, looking equally unhappy.

Hope cried all the way back to her apartment in the taxi. Her heart was breaking over Finn's many lies. She felt sorry for the awful childhood he had endured. But his lying was so extreme. She had no idea what she was going to do.

Chapter 16

Hope spoke to Mark again before she left. The investigators had no further information for the moment, and she had finished all her assignments in New York. She'd been checking on Paul by phone daily at the hospital in Boston. He was about the same, and he was asleep every time she called. She had spoken to his doctor, and he was concerned but not panicked over Paul's health. Paul was weak, but the situation was what it was. He was sliding slowly downhill. And they promised to call her in Ireland if there was any drastic change in his condition. The doctor knew that if there was, she would come back immediately. He had known them both when they were married, and he had always been sorry about the terrible turns of fate that had befallen them, first with Paul's illness, his forced retirement, their daughter's death, and Paul's decision to divorce.

Hope called Finn before leaving New York, to

tell him she was coming and he was ecstatic. It made her sad to hear how happy he was. After the lies she had just discovered, she felt as though the bottom was falling out of their world. She hoped that they could get it on track again, and put it behind them. She wanted to find a way to reassure him that he didn't need to lie about his childhood, or his life, or even problems with his publisher. None of those things would make her think less of him, but lying did. And it unnerved her. She no longer knew what to believe or trust. She wanted to condemn the action, not the man. She still believed that he was a good man. But he still hadn't told her about his current disaster with his contract. It was hard to believe he hadn't said a word about it to her, and that he had taken her out to dinner to celebrate a contract he hadn't signed. She wasn't even angry at him. She was desperately sad. She loved him, and didn't want him to be afraid to tell her the truth.

"It's about goddamn time you came home," he said, grinning broadly, and she noticed that he sounded more than a little drunk. He told her the weather was terrible, and that he had been depressed ever since she left. She wondered if losing his publisher had started him on some kind of downward spin.

"Yeah, me too," she said in a soft voice. It hadn't been a great trip. She hadn't even enjoyed her work this time. She had spent the whole three weeks deeply upset about him. And on the plane, she agonized over what to do about the investigator's report. You couldn't unring a bell. But along with the sound of fear in her head, there was love. And she didn't want to humiliate him by confronting him with the report.

He looked tired when he met her at the airport, and she noticed that he had dark circles under his eyes, as though he hadn't slept. She wasn't even happy to see the house this time. It was freezing cold, and he had forgotten to turn up the heat. And when she went upstairs, she noticed in his office that there weren't more than a dozen pages on his desk to add to his book. He had told her he had written a hundred pages in her absence, and now that she was home she could see that that was a lie too.

"What have you been doing while I was gone?" she asked as he watched her unpack her suitcase. She hung her clothes up and tried not to sound upset when she talked to him. She tried to keep her tone easy and light, but she didn't fool him. He could see that something was wrong the minute she got off the plane.

"What's wrong, Hope?" he asked her quietly, pulling her onto the bed and into his arms.

"Nothing. I've been upset because Paul is so sick." He didn't look happy to hear it, but she didn't know what else to say. She didn't feel prepared or ready to tell him that she now knew that everything he'd told her about his childhood was a lie, and that the ancestral home she'd bought for him really belonged to someone else, and not his family at all. She kept thinking of the tattered photograph of the four little boys in cowboy hats, and she felt desperately sorry for him. He wasn't even an only child as he had said. It was hard to know who he really was, and what it all meant.

"Maybe Paul will get better again," he said, trying to be pleasant, as he slipped a hand under her sweater and fondled her breast. She wondered as he did it if maybe that was all there was. A lot of lies and fantastic sex.

She didn't want to make love to him, but she didn't tell him. She felt as though her world were falling apart, but she tried to pretend to him that nothing had changed. It was so unsettling to know that he had made up so many stories, about his parents, his early life, their house in Southampton, the things he'd done at school, the people he had met. She suspected that he wanted so badly to be accepted and like everyone else. And it probably wounded him to admit that they had been poor, or worse. And trying not to think about any of it, and the things his brother had said about him, she let him slowly peel off her clothes, and in spite of everything that she was thinking, she felt herself become rapidly aroused. If nothing else, he had a magic touch. But even though she loved him, that wasn't enough. She had to be able to trust him as well.

He couldn't get enough of her that night, after three weeks without her. Like a man who had been dying of hunger and thirst, he wanted to make love to her again and again. And afterward, when he finally fell asleep, she rolled over to her side of the bed and cried.

The next morning, over breakfast, he asked her casually when they were getting married. They had been talking about New Year's Eve before she left. He had thought it would be fun to celebrate their anniversary on that night every year. But when he asked about it now, she was vague. With everything she had just learned about him, she needed time to think about it. And she was still waiting to hear the rest. She realized that she didn't want to confront Finn now until she knew it all. Maybe the rest of the story would be different, and closer to the truth as she knew it, from Finn.

"What's that about?" he asked her, suddenly looking anxious. "Did you fall in love with someone else in New York?" It was obvious to him that she didn't want to discuss it, and was no longer willing to make plans and set the date.

"Of course not," she answered his question. "I just feel strange getting married when Paul is so sick." It was the only excuse she could think of, and he didn't like it. It made no sense to him.

"What does that have to do with anything? He's been sick for years." Finn looked annoyed.

"He's gotten a lot worse," she said glumly, shoving the remains of a scrambled egg around her plate.

"You knew he would."

"I just don't feel right having a celebration when he may be dying." She'd had a bad feeling about it when she last saw him, and was afraid she might never see him again. "And besides, no one's coming. That seems so sad. I thought it might be more fun if we do it next summer at the Cape. Our agents could come then, and it would be easier for Michael than coming all the way to Ireland." Finn had told her he wasn't coming for the holidays this year. He was going to Aspen with friends instead.

"Cold feet, Hope? It sounds like you changed your mind." Finn looked hurt.

"Of course not. It just doesn't feel like the right time," she said quietly, staring at her plate.

"We were supposed to get married in October," he reminded her, and they both knew why.

"That's because we were having a baby a month later," she said softly, looking at him.

"And we both know why that didn't happen," he said unkindly. He never missed an opportunity to make her feel bad about it. He had been so incredibly loving to her for the first six months, and now he seemed angry at her a lot of the time. Or maybe he was angry at himself. Nothing seemed to be going right. And he was suddenly putting a lot of pressure on her. Given the lies he had told her, she felt he had no right. But he didn't have even the remotest suspicion that she knew he was lying. Now they were both playing the same game, and Hope hated it, and could hardly look him in the eye.

"I assume you got your period in New York," he asked as she put their dishes in the sink for Katherine to wash later. Hope nodded in answer, and for a moment he didn't comment, but when she turned around to look at him he was smiling. "That means you should be ovulating right about now." When he said it, Hope almost burst into tears. She sat down at the kitchen table and put her head down on her arms.

"Why are you pressuring me about that now?" she asked in a muffled voice with her head down, and then she looked up at him in anguish. "What difference does it make?" As she asked the question, she knew that whatever he answered would be a lie. She could no longer conceive of him telling her the truth. It ruined everything. Mark was right. Finn was a pathological liar.

"What's happening to you, Hope?" he asked gently as he sat down next to her. "Before, you wanted our baby, you couldn't wait for us to get married." She wanted to say that that was before she knew he was a liar.

"I just want a little time to sort it all out. I lost our last baby five months ago. And I don't want to get married while my ex-husband may be dying."

"Those are bullshit excuses and you know it."

Looking at him, she knew she had to tell him the truth. Or part of it at least. "Sometimes I think you don't level with me, Finn. I heard some publishing gossip when I was in New York. Somebody told me that your publisher is suing you, and they wouldn't renew your contract because you didn't deliver your last two books. What's that all about? It was in **The Wall Street Journal** and **The New York Times.** The only one who didn't know about it was me. Why didn't you tell me? And why did you tell me that you'd signed a new contract?" Her eyes were full of questions as she looked at him, but there were others than just these. This was a start. And he looked furious when she asked him.

"Do you tell me everything about your business, Hope?" he was shouting at her.

"As a matter of fact, I do. I tell you about everything that happens in my life."

"That's because museums want to hang you, galleries are begging to show you. Heads of state want you to shoot their portraits, and every magazine in the world wants to buy your work. What the hell is there for you to be embarrassed about? I hit a dry spell for a while, didn't deliver two fucking books, and the next thing I know those assholes are suing me for almost three million dollars. Do you think I'm proud of that? I'm scared shitless, for chrissake, and why the hell do I have to tell you so you can feel sorry for me, or walk out on me because I'm broke?"

"Is that what you think I'd do?" she asked him, looking at him sadly. "I wouldn't walk out on you because you're broke. But I have a right to know what's going on in your life, especially important stuff like that. I hate it when you lie to me. I don't want to hear a better story, the one you can dream up. All I ever want to hear from you is the truth."

"Why? So you can rub it in my face, about how successful you are, and how much fucking money your husband gave you? Well, good for you, but I don't need to humiliate myself so that you can feel better at my expense." He was speaking to her as though she were the enemy, and justifying every lie he had ever told.

"I'm not trying to feel better," she said miserably. "I just want an honest relationship with you. I need to know that I can believe what you say." She almost said something about what she now knew about his childhood, but she wanted to know the rest of the story from the investigator first. Confronting him on any of his lies was going to rock the boat violently, or maybe even sink it. She wasn't ready to face that yet. But it was hard to know what she did now, and not say it.

"What difference does it make? And I didn't lie to you about the lawsuit, I just didn't tell you about it."

"You told me you signed a new contract, and you didn't. You told me you wrote a hundred pages while I was in New York, and you wrote ten or twelve. Don't lie to me, Finn. I hate it. I love you just the way you are, even if you never sign a new contract and never write another page. But don't tell me things that aren't true. It makes me worry about what other lies you're telling me." She was being as honest with him as she could, without totally blowing him out of the water and telling him about the investigator's report. She didn't want to go there yet.

"Like what?" he challenged her, with his face right up against hers.

"I don't know. You tell me. You seem to be pretty creative about it." He had lied about his son too, and the house which he didn't own and had claimed he did.

"What's that supposed to mean?"

"All it means is that I want to know that the man I'm marrying is an honest man."

"I am," he said belligerently. "Are you calling me a liar?" He was goading her to do it and she was trying very hard not to. It would only make things worse.

"I don't know what or who you are sometimes. Just don't lie to me, Finn. That's all I'm saying. I want to trust you. I don't want to wonder if you're telling me the truth."

"Maybe the truth is none of your fucking business," he said, and stormed out of the kitchen, and a minute later, she heard the front door slam, and saw him run down the front steps, get in his car, and drive away. They were not off to a good start, to say the least, but it had to be said. She could no longer pretend that she believed everything he said, because she didn't. But she found herself thinking of Mark's words too, as she walked around the garden to get some air. It wasn't a good idea to corner Finn in his lies. It would only create situations like the one they'd just been in, and all she wanted was for him to tell the truth, so she could believe him again and they could go on with their life. She hadn't given up hope of that yet, even if Mark Webber had after he read the report. Hope still believed they could turn it around, and she wanted Finn to help her do it. She couldn't do it alone.

She walked up the front steps with a heavy heart, as Finn drove up to the house again, and when he got out of the car, he looked apologetic. He came to walk beside her, and turned her around to look at him.

"I'm sorry, Hope. I was an asshole. I just get ashamed sometimes that I don't do things better than I do. I want everything to come out right, and sometimes it doesn't, so I pretend that everything's fine. I want it to be fine so fucking much, that I guess I lie about it." She was touched that he'd admit it, and it gave her hope that the situation could be fixed. And she felt terrible about his childhood and youth, although he didn't know it. She smiled up at him, and he put his arms around her and kissed her. She was even more moved to see that there were tears in his eyes when he did. He had humbled himself to her, and admitted his mistake. She was praying that it meant he wouldn't do it again. All she wanted was the truth.

"I love you, Finn," she said as they walked into the house hand in hand. "You don't ever have to make things better than they are for me. I love you just the way you are, even when things aren't great. What are you going to do about the lawsuit?"

"Finish the books, if I can. I've had a hell of a time with this last one. I've been stuck for months. And my agent is trying to stall them. They just gave me another three months, but I'm screwed without a new contract. I've run out of money. I don't have a fucking dime. Thank God you bought the house. If I were still renting here on my own, I'd be out on my ass. And my great-great-grandfather's house would be in someone else's hands." He had just told another lie, but it was one she would live with for now. If he wanted to tell stories to dress up his childhood, she could let him do that, to save face. He was too ashamed about his real childhood to tell her the truth about it. Compared to her storybook happy childhood in New

Hampshire, his had been a nightmare. She just didn't want him lying anymore about his present life. And she was sorry to hear how broke he was, although it didn't surprise her. She had suspected as much when he hadn't paid his token rent. She knew he would have paid that if he could. It seemed like all the lies he told were out of shame.

"Well, at least you don't need to worry about the money," she said gently. "I can carry the expenses here." She already was.

"And what am I supposed to do?" he asked, looking unhappy as they took off their coats and hung them up in a closet in the front hall. "Ask you for an allowance, or money for the newspaper every day? I'm fucked without a contract." He sounded bitter about it, as they walked slowly upstairs together, but at least he was no longer angry at her. Things were a little better.

"If you finish the book, they'll give you another contract," she tried to reassure him.

"I'm two books behind, Hope. Not one." At least he was being honest about it now.

"How did that happen?"

He smiled ruefully and shrugged. "Having too much fun before I met you. At least now I have more time. I just don't feel like working. I want to be with you all the time." She knew that, but he had also just had three weeks to work without her, and he hadn't. He really needed to put his life back together. While she had been cleaning up his house, he had been doing nothing except hanging out with her.

"It sounds like you'd better get to work," she said quietly.

"Do you still want to marry me?" he asked, and looked like a boy again as he said it, and she put her arms around his neck and nodded.

"Yes, I do. I just want to make sure that we're both being grown-ups about it and have an honest relationship with each other, Finn. We really need that if we want this to work."

"I know," he said. The steam had gone out of him. He was so wonderful at times, and so unreasonable at others. And he had been mean, blaming Hope for the miscarriage, which made her feel awful every time, and was neither loving nor fair. "What do you say we go to bed and take a nap?" he asked, looking mischievous, and she laughed, and then ran up the stairs behind him, and a moment later, he locked their bedroom door, swept her up in his arms like a child, and tossed her into bed, where he followed her a moment later. He got no work done that afternoon, but they both had a great time, and the rift between them seemed to have been repaired. He wasn't always truthful with her, but he was full of charm, and sexy beyond belief.

The following afternoon Finn drove her into Dublin to buy some more fabric and other things she needed for the house. She felt guilty taking him away from his work, but she still wasn't comfortable driving in Ireland, and Winfred was a terrible driver, so Finn volunteered. The atmosphere between them was light and happy again, and they were both in good spirits. They had gotten everything they wanted in Dublin, and Hope was happy to see that Finn was in a good mood. That wasn't always the case these days, and she had the feeling he was drinking more than he used to. And when she had checked with Katherine, she agreed, but Hope didn't say that to Finn. She knew he had a lot on his mind, particularly with the lawsuit in New York and two books to write.

"You know, I was thinking," he commented, as they headed toward Blessington on the two-lane road that ran through the Irish countryside. It still looked like a postcard to Hope, even on a cold November day. "It would make things a lot easier for me, and be less embarrassing for me, if we set up some kind of account that I could draw from, without having to ask you." She looked startled as he said it, although it made sense. But they weren't married yet, and it was a fairly bold request.

"What kind of account?" she asked cautiously. "How much are we talking about?" She could see his point, particularly in his current state of destitution. She assumed he meant a few thousand dollars for minor expenses. She could live with that, although it felt a little awkward to be discussing it.

But they were almost married. She was still hoping to get him to wait till June now, but she hadn't said that to him again, since he got so upset when she did before.

"I don't know. I was trying to figure it out yesterday. Nothing crazy," he said blithely. "A couple of million maybe. Like five, so I have some cushion and don't have to ask you for every little thing I need." She thought he was joking the way he said it, and she laughed. And then she saw the look on his face and realized that he meant it.

"Five million?" she asked, with a look of disbelief. "Are you kidding? What on earth are you planning to buy? The house only cost one and a half." And she had spent that just to make him happy, to buy a house that, it turned out, had never belonged to his family after all.

"That's the whole point. I don't want to have to ask you for every penny, and then have to explain what I want to spend it on." He sounded as though it made sense to him, and she stared at him incredulously, with a sinking feeling in her stomach.

"Finn, a spending account of five million dollars is insane." She wasn't angry, she was shocked. And he hadn't hesitated to ask her for the money, as though it were a ten or a twenty floating around in her purse.

"With the kind of money you have?" Finn suddenly looked annoyed. "What the fuck is that about? Trying to control me by keeping the purse strings to yourself? Five million bucks is small change to you." He wasn't even being nice about it. It was as though everything between them had changed. Suddenly he wanted money, and he alternated between his old sweetness, and being angry and accusatory a lot of the time. This was not the Finn she had fallen in love with. It was a new one who upset her a lot of the time, and then would suddenly revert back to being loving again. But he did not look loving now. This was the new Finn in full bloom, with his hand up to his elbow in her purse. That was very new, and she didn't like it at all.

"That's a lot of money to anyone, Finn," she said quietly. She was not amused.

"All right, make it four. If I'm going to be your husband, you can't keep me on an allowance."

"No, maybe not. But I'm not going to give you millions either, to blow however you want, or I'll be out of money as fast as you are. I'd rather just pay the bills, the way I do now, and keep a few thousand in a petty cash account for you." It was as far as she was willing to go. She didn't want to buy him, and she was no one's fool. She had learned a lot about handling money since her divorce.

"So you're going to keep me on a leash," he said angrily, narrowly missing a truck on a turn in the road, and his driving was scaring her. The road was wet and it was already dark, he was driving too fast, and he was furious with her.

"I can't believe you're asking me for five million dollars in an account for you," Hope said, feigning a calm she didn't feel.

"I told you, four would be fine," he said through clenched teeth.

"I know you're having money troubles, but I'm not going to do that, Finn." She was offended that he had asked her, and even more so that he was in-sisting. "And when we get married, we'll have to have a prenup." She had mentioned it to her attor-neys in New York several months before. They had already done a rough draft. It was relatively simple and said that what was Finn's was his, and what was hers was hers. For obvious reasons, she didn't want to commingle funds with him. Paul had given her that money, and she was keeping good track of it.

"I had no idea you were cheap," he said bluntly, as he took another sharp turn in the road. It was an incredible thing for him to say to her, given what she had done for him with the house. He seemed to have forgotten very quickly her generosity with him. And she wasn't cheap, she was smart. Espe-cially given his newly discovered talent for telling lies. She was not about to turn her fortune over to him, or even a portion of it. Five million dollars was ten percent of what Paul had given her after twenty years.

They drove the rest of the way home in stony si-lence, and when he came to a sharp stop in front, she got out and walked into the house. She was extremely upset by his request, and he was even more so about her refusal. He walked straight into the pantry and poured himself a stiff drink, and she could already see the effect of it when he came upstairs to their room. She suspected he might even have had a second one by then.

"So what would you think is reasonable?" he asked her as he sat down, and she looked at him with a pained expression. Things were going from bad to worse. First his obsession with her getting pregnant, then the lying, and now he wanted a huge amount of money from her. Day by day he was turning into a different man, and then out of nowhere she'd get a glimpse of the old one, who had been so wonderful to her, and just as quickly he'd disappear again. There was something very surreal and schizophrenic about it, and she remembered his brother referring to him as a sociopath in the investigator's report. She wondered now if maybe he was. She also recalled reading an article about something called "intermittent reinforcement," where people were alternately abusive and loving, and their victims were so confused, they became more determined than ever to work things out. She felt like that now. Her head was spinning. His manipulations were a powerful magnetic force. It was almost as though his mask was slipping more and more and what she was seeing behind it was scaring her to death. She still believed that the good Finn was in there somewhere. But which one was real? The old one or the new one, or both?

"I'm not going to give you any money, Finn," she said calmly, and then she saw that he had brought the bottle of scotch upstairs with him and poured himself another drink.

"You don't think you can get away with that, do you?" he asked, turning nasty. "You're sitting on fifty million bucks from your ex-husband, and I'm supposed to hang around, waiting for small change." She had thought he was making a decent living, which would have solved the problem, but even if he wasn't, she wasn't about to start pouring millions of dollars into his accounts. It wasn't right, and she didn't want to buy a man. She realized too that he had complained about his expenses, sending Michael to college, and she wondered now if he paid for anything for his son, or if Michael's grandparents were paying all his bills, and Finn was paying nothing.

"I'm not trying to get away with anything. I don't want to buy a husband, or confuse things between us. I think what you're asking for is unreasonable, and I'm not going to do it."

"Then maybe you should marry Winfred instead. Maybe what you want is a servant and not a husband. If you're only going to put a few thousand in an account and keep the rest yourself, then you should marry him."

"I'm going to bed," Hope said, looking unhappy. "I'm not going to discuss this with you anymore."

"Did you actually expect to marry me, and not level the playing field a little? What kind of marriage is that?"

"A marriage based on love, not money. And honesty, not lies. Whatever happens after that is a matter of good fortune. But I'm not going to make a deal with you, or have you dictate to me to put five million dollars, or even four, in your petty cash account. That's disgusting, Finn."

"Your sitting on fifty million bucks of your ex-husband's money and keeping it to yourself sounds pretty disgusting to me too. And fucking selfish, if you ask me." It was the first time he had ever said anything even remotely like that to her, and she was shocked beyond belief. And she hadn't appreciated the comment about marrying Winfred either, if she didn't want to pay up. Finn was being rude, and mean. And tipping his hand in a frightening way.

Hope didn't say another word to him. She turned around and walked into their bedroom and went to bed. She didn't hear him come in that night. She had lain there for a long time before she fell asleep, wondering what was happening to her and what Finn was doing or turning into, right before her eyes. But whatever it was, it wasn't good.

In fact, things seemed to be falling apart at a rapid rate and getting worse day by day. It was getting harder and harder to believe that things would work out. She felt as though her heart were breaking as she went to sleep.

Chapter 17

From the day Finn first asked her for money, things went steadily downhill. The tension between them was unbearable, the arguments were constant, his drinking increased noticeably, and the conversation was always the same. He wanted four or five million dollars from her, no questions asked, in cash. And now he was demanding more when they got married. He asked her to go to the fertility doctor too, and this time she flatly refused.

The only thing that was keeping her there was the tender memory of how loving he had been with her before. It was almost as though he had temporarily lost his mind, or was having a nightmare, and she was waiting for him to wake up and become himself again. But so far he hadn't. He just kept getting worse, while she clung to the belief that he would once again become the man she'd fallen in love with. And on some days, she wondered if that man, of the first eleven months, was even real. By Thanksgiving, she was beginning to wonder if he ever had been. Maybe the man she had known and loved was an act Finn had put on to suck her in, and this one was the real one. She no longer had any idea what to think. She felt off balance and confused, and she was miserable all the time. It had been going on for weeks.

On Thanksgiving she made a traditional turkey dinner for them, which was ruined when he started to argue with her halfway through the meal. It was the same horrifying conversation about the money he wanted, and why he felt she should give it to him. She finally got up and left the table without finishing her dinner. Listening to him wheedle, rage, and insult her made her feel sick.

As she lay in bed that night, thinking that maybe she should pack her bags and fly home, Finn suddenly turned to her and became loving again. He didn't mention the money, thanked her for a beautiful dinner, and told her how much he loved her, and was so tender with her and kind to her that she actually made love with him, which they hadn't done in days. And afterward, she felt psychotic, no longer knowing what to believe or what was real.

He woke her in the middle of the night, and started arguing with her again, on the same agonizing subject, until she finally fell asleep. She woke up in the morning and he served her breakfast in bed, and was his old attentive, good-humored, loving self. She felt as though she were losing her mind, or he was. But one of them was crazy, and she was no longer sure who. She was most afraid that it was her, and when she said something about his waking her during the night to argue with her, he insisted that he hadn't, and she felt crazier than ever and wondered if she had dreamed it. She needed to talk to someone, to try and make sense of it, but there was no one to talk to. She had no friends in Ireland, and she didn't want to call Mark and worry him. And she didn't want to call the lawyer he had recommended whom she didn't know. Paul was too sick to talk to. The only person she could talk to was Finn, and he had started telling her that she was acting crazy. She really thought and was afraid that she might be going insane.

The only thing that saved her was that on the Monday after Thanksgiving, Paul's doctor called her. Paul had developed pneumonia, and they were afraid that he might be coming close to the end, and if Hope wanted to see him, she needed to come to Boston as soon as she could. Without saying a word to Finn after the call, she packed a bag, and was ready to leave by the time he came home from the village with a bag of things from the hardware store, and some laundry soap Katherine had asked him to pick up. And he had bought a big bouquet of flowers for Hope, which touched her when she saw them, but only confused her more.

He was startled when he saw her, already dressed
to travel, and zipping closed her bag.

"Where are you going?" He looked panicked,
and she told him about Paul. Hope looked upset
about it, and he put his arms around her and asked
if she wanted him to come. She didn't, but she
didn't want to insult him by saying no.

"I'll be fine. I think it's better if I go alone," she
said sadly. "I think this might be the end." The
doctor had said as much to her on the phone. They
had expected it for years, but it was hard to face
now anyway. But the last thing she wanted was for
Finn to come with her. She needed to get away
from him and try to figure out what was happening to her, and who he was. She was no longer sure.
Finn was either accusing her of something now, or
adoring her, kissing her in their bed at night, or demanding money, waking her out of a sound sleep
to argue with her, and then insisting she had
woken him while she staggered around in exhaus-
tion the next day. She wasn't sure, but she thought
he was playing mind games with her, and some of
it was working, because she felt totally confused.
And Finn looked fine and undisturbed.

He drove her to the airport, and she kissed him
and ran for the plane. And as she took her seat in
first class, all she felt was relief to be away from
him, and burst into tears. She slept for the entire
flight, and woke up in a daze as they landed at Lo-

gan Airport in Boston. She felt as though her life with Finn had become totally surreal.

Paul's doctor was waiting for her when she got to the hospital. She had called him on her way in from the airport. And she was shocked when he took her to see Paul. In the short time since she had seen him, he had wasted away. His eyes were sunken, his cheeks were hollow. He had an oxygen mask on, and she wasn't sure if he recognized her at first, and then he nodded, and closed his eyes peacefully, as though he was relieved that she had come.

She sat with him for the next two days. She never left him. She called Finn once, but explained that she couldn't speak to him from Paul's room, and he said he understood and was very sweet to her, which seemed strange to her again. He was mean to her so often now, and then loving at other times. She almost hated talking to him, because she never knew which one he'd be. And afterward he'd blame her for starting a fight, when she was certain it was him.

She called Mark and let him know she was in Boston. She promised to keep him posted, and then finally on the third day Hope was there, Paul quietly slipped away, and as he did, with tears rolling down her cheeks, Hope whispered to him that she loved him, and asked him to take care of Mimi, and then he was gone. She stood next to him for a long time, holding his hand, and then she quietly left the room, heartbroken that he was gone.

Paul had left explicit instructions. He wanted to be cremated and buried with their daughter in New Hampshire, where Hope's parents were as well. It was all over in two days, and seeing him put to rest next to Mimi had an overwhelming finality for Hope. She had never felt so alone in her life. She had no one left now, except Finn. He had been wonderful to her on the phone, ever since Paul died. But now, whenever Finn was nice to her, she wondered how long it would last. He was a different man.

She drove back to Boston from New Hampshire in a rented car, and then flew to New York, and went to her apartment. She felt as though the world had ended, and she sat there alone for days, calling no one, going nowhere. She hardly ate. She just wanted to think about what had happened, and all Paul had meant to her. It was hard to believe that he was gone.

She met with Paul's lawyers. His boat was being put up for sale. Everything was in order. There was nothing for her to do. And afterward, she went to see Mark at his office. She looked drained.

"I'm so sorry, Hope." He knew how hard this was for her. Paul had been all she had left in the world. His secretary poured her a cup of tea, and they sat and talked for a while. "How are things going in Ireland?" At first, she didn't answer and then she looked at him strangely.

"To be honest, I don't know. I'm confused. Sometimes he's wonderful to me, and then he's awful, and then he's loving to me again. He says I'm going crazy, and I'm not sure if I am or he is. He wakes me up at night and argues with me, and then the next day he tells me that's not what happened. I don't know," she said with tears in her eyes. "I don't know what's going on. He was the best thing that ever happened to me, and now I feel like I'm living in a nightmare, and I'm not even sure whose nightmare it is, his or mine." What she described sounded terrifying to Mark, and he was deeply worried about her.

"I think this guy's a lunatic, Hope. I'm really beginning to think so. I think his brother was right and he's a sociopath. I think you have to get out of there, or maybe not even go back."

"I don't know. I need to think about it while I'm here. When he's nice to me, I feel stupid for being upset about it. And then he starts all over again, and I feel panicked. He's been asking for money." Hearing that upset Mark even more.

"How much money?"

"He wants five million in his own account, as spending money." Mark looked furious at that.

"He's not crazy. He's a shit. He's after your money, Hope." Mark was sure of that now.

"I think he's after my mind," she said softly. "I feel like he's driving me insane."

"That's probably what he wants you to think. I don't think you should go back there again. And if you do, I want you to call that lawyer in Dublin first, so you have someone to rely on close at hand."

"I will," she promised, "but I'm going to stay here for a few days." She was still too upset about Paul to want to go back. And she felt better now in New York. Every day her mind got clearer, and the confusion Finn was spinning around her had less effect. He was calling her often, but a lot of the time, she wasn't answering the phone. And then afterward he'd ask her where she'd been and with whom. She usually told him she'd been asleep. Sometimes she just left her cell phone in the apartment and went out.

Mark called her two days later and sounded grim. This time, he offered to come to the apartment to see her. She invited him to come down, and he showed up half an hour later with his briefcase. The investigator had just delivered his final report, and Mark had brought it to her. Mark handed it to her without a word, and waited while she read it. The report was long and detailed, and Hope was shocked by almost everything she read. Most of it was different from what she had heard from Finn. Some he had never mentioned at all.

The report started where the last one had left

off, after his childhood and youth, early jobs, and
went on to tell about his marriage to Michael's
mother. It said she was a model, with some moder-
ate success, and had married Finn when she was
twenty-one and he was twenty. It said that the couple had had a reputation for a heavy party life, with
both drugs and drinking, that she had gotten pregnant, and they married five months before Michael
was born. The report said that they had been separated several times, both had committed infideli-
ties, but had gone back together, and that they had
gotten into a severe accident on the highway, coming back from a party late one night on Long Island. Finn had been drinking heavily that night,
and was at the wheel. Their car was hit by a truck
at an intersection on the highway. It had been
totaled, and his wife had been severely injured. The
driver of the truck was killed. There had been no
witnesses on the scene, and eventually a car driving
by had called the state police from a pay phone just
down the road, and asked for emergency assistance. When the highway patrol arrived, they had
found Finn conscious and uninjured, inebriated
but not extremely, and he had been unable to explain why he had not gone to the pay phone to call
for help himself. To do him justice, the report said
he was in shock and disoriented after a blow to the
head, and he had said he hadn't wanted to leave his
injured wife to walk down the road to the phone.
The accident had occurred half an hour before the

other car drove by, and medical examiners had concluded that if help had been called sooner, Finn's passenger, his wife, would have lived. He had made no effort whatsoever to save her life.

Investigations afterward had determined that their marriage was in trouble, and Finn had asked her for a divorce, which she had refused. There was some question as to whether he had caused the accident, but whether he had or not, he had let her die. Charges had been formally brought against Finn, he was given a five-year suspended sentence and five years probation and had his license revoked for manslaughter for the death of the truck driver. His late wife's death was deemed an accident.

The investigator had contacted the family of Finn's late wife, in California, who were still bitter about it and said that they believed Finn had intentionally killed their daughter, in the hope of inheriting some money. Her father was a wealthy stockbroker in San Francisco, and he and his wife had brought up their daughter's child, who was seven at the time of his mother's death. They said that Finn had flatly refused custody of the child. They had told the investigator that Finn had seen his son twice in the ensuing years before he left for college, and they believed he had seen him a few times since, but had no real role in their grandson's life. They considered him a poor influence on the boy and a dangerous man. He had attempted to extort money from them after their daughter's death, threatening to expose her use of alcohol and drugs and immoral, promiscuous lifestyle. They had reported his extortion attempts to the police, but never brought formal charges against him. They just wanted him out of their and their grandson's life.

They were aware of his literary success in the years since their daughter's death, but nonetheless considered him responsible for her death, and said he was a man without a conscience, who was after money and cared for no one but himself. They said he had claimed to love their daughter in the beginning, and was charming. And he had cried copiously at her funeral. A doctor's report attached said that in his opinion, she would have died anyway, with or without help. Her injuries were too extreme, and she was brain dead.

It was chilling to read the report, and Hope looked up at Mark without comment. His wife's death had in fact been an accident. But he had done nothing to help her. There were several more pages about women he had gone out with. There was also a separate sheet that documented that he had eventually gone after his wife's estate, and sued her parents for support, although they were supporting his child. All his efforts to get money from them, legal and otherwise, for himself had failed. It was certainly wrong of him, but it didn't make him a murderer either. Just a crook or a man desperate for money. He had also attempted to invade monies that had gone to the boy directly from his mother, and her parents were able to stop Finn's attempts to get money from his son as well. Hope couldn't help wondering if Michael knew about that. He knew his father was a liar. But Finn was infinitely worse. He was totally amoral.

Among the women Finn had gone out with were several wealthy women, some of whom he had lived with for a short time, and it was generally believed that they had given him money and gifts. His finances had always been shaky throughout the years, despite his literary success, and his appetite for money was apparently voracious. There was an additional page about his publisher's current lawsuit against him, and a list of other lawsuits that had been filed against him, usually without success. There was one in particular, by a woman he had lived with, who had brought charges of mental cruelty, but she had lost the suit. All together it painted a picture of a man who exploited women, and all the subjects interviewed said he was a pathological liar. Two of them said he was a sociopath, and an unnamed source at his publisher said they considered him unreliable, untrustworthy, unethical, and incapable of following rules of any kind. All of the subjects, including his ex-parents-in-law, said he was charming, but many considered him an unscrupulous, dangerous man, entirely motivated by greed, and who would stop at nothing to get what he wanted. There were no kind words about him in the report, except that he was charming, and was always loving and kind in the beginning, and heartless and cruel in the end. It was what Hope was discovering as well and hoped wasn't true. The report made it hard to deny.

Hope sat back on the couch and looked at Mark after she read it. And added to it, but not in the report, was the girl who Finn had told her himself had committed suicide because of him. So indirectly, he had caused two deaths. And Hope suddenly remembered his question to her when she had found the photograph of Audra, when he asked her if she would ever commit suicide herself, almost as though it would have been a compliment to him. The question had a whole new meaning now. She was surprised to find that she was shaking as she thought about it all and tried to absorb what she'd just read. It was horrifying to think that all those frightening stories and details of his life had slipped through the cracks over the years and become obscured. The investigator had worked hard to unearth them.

"Not pretty, is it?" Mark commented, looking worried.

"No, it isn't," she said sadly. He was charming, as they said, and extremely loving in the beginning, but almost every one of them considered him a dangerous man. "Now what do I do?" she said almost to herself, staring out the window into space, thinking about Finn, wanting with all her heart for him to be who he had been at first.

"I don't think you should go back," Mark said wisely, and she thought about it for a long moment, and how confused she had been when she left. She wondered if he was trying to drive her to suicide, but he wanted the five million dollars first. And if she married him, he would have more. If he had a child with her, he could pump her estate forever, and the child, or her.

"I think I need to go back and sort it out. In my own head at least." He was two people. The one she had fallen in love with and the one in the report. She couldn't help wondering if his late wife's parents blamed him because they couldn't accept their daughter's death, and it was easier to blame him. She wanted to believe that, and was wrestling with herself. She tried to give him the benefit of the doubt, but it was hard to do in light of the report. "We were supposed to get married and for my own sake, I need to find out what is real."

"What if he kills you?" Mark said tersely.

"He won't. He didn't kill his wife. It was an accident. The police report, and the coroner both said so. I think what he wants is to get as much money out of me as he can." That was ugly too, and she still wanted to believe he loved her. "I'll call your lawyer in Dublin before I go back, so I have a contact person close at hand." She felt so alone in Ireland now, and could no longer trust or count on Finn. Whoever and whatever he was, there was a part of him that was evil. Strangely after what she had just read, Hope wasn't afraid of him. She knew that part of him was good too. She still believed that. She also knew she wasn't crazy but there was a possibility that Finn was. It was why he wrote the books he did, all those dark characters lived in his head, and were different sides of him, the ones that didn't show. "I'll be all right. I need to see this through and sort it out," she reassured Mark, handed him back the report, and thanked him. "I'll call you before I leave." She wanted to be alone, to mourn the man she loved, who possibly didn't exist, and never had.

The silence in her apartment was deafening after Mark left. All she could think of now were those wonderful months she had shared with Finn, how completely she had believed and loved him, how real it seemed. Tears rolled down her cheeks, knowing there was a strong possibility now that every moment of it had been a lie. It was hard to believe and harder still to accept. The dream she had lived with him may never have been more than that. A dream. And suddenly it had turned into a nightmare. She no longer had any idea who Finn was. The good man she fell in love with or the ne'er-do-well in the report? All she knew was that she needed to go back, look him in the eye, and find out.

Chapter 18

Hope waited up until four in the morning to call him, which was nine in the morning in Dublin. She held the slip of paper with his numbers in shaking hands. A receptionist answered, put Hope on hold while she listened to music, and then passed her on to a secretary. Hope explained that she was calling from New York, and it was too late for him to call her back, and then finally Robert Bartlett took the call. His accent was American, and he had a pleasant voice. Mark Webber had emailed him, as had the head of their New York office. Johannsen, Stern and Grodnik was an American law firm, with offices in six American cities, and foreign branches around the world. Robert Bartlett had been the managing partner of the New York office when they asked him to take over the Dublin office, because the senior partner died suddenly of cancer. He had enjoyed being in Dublin for several years and was ready to go back to New York in a few months. He was actually sorry to leave Ireland. The situation there had been perfect for him.

He didn't know the nature of the problem, but he knew who Hope was, and that she was an important client of the firm. He was well aware of the hour in New York, and although he didn't know her, he could hear a note of tension in her voice when she introduced herself.

"I know who you are, Ms. Dunne," he said reassuringly as she started to explain. "How can I help you? It's very late in New York," he commented. He sounded easygoing and calm, and he had a surprisingly young voice.

"I'm in a bit of a complicated situation of a personal nature," she said slowly. She didn't even know what she wanted from him, or what she would do yet, and it was a little crazy to ask advice from a total stranger. She knew she needed help, or might, but she wasn't sure with what. He wasn't a bodyguard or a psychologist, if she needed either, and she felt a little foolish calling him. But she wanted a contact in Dublin now in case she needed help. She didn't want to go back without some kind of support available to her there. And he was all she had. "I'm not sure what kind of help I need, if any, at this point. My agent, Mark Webber, thought I should call you." And after reading the investigator's report she thought so too, in case any legal complications arose from her relationship with Finn. She hoped things would calm down with him, but they might not. From what she'd read, more likely not.

"Of course. Whatever I can do to help, Ms. Dunne." His voice was intelligent and kind, and he sounded patient. She felt a little silly explaining it to him, as though what she wanted was advice to the lovelorn, and maybe she did. But this wasn't just about being lovelorn, it was about assessing danger and potential risk. It all depended on who Finn really was, what she meant to him, and how desperate or dishonest he was. Money was clearly important to him. But how important? Maybe this time, for him, their love story had been for real, in spite of all the other horrors she had read in the report. Maybe he truly loved her. She wanted to believe that. But it seemed doubtful at this point, and impossible to assess.

"I feel stupid telling you this story. I think I'm in a mess," she said as she leaped in. It was four o'clock in the morning in New York, her apartment was dark, and it was the heart of the night, when everything seems worse, dangers loom, and terrors grow exponentially. In the morning, the ghosts recede again. "I've been involved with someone for the past year. He lives in Ireland, between Blessington and Russborough, and he has a house in London too. He's a well-known author, very successful, though in a professional and financial disaster at the moment. I took photographs of him in London last year, we went out afterward, and he came to see me in New York after that. To be honest, he swept me off my feet. He stayed with me for several weeks, and we've been together almost constantly ever since, staying at each other's houses, in whatever city. I have an apartment in New York and a house on Cape Cod. We've been everywhere together, though I've been mostly in Ireland lately. He has a house there that he told me he owned, and I discovered he didn't. It turned out that he was renting it." Robert Bartlett was making small acknowledging and sympathetic noises as she told the story, and he was making notes as well, to keep it all straight when they discussed it later. "I discovered that he was renting, although he said he owned it," she resumed after a pause. "He said it was his ancestral home, and he had reclaimed it two years before. That was a lie, he said he was embarrassed to admit he didn't own it. Actually, there were three big lies that I discovered at about the same time, after nine months that were absolutely perfect. I'd never been happier in my life, and he was the nicest man I've ever known, but suddenly after nine months, there were these three big lies." She sounded sad as she said it.

"How did you discover them?" Bartlett interjected, intrigued by the story. She sounded like an intelligent woman, didn't sound particularly naïve, and was a businesswoman, so he knew that if she'd fallen for the lies, the perpetrator was undoubtedly good, smooth, and convincing. Originally, apparently, she'd had no reason to doubt him.

"The lies just kind of popped out of nowhere. He said he was widowed, and had brought up his son alone. His son came to visit us in Ireland, and told me that he didn't grow up with his father, as Finn had told me. His name is Finn, by the way." Bartlett knew who he was on the literary scene, most people did, and he didn't comment. He was certainly an author of major fame, and of equal stature to her in her field. She hadn't picked up some homeless guy off the street. She didn't sound like the type for that. So it seemed like a fair match, on the surface, even if it wasn't, and had probably seemed that way to her too. So it made sense in the beginning. "Anyway, his son told me that he grew up with his maternal grandparents in California and hardly knew his father while growing up, and doesn't see him much now. That's not at all what his father told me. I asked him about it, and Finn said he was embarrassed to admit that he hadn't brought up his son. He has never admitted that he scarcely knew him. He also told me that he and his wife weren't getting along when she died, and they probably would have divorced eventually. She died when their son was seven. But I'll tell you about that later.

"A few months before that, I had found out about the house being rented. He still claimed it was his ancestral home, which I believed, on his mother's side, which it turns out is bullshit. Sorry," she sounded embarrassed, and he smiled.

"No problem. I've heard the word. Never used it myself, of course, but I get the drift." They both laughed, and she liked him. He sounded sympathetic and was listening closely to all she said, despite the fact that it sounded crazy, even to her. "He said he was ashamed of that too, that he was renting. And we were planning to get married by then, so I bought the house last April." She felt a little stupid admitting it to him now.

"As a gift? Did you put it in his name?" It was not a criticism or a reproach, just a question.

"A kind of future gift. It's in my name, but I was going to give it to him as a wedding present when we got married. For now, it's in my name, and I rent it to him for a nominal amount. Two hundred dollars a month, just to keep things clean. I paid a million five for it, and I've put in about the same amount in restoration, and another million in furniture and decoration." Hearing it now, it was a huge amount of money to spend on his house, although technically it was hers, but she had done it all for him. "I drew up papers after we bought it, and it's in my will. In the event of my death, if we are married, it goes to him, free and clear, or in trust to our children, if we have any."

"Does he know that?"

"I can't remember. I think I said it to him once, maybe twice. I told him I would leave it to him. I thought it was his family house then. I discovered a few weeks ago that the house has no relation to him. It was just another lie, among many. But he made a big deal about being embarrassed to have me know he only rented. And I believed his story, hook, line, and sinker."

"To give the devil his due, he sounds pretty good at what he does." So far, he had played on her sympathy every time. He was smooth.

"I also told him what my ex-husband gave me in a settlement in our divorce. I didn't want to keep any secrets. Finn asked me how much, so I told him. It was fifty million dollars, with an equal amount on my ex-husband's death," she said sadly.

"Hopefully not for a long time," he said politely, and there was a pause at her end, while she caught her breath.

"He died this week. He's been very sick for eleven years. That's why he divorced me, he didn't want me to go through that, but I did anyway."

"I'm sorry. But let me get this straight. You have another fifty million coming to you now from your late husband's, sorry, ex-husband's estate. Is that right?"

"Yes." There was a soft whistle at the other end in response and she smiled. "It's a lot. He sold his shares in a company that makes high-tech surgical equipment, and did very well. So Finn knew what I had and what I had coming."

"Has he ever asked you for money?" It didn't

sound like he needed to. He was doing fine anyway, since she'd bought him the house, and promised to pass it on to him, at their marriage or her
death. Either way, he stood to win.

"Only recently," she answered. "He wanted five
million dollars cash, no questions asked. And more
when we get married. He's only asked me for that
in the last month. Before that he never mentioned
money. He's in financial trouble, which was the
third lie that got me worried. He told me he had
just signed a new contract with his publisher, for a
lot of money. We celebrated it, in fact. As it turns
out, he owes them two books, they broke his contract, and are suing him for close to three million
dollars."

"Did he want the money to settle with them, as
a loan of some kind?"

"I don't think so," she said, thinking about it.
"He just wanted it outright and he wanted more
than he's being sued for. Two million more. I don't
know what's going to happen with the lawsuit.
He's trying to stall them, but his name is mud right
now in the business. And he says he has no money,
not a dime. He said he didn't want to ask for an allowance. I suggested some kind of petty cash account, and I pay all the bills anyway, so he has no
expenses. But he wants five million cash in his own
account, with no accounting to me for it. Just a
straight gift, and more when we get married."

"And when was that supposed to be?" He hoped

it was no time soon from the sound of what he was hearing.

"Originally October." She didn't tell him about the baby she'd lost in June. He didn't need to know that, she didn't think it was relevant to the story, and the memory of it still pained her. "We put it off till the end of this month, on New Year's Eve, and I recently told him I wanted to wait till June. He's livid about it."

"I'll bet he is," Robert Bartlett said, sounding worried. He didn't like the story, and just as he was thinking that, it got worse. "He has a lot to gain from marrying you, Ms. Dunne. A house—several houses—money, steady income, respectability. It appears you've been extremely generous with him, and were prepared to be more so, and he has a fairly accurate idea of your financial situation, so he knows what he's gunning for."

"Please call me Hope, and yes, he does," she said quietly, sitting in the dark in her apartment, thinking about it. Finn knew exactly what she had and what he wanted. Maybe all.

"You said you pay the bills right now. Does he make any financial contribution to the household?"

"None."

"Has he ever?"

"Not really. Newspapers, the occasional trip to the hardware store. He usually charges it to me." Nice, very nice. Sweet deal for him, Bartlett thought, but didn't say it. "He was supposed to pay a token rent, but he hasn't. I set up the rent originally to save his pride." Bartlett was convinced by then that Finn had none, just greed. "He's also been very determined that we should have a baby. He was willing to undertake infertility treatments if necessary, for me of course, to make that happen. He took me to a specialist in London."

"And has that happened?" This time Bartlett sounded nervous.

"No . . . well, actually, yes, but I lost it. But he's very anxious to do it again. I wanted to wait, particularly now."

"Please don't do that, Hope. If you have a child, this guy is going to have his hooks into you forever, or the kid. He knows exactly what he's doing."

"Apparently he tried to do that with his late wife's family, and their son when his wife died. I'm not sure the boy knows that. I have a feeling he doesn't."

"Yeah, let's hold off on baby-making right now, if that's okay with you." The more she talked to him, the more she liked him. He sounded like a decent, down-to-earth person. She was using him as a sounding board, she realized, to try and make sense of it herself.

"Fine with me. And another thing was that I found a photograph of a woman he went out with when he was young, a long time ago. He said she killed herself and was pregnant by him. She committed suicide, and he asked me if I would ever do that. I got the creepy feeling that he felt somehow that that was a tribute to him and how much she loved him." He didn't tell Hope that, but listening to her, for the first time, Robert Bartlett was scared. This was beginning to sound dangerous to him, and familiar. Strung all together it was the classic portrait of a sociopath. And she was his ideal victim, she was isolated with him in Ireland, had no family or friends nearby, she was in love with him, she had money, a lot of it, and was entirely at his mercy, and would be much more so if they got married. Robert was very glad Hope had called him. He asked her then if she had children. There was another brief silence at her end. "I had a daughter who died four years ago, of meningitis. She was at Dartmouth."

"I'm so sorry." He sounded like he really meant it, which touched her. "I can't imagine anything worse. My worst nightmare is something like that happening. I have two kids in college. Just their going out at night and driving drives me crazy."

"I know," she said softly.

Robert Bartlett also realized now that she didn't have kids to observe what was happening, be alert, or warn her. Hope was every sociopath's dream, a woman without family or protection, and a hell of a lot of money. And worse yet, he could sense that she loved him, maybe even now. There was a quality of disbelief to what she was telling him, as though she wanted to piece the puzzle together for him, and have him tell her there was nothing to worry about, and it was not what it appeared to be. So far he couldn't do that for her. It sounded pretty bad, and frightening. And there was a seeming innocence to her that alarmed him even more. Just knowing this much, he thought she was in real danger. Finn O'Neill sounded like a con artist of the first order. The suicide of the previous girlfriend concerned him, as did O'Neill's determination to get Hope pregnant. At least it meant he didn't want her dead. Right now, she was more useful to him alive, married, and pregnant. Unless she gave him trouble, or interfered with his plans, which was what she was currently doing. She had postponed the marriage, refused him money, and didn't want to get pregnant again at the moment. All bad news for him. It meant he would have to work harder to convince her, and if he couldn't, she was going to be in serious danger. And the worst thing about sociopaths, Bartlett knew, was that they induced their victims to destroy themselves so they didn't have to do the dirty work, like Finn's old girlfriend. But so far, Hope still sounded sane. He was doubly glad she had called him, and that her agent had given her his number. He had dealt with situations like this before, although Finn seemed like a particularly able pro at the game. He was good.

"So those were the lies I discovered on my own,"

Hope went on. "But the last one made me nervous, the lawsuit and his publishing contract. He told me that time too that he was ashamed to tell me the truth, in contrast to my own success. He always uses that same excuse about being embarrassed so he didn't tell me. The truth is, I think he just lies. Everything was fine between us until last June when I lost the baby. He blamed me for it, and said I wasn't careful enough so I caused the miscarriage. He was pretty nasty, very disappointed, and very angry. And he wanted me to get pregnant again right away. My doctor wanted me to wait, because I almost died." Bartlett winced as he listened. It sounded grim yet again.

"But before all that, he was wonderful to me, and thrilled about the baby. We didn't have fertility treatment by the way, it happened on its own. We knew that I was ovulating, he got me drunk, and we had sex without protection. He knew what he was doing." Bartlett was convinced of that by now, she was preaching to the choir. "And it worked. Anyway, for six months everything was wonderful, and after the miscarriage, it was fine again for the summer. But now, he's angry at me all the time, or most of the time. Sometimes he's absolutely wonderful to me again, and then he gets vicious. He's drinking more than he used to. I think he's pretty stressed about the lawsuit, and he's not writing. And he's really angry that I've been postponing the wedding. All of a sudden, we're fighting all the time, and he's always pushing me about something. He never did that before. It was perfect, he was wonderful to me, and he still is sometimes, but it's bad more than it's good now. And sometimes it changes so often and so suddenly, he goes from bad to good to bad to good again, my head is spinning. By the time I left Dublin a week ago, I was so confused, I didn't know what to think. And he kept telling me I was going crazy. I started to believe him."

"That's what he wants you to believe. I can tell from talking to you, Hope, you're not crazy. But I'm equally sure he is. I'm no psychiatrist, but this guy is a textbook case in sociopathy. This is very scary stuff, particularly trying to brainwash and confuse you. When did he ask you for the money?"

"A few weeks ago. He just came right out and asked for it. I said no, and we've been fighting ever since. It concerned me, so when I came to New York in November to do some work, I had my agent hire someone to do an investigation." She sighed then, and told him what the report contained. "His brother thinks he's a sociopath. Even his saying he was an only child wasn't true, he had three brothers. His mother was a maid, not an aristocrat, his father died in a bar fight and wasn't a doctor. Absolutely nothing he told me about his history is true, which is how I know the house in Ireland isn't his ancestral home. And everybody else who's ever known him says he's a pathological

liar." That much they both knew was true from
what she had told him so far. "The rest of the report came yesterday, and it's no better. His wife
died in an accident. He was driving drunk. He had
told me she was alone in the car and died. The report says that he was with her, she was alive at the
time of the accident. He had a concussion and
didn't call for help and she died. Although to be
fair, the medical report said she would have died
anyway." Even now, she was trying to be kind to
Finn. Robert Bartlett considered it a bad sign. She
was still in love with him, and hadn't fully assimi-
lated the new information she'd gotten. It was too
shocking, and hard for her to accept. "He got a
suspended prison sentence for manslaughter and
five years' probation for killing the other driver,"
she went on. "And there are some other minor upsetting stories. His wife's parents think he was responsible for her death and wanted her money. He
tried to get it, and what she left their son. And now
he's after my money. Indirectly, he has been responsible for the death of two women. His wife's
death in the car accident and the earlier suicide. He
has lied to me about everything. I just don't know
what to believe about him anymore." Her voice
shook on the last words. Robert Bartlett would
have been stunned by what she had just said to
him, except that he had heard it before, and it was
the nature of a sociopath and his victim. The confusing evidence and contradiction between their

calculating viciousness and their extreme attention, kindness, and seduction paralyzed their victims, who wanted to believe that the good parts were true and the bad ones only a mistake. But with more and more evidence, it became harder to believe. He could tell that Hope was at that stage. She was waking up and starting to see Finn for what he was, but, understandably, didn't want to believe it. It was hard to accept all of that about someone you loved, and who had been so loving at one time.

"I don't want you to be his next victim," Robert said in a sobering tone. She already was in many ways, but he was seriously afraid that if she crossed him in some serious way, or became useless to him, Finn might kill her, drive her to suicide, or cause an accident to happen.

"Neither do I. That's why I called you," Hope said in a heartbroken voice.

"You know, what you saw in the beginning, when he was so wonderful to you, is called 'mirroring,' when a sociopath will 'mirror' back to you everything you need and want and want them to be. And then later, much later, the truth of who they are comes out," Robert told her. "What do you think you want to do, Hope?" he asked her then gently. He felt deeply sorry for her, and understood better than most people how hard it was to face this kind of thing and take action.

"I don't know what I want to do," she admitted. "I know that sounds crazy. It was so wonderful for nine months, and suddenly all this awful stuff is happening. No one had ever been as nice to me, or as loving. I just want it to go back to the way it was in the beginning." But she was trying to raise the **Titanic,** and she was beginning to see it. She just didn't want to believe it. Not yet. She wanted Finn to prove all of it wrong. She wished she'd never gotten the report and still believed the dream. She wanted to but didn't. But she felt she had to go back and see for sure. Anyone listening to her would have thought she was insane, except Robert Bartlett. She had been lucky to find him.

"That's not going to happen, Hope," he said gently. "The man you saw in the beginning and fell in love with doesn't exist. The real one is a monster, without a heart or a conscience. I could be wrong, of course, and he could just be a very troubled guy, but I think we both know what we're seeing. That man in the beginning was an act he put on for you. That act is over. This is the third act, where the villain goes in for the kill." It was the theme of everything Finn wrote. "You can go back and take another look to be sure, no one can stop you, but you could be putting yourself at risk. Maybe great risk. If you do go back, you've got to be ready to get out fast, and run like hell if you smell danger. You can't stick around to negotiate with him. I don't usually tell people this, but I've been there. I was married to an Irish girl, the most beautiful woman you've ever seen, and the sweetest. I believed every word she told me, and her story sounds a lot like Finn's. She had a miserable childhood, her parents were both drunks, and she wound up in foster homes where people did awful things to her. She had the face of an angel and the heart of a devil. I defended her on manslaughter charges a few years after I got out of law school. I had absolutely no doubt of her innocence then. She killed her boyfriend and claimed he tried to rape her, and there was evidence to support it. I believed her. I got her off, but today I wouldn't tell you the same thing. Eventually, she left me, took every penny I had, broke my heart, and took our kids with her. I married her right after I defended her.

"Eventually she tried to kill me. She came back during the night and stabbed me, and tried to make it look like an intruder, but I knew it wasn't. I knew it was her. And I still went back to her two more times, trying to make it work, ignoring everything I knew. I loved her, I was addicted to her, and all I wanted to do was save our marriage and keep my kids. She eventually kidnapped them to Ireland seven years ago, and by some miracle they needed someone to head up the Dublin office at the time, so I jumped at it, to be close to my kids. I couldn't force her to come back to the States. She's very clever, and thank God, my kids are okay. The youngest one just left for college in the States two months ago, and I'm going back to the New York office this spring. Nuala has married two men since me, both for money, and one of them died two years ago, from a medication he was violently allergic to, which she administered to him, and convinced the judge at the inquest that she didn't. She inherited all his money. And she's going to do it to the man she's currently married to or some other guy one of these days. She has absolutely no conscience. She belongs in prison, but I don't know if she'll ever get there. She is so profoundly disturbed that she is willing to cross any line and has a deep need to get back at the world for what was done to her. No one is safe from her.

"So I know what you're dealing with here, and I think I know how you feel. It took me years to understand that the good Nuala was only an act she put on for me, but it was so goddamn convincing that I always believed her, no matter what lies she told me or what awful things she did. The kids eventually moved in with me, which didn't bother her. People like that don't make terrific parents. Their children are either accessories to their crimes, or their victims. She doesn't even see my girls now, and I don't think she cares. She's busy spending her late husband's money, the guy she killed by giving him the wrong antibiotic out of the medicine chest. It stopped his heart cold as she knew it would, and she waited an hour to call the paramedics because she 'was so upset' and claimed she was sound asleep and didn't hear him dying.

And they believed her. No one has ever cried as hard as she did at the investigation. She was inconsolable. She married her defense attorney, again, and one of these days, she'll do the same thing to him or someone else. But every man she's ever left, except the dead ones, have mourned her. And so did I.

"It took me years to get over her, give up on her, and not give a damn anymore. Until then, I went back a hundred times for more. So, I get it. If you still need to turn the boat around, no matter what the evidence, no one can stop you. You have what you saw for nine months, and felt for him, and then you have that investigator's report and what everyone who knows him, and has experienced him, said. But if you go back, Hope, be smart. With people like that, when he turns on you, all you have time to do is run. That's the best advice I can give you. If you go back to him for another round, wear your track shoes, listen closely, trust your instincts, and if something happens that worries you or scares the shit out of you, trust yourself and get the hell out. Fast. Don't wait to pack a suitcase." It was the best advice he could have given her, based on his own experience, and she was stunned. It was a terrifying story. But so was Finn's.

"He's all I have now," she said sadly, "and he was so good to me for all those months. Paul was the only family member I had left, and now he's gone, and so's my daughter." She was crying as she spoke.

"That's the way these people work. They prey on the naïve, the innocent, the lonely, the vulnerable, and the solitary. They can't work their voodoo in a group with people watching them. They always isolate their victims, like he has you, and they pick them well. He knew that all you had was your ex-husband, who wasn't around anymore and was very sick. So he got you over to Ireland, where you have no family, no friends, no one to look out for you. You're his ideal victim. Just be aware of it when you come back. When are you coming?" He didn't ask her if but when. He knew she would. He had done the same thing, and he could tell she wasn't ready to let go yet. She needed another dose of Finn to shock her, because the evidence of the good Finn, and the memory of it, was so strong. It was a perfect example of cognitive dissonance, two sets of evidence in direct conflict with each other, all the love they lavished on people at first, and from time to time later, and the brutal, uncon-scionable cruelty when they took off the mask, and then put it back on again, and confused their vic-tims even further, and tried to convince them they were insane. Many sociopaths caused suicides as a result, when perfectly sane victims couldn't figure out what was happening to them, and got pushed over the edge. He didn't want that happening to Hope. His only goal now was to be there for her, keep her alive, and help her get out when she was ready, which he could tell she wasn't yet. He knew only too well that only someone who had been there would understand. And he had been.

Hope was deeply impressed by Robert's story, his willingness to tell it to her, his honesty, and compassion for her dilemma and love for Finn. It was so hard to assimilate the evidence and the extreme contradiction between how he had treated her in the beginning and all she felt for him, and what everyone else said about him, and her own concerns about him now. It was the very definition of confusion and contradiction. And no one could understand it unless they had been in a similar situation themselves, as Robert had. Her willingness to go back and look again was incomprehensible to Mark.

"Thank you for not telling me how stupid I am for going back. I think I keep hoping he'll be the way he was in the beginning."

"We all hope that in matters of the heart. And more than likely, he will be, for a night at a time, or a few hours. He just won't stay that way, because it's all an act, and a way of getting what he wants. But if you get in his way, or don't give it to him, you're going to be in big trouble, and he'll strike like lightning. Hopefully, the worst he'll do is scare the shit out of you. Let's try to keep it at that." That was his only goal now. Hers was still the hope that Finn was what he had seemed, and would straighten up and treat her right. Robert knew there was no chance of that, but Hope had to experience it for herself. Maybe more than once. He hoped not. She was the classic victim of a sociopath. Isolated, confused, incredulous, vulnerable, inordinately hopeful, and not yet ready to believe the evidence at hand. "Why don't you come and see me before you go back? You can stop in at my office on the way back to Russborough when you get to Dublin. I'll give you all my numbers, we can have a cup of coffee, and then you can go back to Jack the Ripper." He was teasing her and she laughed. It was not a pretty picture, and she felt a little foolish, but he was right. "I'd offer to come and see you at the house, but my guess is that that would get you in trouble. Most sociopaths are extremely jealous."

"He is. He's always accusing me of flirting with someone, even waiters in restaurants."

"That's about right. My wife was always accusing me of sleeping with my secretaries, the au pair, women I'd never even met, and eventually she started accusing me of sleeping with guys. I was constantly defending myself and trying to convince her that I wasn't. As it turned out, she was." It was projection at its best.

"I don't think Finn cheats on me," Hope said, sounding certain of it. "But he accuses me of sleeping with just about everyone in the village, including our workmen."

"Try not to get him excited about anything for the moment, if you can help it. I know that's hard.

The accusations are never rational or based on fact, or rarely, unless you give him something to worry about." But she didn't sound like the type. She sounded honest, honorable, and straightforward, and she was feeling much better since their conversation, and no longer crazy. "My guess is that you'll get into it with him over the money. That's bound to be his number-one goal, and the wedding, and maybe a baby." He didn't tell her that most sociopaths were extremely sexual. Nuala had been the best thing in bed that had ever hit him. That was one of the many ways they got control of their victims. In his ex-wife's case, she screwed them blind. So blind they didn't know what hit them, and then she killed them. He had narrowly escaped that fate at her hands. A good therapist and his own common sense had saved him. And even though she was still in love with Finn and her illusion of him, Hope sounded sensible to him too. The truth was very hard to swallow and believe, and the dichotomy too extreme to make sense to a sane person, so she was giving him the benefit of the doubt, which their victims often did. It wasn't stupidity on her part, just hope, naïvete, faith, and love, however undeserved.

As Hope thought about it while talking to him, she decided to fly back the next day, on the night flight she liked to take, which would put her in Dublin the following morning. And she liked the idea of seeing Robert Bartlett before she went back to the house. It would ground her. She made an appointment with him for ten o'clock that morning, after she got through immigration and customs, and came in from the airport.

"That's fine. I'll be clear all morning," he assured her. And then he had another thought. "What do you want to do with that house when this is over, when that happens?" This wasn't a divorce where she owed him a settlement to end it.

"I don't know. I've thought about it, and I can't decide." She still hoped it wouldn't come to that but was well aware now that it might, and had to give it some thought. "I could keep it and keep renting it to him, but I'm not sure I'd want to. It could turn out to be a link to him I don't want. But I feel mean just throwing him out." Robert knew it was all Finn deserved, but Hope clearly wasn't there yet. And she still wished that would never happen, but Robert wanted to bring it up.

"You don't need to worry about it now. Enjoy New York, and I'll see you day after tomorrow." She thanked him again and hung up. It was six-thirty in the morning by the time she finally went to bed, feeling calmer than she had in months. At least now she had a support system in Ireland, and Robert Bartlett clearly knew the subject. It sounded as though what he'd been through with his ex-wife was far worse. She was an extreme example of the breed, but with two women dead because of him, and a lifetime of lies, Finn wasn't much better. Hope could see that. The sad thing was that in spite of all she knew about him now, she still loved him. She had believed everything that he had been to her in the beginning, and it was hard to give up that dream. She was deeply attached to him, particularly now with Paul gone. Finn really was the only person she had left in the world, which would make it that much harder to give him up. It would mean she was entirely alone for the first time in her life.

Finn called her twice that morning as she slept. She stirred and saw his number on her cell phone, turned over, and didn't answer. And when she went back to Ireland, because she would see Robert Bartlett on the way, she wasn't going to tell Finn she was coming, and she would surprise him when she got back to the house. But she wanted a few hours alone with Robert Bartlett in Dublin first.

Chapter 19

As it turned out, it snowed the night Hope left New York, and her plane sat on the runway, delayed, for four hours, waiting for the storm to lessen. They eventually took off, but the winds were against them, and it was a long bumpy flight to Dublin. There were delays getting the bags off the plane, and instead of arriving at Robert Bartlett's office at ten in the morning, she arrived at two-thirty in the afternoon, tired and disheveled, dragging her finally retrieved suitcase behind her.

"I'm so sorry!" she apologized as he came out to greet her. He was a tall, slim, distinguished-looking man with graying sandy-blond hair, green eyes, and a cleft in his chin that was more noticeable when he smiled, which he did often. He had a friendly face, and a warm demeanor. He made tea for her while she settled into one of the comfortable chairs in his office. The law firm was in a small historical building in Southeast Dublin, on Merrion Square, near Trinity College. There were lovely Georgian houses and a large park. The floors of his office were crooked, the windows were off center, and the general atmosphere was one of cozy disorder. It was a far cry from their fancy, sterile New York office. Robert liked this much better, and was almost sorry he was going back. And after seven years in Dublin he was very much at home there, and so were his children. But he wanted to be closer to his children, both of whom were in college now at Ivy League schools on the East Coast, although he said that one of them wanted to come back to Ireland after college.

He and Hope talked for hours about the vagaries of Finn, the lies he had told, and her hope that somehow, magically, things would get better. Robert knew not to argue with her, but he kept reminding her of the evidence she did have, and the unlikelihood that Finn would mend his ways now, even if he loved her. Robert knew it was a slow process giving up the dream, and all he hoped was that Finn didn't do something really terrifying to her in the meantime. He reminded her again and again to trust her instincts, and get out if she felt she should. He couldn't say that to her often enough, and wanted to impress her with it. It was essential, and she promised him that she wouldn't stay if she was uncomfortable, but she didn't think Finn would harm her physically. His style these days seemed to be more psychological torture. And she hadn't told him yet that she was coming back, and surely not that she was spending the day in Dublin with an attorney before she did.

By the time they had finished talking, it was five o'clock and Robert told her that he wasn't comfortable with the idea of her going back to Blaxton House in the evening. She had to rent a car, which would take time, and then get there, and she had already said how uncomfortable she was driving in Ireland, particularly at night. Worse than that, she might arrive when Finn was in a black mood or drinking. Winfred and Katherine would have gone back to the village for the night. He just didn't think it was smart. He suggested she stay at a hotel in Dublin that night, and go back in broad daylight the next morning. And as she thought about it, she agreed with him. She was anxious to see Finn, although nervous about it, but getting there late in the evening could mean putting her head in the lion's mouth if he'd been drinking. It just wasn't smart, and she agreed.

Robert suggested a hotel she knew, and his secretary made a reservation for her. It was the best hotel in Dublin. And since he was leaving the office, he offered to drop her off with her suitcase, which she gratefully accepted. It had been a pleasant afternoon talking to him, although the subject was difficult. What was happening in her life was so disappointing and painful. As hard as it was to justify or explain, she was still in love with Finn, the one she had known in the beginning, not the man he was now. It was hard to believe and absorb all the terrible things she'd heard about him, yet she had doubts about him herself. But when she had asked for the investigation, she hadn't expected to get the kind of information she did. Now she had to decide what to do about it. But sadly, it didn't change how attached she was to him, which only made the distressing discoveries hurt more. It seemed like a huge problem. Robert had said to her that afternoon that ultimately the situation would take care of itself. It was the kind of thing her teacher in India would have said, or her favorite monk in Tibet. And for the rest of the way to the hotel, she talked about her travels. Robert was impressed, and they had a very agreeable conversation.

The doorman took her bag when they reached the hotel, and Robert turned to her with a kind expression. He knew this was a hard time for her, and she was anxious about seeing Finn the next morning. She had no idea what to expect, or what kind of mood he'd be in. There was no way to know if she'd be meeting the good Finn or the bad Finn, the old Finn or the new Finn, and she had admitted to Robert that she was feeling very stressed about it, particularly after his many warnings about what potentially lay ahead.

"Would you like to go out for an easy dinner

tonight? Pizza? The pub? There's a halfway decent Chinese place not far from here. And a really good Indian one, if you like hot food. I've got a court appearance tomorrow, and I know you want to get on the road early, so if you want to grab a bite, I could pick you up in an hour. I only live a few blocks from here." She actually liked the idea. He was a nice person, and she was feeling jangled by everything she had in her head. She didn't really want to eat alone in her room, or go out on her own in Dublin, it seemed too depressing, and it would be friendlier dining with him. He was just an ordinary decent man, but a smart one, and Mark had said he was an excellent attorney. She appreciated his advice so far, a lot of which wasn't legal, but even more useful to her, given the situation she was in.

"I'd love that," Hope said gratefully, looking tired and worn out.

"Terrific. Put on a pair of jeans, and I'll pick you up in an hour."

She checked into her room, which was small, elegant, and clean. She didn't need anything fancy, and she lay down on the bed for a few minutes, before taking a shower, putting on jeans, and brushing her hair. He was back in exactly an hour, as promised. And as she looked at Robert as they drove to the restaurant in his car, it was hard to imagine him in the clutches of the evil Nuala, or even besotted with her. He looked like an even-tempered, sensible person. He had worn jeans that night too, with a sweater and a pea coat, and he looked younger than he had in a suit. She guessed him to be about Finn's age, and close to hers. He said he was originally from California. San Francisco. And had gone to Stanford, followed by Yale Law School. She told him about her father teaching at Dartmouth, and he laughed and said he loved beating them when he played football for Stanford. He said Dartmouth had a great team. He had played amateur ice hockey too, at Yale, and still looked fit and healthy, although he claimed he wasn't. But he said he loved to go skating with his girls, both of whom were on sports teams in college. He was looking forward to seeing them for Christmas. They were all meeting in New York for the holidays, staying at the Pierre, and he was planning to start looking for an apartment, since he was moving back in March or April.

Hope had no idea where she'd be by then. Either back in New York, heartbroken, or still in Ireland, things having settled down with Finn, maybe even married. She sounded hopeful, and Robert nodded and didn't comment. He had said enough on the phone and that afternoon. Hope had all the information she needed, and he hoped that when she was ready, she'd use it. It was all he could do. There was nothing for him to do for her legally at the moment, except be available to her. She now had his office, home, and cell phone numbers written down on a piece of paper in her bag. And he told her to use them, and not be shy if she needed advice or help at any hour. That's what he was there for, and he was happy to help.

The curry was delicious and they talked about her travels again. He was fascinated by her stories, and her work, and said he had never been anywhere exotic. Just Europe and Scandinavia, mostly on business. He looked like a typical Ivy League suburban husband, with an extra dose of kindness in his eyes.

They finished dinner early and he took her back to the hotel, and wished her luck for the next day, and a good rest that night.

"Remember, you're not alone now. I'm an hour away at any time. If you get in real trouble, call me, and I can get help to you in minutes. Or call the police. Or just get out." She smiled at what he said, it was like preparing for a war, and she didn't think that Finn would ever be violent with her, or dangerous. He would be upsetting, and argue with her, or drink too much and then pass out, but it wouldn't get worse than that. She knew him well and reassured Robert. His wife had been an exceptional case.

Much to her surprise, Hope slept extremely well that night. She felt peaceful and safe, and it was reassuring to know that she had a friend in Dublin. Everything Robert had said had made her feel less isolated, and she called his office before she left the hotel and left a message, thanking him for dinner. She was careful to leave the hotel by nine A.M. for the car rental place. She wanted to be heading for Russborough by nine-thirty. When she flew in, they normally got to the house by eleven, and she was planning to tell Finn that she had arrived on the morning flight to surprise him. She had sent him a loving text message the night before, and he hadn't responded. She hoped he was writing. And she had no intention of telling him that she had spent the night at a hotel in Dublin. That would make him suspicious and inevitably jealous. She looked neat and rested as she drove toward Blessington, and then Russborough, and as though perfectly timed, she arrived at Blaxton House at ten to eleven. There was no one outside, and it was a wintry December day, with a light veil of snow on the ground.

She left her suitcase in the car, bounded up the front steps, and saw Winfred as soon as she walked into the house. He touched his brow in a gesture of respect, smiled broadly, and went out to get her bag, while she rushed up the steps to their bedroom. Suddenly, she was excited to see Finn. It was as though all the terrible things people had said had disappeared. They couldn't be true about Finn. She loved him too much for any of that to be true about him. It was all a mistake. It had to be.

She tiptoed to their room and opened the door. It was dark, he was asleep in bed, and there was an empty scotch bottle on the floor beside him, which explained why he hadn't responded to her text message the night before. He had obviously been drunk.

She slipped onto the bed next to him, looked at his handsome face for a long moment, loving him all over again, and gently kissed him. She was under his spell again the moment she saw him. He didn't stir until she kissed him once more, and then he opened an eye, saw her, and gave a start, and then he beamed at her and pulled her into his arms. He reeked of scotch, but she didn't care as he kissed her. He smelled like an open bar, which worried her for him, but she didn't say anything about it. She wondered how the writing was going, and how close he was to delivering at least one of the two manuscripts he owed them. They were going to uphold the lawsuit if he didn't, and she didn't want that to happen to him.

"Where did you come from?" he asked with a slow, sleepy smile, stretched, and then turned over.

"I came home to see you," she said tenderly as he put his arms around her and pulled her closer, and as he did, all the good advice she'd been given was forgotten, as Robert Bartlett knew it would be. But he also knew she'd have it in her head when she needed it, at the right time.

"Why didn't you call me? I'd have come to pick you up," he said as he pulled her into bed with him, took her clothes off, and she didn't fight him.

"I wanted to surprise you," she said sweetly, and he forgot about what she was saying. He had a much better surprise for her, but it was no surprise. Their sex life had been fantastic from the first, which was part of the excitement of being with him. It was irresistible, even if she knew better than to fall for his seductive charms again. He was hard to resist. And minutes later they were making wild, passionate, insatiable love, as though the world was about to come to an end, and for a moment it always felt as though it might.

It was afternoon when they got up, bathed, dressed, and he looked at her. He was being so sweet to her again. It was hard to believe that he could ever tell a lie, hurt anyone, or make anyone unhappy, even her.

"I missed you so much," he said, and she could see that he meant it. He really did. She had found five empty scotch bottles under the bed. He had drowned his sorrows while she was gone, or his fears. He was like a child sometimes.

"I missed you too," she said gently. And then they went downstairs together and went for a walk before dark. It was snowing lightly, and looked beautiful. They were going to spend Christmas there alone. Michael was going skiing in Aspen with friends. And Hope had no one now. Only Finn.

"I'm sorry you had to go through all that with Paul. It must have been rough." He looked sympathetic and she nodded, as they held hands and walked. She tried not to think about it, or it would have panicked her that Paul was gone. And then he asked her a question that startled her in its bluntness. He wasn't usually that crude. "What's happening with the estate?"

"What do you mean?" She looked at him, shocked.

"You know . . . what happens now? . . . do they just give you the money, or do you have to wait until they sell stock or something?"

"That's a strange question. What difference does it make? It takes a while to probate the estate. Months, a year. I don't know. I don't care." And she didn't know why he would. They weren't dependent on Paul's money. Hope had enough, from what he had given her before. More than enough, as Finn knew only too well, since she had told him. "I just miss him," she said sadly, changing the subject. His interest in her money, and now Paul's, unnerved her and brought reality home to her again.

"I know you do," Finn said sympathetically, and put an arm around her shoulders, pulling her closer to him. "You're all alone now," he said, although he didn't need to rub it in. She was well aware of it herself, too much so. "All you have is me." She nodded and said nothing and wondered where he was going with what he was saying. "We have each other. That's all we have." She thought of his old fusion theory. He hadn't mentioned it in a while.

"You have Michael," she reminded him. And the next thing he said hit her like a punch in the solar plexus, and he was a big man and packed a powerful punch.

"And Mimi's gone," he said softly, as Hope tried to catch her breath and steady herself from the blow. It was his stock-in-trade now, putting her off balance and making her unstable, hurting her when she least expected it, in all the ways that hurt most. "That just leaves me," he repeated for emphasis. Hope didn't answer, and they walked along in the falling snow. But he had hit his mark. She felt even sadder than she had before, and then they went back to the house. He had been reminding her that she was dependent on him now, and without him she was alone. It was a shot across her bow. And she suddenly found herself thinking of Robert and his many warnings. They had agreed that he wouldn't call her, so Finn didn't get angry or upset. But if she needed Robert, she knew where to reach him. She had all his numbers in her purse.

She and Finn cooked dinner together that night, and he went upstairs to work while she got things ready, and he was wearing an odd expression when he came back downstairs to the kitchen in the basement. They still needed to restore that. It was functional, but grim. Most of the time they used the pantry on the main floor, but not that night.

Just as they sat down at the kitchen table where the servants used to eat, Finn turned to her with a glint in his eyes, and she wondered if he'd had a drink after their walk, or maybe even before. He was drinking way too much these days. He never used to, but he did now. She wondered if the pending lawsuit was causing him to drink.

"Where were you last night?" he asked her innocently.

"On the plane. Why?" She could feel her heart race, and looked blank as she served him pasta from a large bowl.

"Are you sure?" he asked, looking her in the eye.

"Of course I am. Don't be silly. Where else would I have been? I got here this morning." She dug a fork into her pasta, and he slammed her passport and a notepad onto the table next to her plate.

"Tell me about it. You stayed at a hotel in Dublin. I found this notepad in your purse when I was looking for something. I called them. And you were there last night. Your passport says you arrived in Ireland yesterday. Not today." And then he produced the piece of paper with Robert's numbers. She had written down only "Robert," no last name. Finn was an excellent detective. And Hope felt like she was going to have a heart attack. It was hard to explain. She had taken the notepad off the desk at the hotel without thinking. And Finn had found it. It never occurred to her to ask what he was looking for in her purse, she was too scared. Her night in Dublin was going to be hard to explain.

She had no choice but to be honest with him. She always had been until now. It was the first time she had ever lied to him, about her arrival, or anything else. "You're right. I arrived yesterday. I wanted a night to myself in Dublin. And I met with an attorney from my New York law firm. They thought I should see a lawyer here, about taxes, residency issues, this house. I met him, stayed at the hotel, and drove here this morning. End of story. I'm sorry that I lied." She looked remorseful, and she was not going to tell him about dinner with Robert, or Finn might go into a jealous rage, and there was no way he would believe it was innocent. He never did. In spite of herself, Hope looked frightened and was shaking.

"And Robert?"

"He's the attorney."

"He gave you his home and cell numbers? You fucked him at the hotel, didn't you, you little slut. And who were you fucking in New York? Your agent? Or some guy you picked up at a bar? A trucker on Tenth Avenue maybe while you took his picture." He knew she went to places like that to take photographs, and he used it against her now. "Did you take pictures of his cock?" He spat the words in her face, and Hope started to cry. He had never talked to her like that before, or been as crude. He was starting to cross boundaries he never had. Robert had warned her that he would, and she didn't believe him. "What about Robert? Was he good? Not as good as I am, I'll bet." Hope didn't comment. She just sat there at the table looking paralyzed and ashamed. He made her feel like a tramp, and she had done nothing wrong. She had seen a lawyer and had dinner, and would never have considered doing anything more. It didn't cross her mind. That wasn't who she was. But he accused her of it, with venom in his eyes and poison in his mouth.

"Nothing happened, Finn. I met with a lawyer, that's all."

"Why didn't you tell me about it?"

"Because sometimes my business is private." And even if it had been business, he would have insisted on coming with her. He never let her do anything alone. It was all about control. He even wanted to go to the doctor with her, as he had to the fertility doctor in London. He was intrusive, and wanted to be in full control of her at all times.

"How private was it?" he asked, looking at her, and this time she was sure he'd been drinking. If not, he was insane. And maybe he was that too. He looked like a crazy person as he glared at her, knocked his chair back until it fell, and paced around the kitchen, while she watched him, trying not to anger him further. She sat very still, praying that he'd back down.

"You know I wouldn't do anything like that," she said, trying to sound calmer than she felt.

"I don't know shit about you, Hope. And you know even less about me." It was probably the most honest thing he had ever said to her about himself, but the way he said it wasn't reassuring. "For all I know, you're a whore who blows every guy you meet whenever I'm not around." If Hope had dreamed of finding the old Finn when she got there, she had encountered the new Finn instead, an even newer one, who was worse. The real one.

"Why don't we calm down and eat dinner. Nothing happened in Dublin. I spent the night in a hotel alone. That's all." She sat straight in her chair, looking dignified and small, and before she knew what had happened, he grabbed her out of her chair, and slammed her up against the wall. She nearly flew across the room in his grip, and let out a gasp as she hit the wall with her back, and he lowered his face next to hers.

"If you ever fuck anyone, Hope, I'll kill you. Do you understand that? Is that clear to you? I won't put up with that from you. Get that through your head right now." She nodded, unable to speak, while tears choked her throat. She could hear a grinding in her ears from when he'd slammed her against the wall, and she was sure it was the sound of her heart breaking. "Answer me! Do you understand?"

"Yes," she whispered. She was sure that he was

drunk. He wouldn't behave that way if he weren't. But if so, they had to do something about it. Or he did. He was under a lot of stress over the lawsuit and the books he had to write. It was obviously driving him over the edge, and now her with it.

He slammed her back into her seat then, and glared at her while she pecked at her dinner. The look in his eyes was not one she recognized. She had never seen him that way before, and it occurred to her as she moved the pasta around her plate and pretended to eat it that she was alone in the house with him. Winfred and Katherine went home at dinnertime, and she was alone with Finn every night until morning. It had never worried her before, but it did now for the first time.

There were no more outbursts during dinner. He didn't say a word to her. He took the piece of paper with Robert's numbers on it, shredded it, and then shoved the pieces into the pocket of his jeans so she couldn't find them. He left the pad and passport on the table. And then without a word, he left the room, and left her to clean up. She sat for a long time at the table, with tears streaming down her cheeks and choking on sobs. And he had made the point earlier. She was alone in the world now. All she had was him. She had nowhere to turn, and no one to love her. With Paul gone, she felt like an orphan in a fairy tale, and the handsome prince was turning into a wild beast.

It took her an hour to calm down and clean up

the kitchen. She spent most of it crying, and was afraid to go upstairs, but she knew she had to. And when she thought about it calmly, she realized that the fact that she'd spent the night in Dublin didn't look good. The piece of paper with Robert's numbers on it looked suspicious. She could see why he was upset, since she had lied to him about it when she'd arrived. She realized that she should have told him the truth about when she was coming, but if she had, she would never have been able to meet with Robert and she was glad she had. It had been helpful and good to know that she could turn to someone somewhere, if she needed to, to help her. And he was at least nearby. But she could also understand that Finn was upset that she had disappeared for a day and lied to him about her arrival. Although it had been innocent, she felt guilty about it, and in some way didn't blame him.

She dreaded going upstairs to see him, and was surprised to find when she did, that he was sitting in bed waiting for her. He looked peaceful and as though the scene in the kitchen hadn't happened. Seeing him go from one mood to the extreme opposite like that was terrifying. One moment brimming with rage like a dragon, the next calmly in bed, smiling at her. She wasn't sure if he was crazy or she was, and she stood looking at him for a moment, with absolutely no idea what to say.

"Come to bed, Hope," he said, as though they'd had a pleasant evening, which they certainly hadn't. It had been anything but that, and now he looked like it had never happened. Watching him lie there, all innocence, made her want to cry.

She got into bed cautiously beside him a few minutes later, after brushing her teeth and putting on her nightgown. She glanced at him as though he were a poisonous snake about to strike.

"Everything is fine," he said to her soothingly, and put an arm around her. It was almost worse than if he were still angry at her. This was just too confusing. "I was thinking," he said easily, as she lay there stiffly beside him, waiting to see what would come next. It was impossible to relax now. "I think we should get married next week. There is no reason for us to be waiting. We're not going to have a wedding anyway, with people coming from far away. And I don't want to wait any longer. We're all alone in the world, Hope, you and I. If anything ever happens to either of us, like what just happened to Paul, we should be married. No one wants to die alone."

"Paul was very sick, for a long time. And I was with him," she said in a choked voice.

"If either of us has an accident, the other would be unable to make decisions. You don't have kids or family. Michael's not here for me. We only have each other." It was a recurring theme for him tonight, to emphasize her solitude and remind her that she only had him to rely on. "I'd feel better if we were legally married. We can always have a party later, in London, New York, or Cape Cod. It's time, Hope, it's been a year. We're grown-ups. We love each other. We know what we want. There's no point waiting. And we need to get going on the baby project again," he said, smiling at her. It was as though the scene in the kitchen had never happened. An hour before, he had been threatening her and slamming her into a wall, and now he wanted to get married in a week, and get her pregnant. Listening to him, Hope felt insane. "It's been six months since you lost the last baby," he reminded her, and for once he didn't say it was her fault. It was as though he had cleared his pipes in the kitchen, and now he was his old self again. The good Finn was back with them, tucked into bed with her. But she no longer believed what she was hearing. She didn't trust it, or him. Not at all.

And she wasn't ready to marry him, by any means, and she had the strong impression this was only about money. If he was married to her, and anything happened to her in that isolated house in the Irish countryside, he would be the heir to her fortune, and to Paul's once that came to her. And with a child, she would be even more locked in. Robert had pointed that out to her the day before in his office, and it was obvious to her too. But she didn't want to get Finn mad at her again by saying she wasn't ready to get married. At least not tonight. She'd feel better talking about it in the morning, with Winfred and Katherine around, in broad daylight. Not when she was alone in the house, and he might fly into another rage like the one in the kitchen. She'd had enough excitement for one night.

"Can we talk about it tomorrow?" she said evenly. "I'm exhausted." The scene with him at dinner had made her feel like she'd been hit by a bus. For several minutes, she had been terrified of him. But he seemed totally calm now, and even loving. She felt as though he had ripped through all her gears, and she was still trembling inside and felt very tense. She tried not to let it show.

"What's to talk about?" he asked, putting an arm around her. "Let's just do it." She could tell that this was going to be the subject of their next big fight.

"We don't have to make that decision tonight, Finn," she said softly. "Let's go to sleep." It was still early, but she just couldn't deal with it anymore. She was too hurt, too upset, too disappointed, and had been too frightened to want to talk about any-thing with him. All she wanted to do was go to sleep, or maybe die. She knew suddenly that this wasn't going to get better, and it was going to be one fight after another. After his attack on her at dinner, she was losing hope, however nice he was now. It wasn't likely to last long.

"You don't love me, do you?" he asked in the voice of a small boy. Suddenly he was the injured child, and not the man who had terrified her, and all he wanted was to be loved. This was getting very sick. He cuddled up to her like a two-year-old nestled at her side and put his head on her shoulder. She sighed as she stroked his hair and face.

She loved him, but the roller-coaster ride was taking her breath away. He continued to snuggle up against her, and she turned off the light, and moments later he was pulling up her nightgown and wanted to make love. She was so upset and overwrought, she didn't want to, but she was afraid that if she denied him, he'd start a fight with her again. And he was so expert at what he did that within moments, her body responded, even though her mind wanted to push him away, and her heart was totally confused. But her body suddenly wanted him. And he made love to her with such infinite gentleness and caring that there was no way to believe that this was the same man who had attacked her only hours before.

After they made love, she lay awake for hours while he snored. And she finally fell asleep, totally exhausted, at dawn. She had been crying silently all night, and she felt dead inside. He was killing her by inches. She just didn't know it yet.

Chapter 20

Finn was already up when Hope awoke the next morning. She got out of bed feeling drained and beaten, and her spirits were as gray as the weather. She looked tired and pale when she met him in the pantry eating breakfast. He looked full of energy and cheer, and told her how happy he was to have her home. He even seemed as though he meant it. She no longer knew what to believe.

She was cautiously sipping a cup of tea, when he mentioned the wedding again. He suggested they go in to talk to the vicar in the village, and said they had to go to the embassy in Dublin to get permission for her to be married in Ireland. He was an Irish citizen, but she wasn't. He had already called the embassy to find out what they needed. And she realized that unless she was willing to marry him, she had to say something to him.

She set her teacup down and looked at Finn. "I can't," she said sadly, for reasons she couldn't begin to broach with him. "Paul just died. I don't want to start a new life right after something so sad." It seemed like a reasonable excuse to her, but not to him.

"You were divorced, you're not his widow," he said, looking faintly annoyed. "And no one's going to know the difference."

"I do," she said quietly.

"Is there some reason you don't want to marry me?" he asked, looking hurt. There were an increasing number of them, but she wasn't willing to discuss any of them with him. His many lies, the investigator's report, the two women whose deaths he had indirectly caused, his recent demand for money, and his attack on her the night before. All seemed good reasons to her to think long and hard before she married him, or not do it at all. But then why was she living with him? Things between them were not as they had been before, even in their best moments now. There was always an undercurrent of something wrong. Things hadn't been normal between them in well over a month, or more, ever since he'd asked her for the money.

"It's not a simple matter," Hope said patiently. "We have to get a prenuptial drawn up, sign papers, talk to lawyers. I've mentioned it to them, but it takes more than a couple of days. And I'd really rather get married in New York."

"Fine," he said, changing tacks unexpectedly, and for a split second, she was relieved. That had been easier than she thought. "Then how about you set up the account we talked about before? And we can wait to get married till the summer." It was back to that again.

"What are we talking about, Finn?" She remembered the amounts, but she was wondering if anything had changed.

"I told you I'd settle for four million dollars, although I'd rather have five. But that was before Paul died. Given what he's leaving you, I really think it should be ten." Hope let out a sigh as she listened. This was exhausting, and none of it made sense, or maybe it did. Maybe this was all it had ever been about. She felt like she was fighting for her life from the moment she woke up until she went to sleep at night. "I know you don't have the money from Paul yet. So let's do five now, and five after the money from Paul comes through." It seemed perfectly reasonable to him. He said it as though he was asking her to stop at the hardware store, or get him a subscription to a magazine. And he acted as though he expected her to do it, without question, and was sure she would.

"So you want five now, and five later," she said, sounding like a robot. "And what kind of arrangement when we get married?" She figured she'd get it all on the table now, instead of waiting for him to ambush her with it.

"I can have my lawyer talk to yours," he said pleasantly. "I think some kind of annual amount would be fair, maybe a signing bonus when we get married," he said with a broad smile. "And I guess these days people prenegotiate a divorce, in case there is one, alimony and a settlement." It sounded like a great arrangement to him, and the outrageousness of it didn't strike him for a minute. "And let's face it, Hope, I'm a lot more famous than you are, a rare commodity, and a hell of a deal for you at any price. At your age, guys like me don't come along. I could be the last train out of the station for you. I think you need to keep that in mind." What he said to her was breathtaking, and it was the first time he had made an issue of his fame, and belittled hers. She was surprised, but thought it wisest not to comment on any of it, but it was shocking, even to her.

"Sounds like an expensive deal," she said quietly, as she poured herself another cup of tea, still stunned by what he'd said and what he was doing.

"I'm worth it, don't you think?" Finn said as he leaned over and kissed her, as Hope looked at him with eyes full of tears. He was insane. Even she knew it now. "Something wrong?" He saw the expression on her face and the sag of her shoulders, which seemed surprising to him.

"I think it's very depressing to be talking about money instead of love and the years we want to spend together, and prenegotiating alimony and a divorce. That's a little too businesslike for me," she answered, looking at him sadly.

"Then let's just get married and forget the prenup," he said simply. But there was no way they could do that. She was worth a substantial fortune, and Finn had nothing but debts, bills, and a lawsuit. She couldn't be that irresponsible. Without a prenup, she'd be completely vulnerable to him financially, and he knew it. The whole conversation made her feel sick. There was no way they could ever marry. Finn was in a very good mood. He thought he had her trapped.

In the end, to pacify him, Hope said that she would think about it and let him know what she thought. She didn't want to set him off by telling him there was no question of his getting the money he wanted, or her marrying him, and she didn't want to give it to him either. She thought about his demands all day, as she edited some photographs, went to the FedEx office, and went for a walk alone in the woods. She didn't see Finn again until late that afternoon. And he was as loving as he ever had been. The trouble now was that Hope no longer knew if it was about love or money, and she never would, he was slowly wearing her down, demoralizing her, and making her feel crazy and off balance. His financial demands were insulting and insane. She was trying to stay calm, but it was just too hard fighting with him all the time. He always had some obsession, whether it was getting her pregnant, getting married, or giving him millions of dollars for his own use. Hope was feeling overwhelmingly sad. The dream of love and trust that she had shared with him was crumbling in her hands like butterfly wings. They went from one upsetting subject to another, and had resolved nothing so far. It was all about money now, and he had asked her to prove her love for him by putting five million dollars in an account in his name. That was a lot of love. And what was he planning to give in return, other than his time? Even Hope herself was well aware that she was getting screwed. Worse than that, she felt like she was trapped in a spider-web of deceit. He was the spider and it was becoming ever more clear that she was the prey.

Finn invited her to dinner in Blessington that night. She agreed to go, for distraction in her despair, and for once not a single difficult subject came up. Not money, not babies, not weddings. She was depressed at first, and surprised that they had a good time together like in the beginning, and once again, it gave her hope. She was constantly ricocheting now between hope and despair. And she was having more and more trouble getting up each time she got knocked down. Ever since Paul had died, she was tired. And Finn was slowly beating her down.

But miraculously, for the next several days, just as she had begun to lose hope, everything seemed to be all right again. Finn was in a good mood. He was writing. She was starting a new book of photographs of Ireland, and enjoying some projects in the house. It was beginning to feel like the early days when she had first bought the house. And she tried to put out of her mind the outrageous things he'd said to her, and the money he had asked for. Just for now. She needed the respite. And then a letter came by FedEx from New York. She took it up to Finn and left it with him, and when he came out of his office again, he looked like a black cloud.

"Bad news?" she asked, looking worried. Given the expression on his face, it would have been hard to believe it was good.

"They're telling me that even if I deliver the book now, they won't publish it. They're going ahead with the suit. Fuck. And this is one of my best books."

"Then someone else will publish it, and you may get a better deal." She tried to sound encouraging, but he looked incredibly angry.

"Thank you, Little Miss Cheerful. They want their money back, and I've already spent the advance."

Hope put a gentle hand on his shoulder, as he poured himself a stiff drink and took a long sip. He felt better when he did.

"Why don't you let me ask Mark Webber to handle this, and see if he can negotiate something for you."

Finn looked at her then with fury. "Why don't you just fucking write them a check?" She didn't like the way he had spoken to her, but she didn't say anything to him about it, and refused to react in kind. She didn't want another fight.

"Because a good lawyer can make a deal, and then we'll see what we have to do." She was trying to reassure him, without committing herself. It was hard to know these days where things were going to go with them. She was still hopeful, but realistically, less and less. Things weren't going well. It was all about greed now, getting his hands on her money, and covering up old lies. As it said in the Bible, their house was built on sand.

"Is that a royal 'we'?" he asked her in a nasty tone. "Or are you going to pay up, and stop making me hang by the neck about it? I need money. And I want my own account." She was already clear about that. He had been saying it for weeks.

"But we don't know how much you need," she said quietly. Hope always got quiet when she was upset, either angry or scared.

"That's beside the point. If you want me to stick around, I don't want to be accountable to you. What I spend, how much, and what I spend it on is my business, not yours." And yet he wanted her money to do it, but figured it was none of her business. It sounded pretty ballsy, even to her. "Let's be honest about this, Hope. You're forty-five years old, not twenty-two. You're a pretty woman, but forty-five isn't twenty-five or thirty. You don't have a living relative in the world, no siblings, no parents, no cousins even, your only child is dead, and the last person you considered yourself related to, your ex-husband, just died last week. So who do you think is going to be around, if something happens to you, you know, say if you got sick? And what do you think would happen if I walk out on you, maybe because I found a twenty-two-year-old? Then what happens to you? You wind up fucking alone, probably forever, and one day you die alone. So maybe what you need to think about, if you don't want to put that money in an account for me, is what your life is going to look like ten years from now, or twenty, when no one else is around, and you're all alone. Looking at it from that perspective, you just may want to give some serious thought to making it attractive to me to stick around." As Hope listened to him, she looked like she'd been slapped.

"Is that supposed to be a declaration of love?"

"Maybe it is."

"And how do I know, if I set up these accounts for you in the right amounts, that you actually will stick around? Let's say I do that, for five or ten million, and whatever you want when we get married, and then you meet the perfect twenty-two-year-old."

"Good point," he said, smiling. He looked as though he was enjoying the moment. Hope clearly wasn't. "I guess you pays your money, you takes your chances. Because if you don't put that money in the accounts, when Miss Perfect Twenty-Two-

Year-Old shows up, especially if she's some kind of an heiress or a debutante, then guess who won't be sticking around to hold your bedpan in your old age." She couldn't imagine him doing that in any case, and the conversation they were having was beyond disgusting. She had never been so upset.

"So you're basically suggesting that I buy you, as an insurance policy for my old age."

"I guess you could say that. But look at the perks you'd be getting and already are. Sex anytime you want it, hopefully a baby, maybe even a couple of kids, if you take care of yourself. And I think we have a pretty good time."

"Funny," she said, the violet eyes shooting sparks, "you haven't mentioned love. Or is that not part of the deal?" She had never been so insulted in her life. She was supposed to buy herself a guy. If she wanted Finn, there were no two ways about it, she had to pay the price.

And with that, Finn came and put his arms around her. He had seen the look on her face. "You know I love you, baby. I just have to cover my ass. I'm no kid either. And I don't have the kind of money you do. There's no Paul in my life." But now he wasn't in hers either. And Paul hadn't made his fortune so that Finn could spend it screwing around, or maybe buying himself a few blondes, no questions asked. The very fact that Finn had asked her for this kind of money disqualified him, or should have. But she didn't want to blow her top. If she did, she'd have to see it through, and end it with him, and she just wasn't up to it. She felt destroyed, and paralyzed by his abuse.

"I'll think about it," she said, looking somber, trying to buy time and put him off, "and I'll let you know tomorrow." But she also knew that if she didn't give Finn the money, their relationship would blow sky-high and it would be over. She hated everything he had said, the barely veiled threats to leave her for a younger woman, trying to scare her about being alone in her old age, reminding her that there would be no one to take care of her if she got sick. But was she truly ready to be alone forever? She felt like she was between a rock and a hard place and both were awful. Ending it or staying. And instead of telling her that he loved her and wanted to be with her forever, he was making it very clear that if several million dollars weren't forthcoming, sooner or later he'd be out the door when a better deal came along, so she'd better ante up, if she knew what was good for her and didn't want to wind up alone. He had certainly spelled it out. And she had no desire to buy a husband or lose him entirely yet. She was wandering around the house like a zombie, in a permanent state of silent distress.

Finn was in great spirits for the rest of the afternoon. He had delivered his message, and thought it had been fairly well received. He didn't know Hope as well as he thought. She was depressed and angry all day, and stayed busy scrubbing and polishing several bathrooms on the second floor to keep distracted from the agonizing situation she was in. And Finn was affectionate with her. She wondered if that was what life would be like if she paid his price, which she was not inclined to do. But if so, would he always be sweet to her? Warm and loving as he had been in the beginning? Or would he still be jealous, threaten her if he felt like it, and ask for more when he blew the five or ten million dollars and needed the account filled again, no questions asked? It was hard to know what she'd be getting, if she decided to pay him what he wanted. If anyone had told her she'd be thinking about giving him the money, she would have told them they were insane. All she wanted was the old Finn back, the first one, but even she knew you couldn't buy that.

The whole conversation saddened her, and she went for a walk alone that afternoon to clear her head. Finn saw her go out, and decided that it was better to let her come to her own conclusions, on her own. She really didn't have much choice, as far as he was concerned. He was very sure of himself, and believed that she was firmly hooked. He had all the grandiosity and sense of entitlement of sociopaths, as Robert had said to her. Finn was certain that if Hope loved him, she'd pay up. She didn't want to be alone. He knew she loved him, and didn't want to lose him. To him the answer was clear. And he was sure it would be to her too. He was feeling increasingly secure and had made himself clear. He thought she might need to be pushed a little, and be reminded of the alternative again. But ultimately, unless she was willing to risk being a lonely old lady in a nursing home, Finn knew he was the better deal and she had no choice. And with him, she could have more kids. He had almost called it "stud service" when he talked to her, but decided that might put her off. The rest seemed okay to him. And as far as he was concerned he was worth every penny he was asking. Hope knew he believed that too. It all made sense to him, and he was sure she'd be sensible about it, and too scared not to. He looked jubilant as he sat at his desk and watched her back from the window, as she walked toward the hills. He didn't see the rivers of tears rolling down her face.

As Hope sat in a warm bath before dinner, she was seriously depressed. He had planted the seeds of some really melancholy observations, about what her future would look like without him. He was right. She didn't have a soul in the world, except him. If she left him, there might be someone else. But that was beside the point. She loved him, and had for a year, enough to want to marry him at one point and have a child. She wanted neither of these now. She just wanted to feel sane again and for things to calm down.

She had no one in her life except Finn. And

saddest of all was that she had truly loved him, even if it was turning out that she was only a piggy bank to him. It was a lot to pay for a guy who was demonstrating that he only wanted her for her money, and was fabulous in bed. All she really wanted from him was his heart. And Hope no longer believed that Finn had that particular piece of equipment. It just wasn't there. Her eyes filled with tears as she thought about it. She had loved him so much. Why did it have to be so damn complicated and turn out like this? She knew she'd have to deal with it soon. She couldn't stall him forever.

She decided to put a good face on it, and dressed in a nice dress for dinner. She put on high heels, brushed her hair back, added earrings and makeup, and when she got downstairs to the pantry where Katherine had left a tea tray for them, Finn looked at her and whistled. And when he pulled her into his arms and kissed her, he looked as though he loved her, but who knew now? She no longer believed anything. It was a sad place to be in.

They decided to make do with Katherine's sandwiches and a pot of tea, instead of dinner. And Finn looked animated as he started telling her about a new book he'd been thinking about that afternoon. It was for the second book due in his contract. He said he had almost finished the first one, but she wasn't sure she believed him, since his relationship to the truth had proved flimsy at best.

⟩(As they ate Katherine's sandwiches, Hope listened to him tell the story. It was about two newly married people who had bought a château in France. The woman was American, and the hero of the story was French, a very handsome older man. Finn said he was a dark character who had already had two wives who had mysteriously died. And what the hero wanted more than anything was a child. It was beginning to have a familiar ring to it, as Hope listened, but she figured he would spin it off eventually into one of his typically scary tales with ghosts, murderers, people imprisoned in basements, and bodies hidden in the woods. It always intrigued her how he came up with the stories, which, for years, critics had said were the product of a troubled, brilliant mind. Initially he had seemed surprisingly normal, considering the twisted tales that he told. Now she was no longer so sure.

"Okay, so then what happens?" she said, listening with interest, trying to concentrate on this book. It was something to talk about, other than money, and as a result, it was a relief.

"She gets pregnant, so her future is assured, at least until she has the child. She's an heiress, and her father gets kidnapped later in the book." Hope smiled. It already sounded complicated to her. "As it turns out, she and her brother have been stealing money from their father for years. Her husband finds out and blackmails her, and asks her for ten million dollars. She talks to her brother, and they decide to call his bluff. They don't give him the money," he said, with a small evil smile at Hope, and then he kissed her neck.

"Then what?" she asked, with an odd chill running down her spine from his kiss.

"He kills her," Finn says with a look of pleasure. "First he kills her. Then the baby." She shivered as he said it.

"That's awful. How can you write that?" She gave him a disapproving look, and Finn seemed amused. "How does he kill her, or do I want to know?" Some of his books had been gory and perverted beyond belief. They were strong stories, but some of the details made her sick. They were always thoroughly researched.

"It's pretty clean. He uses an undetectable poison. And he inherits the entire fortune. Or her half anyway, then he kills the brother. And when their father is kidnapped later, the hero doesn't pay the ransom, because he's been a shit to him. So he lets the kidnappers kill him. One by one, he kills the entire family, and winds up with all their money. Pretty cool for a poor boy from Marseilles, don't you think? He even buys himself a title that comes with the château." It sounded like Finn's fantasy to her, and some of his earlier lies about the house.

"And he winds up alone?" Hope asked innocently. The plot sounded pretty sick to her, but very Finn.

"Of course not. He marries a young girl from the village, who he was in love with in the first place. She's twenty-one, and he's fifty at the end of the story. So what do you think?" He looked pleased with himself.

"Pretty scary." She smiled, thinking of the twists and turns he described. "I think killing the pregnant wife is a little much and may upset your readers. Most people have sensibilities about those things."

"She didn't pay him the money," Finn said, looking straight at her, deep into her eyes. "The brother would have, but she convinced him not to. And in the end, he got the money anyway, all of it, not just her share, and far more than he originally asked for. The moral of the story is that they should have paid him when they could, before he killed them all." He was good at complicated, layered stories of psychological terror, and frightening murders of retribution.

Hope asked, looking him in the eye, "And that seems fair to you?"

"Completely. She had all the money, why should she get everything and he has nothing? And in the end, he's avenged, and the poor boy gets everything."

"And a lot of dead bodies in the basement."

"Oh no," he said, looking offended. "They all had proper burials. Even the police never figure out they were murdered. They suspect it, but they can

never prove it. There's a very clever French inspector, and in the end, François kills him too. François
is my hero. The inspector's name is Robert. He
buries him in the woods, and no one ever finds
him." And as he said the inspector's name, the
story clicked for Hope. It was no accident that the
rich wife was killed, the poor boy wins, and the inspector had the name of the lawyer Finn had found
on the piece of paper in her purse when she first
came from Dublin. All the puzzle parts fit together
seamlessly, and the threat to her was clear.

She looked straight at Finn then. "Is there a message there for me?" She didn't flinch as their eyes
met, nor did he. He shrugged his shoulders and
laughed.

"Why would you say a thing like that?"

"Some of the story seems a little close to home."

"All writers inspire themselves somewhat from
real life, even if they don't admit it. And there are
differences. The wife he kills is pregnant. You're
not. You don't have a brother. Or a father. You're all
alone. That would be a lot more scary. But very
boring for the reader. You need layers, subplots,
and more people to make a story work. I just
found it interesting what happens to her when she
won't give him the money. It proves that trying to
hang on to it doesn't pay. You can't take your
money to the grave." What he was saying to her
was frightening, given their situation, but he said it

with a smile, and he was clearly mocking her. But his message to her was clear. Pay up or die.

He didn't mention it further, and she put their dishes in the pantry sink, trying to act normal. They started talking about Christmas, which was two weeks away. Hope said she wanted to go to Russborough to get a tree the next day, and Finn said he would rather chop one down himself. He had an ax in the stable, which sounded ominous to her too. His story had unnerved her, and she suspected that was the point. Finn knew exactly what he was doing. The night before he had reminded her of how alone she was. And now he had told her a story he had created about a man who kills his wife when she doesn't give up her fortune to him. The message was extremely clear. And the hair stood up on her arms when she thought about it. They read side by side in bed that night, clinging to the appearance of normalcy, and Hope said nothing to him. She was thinking of his story and couldn't concentrate on the book in her hands. For an odd moment, she began to wonder if she should run like hell, as Robert had said, or just pay Finn, and give in. If she didn't, he was right, she would be alone forever. And if she paid him, then what would happen? Would he be nice again, and calm down? Maybe if she gave him the money, things would go back to the way they were in the beginning and they would stop fighting. And Finn was right. He was all she had in the world. She didn't like the idea, but maybe she had no other choice. She felt cornered, beaten, and trapped. She was tired of trying to swim against the tides. She felt like she was drowning. Finn was too powerful for her. He was trying to destroy her mind. He almost had. She could feel it. He was winning.

"So what do you think about my story?" Finn asked her when she put down her book and stopped pretending to read it. She looked at Finn then, with a dead look in her eyes.

"To be honest, I'm not sure I like it. And I get the message. I'd like it a lot better if they all kill the poor boy from Marseilles. Then I wouldn't feel so threatened." She looked right at him as she said it.

"It doesn't work that way," he said cleverly. "He's much smarter than they are." And more willing to take risks, and cross lines.

"I'll give you the money, if that's what you want to know," she said bluntly. She had no illusions anymore. This was about survival. He had defeated her. She felt dead inside.

"I thought you would," he said, smiling at her. "I think it's a good decision." And then he moved toward her and kissed her ever so gently on the lips. She didn't respond. For the first time since she'd known him, she hated his touch. "I'll make you happy, Hope. I promise." She no longer believed it, or even cared. She was selling her soul, and she knew it. But being alone in the world seemed worse. "I love you," he said gently, looking pleased. She no longer believed that either. She knew exactly what he had done. He had terrorized her. And it had worked. "Don't you love me?" He had on his little-boy voice, and for a moment, she hated him, and she wished he would kill her. It would be so much simpler in the end.

"Yes, I love you," she said in a dead voice. He didn't know the meaning of the word. There was no coming back from what she knew now, or what he had implied that night at dinner. "We can get married next week if you want, if the embassy can get the papers ready. I'll call the lawyer in Dublin about the prenup." She sounded like a robot and felt like a corpse.

"Don't put too many teeth in it," he warned. She nodded. He had the upper hand now. And she was alone with him at the house. There was a stiff wind outside, and there was a snowstorm expected that night. She didn't care. About anything right now. He had killed something inside of her that night. Any hope she had of being loved. All she was buying was his presence, not his heart. The only heart involved was her own. And it was broken beyond repair. "We'll have beautiful babies, I promise. We can spend our honeymoon in London and see the doctor."

"We don't need the doctor," she objected.

"If you let her give you the shots, you could have twins or triplets." His electric-blue eyes lit up at the thought. It sounded frightening to Hope. It had been hard enough for her to have one baby when she had Mimi. She was a tiny woman. The thought of twins or triplets was terrifying, and then she looked at Finn. He owned her now. She had sold her soul to the devil, and he was it.

"Does he kill her if she has twins?" she asked him with wide, frightened eyes. And Finn grinned.

"Never. Not if she gives him the money." Hope nodded in response and said nothing, and a little while later, Finn wanted to make love to her, and she let him. The wind was howling outside, and this time, she just lay there, letting him do whatever he wanted, even the things she had never let him do before, and some of them she enjoyed. He was excited by everything that had happened between them that night, his bloodlust had been satisfied, and his need to own her. She had finally surrendered, and it heightened his sexual desire for her. He took her again and again. He owned her in every way now. And just the way he wanted, Hope was his.

Chapter 21

Hope woke up at five A.M. when the wind smashed a tree limb against the house. The storm was in full swing. Finn had heard nothing, and as Hope awoke she felt as though her heart had been ripped out through her lungs. She was instantly awake and remembered everything that had happened the night before. Everything. Every word. Every sound. Every innuendo. Every nuance of Finn's story about the young wife the poor boy killed. She understood all its implications, what she'd done, and what he'd done to her the night before, to her head, not just her body. He had brainwashed her. And every fiber of her being was screaming. She had sold her soul to the devil, or planned to, and he was asleep beside her in the bed. He was worn out from their sexual acrobatics that had only ended two hours before. Hope was still sore and knew she would be for days. And suddenly as she thought of all of it, she knew that as bad as being alone might be one day, this was infinitely worse. What she had just signed on for, and had been living for the past few months, was worse than death. She had bought her ticket to hell the night before, and as she thought of it, she remembered everything Robert Bartlett had said too . . . trust your instincts . . . when you know . . . run, Hope, run . . . run like hell . . .

Hope slipped out of the bed by millimeters. She had to go to the bathroom, but didn't dare. She found her underwear on the floor, the dress she had worn the night before, a sweater of Finn's, she couldn't find her shoes, but she grabbed her purse, and slipped through the crack in the barely open door on bare feet. She ran quickly down the stairs, praying they wouldn't creak, but the wind and the sounds of the storm were so loud that it covered everything else, and she never looked back, fearing he would be standing in the doorway, watching, but no one stopped her. He was sound asleep and would be for hours. She found a coat on a peg next to the back door, and the boots she wore in the garden. She unlocked the door, and ran out into the night, taking big deep gulps of the icy air. She was freezing and it was hard to run in the boots, but she didn't care. She was doing just what Robert had told her, she was running for her life . . . to freedom . . . She had known the minute she woke up that if she didn't, he would kill her. He had made that clear the night before. And she didn't doubt it for a minute. Two women were dead because of him, she was certain of it, and she didn't want to be the third. Even if she was alone forever. She no longer cared. About anything. Except getting out.

She walked for miles in the storm, with snow blanketing her shoulders; her legs were freezing in the thin dress, but she didn't mind. Her hair was matted to her head. She passed houses and churches, farms and stables, a dog barked when she ran past. She ran and walked, and stumbled in the dark. But no one followed her. She didn't know what time it was, and it was still dark when she got to a pub outside Blessington. It was closed, but there was a woodshed behind it. She walked into it, and closed the door. She hadn't seen another human on her route, but she kept expecting Finn to yank open the doors of the shed, drag her home, and kill her. She was shaking violently, and not just from the cold and the storm. She knew she had been snatched back from the jaws of death by the hand of Providence and the memory of Robert's words. She dug in her bag, and opened the door of the shed a crack so she could see by the light of a streetlamp. She found the tiny scrap of paper she was looking for. Finn had torn the one with Robert's numbers to shreds, but Mark had written them on a notepad in New York and given her the same numbers. She forgot she had it until that moment, and with trembling, frozen hands, she found her cell phone. His cell phone number was on the paper; she pressed the buttons and listened while it rang. He answered in a deep sleep-filled voice, and her teeth were chattering so hard he didn't recognize her when she said hello.

"Who is it?" he shouted into the phone. There was a terrible shrieking from the wind, and he was afraid it was one of his children. It was just after six in the morning in Ireland, and after one in the morning on the East Coast of the United States where his daughters were.

"It's Hope," she said, shaking violently. She had had trouble saying her own name, and she could hardly speak above a whisper . . . "I'm out . . ." she said in a shaken voice, and instantly Robert was awake and knew who was calling. She sounded like she was in shock.

"Where are you? Just tell me. I'll come as fast as I can." He was praying that Finn didn't find her first.

"Thhe Whhhite Horse Pubbbb in BBBllesssington, south edge of town. I'm in the wwwooodd-shedd," she said, starting to cry.

"Just hang on, Hope. You're all right. You're going to be fine. I'm coming." He jumped out of bed, raced into his clothes, and five minutes later, he was in his car, speeding south out of Dublin on slippery, deserted roads. All he could think of was that she sounded the way he had the night Nuala had stabbed him. It was over then, and he never went back, although he knew others did in similar conditions, and worse. He just prayed that Hope wasn't hurt. At least Robert knew she was alive.

The roads were icy, and it took him fifty minutes to get there. It was seven in the morning by then, and there was the faintest gray light coming through the sky. The snow was still falling, but he reached the southern edges of Blessington, and drove around looking for the White Horse Pub, and then he saw it. He got out of his car, walked around it, and saw the shed in the back. He hoped she was still there, and Finn hadn't found her. He walked to the doors of the woodshed, pulled the doors slowly open, and saw no one, and then he looked down and saw her crouched on the ground, soaking wet, with her thin dress plastered to her legs, and eyes full of terror. She didn't get up when she saw him, she just crouched there, staring at him. He leaned down gently and pulled her slowly upright, and as she stood up, she started to sob. She couldn't even speak to him as he put his own coat around her and led her to his car. She was frozen to the bone.

She was still sobbing when they got to Dublin an hour later. He had driven more slowly on the way back. He was debating about taking her to the hospital to have her checked out, or take her to his home and sit her in front of the fire in a warm blanket. She still looked terrified and she hadn't said a word. He had no idea what had happened, or what Finn had done to her, but she had no obvious injuries or bruises, except to her soul and mind. He knew it would be a long time before she felt whole again, but he knew from talking to her before that she would survive, and even recover, no matter how long it took. It had taken Robert several years.

He asked Hope if she wanted to go to the hospital, and she shook her head. So he took her home with him, and when they got there, he gently undressed her as he would have one of his daughters when she was a child. He rubbed her down with towels as she stood there and cried, handed her a pair of his pajamas, wrapped her in a blanket, and then put her in his bed. He had a doctor come by to look at her later that morning. And she was still looking wild-eyed, but she had stopped crying. All she said to Robert when the doctor left was "Don't let him find me."

"I won't," he promised. She had left everything there, and she had done what Robert had said. She ran like hell for her life, and she knew with total certainty that if she hadn't, sooner or later, she would have died.

Robert waited until the next day to talk to her, and she told him everything that had happened. Every word that Finn had said. His pressure for the money. The outline of the story he had described to her, and the implications of it weren't lost on Robert either. Finn had almost succeeded in getting everything he wanted, but the golden goose had run away during the night. Finn had started calling on her cell phone within hours of her escape. He woke up early in the storm and couldn't find her, and when she didn't answer her phone, he started sending text messages. He kept telling her he'd find her, that he wanted her to come home, at first that he loved her, and later when she didn't respond, his messages were full of thinly veiled threats. Hope didn't answer, and Robert finally took her phone so she didn't have to see them. She shook violently every time one of them came in. Robert gave her his bedroom, and he slept on the couch.

And on the second day of her escape, he asked her where she wanted to go, what she wanted to do, and what her plans were for the house. She thought about it for a long moment. In some part of her she still loved the way Finn had been at the beginning, and knew she would for a long time. It wasn't over yet. She would never forget or stop loving the man she had loved for the first nine months, but the demon he had become after that had nearly cost her her soul, and would have cost her life. She had no doubt of it now.

"I'm not sure what to do about the house," she said sadly. Making major decisions about anything was too hard for her right now. She was still too shaken by everything that had happened.

Robert looked at her quietly. She needed a guide

to get through the dark forest of what she was going through. "The man threatened to kill you. That was not a story for a book, it was a message to you." She had told Robert all about it.

"I know," she said, with tears in her eyes. "He killed the woman's baby too, so he could get all her money." She spoke about them as though they were real people, which they had become to her, instead of an allegory for her, which she understood clearly in the end.

"I'd like to give him thirty days to pack up and get out. People like him always land on their feet again. They tell enough lies and screw over enough people, and the next thing you know, they turn up somewhere else," Robert said. He was sure that Finn would too. "Can you live with that? Thirty days for him to figure out his plans and pack up." Robert would have preferred to kick him out in twenty-four hours, but he knew that it would be too stressful for Hope to contemplate doing that.

"Okay," she agreed.

"I'll go out there and pack up your things sometime this week."

"What if he follows you back here?" Hope asked, looking terrified again, and Robert thought about it. Hope knew he didn't have Robert's name or numbers, because he had torn up the piece of paper and thrown it away, and he was still text-messaging her to no avail. Robert still had her phone. He handed it to her later that day, and saw her reading all the frantic text messages from Finn, and when she turned it off, she cried. It was awful what loving a man like that did to another human being. He had gone through the same thing when he finally walked away from his wife. There was no other choice. They were people who had been stolen by aliens sometime in their youth, destroyed, turned into twisted machines, returned, and then walked the planet destroying other lives. They had virtually no conscience and no heart, and very sick minds.

Hope was afraid that Finn was combing Dublin for her, and Robert knew it was possible. There was no limit to what a sociopath would do to reclaim his prey. So she sent Robert shopping for her, and she gave him all her sizes. He came back with enough clothes to keep her going for a few days. She hadn't decided where to go yet, but she knew that Finn might look for her in New York or Cape Cod. He would think nothing of getting on a plane to find her. And his text messages were getting increasingly desperate, alternating between threatening and loving. When a sociopath lost his prey, or any perpetrator, they went insane looking for them so they could torture them again. Robert had seen it all before. His wife had been similarly desperate, and the last time he had left her, he never went back. He wanted this to be the last time for Hope and she said it was. Whatever she still felt for him, she knew there was no other choice. She had barely come out alive. If he hadn't killed her, she would have killed herself. She was certain of that. She remembered thinking about it on the last night, and knowing she had surrendered her soul to him, she would have welcomed death, or sought it herself.

Robert was bringing in food for her, and she was too afraid to leave the house. They were sitting in his kitchen eating dinner, when he gently asked her where she thought she might like to go. She'd had an idea all day, and since she didn't want to go back to New York or Cape Cod yet, it seemed like it might be the right choice. She didn't want to go to a strange city and hide. And there was no telling how long Finn would look for her or how desperate he would get. And she didn't want to give herself the temptation of seeing him again. Every time she read his loving text messages to lure her back, her heart ached and she cried. But she knew that whoever was writing them was not the same man she would find if she went back. The mask was off for good, and as everyone who knew him had said, he was a dangerous man. He was everything they had described and worse.

She had Robert's secretary make a reservation for her to New Delhi. It was the only place she wanted to go, and she knew she would find her soul again there, just as she had before. She wanted to hide, but she also needed to put herself back together again. She still shook violently every time she heard the phone ring, and her heart stopped every time Robert let himself into his home. She was terrified it would be Finn.

Her reservation to New Delhi was for the following night, two days after she had walked to Blessington in the early-morning snow. And listening to Hope tell him about the ashram over dinner, Robert thought it was a good idea. He wanted her as far away as possible from Finn. He was planning to go to Blaxton House himself after she left, and serve Finn with eviction papers. They were giving him thirty days to get out, and after thinking about it, Hope told him to sell the house. She never wanted to see the place again. It was too intimately linked to Finn. She knew she had to close that chapter of her life for good.

The day she left for New Delhi, she called Mark Webber in New York and told him what had happened. He asked if she had called Robert Bartlett, and she said she was staying in his house and he had been wonderful to her. She didn't tell him that he had been particularly helpful to her because he had had a sociopathic wife. But Mark was relieved to know she was in good hands. She told Mark she was going back to the Sivananda Ashram in Rishikesh, where she had been before, and he thought it was an excellent idea. The photographs she had taken there had been the most beautiful of her career, and being there had restored her before. He asked her to stay in touch, and she promised that she would.

And then, trembling from head to foot, she called Finn before she left. She had to say goodbye. She needed closure, and couldn't leave without saying something to him, even if only that she loved him, and was sorry she couldn't see him again. It seemed only fair. But fair was not an operative word for Finn.

"This is about the money, isn't it?" he said, when she called him.

"No, it's about everything else," she said, feeling broken as she talked to him. Hearing his voice ripped out her heart and reminded her of the agony she'd been through at his hands. "It wasn't right. I couldn't do what you wanted me to. You frightened me with that story the last night." He had intended to, to get out of her what he wanted.

"I don't know what you're talking about. It was just a story for a book, for chrissake. You knew that goddamn well. What the fuck is this all about?" It was about saving her life. She knew it then, and even when she heard his familiar voice, and his denials, she still knew it now.

"It wasn't just a story, it was a threat," she said, sounding more like herself.

"You're sick. You're frightened and paranoid and neurotic and you're going to wind up all by yourself," he threatened her.

"Possibly," she admitted to him and herself. "I'm sorry," she said, and he heard something in her voice that concerned him. He knew her well. It was how he did what he did, by knowing people's underbellies and their weaknesses and how to play them. He could hear a note of apology in her voice.

"What are you doing about the house?"

"You have thirty days," she said in a choked voice. "And then I'm putting it on the market. I'm going to sell it." There was no other choice unless he wanted to buy it himself. And there was no way he could. All his plans to bilk her out of money had gone awry. He had shown his hand too early and played it too hard. He had been so sure of himself that he had blown all his Machiavellian schemes to smithereens. "I'm sorry, Finn," she said again, and all she heard after that were two words.

"You bitch!" he said, and cut the line. The words were his final gift to her, and somehow made it easier to leave.

Robert drove her to the airport that night, and she thanked him again for everything he had done, including the use of his bed and his good advice.

"It was nice to meet you, Hope," he said, looking at her kindly. He was a very decent man, and had been a good friend to her. He would never forget finding her in the woodshed in Blessington, and she would never forget looking into those gentle eyes. "I hope to see you again sometime. Maybe when we're both back in New York. How long do you think you'll stay in India?"

"As long as it takes. It took six months before. I don't know if I'll stay longer this time or not." Right now, she never wanted to come back. And she never wanted to see Ireland again. For the rest of her life. She was afraid she would have nightmares about it for years.

"I think you'll be fine." He thought she had made remarkable progress in the past two days. From the broken woman she had seemed two days before, the shell of who she had been before was already beginning to emerge. She was stronger than she thought, and she had been through worse, but not much. Falling in love with a sociopath was one of those experiences you never forgot, if you were lucky enough to survive at all. And the worst was that they seemed so human, and sometimes acted so mortally wounded themselves, but when you reached down to help them on the ground, they pulled you into the swamp and drowned you if they could. Their killer instincts couldn't be cured. Robert was glad she was going as far away as she could, and the place she had described sounded like heaven to him. He hoped it would be for her.

They hugged each other as he left her at security with her small bag, full of the clothes he had bought for her to wear.

"Take care, Hope," he told her, feeling the way he had when he sent his daughters off to camp.

She thanked him again, and as he walked back to his car in the garage, he knew that whatever happened to her next, she would be all right. There was a spirit in her and a light that even a man like Finn O'Neill couldn't kill.

He was in his house, sitting in front of the fire, thinking about her and his own experience with his wife, when the plane Hope was on lifted off the runway and headed for New Delhi. She closed her eyes, laid her head back against the seat, and thanked God that she was safe. And then she wondered how long it would take for her to stop loving Finn. She didn't have the answer to that question, but knew she would one day. When the flight attendant handed her the newspaper, Hope took it and sat staring at the date. She had met him a year ago today. It had started exactly a year before, and now it was over. There was a symmetry to it, a perfect seamlessness. Like a bubble floating into space. The life that had been hers and Finn's was over. It had been beautiful at first, and terrifying at the last. She sat staring at the sky as they burst through the clouds over Dublin, and she could see stars in the sky. And as she looked at them, she knew that however broken she still felt, her soul had reentered her body, and one day she would be whole again.

Chapter 22

The chaos in the New Delhi airport felt wonderful to Hope. She looked at the women in the familiar saris, some of them wearing bindis. The noises and smells and brightly colored costumes all around her were just what she needed. It was as far from Ireland as she had been able to come.

Robert's secretary had hired a car and driver for her, and she traveled the three hours north to Rishikesh in comfort. And then they traveled a smaller road to the ashram where she had spent half a year before. It felt like coming home. She had requested a small room by herself. She had asked for time with the swamijis and monks so that she could continue the spiritual seeking she had pursued before. The Sivananda Ashram was a holy place.

She could feel her soul sing when she saw the River Ganga, and the Himalayan foothills where the ashram rested peacefully like a bird in its nest.

The moment Hope stepped out of the car, it was as though everything that had happened to her in the past year faded into the mists. The last time she had come here, she had been heartbroken over Mimi, and devastated by the divorce from Paul. This time the pieces of her had felt so broken in Dublin, and the moment she walked into the ashram it was as though all else was stripped from her life and she could feel her essence come alive again like a brightly burning flame. It had been the right place to come.

They had passed several ancient temples on the way to the ashram, and just being there filled her soul. She fasted that night to purify herself, and did yoga in the early morning, and as she stood at the edge of the river afterward, she told her heart to let Finn go. She sent him with her love and prayers down the Holy River Ganga. She released him. And the following day she did the same with Paul, and she wasn't afraid to be alone anymore.

She met with her beloved master every morning after she did her meditation and yoga. She was up each day by dawn, and her master laughed when she told him she had been broken. He assured her that that was a great gift, and she would be stronger now. She knew that what he said was right and she believed him. She spent as many hours with him as he would allow her. She could never get enough of his wisdom.

"Master, the man I loved was totally dishonest,"

she explained to him one day, as she thought of Finn. He had been on her mind all morning. It was January by then. The Christian holidays had come and gone, with very little meaning for her this year. She was grateful not to have to celebrate them, and had slipped into January peacefully. She had been at the ashram for a month by then.

"If he was dishonest, he was a great lesson for you," the swamiji answered her after a long pause for thought. "We are always better than before when those we love inflict wounds on us. They make us stronger, and when you forgive him, you will no longer feel the scars." She was aware still that she did feel them, along with the regrets. And part of her still loved him. Her memories of the early days were the hardest to give up. She was more willing to forget the pain. "You must thank him for the pain, deeply, sincerely. He gave you a great gift," the swamiji told her. Hope found it hard to see it that way, but hoped that eventually she would.

She thought of Paul a great deal too. She missed him, and being able to call him. He was always in her thoughts, somewhere, in the past behind her, along with their daughter, who was a gentle memory now. She had been for a long time.

Hope walked in the foothills. She meditated twice a day now. She prayed with the monks and the other guests at the ashram. And by the end of February she felt more serene than she ever had in her life. She had no contact with the outside world, and missed it not at all.

She was startled when she heard from Robert Bartlett in March. He apologized for calling her at the ashram. They had brought her to the main office for his call. He needed a decision from her. It was about the house in Ireland. They'd had an offer, for the same amount she'd paid for it, which meant that all her improvements would be a loss. But they were willing to buy the furniture for a fair price, which was a loss as well. He said it was a young couple who had fallen in love with it, and were moving from the States. He was an architect and she was an artist, they had three young children, and the house was perfect for them. Hope wished them well and didn't care about the losses. She wanted to get rid of it, and it was good to know it would be in the right hands. He said that Finn had left right after Christmas, and said he was moving to France. Someone was lending him a château there, in Périgord.

"Did he give you any trouble?" she asked cautiously. She wasn't sure she wanted to know. She had spent so much time pushing him from her mind that she was hesitant to think about him now, for fear that he would poison her again. She had worked so hard to heal the wounds, and didn't want thoughts of him opening them again. Everything about him was toxic for her.

"No, he was all right. Kind of pompous and dif-

ficult, but he got out. It doesn't matter. How are
you, Hope?" He was happy to talk to her. He had
thought of her often and the day he had put her on
the plane to India. She looked so small and fragile,
and so brave. He admired her enormously. Getting
out the way she had, taking nothing with her, and
running for her life through the night took
tremendous courage. He knew it all too well.

"I'm fine." She sounded happy, and free. "It's so
beautiful here. I never want to go back. I wish I
could stay forever."

"It must be beautiful," he said wistfully.

"It is." She smiled as she looked out the window
at the hills around them, and wished he could see
them through the phone. It was a long, long way
from Dublin, which she hoped never to see again.
It had too many ugly memories for her. She was
glad he had been able to sell the house. He had said
the new owners were keeping Winfred and Katherine, and Hope was glad to hear it. She had written
them both letters of thanks and farewell from the
ashram, with apologies for not saying goodbye to
them. She was still paying them until the house
was sold. "When are you leaving Dublin?" she
asked him. It was nice talking to him. He had been
part of such a strange time, and had saved her life
with his wise counsel. He had been the swamiji of
that hour in Dublin. Thinking that made her
smile.

"In two weeks. I'm taking my girls to Jamaica for

their spring vacation, and then I have to go back and settle in. It'll be strange working in New York again. I'm going to miss Dublin. I'm sure you don't have decent memories of it, but it's been nice for me working here for all these years. It sort of feels like home."

"I almost feel that way here."

"When are you coming back?" he asked her.

"I don't know yet. I've been turning down assignments. I think Mark's getting mad at me, but I'm in no hurry to rush home. Maybe this summer. Monsoon season starts in July. It's not so great here then. I could go to the Cape." She had told him about her house there.

"We go to Martha's Vineyard in the summer. Maybe we could sail over to see you."

"That would be nice." He had told her about his girls. One was a dancer, like Mimi, the other one wanted to be a doctor. She remembered their talks about them during those strange days before she left for New Delhi. It all seemed very surreal now. The only thing that still seemed real to her were the early happy months with Finn. It really had been a dream that turned into a nightmare. She wondered who his next victims would be in Périgord or elsewhere.

Robert promised to keep her informed about the sale. And a week later she got a fax. It had gone through at the price she'd paid for it. Blaxton House was no longer hers. It was an enormous relief to her. Her last tie with Ireland and Finn O'Neill had been severed. She was free.

Hope stayed at the ashram until late June. The monsoons were coming, and she savored her last days there like a gift. She had done a little traveling this time with other seekers from the ashram, and had discovered some beautiful places. She had taken a boat trip on the River Ganga. She had bathed in the river many times to purify herself, and she had taken spectacular photographs again of the pink and orange colors at the ashram and along the river. She had worn saris for the last several months. They suited her, and with her jet-black hair, she looked completely Indian. Her teacher had given her a bindi, and she loved to wear it. She felt so much at home here. She was sad for days before she left, and spent many hours with her favorite swamiji on the last day. It was as though she wanted to store up all his knowledge and kindness to take them with her.

"You will be back, Hope," he said wisely. She hoped he was right. It had been a healing place for her for the past six months. The time had flown by.

On the last morning, she was praying long before the sun came up, and meditating. She knew she was leaving a piece of her soul here, but as she had hoped to, she had found other pieces of herself in exchange. Her teacher had been right in the beginning. Her scars had healed here, faster than she expected. She felt like herself again, only more and better, stronger, wiser, yet more humble. Being there made her feel pure. She couldn't imagine going back to New York. And she was planning to spend two months on Cape Cod, before starting work in New York in September.

When she left the ashram, they drove through sleepy Rishikesh. She wanted to cling to every moment, every image. She had her camera over her shoulder, but didn't use it. She just wanted to watch the scenery she loved so much slide by. She had very little with her, except for the saris she had worn, and a beautiful red one she had bought to wear to parties at home. It was prettier than any dress she owned. Robert had sent her camera to her when he retrieved her belongings from the house in Ireland. On her instructions, he sent the rest to her apartment in New York. She had been happiest at the ashram with almost no possessions to weigh her down.

She felt light and free when she boarded the plane in New Delhi. The flight stopped in London on the way back, and she bought a few silly things in the airport. This trip hadn't been about acquiring objects, it had been about finding herself, and she had. As she flew home she knew that at long last she was whole, possibly more than she ever had been in her life.

Chapter 23

When Hope left India, she flew straight to Boston. She wasn't ready for New York yet. Predictably, it was a shock to her system. People looked so drab here, there were no saris, colorful clothes, or beautiful women. There were no pink and orange flowers everywhere. There were people in blue jeans and T-shirts, and women in short hair. She wanted to put her sari on and wear her bindi. And she wished she were back in New Delhi when she went to rent a car at the airport.

She drove to the Cape, thinking quietly to herself, and for a moment she looked around the house when she got there, and thought of her time there with Finn, and then she opened the shutters and forced him from her mind.

She went to the market that afternoon and bought flowers and groceries, and then put the flowers in vases around the house. She went for a long walk on the beach and felt peaceful being alone. It had been Finn's greatest threat to her, that if she didn't give him what he wanted, he would abandon her and she would be alone forever. And instead she had embraced it, and now she enjoyed her solitude. She took her camera with her when she went walking on the beach and she never felt lonely, only quiet and happy and serene.

She saw her old friends there, and went to a Fourth of July picnic. She was still meditating every morning and doing yoga, and she was happy to hear from Robert Bartlett in the second week of July. She had been at the Cape for three weeks then. She had adjusted to some of the culture shock from being back from India. And she still wore simple saris sometimes at night when she was alone. It was a way of reminding herself of her time at the ashram, and she would instantly feel a sense of peace come over her when she wore them. And in the mornings she did yoga on the beach.

"So how is it being back?" Robert asked her when he called her.

"Weird," she said honestly, and they both laughed.

"Yeah, it kind of is for me too," he admitted. "I keep wondering why people don't have brogues when I buy my groceries."

"Me too," Hope said, smiling. "I keep looking for saris, and monks." It was nice to talk to him. He no longer reminded her of a bad time. He was just a friend now, and she invited him and his

daughters to come for lunch that weekend. They
were coming by sailboat from Martha's Vineyard,
and she told him where they could anchor. She
would pick them up at the marina, and then bring
them back to the house for lunch and the afternoon.

It was a gloriously sunny day when they sailed
over from the Vineyard, and she smiled when she
saw his daughters stepping off the boat in bare feet
onto the dock. They were carrying their sandals in
their hands, and he was shepherding them around
like a mother hen, which made her laugh. He was
reminding them to put on sunscreen, take their
hats with them, and put their shoes on so they
didn't get splinters on the dock.

"Dad!" His oldest daughter scolded him, and
then he introduced them both to Hope. Amanda
and Brendan. They were very pretty girls, and they
both looked a lot like him.

They loved her house. And they sensed the
peace there, and the warmth. That afternoon all
four of them went for a long walk on the beach.
The two girls walked far ahead of them, and
Robert and Hope brought up the rear.

"I like your girls," Hope said, as they walked
along.

"They're good girls," he said proudly. He knew
that she had lost a daughter who was about the
same age and he wondered if it was hard for her being around them, but she said it wasn't, it brought

back happy memories for her. He thought she looked like a different woman from the shattered soul he had rescued in Blessington seven months before, in a woodshed behind a pub. The memory struck them both. She had never been as happy to see anyone in her life. And he had been so kind to her when he took her to his house, and let her sleep in his bed, while he slept on the couch.

"You recovered a lot faster than I did when it happened to me," he said quietly. He admired her a lot for all that she'd been through and survived.

"India will do that for you," she said happily. She looked like a free woman, as they turned finally and went back to her house, and then he had an idea.

"Do you want to sail back to the Vineyard with us? You can stay with us for a few days if you like." She thought about it for a minute. She had nothing else to do, and it sounded like fun to be on the sailboat with them. They'd be back at the Vineyard by that night. And she could rent a car to get her back to the Cape.

"Are you sure?" she asked him cautiously. She didn't want to intrude. She knew from what he'd said how precious his time with his daughters was, now that they were away at school most of the year. He talked a lot about how much he missed them all the time. But he insisted that he wanted Hope to join them, and the girls added their voices to his. They said it would be fun.

Robert helped her close the house. She packed a small bag and put the alarm on when they left. She drove them back to the marina and parked her car. She liked being with them. It was like being a family again. She was so used to being alone now that it didn't bother her at all. But having opened her arms to it, as the swamiji had instructed her at the ashram, she found suddenly that being in a group like theirs was a precious gift.

She helped them toss the lines when they set sail, and then she stood next to Robert as they sailed slowly up the coast. And for some odd reason she thought of Finn then and his dire threats about how lonely she would be if she didn't stay with him, reminding her of how alone she was and that she would have no one now. She looked at Robert then, and he smiled at her and put an arm around her shoulders and it felt right.

"Are you okay?" he asked her with that same kind look in his eyes she had noticed the first time she met him in Dublin, and she nodded with a smile.

"Yes, I am," she confirmed. "Very much so. Thanks for bringing me along." He had noticed the same thing she did, that the four of them seemed like a nice fit. The girls chatted with her as they made their way slowly to the Vineyard. The sun was setting as Robert trimmed the sails with Amanda's help. Hope and Brendan went below to get snacks for all of them. It was one of those perfect moments when you wanted to stop time, and when they came back on deck, Hope took pictures of the girls. She wanted to give copies to Robert, and she got a lovely one of him in profile with the sails behind him, and his hair ruffled by the breeze. He quietly reached over and took her hand then. She had come a long, long way from where he'd found her on that terrible morning. And as he looked at her and they exchanged a smile in the balmy evening, she discovered that her master had been right, all her scars had disappeared.

"Thank you," she whispered to Robert, and he nodded, smiling back at her, and then they both looked at his girls. They were laughing at something one of them had said to the other, and as Robert and Hope looked at them, they started laughing too. It was just one of those times when everything felt good. A wonderful day, a perfect evening, the right people, a moment to be cherished, and a feeling of rebirth.

LIKE WHAT YOU'VE SEEN?

If you enjoyed this large print edition
of **MATTERS OF THE HEART,** here are a
few of Danielle Steel's latest bestsellers
also available in large print.

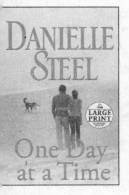

ONE DAY AT A TIME
(paperback)
978-0-7393-2824-7 • 0-7393-2824-8
$27.00/$32.00C

A GOOD WOMAN
(paperback)
978-0-7393-2807-1 • 0-7393-2807-7
$27.00/$32.00C

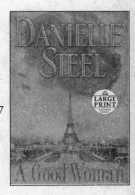

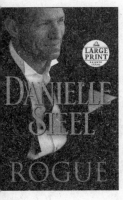

ROGUE
(paperback)
978-0-7393-2792-0 • 0-7393-2792-5
$27.00/$32.00C

HONOR THYSELF
(paperback)
978-0-7393-2774-6 • 0-7393-2774-7
$27.00/$32.00C

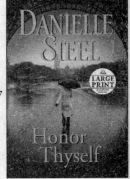

Large print books are available wherever books
are sold and at many local libraries.

All prices are subject to change. Check with your
local retailer for current pricing and availability.
For more information on these and other large print titles,
visit www.randomhouse.com/largeprint.